IMPERIAL

SUNSET

Ashes of Empire #1

WE SHALL PREVAIL

ERIC THOMSON

Imperial Sunset
Copyright 2018 Eric Thomson
First paperback printing July 2018

Published in Canada
By Sanddiver Books
ISBN: 978-1-775343-26-4

Sanddiver
Books

PART I - EXODUS

—1—

"Crap." Centurion Eve Haller pulled out her earbug and tossed it aside in disgust. "The damned rebels just breached our outer defensive line. I was hoping Her Imperial Majesty's 14th Guards might hold on a little longer, if only for the honor of the Crown."

Lieutenant Colonel Brigid DeCarde gave her battalion operations officer an ironic smile.

"If that was the explosion we just felt, then I'd say they didn't merely breach the outer ring but flattened it entirely, so don't be too hard on the Guards."

Haller made a dismissive gesture. "One can never be too hard on the Guards, sir. Useless gits that they are. Good thing we pulled our people back to the inner line last night. And too bad for the 14th, but they wouldn't listen. I'd say the final round is about to start."

"Do you intend to inform her nibs?" Major Piotr Salmin, the battalion's second in command asked. "Before she drinks herself into a stupor, seeing as how it's almost lunchtime? Or will you leave that unpleasant duty to the Guards?"

DeCarde, a muscular, square-faced blonde with deep blue eyes beneath short, sandy hair, exhaled noisily. "At least when our dear governor general is sloshed, she's not trying to play tinpot general based on her three years as a reserve officer in the 1st Imperial Guards forty years ago."

"Considering the morale of the 14th Guards Regiment these days, I figure she only has to order one more suicide mission before what's left of it defects to the enemy. Then, we'll be the last thing standing between a bloodthirsty mob and Countess Klim's scrawny throat."

Haller's macabre laughter bounced off the command post's solid rock walls. "If those bastards think the rebels will accept them with open arms, they're delusional. After what they did? They'll be lucky if the only thing they get is summary execution and not the sort of treatment the Guards supposedly inflicted on rebel prisoners when we weren't watching."

"So will we." Regimental Sergeant Major Cazimir Bayn, a barrel-shaped veteran of the Imperial Marines muttered. "Rebels won't differentiate between the Guards and us, even if we took no part in the atrocities. Hell, we weren't even on Coraline when the worst of them happened."

"True," Haller nodded as she picked up the earbug and reinserted it. "It'll be a repeat of the 3rd Marines' last stand at Fort Wagner. No survivors."

"Except there won't be an Imperial Marine Corps left to commemorate our noble deaths," Salmin, a solemn-looking, dark-haired, dark-eyed, forty-something career officer said. "Or strike our unit permanently from the order of battle."

Haller tilted her head to one side and held up a hand.

"B Squadron reports a rebel battalion moving up to seize the breach, but the survivors from the Guards companies manning the outer defenses are running away instead of trying to delay them. Major Pohlitz figures their panic will infect the Guards companies holding the inner defensive line and would like to move his squadron into the fortress before the inner defensive line turns, and I quote, into a massive clusterfuck that'll leave my ass hanging in the wind for no damn reason."

DeCarde turned her eyes back to the status board where the tactical diagram was shifting in response to fresh data. "Permission granted. Tell him to try and be inconspicuous."

She mentally cursed the blinkered idiots who sent her battalion to Coraline when they knew the entire Shield Sector was in full revolt against the imperial government. At last count, half or more of the Marine Corps and Navy had declared for the rebellion against Empress Dendera. But her Imperial Pathfinders were elite strike troops, not cannon fodder to be wasted on forlorn hopes, such as saving Countess Klim from a fate DeCarde thought was thoroughly merited.

If it weren't for an inability to break her oath, something baked into the family DNA, she might have turned her battalion, the 6th of the 21st Imperial Pathfinder Regiment, against the empire herself. Of course, since her Marines now shared the final redoubt with the last loyal unit on Coraline, there would be no going over to the rebellion. Klim's vicious response to the first sparks of disaffection, as per Empress Dendera's orders, made every imperial trooper share in the guilt. And the rebels would make sure her troops shared in the punishment alongside the 14th Guards Regiment.

A lengthy, though muted rumble echoed through the empire's last redoubt on Coraline, a massive fortress carved out of the Talera mountain range long ago, well before humanity left its native world. DeCarde knew nothing of the civilization that built it but admired their handiwork and believed nothing short of a kinetic strike from orbit might dent stone rendered almost impervious to any damage. The grim fortifications overlooked rolling foothills crossed by a sluggish river that drained the surrounding countryside until it met the Western Ocean near Alexandretta, the half-destroyed colonial capital fifty kilometers away.

"Did our rebel friends find a stash of artillery ammunition we missed, or are the factories back in operation?"

The last loyal Navy ships to pass through the Coraline system weeks earlier carried out a savage orbital bombardment of rebel-held areas at Governor General the Countess Klim's orders, enough to destroy any semblance of modern technology. It was one more item on the long list of sins committed against the citizens of Coraline in the name of a distant empress willing to kill billions if it would help prop up her rule over a fractious empire.

"I doubt they repaired factories, Colonel. Our last drone overflight didn't show evidence of rebuilding."

And it was the last drone overflight, period. Nothing flew on Coraline or orbited the planet. Between them, the 6th of the 21st and the 14th Guards Regiment shot down everything the rebels captured or commandeered, a favor the latter returned with interest. The rebellion's shock troops on Coraline came from the 118th Imperial Marine Regiment which had mutinied months earlier, and they proved to be tough, capable enemies.

"Meaning they can't keep hammering away at Klim Castle." DeCarde used the ironic name her troopers gave the ancient fortifications. Its formal designation was Talera Fortress. "For the good it'll do them. Whoever built this place knew a thing or two we can't even begin to understand."

"Until a Navy task force loyal to the rebellion appears overhead." Sergeant Major Bayn, not a cheerful soul at the best of times, sounded positively glum. "Then, it's a quick jump to Valhalla for the likes of us."

"Did you intend to live forever, RSM?" Salmin gave the old noncom a sardonic grin. "Besides, where would we go if we escape the countess' hospitality? Maybe the empress destroyed the wormhole network *and* blew up every antimatter cracking station in the sector, effectively halting FTL travel. Right now, I figure the pro and anti-rebellion forces are probably duking it out above the sector capital, turning each other into so much orbiting scrap metal."

"That's what I always liked about you, Major, sir," Bayn replied. "Your optimism."

"Uh-oh." Centurion Haller raised a hand to catch DeCarde's attention. "Her nibs is summoning a command conference. Perhaps the latest rebel advance knocked her brain cells back into alignment."

"Let's hope she's already well into her cups. Otherwise, our dear countess might just decide on a sortie to end this siege in a blaze of glory, and I don't have the patience to talk her out of it. When is this blessed event to occur?"

"In ten minutes."

DeCarde sighed. She picked up her brimmed field cap, adorned with the regimental insignia of the 21st Imperial Pathfinder Regiment, a crown-topped winged dagger with the numeral 21. Until last century, the Imperial Marine Corps boasted twenty-two elite Pathfinder Regiments. But the current empress' dynasty, founded by a power-mad, greedy senator who led a coup against a weak emperor and seized the throne for himself, disbanded half of the Marine Corps' Special Forces and eliminated the Imperial Army altogether.

To replace them, he created an Imperial Guard Corps loyal to his person rather than the constitution, unlike the Navy and Marines whose allegiance was not to the person on the throne. Now, only five Pathfinder Regiments remained. Or perhaps not even that many. Her battalion could well be the last of its kind remaining. DeCarde didn't doubt that given a chance, her regimental commander would have gone over to the rebellion and broken the crown off his insignia. Would that she could do the same, but Klim's actions ensured no further imperial troops would dare make overtures to the rebels, lest they be massacred out of hand.

She gave her second in command a weary grin. "The battalion is yours if I blow Klim's head off and end up in front of a Guards firing squad."

"You realize the idea of taking command at this juncture simply thrills me." Salmin grimaced with distaste.

"If the colonel shoots her nibs, you'll not need to worry about that particular burden, Major."

DeCarde gave her sergeant major a tight grin. "Now who's being an optimist?"

—2—

"The flagship, sir — it's gone." Disbelief, mingled with outrage and not a little fear.

Captain Jonas Morane, commanding officer of the Imperial Starship *Vanquish,* turned tired, blood-shot eyes on the cruiser's combat systems officer. His angular face bore the weary, almost resigned expression of someone who knew his life was changing forever. If they survived the next few hours or days.

"What?"

"*Valens*' subspace beacon vanished. She's either been taken or destroyed."

"I guess we'll find out which it is when the visuals reach us. In approximately three minutes, right?"

Lieutenant Commander Annalise Creswell nodded. She was an athletic redhead whose normally bright green eyes were dulled by the stresses of fighting a losing war. Fatigue and worry lined Creswell's pale features, giving her the appearance of someone ten years older.

"Three minutes, sir."

Subspace radio was practically instantaneous within the confines of a star system. But it still took coherent light a second to travel three hundred thousand kilometers, and Morane's ship was fifty-four million kilometers from the main force engaging the rebels near Toboso, the Cervantes system's sole inhabited planet.

Vanquish, a long, wedge-shaped fast attack cruiser and its three consorts sat athwart the 197th Battle Group's escape route, waiting for the main force to disengage from a rebel ambush so they could flee through Wormhole Cervantes Two. Hopefully toward a system still in the hands of naval units loyal to the empire, although they were getting fewer each day.

"What about the others?"

"Still transmitting." Creswell hesitated. "Cancel that. *Stilicho* just went dark as well."

"Damn." Morane ran a hand through his short, black hair as his mind tried to deal with the rapidly deteriorating situation. Two more heavy cruisers either taken or destroyed by Admiral Loren's rebel fleet. On top of their earlier losses.

He'd told Rear Admiral Greth, the 197th's commanding officer, it was too risky entering the Cervantes system. The rebels surely controlled such a significant wormhole junction and were ready to attack any unwary loyalist vessels passing through. But Greth wouldn't hear about falling back toward the imperial capital and saving his battle group's strength until they could join others still faithful to their oaths.

For the sin of objecting to aggressive action against the rebellion, Morane and his fast attack cruiser were left out of battle. Their mission was to protect the 197th's most vulnerable units, the replenishment ship *Narwhal* and two frigates damaged in their previous engagement with Loren's forces, *Nicias* and *Myrtale*. Greth considered it a punishment for lacking the right fighting spirit.

Morane, who was increasingly doubtful about the wisdom of fighting the rebellion head-on, voiced no objections. He didn't want to court a needless death. If that made him a coward in some eyes, so be it. The empire was finished, he could feel it in his gut, and the rebellion wouldn't fare much better. No entity born of such violent dissolution could last.

Now another pair of the 197th Battle Group's remaining heavy cruisers were gone, their crews dead. And for what? So a psychotic ruler could cling to her throne for another few weeks or months?

Morane kept his eyes on the combat information center's primary display, waiting for the moment visual evidence of the flagship's fate reached *Vanquish*. With Greth gone, command would pass to the senior of the captains in the main strike force, though it wouldn't be Tanaka, of *Stilicho*.

"We just lost subspace contact with *Belisarius* as well, sir." A pause, then a gasp.

The command cruiser *Valens'* image vanished in a blinding flash of light. Seconds later, another flash announced the destruction of her consort, *Stilicho*.

"What the hell is happening around Toboso?"

"Perhaps Admiral Greth stumbled across several rebel battle groups concentrating for a large-scale attack. If they were running silent, he wouldn't have noticed them until the last minute, now we've lost both of our scouts." Creswell's matter-of-fact tone belied the somber blanket of defeat settling over *Vanquish*'s combat information center.

Morane grunted. "I'd call that a massive blunder rather than a stumble, Annalise." He didn't need to add that he'd warned Greth against charging in headlong. There was no need. All of his senior officers had been present during that unpleasant discussion.

Two minutes later the stunned CIC crew watched *Belisarius'* shields collapse after sustaining more anti-ship missile hits than its defenses could handle. Several more volleys slammed into her massive, curved hull. Then, she too became a miniature star with a very brief lifespan as her antimatter containment bottles ruptured.

"I still can't believe we're killing each other like that, Captain." Combat Systems Chief Petty Officer Lettis' subdued voice sounded almost mournful. The gray-haired spacer shook his head.

"Family quarrels are often the most vicious of all, Chief, and civil war is the ultimate family quarrel."

"Too bad we can't find a rogue wormhole, go back in time, and kill Dendera before she becomes empress."

"You'd have to go back another three generations and kill Stichus Ruggero, I'm afraid. The empire's fate was sealed when the Senate and the Fleet failed to oppose his accession to the throne."

Another bright light flashed across the display and Creswell consulted her status board. "That was probably *Theodosia.* She's no longer transmitting. The remaining ships have come around Toboso and are accelerating back toward us."

"With the rebels in pursuit." Chief Lettis cursed volubly in five languages. "The escorts are gone. Vanished."

Morane took a deep, calming breath to fight back the despair welling up his throat. Only two heavy cruisers remained of the six that exited Wormhole Cervantes Two forty hours earlier. And the ailing frigates sheltering under *Vanquish's* guns were the last of the 197th's smaller combatants. His own ship was the sole survivor of the battle group's half-dozen more nimble fast attack cruisers, just as *Alcibiades* and *Hephaestion,* now desperately accelerating away from Cervantes, were the last of the heavies. Five ships left of a battle group that started out with eighteen.

According to the latest intelligence report, one only Greth and the starship captains were allowed to see, this scenario was repeating itself in sector after sector. Dendera might hang on to Wyvern and a few of the core systems, but the rest of the empire was plunging into anarchy as warlords fought each other for supremacy. Few of the rebellious admirals could claim Loren's brilliant grasp of politics, let alone his charisma. Fewer even would be able to hold their sectors once the disintegration started in earnest.

And once sundered, the empire would not be reunited in his lifetime. It might never be reunited at all if this civil war brought down the long night of barbarism some human historians had foreseen. And civil wars always became the epitome of savagery.

With a heart grown heavy at the notion something would end here, today, he came to the decision he'd been contemplating for months while waiting for the right time.

"Signals, order the rearguard to execute the planned turn and set course for Wormhole Two. We need to get there before the rebels come any closer. Bridge, captain here."

A tiny holographic projection of Morane's first officer, Iona Mikkel, appeared in midair by his command chair.

"Sir?"

"Turn the ship toward the wormhole and hit the accelerator. We're out of here."

Mikkel nodded. "I figured as much. Do you think *Alcibiades* and *Hephaestion* will make it?"

"Depends on what sort of acceleration the rebels can manage and with what weight of ordnance. A stern chase is a long one. But I don't want to stick around and find myself within range."

"Since you're now the senior surviving captain in the 197th, no one will be able to fault you for withdrawing."

"Am I?"

Mikkel's laughter held a grim edge. "We first officers keep track of such things. And may I suggest that the remains of our magnificent battle group haul its ass back to Wyvern where we can lick our wounds under the orbital station's guns?"

Morane slowly shook his head. He activated the invisible privacy screen that would keep his words from reaching the CIC crew's ears and waited for Mikkel to do the same on the bridge. Once the applicable telltale turned green, he said, "We'd never make it. Too many systems between here and the capital have fallen into rebel hands."

"Then we defect."

"And merely prolong the agony or tear our crews' loyalties apart? Besides, to which of the self-proclaimed sector rulers do we pledge ourselves? Loren isn't the only admiral to renounce his oath. According to a report the flagship received a few days ago, almost every sector except Wyvern's is in revolt. Each rebellious admiral, general or viceroy is trying to steal a march on his or her neighbors and proclaim themselves the one true ruler. If the Shrehari weren't going through similar troubles while fending off their former Arkanna allies, we'd surely face an invasion by now as well, or at least the Rim Sector would. Sorry to spring this on you, but Greth wanted us captains to be the only ones who knew. The empire is gone just as surely as the 197th's heavies."

Mikkel's hologram stared at him in silence for what seemed like an eternity. "Somehow, I knew this would come sooner rather than later. If we can't make it to Wyvern and don't want to join one of the rebellious fleets, what then?"

"We quit the whole shebang."

—3—

The lonely walk to Governor General the Countess Jessamyn Klim's inner sanctum through bleak corridors burned out of living granite always gave DeCarde an impression of entering the nine circles of hell, one after the other. Klim's appointment as regent of Coraline followed a pattern familiar since Senator Stichus Ruggero became Emperor Stichus in flagrant violation of the constitution more than a century ago.

Of minor, if not quite penniless nobility, Klim was the sort who would sell her soul in return for preferment at court. Appointment as governor general in one of the five hundred star systems colonized by humans was enough for an oath of undying loyalty even to a sociopathic sovereign such as Stichus' great-granddaughter Dendera.

Competence, a sense of responsibility or even basic morality were not required. Greed, lust, gluttony, wrath, and treachery, on the other hand, were virtues in her circles. And thus, humanity's long, golden age of peace and prosperity was coming to a violent end. A thousand years of empire undone in less than a thousand days.

It irked DeCarde profoundly that she was caught in the treacherous rapids of disintegration with nothing more than death awaiting her and the 6th of the 21st at the end. Would matters be different if Fleet HQ sent her elsewhere, or even kept her battalion at home? Perhaps not. The Imperial Pathfinder Regiments were the Fleet's quick reaction force, used to quell trouble anywhere at short notice. If not Coraline, then another, equally rebellious star system in the Shield Sector.

Klim's conference room seemed to float at the center of the fortress as if it was a world apart, as did her private quarters. Her staff moved every precious hanging, piece of furniture and knick-knack into the last redoubt from her official residence when she evacuated Alexandretta ahead of the advancing insurgents. Transport better used to bring more ammunition and supplies instead pandered to Klim's vanity. A cloying smell of perfume assailed DeCarde's nostrils as she entered, something the governor general's aides sprayed to cover the earthier aromas of Guards and Marines whose personal hygiene weren't up to Klim's delicate standards.

DeCarde's Imperial Guards counterpart, Lieutenant Colonel Dagon Verkur already sat at a massive table carved from a single piece of dark, lustrous native wood. His regiment lost more than half its strength during the vicious fighting of the last few months, including its commanding officer, a minor baronet with the tactical sense of an amoeba. But he was adept at playing politics and enforced Klim's decrees with utter brutality.

Verkur, the regiment's senior surviving officer, wasn't much better than his former CO even though his family couldn't claim more than the odd knight in its lineage. He knew DeCarde considered him a butcher and gave her a silent sneer when she slid into a chair across from him.

"I hear your soldiers were practicing the four hundred meter sprint earlier today, Dagon. How will they get their exercise once the rebels finish pushing us all the way back into Klim Castle, I wonder?" Verkur, a round-faced, middle-aged man with a weak chin and a receding hairline, made an obscene gesture at her. DeCarde laughed, but without humor. "I love you too. Any idea what she wants now? Is she running out of gin and needs us to do a sortie so we can capture the nearest distillery?"

"One day your smart mouth will buy trouble your ass can't afford, DeCarde. Even if you are one of Her Majesty's super-warriors."

"The way things are shaping up, I think we'll be leading the final charge before that happens. Unless you intend to commit suicide, which probably isn't a bad choice in your case."

The door to Countess Klim's private apartments, a plastic panel fitted into a smooth opening carved by an alien civilization long ago, swung back. A tall, thin, patrician woman swept through and sat at the head of the table. Both DeCarde and Verkur examined her carefully for signs of inebriation so they might know what to expect. She, in turn, studied them with deep-set, cold, dark eyes beneath perfectly coiffed silver hair.

"Which of you would like to tell me we're successfully holding off the rebel scum while we prepare to retake the initiative and sally forth to our final victory?" Her querulous voice betrayed the unsteadiness of someone overwhelmed by events and self-medicating in the most time-honored fashion. "That explosion was our Guards Regiment dealing the enemy a deadly blow, wasn't it?"

"The rebels breached the outer perimeter," DeCarde said without preamble. "We withdrew to the inner line, but at this rate, the rebels will force us back within the next forty-eight hours because it seems they found a fresh stock of artillery ammunition. Since our own counter-battery capabilities are gone, the only thing we can do is hunker down and wait for them to run out. This morning's attack, thankfully, caused my unit no casualties. How about you, Dagon?"

"Nine dead, twenty-three wounded," he said in a flat tone. "I'm afraid Brigid is right. The rebels can apply pinpoint pressure on us at a ten to one ratio. Even the best troops in the empire will eventually give way."

He did not, DeCarde noted, mention the possibility that his panicked soldiers might withdraw from the inner defensive line and into the fortress without even waiting for that pinpoint pressure. Which was just as well because she'd ordered her own troops to pull back so they could avoid needless casualties.

A vexed air further pinched Klim's narrow, bird-like features. "Surely the Navy will be back to relieve the pressure. Someone will have heard our distress call before the rebels destroyed our subspace transmitters."

DeCarde shrugged. "The last starships to visit Coraline, other than smugglers, were the one that bombarded the rebels from orbit. Either someone is blocking the wormholes, or anything that can go FTL is busy dealing with worse messes than what we're facing. Or the entire sector has gone over to the rebellion and is now under Admiral Loren's control. Which means the next Navy vessels we'll see will probably be keener to destroy this fortress than the people besieging it."

"You're a cheerful little person, aren't you, Colonel DeCarde." Klim glared down her nose at the Pathfinder who was anything but small.

"Reality doesn't care whether it makes you happy, Countess. Reality merely demands we acknowledge it. And the reality is that we're fucked, with a capital F."

"And defeatist to boot, which the Crown has decreed is a capital crime."

DeCarde felt anger and exasperation clamoring for release. "Thanks to your cack-handed application of our psychotic empress' short-sighted, idiotic policies, the rebels hoisted the black flag. Otherwise, I'd recommend asking for terms. Heck, I'd go out there myself and at least negotiate my battalion's surrender. But I can't. The rebels want to see every one of us hang even though we Imperial Pathfinders did not take part in the atrocities your 14th Guards Regiment perpetrated. That's what serving the empress has come to — collective guilt, followed by collective punishment."

Klim and Verkur stared at her in shock for daring to criticize the sovereign. Finally, the latter said, "That's treasonous talk, DeCarde. And it's enough to see you garroted."

"Good luck trying." She gave them a contemptuous glare. "But you've given me an idea. Perhaps I should simply order my Pathfinders to kill every single guardsman, then offer our beloved governor general to the rebels in exchange for letting us leave unharmed."

An appalled look twisted Klim's pinched face. "You wouldn't dare."

"In a nanosecond." She nodded at Verkur. "And he knows we can do it too."

"I do not."

DeCarde pointed her finger at the Guards officer and mimed firing a gun.

"Whatever helps you sleep at night. Now, if this meeting was merely so you could vent your spleen, Countess, I'll be on my way. I have plans to make, and Dagon has casualties to visit. Then we need to figure out ways of prolonging this clusterfuck, so the rebels find a new hobby and bugger off. Preferably before we run out of ammunition and rations." She climbed to her feet. "Especially rations. Enjoy your afternoon gin, Countess."

**

"That probably wasn't the smartest thing to say, Colonel." Piotr Salmin shook his head in mock dismay after DeCarde related her meeting with Klim and Verkur.

"No, but considering the situation, it might be our only way out."

"And then what? We're stuck on Coraline. The rebels will be able to massacre us at their leisure. Do you think they'll ever accept our defection? After the last few weeks of fighting?"

DeCarde made a face. "I suppose not. It would have been better if we defected the moment we set foot on Coraline instead of tainting our colors with Klim's stench."

"Hindsight is always perfect. We didn't know how bad things were until our window of opportunity slammed shut, thanks once more to the Fleet's blind, dumb and deaf intelligence service."

"In fairness, Piotr, the sector is a hopelessly chaotic disaster beyond even the best intelligence officer's abilities. Perhaps even the entire damned empire."

"May the devil take that bitch Dendera and her entire clan."

DeCarde raised her tea mug. "I'll drink to that. Somehow uttering treasonous words seems to cheer me up."

"Should we break the crown off our badges? You know, take it a step further and declare our own rebellion against the empire?"

"And make the battle for Coraline a three-sided mess? Are you sniffing antimatter fuel, Piotr?"

"Just trying to find an exciting end for the 6th of the 21st. Something for the ages. A story they'll be telling until the last Marine passes away."

A profound sigh escaped DeCarde. "I never figured I'd be re-enacting the Farhaven disaster when I took my commission."

"It's time someone adds a new holy day to the Marine Corps' calendar celebrating our most heart-rending defeats."

"Pass."

"Not your call, boss. Make the bugler sound the charge."

"We don't have a bugler, Piotr."

DeCarde's second in command snorted. "Give me two minutes, and I'll solve that little problem."

"Drafting one of Dagon Verkur's toy soldiers doesn't count. There's too much blood on their instruments."

"I wouldn't dream of it. Lance Corporal Yorig in D Squadron apparently plays a mean bugle."

She nodded while a small smile danced on her lips. "I'd heard something to that effect. He plays in a brass combo, right?"

"Nothing but the best thirty-second-century classical jazz."

"Not my sort of music. At least not right now."

"Too old or not old enough?"

"Neither, although four hundred years old isn't classical, Piotr. It's damned ancient."

Salmin snorted. "Depends on your definition of the word."

"Right now, I feel ancient, but that's probably because we're fighting for a lost cause that wasn't worth the life of a single Pathfinder in the first place." When Salmin opened his mouth to speak, DeCarde raised her hand. "And don't give me that 'ours not to reason why' crap. I didn't buy it when I was a noncom, and I don't buy it now."

Salmin took a sip of his tea and grimaced. "It's a real shame we'll go down fighting with this swill in our guts rather than a proper brew."

"Can't be helped."

Centurion Haller chose that moment to stick her head into DeCarde's makeshift office. "Observation post Theta Four reports movement behind the rebel lines. It looks like they're bringing reinforcements across the river."

"Already?" Salmin sounded incredulous.

"I guess whoever's commanding the 118th these days believes in keeping the initiative." DeCarde drained her tea and stood. "The bastard wants to make sure we're bottled in tight so he can starve us into surrendering. Warn the Guards please, Eve."

"Wilco, sir." The centurion tossed off a quick salute and retreated into the operations room.

—4—

Commander Iona Mikkel stared at her captain as if he'd just grown a second head. "Pardon?"

"If my reading of the situation is correct, we're facing a civilization-level collapse the likes of which humanity has never seen before. And it will happen very quickly. No matter where we go or who we join, our future is bleak at best. Give it a few decades, and we might well see star system after star system lose its technological base, either to orbital bombardment by rivals, lack of maintenance as interstellar trade grinds to a halt or simple neglect. Once that happens, we'll lose the ability to build and fuel FTL ships, and that means the end of our interstellar civilization."

"Isn't that just a bit overly pessimistic, sir?"

"Is it? Since Loren proclaimed the Shield Sector's secession from the empire, we saw people wearing the same uniform as you and I kill countless thousands of their former comrades and destroy some of the most advanced starships ever built. Do you think they'll hesitate to bombard planets resisting them, or destroy trade to starve holdouts? And then we'll see scavengers come around, the human and non-human slavers, pirates, reivers and corsairs who lurk beyond the frontiers.

"They'll be looking to feed off humanity's remains and take what we didn't destroy ourselves. Then, at a given point, if we're not there yet already, destruction and death will amplify each other in a closed loop and grow until no one can stop the madness. As history has proved many times, this ends only when nothing remains. The Four Horsemen of the Apocalypse are riding across the galaxy, Iona. And they won't leave until they're sated."

"War, famine, pestilence and death."

"Pretty much in that order. The colonies that aren't self-sustaining will die off first. They'll likely be the lucky ones. The more advanced star systems will die a lot harder because their fall comes from a greater height."

Mikkel's image seemed to shiver, although that could be an unsteady holographic projection. "What is your intent, sir?"

Before Morane could reply, Creswell raised her hand. "*Alcibiades* is taking damage from rebel missiles. She..." The combat systems officer swore. "She's gone."

"Is everyone on the new course?"

Lettis nodded. "Aye. They report ready for a jump to the wormhole's entrance whenever we give the word."

The jump, a sprint in hyperspace to reach their escape route was the most the injured frigates could manage. Fleeing the Cervantes system via old-fashioned FTL travel through interstellar space was beyond them.

"The word is given."

A klaxon sounded and seconds later, the universe tumbled into a kaleidoscope of colors and sensations. Morane felt the usual transition nausea twist his guts for a few moments. Then everything settled, but *Vanquish* was no longer in contact with her consorts, nor could her sensors track the last remaining heavy's forlorn attempt to escape.

Morane felt for the people aboard *Hephaestion*, watching the 197th Battle Group's remains vanish, but his first responsibility was to the ships in his charge and their crews.

Now that he'd come to a decision, Morane felt strangely liberated, as if the imperial crown on his naval insignia and on the cruiser's hull were gone. He no longer belonged to Empress Dendera's Navy or to anyone else's. The same held true for everyone aboard *Vanquish*, the supply ship *Narwhal* and both frigates, but they didn't know it yet.

Mikkel's hologram shimmered with a waving hand. "You were about to tell me what you planned, sir."

Morane checked the privacy screen, then said, "Are you familiar with the Lyonesse system?"

The first officer shook her head. "I'd have to look it up."

"So would ninety-nine percent of the Navy's officers, Iona. It's a wormhole cul-de-sac. One connection only, leading to Arietis via two sterile systems, each with only two mapped wormhole termini. Lyonesse is an Earth-norm planet, a minor colony that achieved level two self-sufficiency ten years ago. Better yet, a corrupt sod in the Imperial Procurement Service established a Fleet supply depot on its surface, near the main settlement."

"A supply depot in a wormhole cul-de-sac? That's hardly practical."

"No, but apparently it was profitable, and another sign of the empire's decline."

"That's where you're taking us?"

"Lyonesse is the only system within our reach that might survive the chaos because it's a minor dead-end in the wormhole network. It also has enough resources to support a technologically advanced society if the worst happens and interstellar communications, travel, and trade collapse for centuries."

"What about those who don't want to come along into what sounds like permanent exile, but instead would rather try to return home and be with their families? Not everyone is a confirmed career hound without close loved ones like you or me, Skipper."

Morane grimaced. He was expecting the question to come up. It had plagued him ever since he planned their escape in case matters turned for the worst.

"Once we're away from Cervantes, I'll speak to whatever's left of the 197th and offer everyone who doesn't want to come with us a chance of landing on a suitable world somewhere between here and the Lyonesse wormhole. It's up to them after that. If enough want to split away, perhaps we can exchange crews with one or both of the frigates and cut them loose."

"Harsh, but I suppose it's the only thing we can do."

"I assume you're with me, Iona?"

"Of course. And I daresay most of our crew will be too. They can see what's happening just as clearly. There's no better sign from the Almighty than watching people who once held allegiance to the same Crown destroy your battle group." She paused, then asked, "How do you estimate our chances of running the gauntlet from here to Lyonesse? We'll pass through dozens of wormhole junctions and the rebels will hold many of them."

"Stealth. Pretending to be rebels in rebel-held systems and loyal in systems still under Crown control. And a circuitous route, through sterile systems, those without wormhole defense arrays and systems without a permanent naval presence. The only junction I'm apprehensive about is Arietis. At last news, it was home to a task force. Maybe even a full battle group.

"If the admiral in charge of the Coalsack Sector has mutinied, our run across that system could be interesting.

What I'd really like is to pass unnoticed and avoid tempting anyone into following us. If no one realizes a handful of Navy ships took a minor wormhole out of Arietis, one leading to an equally minor colony, so much the better. But first, we get out of here, Iona. Then we'll worry about the rest."

"Hopefully, the rebels didn't slip a few ships between our emergence point and the wormhole."

"They may not even have known we were in the system until we jumped just now, what with their attention focused on the heavies."

"Whistling through the graveyard, Skipper?" Mikkel gave him a mischievous smile.

"Working the odds, nothing more, Iona."

"And *Hephaestion*?"

"If she survives, she can catch up with us after we make the wormhole transit to the next system. If not... I know that sounds cold-blooded, but whatever force killed six heavy cruisers and their escorts in such a short time will turn us into debris without so much as an afterthought."

Mikkel raised both hands in surrender. "You'll not hear a word of disagreement from me. My aspirations don't including dying nobly for a lost cause."

**

The public address system startled Morane from his silent contemplation of the wormhole network.

"Now hear this. Emergence in five minutes. I repeat, emergence in five minutes. That is all."

Unable to sleep, he had spent the ten hours since *Vanquish* went FTL with busywork and fighting off self-doubt.

Tired legs carried him from his day cabin to the CIC before the jump klaxon sounded three times. Once more ensconced in his command chair, Morane braced himself for the inevitable nausea. When it passed, his eyes were drawn to the tactical projection, searching for *Narwhal, Nicias,* and *Myrtale* as well as any rebel ships blocking their way.

"Everyone made it and no enemy contacts," Creswell announced.

"What about *Hephaestion*?"

A long pause while the combat systems officer checked her status board. "Nothing. Her subspace transponder is no longer there. I'm not picking up any enemy ship signatures near *Hephaestion*'s last known position. They either broke off the chase or went FTL to intercept us."

Morane let out a long, almost mournful exhalation and briefly closed his eyes. Over three thousand spacers dead in the space of what? A few hours? All because the late and unlamented Rear Admiral Greth, Peer of the Realm and Knight of Wyvern, wanted to teach a lesson to what he thought was only a motley bunch of rebels. Instead, he found several battle groups and an inglorious end.

"Get our ships synced and ready for wormhole transit, then go to silent running and stand by. I want no one to hear us pop out on the other side."

"Aye, aye, sir."

The better part of an hour passed while Morane did his best to avoid fidgeting before the signals petty officer reported, "All ships confirm silent running and ready for wormhole transit."

"We are synced," a disembodied voice reported from the bridge, "and ready to cross the event horizon."

"Start the countdown to final burn."

"Starting the countdown to final burn," *Vanquish*'s navigation officer replied. "Burn in sixty, that's six zero seconds. Event horizon in thirty that's three zero minutes."

Precise to the second, Wormhole Cervantes Two swallowed the 197th Battle Group's survivors half an hour later. For a few hours, they disappeared from the face of the galaxy as they crossed a dozen light years without knowing what waited at the other end.

In the eyes of Captain Jonas Morane, formerly one of her Imperial Majesty's officers, it was the first step on a long and perilous journey to a sanctuary he'd only ever seen in his mind's eye. A refuge he believed might become humanity's best, if not only chance of avoiding a darkness that could last for thousands of years. Or perhaps even forever.

—5—

"Who are you? What do you want?" A querulous male voice erupted from the command post's central communications unit. "Fucking imperial scum."

"I am Lieutenant Colonel Brigid DeCarde, of the 6th Battalion, 21st Imperial Pathfinder Regiment and I want to discuss terms with the commanding officer of the forces besieging Talera Fortress."

"He doesn't speak with butchers and war criminals."

DeCarde expected that sort of reaction, but for her troopers' sake, she had to try. "You know we didn't take part in the counterinsurgency operations on Coraline. The 14th Guards Regiment is solely responsible."

"You fought alongside them when we rose to take back what was ours. That makes you complicit after the fact."

"How about I discuss this with your commanding officer? I'm sure he'd like to know how we can help you folks avoid any more unnecessary casualties."

"General Tymak can't be disturbed."

DeCarde glanced at Salmin and mouthed, "General?" Her second in command merely shrugged. The 118th

Marines listed a Tymak among its senior officers from what she recalled of the intelligence briefing the Guards Regiment gave them upon arrival. A major or lieutenant colonel.

That the rebels were giving themselves promotions and new titles meant they didn't expect the empire to regain control of Coraline. Maybe they also now had a sovereign or a president, someone whose face replaced Dendera's on official portraiture. It might even be an aesthetic improvement. DeCarde didn't like the empress' crazy eyes. She always felt as if they were following her across the room, looking for an excuse to order her arrest and execution.

"Not even if we offer him Countess Klim on a silver platter?"

"You'd betray Dendera's personal representative?" The rebel's tone took on a derisive edge. "What about the Imperial Pathfinders' traditional loyalty?"

"Our oath is to the Crown as guarantor of the empire's constitution, not to any governor general or viceroy. Or to the empress herself. My troops and I would rather not be massacred for the sins of the countess and her Guards Regiment."

"They why don't you simply walk out of the fortress under a white flag?" The mocking tone grew stronger.

"Because I can't trust you to treat us as prisoners of war under the Aldebaran Convention. Not after what happened to the loyalists who stayed behind, thinking you'd treat them as non-combatants."

"So you know about that, do you? It's no more than what they deserve."

"Look, both sides committed excesses. We can stop the killing and the dying now if General Tymak is open to negotiations."

"And Klim? Or her damned Guards Regiment?"

"You'd be in your rights to investigate and prosecute them for war crimes."

"Why bother with the legal niceties Klim and her minions ignored?   They've already condemned themselves to death."

"But not us Marines." She paused. "Listen, I won't offer to change sides because you won't accept us. However, I can offer a cessation of hostilities. What I'm asking is for your permission to withdraw in good order, with our arms and equipment, to a sanctuary where we can wait for a starship that will take us home."

The man laughed.

"A starship? Is that everything? Not one damn Navy vessel has passed through in months. The system's subspace radio relay is gone, and for all we know, parts of the wormhole network might have collapsed. No. We can't allow you to sit around with your guns and armor forever, and we sure as hell won't send you out on any of our remaining FTL ships. The longer you hang around, the more you might get it in your heads to try something against the Coraline government.

"So you see, we can't afford to let the empire's super-soldiers roam free. Walk out of the fortress under a white flag, without weapons or armor. Otherwise, you can stay with Klim and the rest while we wait until starvation does the job for us. It'll be entertaining to see who survives the coming outbreak of cannibalism. My bet is on you Pathfinders."

DeCarde glanced at Salmin again. Did the unnamed rebel just give away their game plan? That once the imperial forces were truly and well stuck inside the ancient alien redoubt, they'd be allowed to wither on the vine?

"And if we come out under a flag of truce? We join the surviving loyalists in your concentration camps. Or are they actually extermination camps? We've not heard much about them in your provisional government's news broadcasts."

When the man didn't immediately reply, DeCarde gave Salmin a knowing look. "So that's the plan, is it? Murder anyone who still has an allegiance to the empire so you can cleanse Coraline? That way, if an expeditionary force shows up to retake the system, it'll face a uniformly hostile planet and think twice. Are you smoking Coraline wacky weed? An imperial task force will retake this system in a matter of days. Do you understand what sort of the damage small, iron core asteroids will do if they're dropped on your cities from orbit? Your provisional government won't be begging for mercy because it'll be wiped out in the first few hours."

A loud, derisive snort. "What do you care? You'll be dead by the time Wyvern bestirs itself and sends what's left of the Imperial Armed Services to retake the sector. Which I doubt will ever happen. The final newscast we received before the subspace relay died made it clear that most of the outlying sector commanders imitated Admiral Loren and rebelled. Your empire is finished. Too bad you didn't figure it out before tainting yourself with the Guards' stench. We might have welcomed you back then. Now was there anything else?"

"Please inform General Tymak of my offer. His opinion might differ."

The man chuckled. "General Tymak was expecting you to try something like this after we cut off any chance of escape. I just gave you his opinion and his answer. Feel free to surrender once you realize that a quick death is preferable to a slow agonizing one."

"So you are running extermination camps?"

"That's how one deals with imperial vermin. Enjoy what's left of your life, DeCarde."

Dead silence descended on the command post. Haller glanced up from the communications unit. "They've broken the connection. Do you want me to try and relink us?"

DeCarde shook her head. "I think he was pretty clear about rebel intentions."

"What now?" Salmin asked. His expression betrayed no emotions, but DeCarde could read dismay in his eyes.

"We're certainly not about to start sizing up our comrades from the 14th Guards Regiment as long pig for when the rations run out." She climbed to her feet. "While there's life, there's hope, right? Let's do what I should have thought about weeks ago when it was becoming clear we were on the losing side of this family spat. Eve, please set the communicator to broadcast an automated message at the heavens on every Navy frequency, using the most recent encryption algorithm, and put it on a repeat cycle. If a ship passes through the system on its way from one wormhole to the other, it'll hear us."

"What should the message say, sir?"

"The 6th Battalion of the 21st Pathfinder Regiment is surrounded by hostile forces intent on annihilation and requires immediate extraction."

A faint smile appeared on Salmin's lips. "Doesn't our unit title include the word 'Imperial,' Colonel?"

"If one of Admiral Loren's ships receives our message instead of a loyal unit, perhaps their first reaction won't be to bombard the fortress from orbit if they think we switched sides and broke the crown from our insignia. Right now, I'll make nice with anyone not intent on shooting us out of general principles."

"That's what I thought. And if they decide to strike at us anyway?"

"Then we won't die at the hands of the Coraline rebels or from consuming rancid Guards Regiment meat."

Centurion Haller made a retching sound. "I'd rather blow my own head off than eat that species of long pig. Or any sort, really."

"Oh, I don't know," Salmin said. "If we run it through the nutritional processors, you won't know the difference."

"Not even in jest, Major."

**

"Do you think they'll make it?" Commander Mikkel nodded at the primary display in Captain Morane's day cabin. It showed the frigate *Nicias*, her imperial insignia removed, leaving the 197th Battle Group. She was headed for the first of several wormhole transits on a journey to Aramis, the sector capital where her captain would join Admiral Loren's rebel forces, though many aboard no doubt harbored different ideas.

"I don't know, Iona." Morane's tone held an undercurrent of sadness. He looked up at his first officer, a forty-something, olive-skinned brunette whose features were as deeply etched by worry and fatigue as his own. "I hope so, but if they run across anything bigger than a corvette whose crew is still loyal to the Crown..."

"In a sense, I can understand those who prefer joining the insurrection rather than go into exile with us. Your speech made it clear the chances of ever seeing our native worlds, our friends or our families again once we hole up in the Lyonesse system were damned slim. At least on Aramis, those disinclined to fight for Loren can desert and find their way home again before interstellar travel becomes too difficult, or if you're right, collapses altogether." Mikkel chuckled. "But I liked the way you explained how those of us bowing out of the empire altogether might become a human knowledge vault like one of those ancient seed vaults we read about in historical texts."

"As long as forces from either side in this civil war don't reach Lyonesse."

"Or anyone else intent on creating chaos, and that sort isn't exactly in short supply at the best of times."

Morane shrugged. "There are no guarantees. However, I'd rather try something that doesn't involve slaughtering other humans in job lots."

"Me too, Skipper, and I daresay most of those who stuck with this battle group feel the same. I was surprised so few elected to leave, but perhaps I shouldn't have been. You sure know how to make a persuasive speech."

"With the galaxy going to hell, settling at the end of a wormhole cul-de-sac in an era when no one spends time and fuel traveling between the stars in hyperspace anymore looks pretty good. But I expect a number of our people will regret their decision once the herd instinct of remaining with trusted shipmates wears off and they miss the old homestead and kinfolk."

Mikkel cocked an amused eyebrow at her captain. "Homestead? Kinfolk? Are you turning colonial on us already? What if they don't talk like that on Lyonesse?"

Morane shrugged. "Then I start a new trend. And we should think about heading off." He nodded at the telemetry beneath the frigate's image. "*Nicias* is almost at the event horizon, so she doesn't need an escort anymore. But we must still cross this system to Wormhole Four, and if the rebels are following us from Cervantes..."

"Aye. They could appear at any moment." She climbed to her feet. "I'll order the officer of the watch get us underway. Hopefully, we'll manage a clean break."

"And even if the rebels see us before we cross the event horizon, we're passing through two uninhabited systems with three termini each before we reach Coraline and the first wormhole connecting to the Coalsack Sector. Since they probably concentrated around Toboso for a major operation, they won't waste time chasing us any further. We're not much of a threat to anyone."

"From your lips to the Almighty's ear, sir."

"I don't think the Almighty is listening to us these days, Iona. Otherwise, why let humanity retake the path of self-destruction?"

Mikkel gave him a tight smile. "It's that pesky free will thing, sir. Either that or He figures we're due for another cleansing by fire and sword after we drowned our glorious thousand year empire under a wave of self-satisfied degeneracy. Or at least our supposed betters did."

With that observation, she left Morane to stare at the stars on his cabin's display. A few minutes later, the jump klaxon sounded, and the 197th's three remaining starships jumped across the system before heading down another wormhole and further away from the sector capital that gave birth to the rebellion.

— 6 —

Shortly after emerging from Coraline Wormhole Two, several days and wormhole transits later, the CIC signals petty officer raised his hand to attract Morane's attention. "Sir, I'm picking up a distress signal on standard Fleet radio frequencies, plural, from Coraline. It's encrypted with a four-month-old algorithm, but there's no subspace carrier wave. The Coraline system's relay is either down or destroyed, and none of the wormhole traffic control buoys are broadcasting."

"What sort of signal?"

"Text only. It says the 6th Battalion of the 21st Pathfinder Regiment is surrounded by hostile forces intent on annihilation and requires immediate extraction from Coraline."

"Pathfinders? What the hell is a battalion of Pathfinders doing here?"

"More to the point, sir," Mikkel said, "why aren't they identifying themselves as Imperial Pathfinders. Our Marine Corps siblings are punctilious to a fault about proper protocol."

"Perhaps they renounced their allegiance to the Crown." He thought for a moment, then touched the command chair's arm. "Captain to the CIC."

Creswell's voice replied almost at once. "CIC, sir."

"I need a close scan of Coraline and its immediate environs."

"Will do. Is that related to the distress signal we picked up?"

"Aye, Annalise. I'd like to swing by Coraline instead of making directly for the next wormhole terminus. Finding a battalion of Pathfinders marooned in a minor system like this and calling for help intrigues me. Especially since it seems they dropped part of their regimental title, the same part we've shed."

"You're thinking kindred spirits?"

"Perhaps." Morane turned to his navigation officer. "Tupo, plot a course to take us within four light minutes of Coraline. That'll cut the time lag and still give us enough of a standoff in case rebel ships are hiding in orbit. Once the CIC confirms there are no clear threats, we'll jump."

"Aye, aye, sir." Lieutenant Hak replied.

"Signals, the moment we drop out of FTL, send a reply merely identifying us as the cruiser *Vanquish* and ask for a full situation report. Use the same encryption." He climbed to his feet. "Officer of the watch, you have the con. I'll be in my day cabin. Iona, with me."

"I have the con." Lieutenant Vietti took the command chair.

Once in his sparsely furnished and decorated office, halfway between the bridge and the CIC, Morane drew two cups of tea from the samovar sitting on a sideboard.

"What are you thinking, Skipper?" She accepted a mug and sat in front of Morane's desk. "I see that look on your face."

"I'm not sure. According to the latest order of battle, the 118th Marines, as well as the 14th Guards Regiment, make up the ground forces garrison on Coraline. Why did HQ send a Pathfinder battalion? And why are they facing annihilation? Interesting choice of words, by the way?"

Mikkel shrugged. "Could be the 118th Marines did like a lot of regiments in the Shield Sector. They rebelled and set out to remove the local governor general when Admiral Loren shot Viceroy Rewal and abjured the Crown. When that happened, the 14th Guards would have objected and called for help. Perhaps Wyvern sent the Pathfinders as reinforcements for the Guards, since units like the 21st come under Fleet HQ, not sector command."

"Now they want out of a mess not of their creation."

"Perhaps. I can't see Pathfinders getting along with Guards."

"No one gets along with Guards, Skipper."

"Nor can I see rebellious line Marines being anything other than suspicious of elite troops renowned for their loyalty to the empire, if not necessarily to the person of the sovereign."

"Are you thinking of recruiting them to our cause?"

"It's worth checking out. Lyonesse would at best have a reserve unit for ground defense, seeing as how it's a thoroughly uninteresting system. If we're to set up a human knowledge vault, then who better to help than the Corps' finest? Since they're reputed to be even more bereft of familial and homeworld attachments than us spacers..."

"Don't get too excited, sir. They may not be our sort of people, and by that I mean the sort who've renounced their allegiance. You just said yourself that these Pathfinders are renowned for their loyalty."

Morane gave her a thin smile. "When you're facing death, loyalties can become fluid. If that death is for a cause you no longer support, then why stick around?

They wouldn't put out a distress signal on normal radio channels hoping a passing ship might pick it up if they were ready to die in the name of the empire. Otherwise, why bother with such a forlorn hope?"

"Okay. Let's say they'll be happy to join our merry band. How big is a Pathfinder battalion?"

"Six or seven hundred, I suppose. Less if they've suffered casualties. And I know where you're going with this Iona."

"Good. Then consider this. We can take maybe two-and-a-half companies worth, say three hundred at a pinch, aboard *Vanquish*, since our Marine barracks are vacant. That means the rest will have to go aboard *Narwhal*. She has internal space, but to carry things, not people. Her environmental systems might not be able to accommodate a hundred percent increase in living, breathing, shitting human beings. I won't even mention *Myrtale* since she can't carry much more than a platoon or two at best. Then, there's the matter of food. Do we carry enough to feed another six hundred for however long it'll take us to reach Lyonesse? We should assume they won't be bringing much with them. Finally, there's the little matter of lifting that many armored troops, potentially under hostile fire, with our shuttles."

Morane grinned at her. "Spoken like a true first officer. How about you make a quick survey of the battle group's capacity for carrying extra passengers in terms of both space and rations? I'll ask Annalise to look at how we might pick up a few hundred stranded Marines and their gear with whatever lift we can muster between us, *Narwhal* and *Myrtale*. That way we'll be ready to discuss specifics once we're within a reasonable distance for a radio conversation."

"CIC to the captain. We can't detect any threats. There may be ships running silent, but Coraline's orbit appears devoid of everything except debris."

"Thank you, Annalise. Captain to the bridge."

"Officer of the watch."

"Execute the planned jump to four light minutes from Coraline when everyone reports ready."

—7—

Dagon Verkur intercepted DeCarde on the way to Klim's conference room where they'd been summoned for yet another useless command conference.

"A little birdie told me you made overtures to the rebels. Without the governor general's knowledge." He tut-tutted. "There's a word for that."

"Nonsense?"

"No." A vicious smile spread across the man's bloated features. "Treason. Punishable by death. You know, a drumhead court-martial followed by a quick execution."

DeCarde made a dismissive gesture. "Since we will die anyway, why bother?"

"To make an example."

"And you think your Guards will arrest me?" She chuckled. "Perhaps you should try, Dagon. If we thin out your ranks, there will be more food left for us. Since the rebels won't bother assaulting the fortress now that they can starve us into submission, it might allow my unit to last long enough for rescue by a loyal Navy task force."

Verkur gave her a suspicious stare. "How do you know they want to let us starve? Did the rebels tell you?"

"It stands to reason, Dagon. Why risk massive casualties to seize this place once we're unable to break out? Let nature take its course. Didn't you pay attention during your advanced tactics course? Or are Guards officers promoted past lieutenant without the sort of training foisted on us Marines? It would explain how we ended up in this mess. I can understand Klim being an idiot with delusions of military adequacy, but I expected better from the Guards. Not much, but a little."

"Keep talking yourself into a treason charge, Brigid." His lip curled up in a sneer.

"Since I can't talk my way out of Klim Castle without getting shot by the rebels, thanks to your poor grasp of counterinsurgency operations, showing disrespect for her nibs is the next best thing."

"Oh? Would you have done better under the circumstances?"

"Here's a hint, if ever you're reincarnated as something more evolved than a louse. Reprisals against civilians are a great way to help rebel recruitment drives."

"We had orders from Wyvern."

"I know. Dendera's another idiot with delusions. Except she has a nasty streak of sociopathy instead of a fondness for gin."

"That's 'Her Majesty the Empress' to you, DeCarde. She's still your sovereign and commander-in-chief."

"I guess you subscribe to the notion of *dulce et decorum est pro patria mori*?"

"What now?"

"So... No mandatory history studies in the Guards either, eh? What was Senator Ruggero — pardon me, Emperor Stichus thinking when he converted half of the Army's line regiments into Guards units? At least he gave us the others, and we didn't waste them on toy soldier nonsense. Here, let's take well-educated, well-rounded officers and turn them into mindless automatons? Or does swearing an oath to the sovereign's person instead of the constitution turn you into *nekulturny*?"

"And yet you're the one who's not making a shred of sense, jarhead."

"Well, they do say it's impossible to communicate with someone whose IQ is two or more standard deviations below yours. Shall we take our seats so the countess can grace us with her tactical brilliance?"

"Did you or did you not speak with the rebels?"

"At this point, what does it matter? They've made it quite clear they want everyone dead. Our only options are to die slowly inside Klim Castle or more quickly kneeling beside a ditch, waiting for a shot in the back of the head." DeCarde stepped around Verkur and entered the conference room. "I doubt the rebels will bother running us through their extermination camps for shits and giggles. Or at least they won't try it with my people. Yours? Perhaps."

"Why?" Verkur slipped into his usual seat.

"They want us dead merely because we stayed loyal to the empire. It's nothing personal, just business. The 14th Guards Regiment, however? They hate you with a passion, and should the rebels seize any of your troops alive, they'll take delight in making them suffer. You can call that the wages of brutality if you like."

"They wouldn't dare violate the Aldebaran Convention."

"In a Wyvern minute, Dagon. What do you think happened to the loyal bureaucrats, landowners and law enforcement types who couldn't join our withdrawal to Klim Castle?"

"I don't remember you objecting to the governor general's scorched earth policies when we withdrew."

The door to Klim's apartments opened at that moment, but DeCarde, throwing caution to the wind, didn't bother swallowing her reply.

"Military targets only, Dagon, remember? We didn't subscribe to your and her nibs' interpretation of the order."

"I hope you're not referring to me as 'her nibs,' Colonel."

"It's the most flattering term used by my Marines, Countess. You don't want to hear what else they call you."

"Do tell." There was a slight, but unmistakable slur in her voice, proof of an ethanol-laden breakfast. "An uncouth Marine is hardly news. But so long as they fight, I don't care. Not everyone has what it takes to join a Guards Regiment."

"You mean disregard for common decency, human rights and basic morality? I agree."

"Careful, DeCarde," Verkur growled. "The countess might just decree your battalion is due for a change of command."

"Enough!" Klim struck the heavy tabletop with the flat of her hand. "I won't tolerate any more bickering. We need to find a way out, not ways of doing each other in."

DeCarde's face hardened. "Perhaps we might establish a basis for negotiating our surrender under the Aldebaran Convention if you voluntarily surrendered yourself to the rebels, Countess."

"Are you mad? They'd execute me on the public square. If they don't tear me limb from limb beforehand."

"Of course they will. And I'll cheer them on. But consider that your sacrifice might save many lives. Considering the rebels hoisted the black flag, your death is inevitable. Why not die hoping to save the men and women who fought to protect you and your government?"

Klim snorted. "Fat lot of good they've done me so far. You forget that my value as the empress' representative is incalculable, especially for loyalist morale."

DeCarde bit back a pungent reply. Instead, she said, "I'm merely looking at every option."

"That isn't an option, Colonel and please don't speak such nonsense again. Find a way to make sure of our final victory instead. The rebels face the combined fighting abilities of a Guards and a Pathfinder unit. They shouldn't stand a chance."

It was an old argument, one DeCarde didn't intend to rehash. Klim seemed unable to grasp that the 14th Guards weren't anywhere near as capable as the rebellious 118th Marine Regiment. And by the time her battalion landed on Coraline, the advantage was already heavily weighted against them, not least because of policies that drove most colonists into supporting the revolt.

But before the Pathfinder could formulate a response that wouldn't trigger another lengthy, semi-coherent rant from the countess, her earbug came to life. Though only she could hear the transmission, DeCarde was careful to keep her expression neutral, so neither Klim nor Verkur would know the battalion's command post was calling.

"Colonel, we just received a reply to our distress call."

**

The rest of the desultory command meeting seemed to drag on forever before Klim released them to achieve that entirely mythical victory she still believed possible. DeCarde kept from fidgeting with impatience, but once out of the conference room, long strides through corridors festooned with ceiling conduits, light globes, and propaganda holograms, took the Marine back to the battalion's unit lines. As was her habit, she visited a few of the fighting positions along the way, so she could chat with her troopers and get a first-hand look at enemy activity through observation slits cut into the rock.

Once back in the windowless space Centurion Haller chose for her command post when Countess Klim decreed their withdrawal to the fortress, DeCarde dropped into a field chair by the status board. She looked at Haller with an air of impatience on her angular face.

"Talk to me."

"By some miracle, the cruiser *Vanquish* heard our signal. They replied with the encryption protocol we used, stated they were four light minutes from Coraline, and asked for a situation report."

"That's it?"

Centurion Haller projected the message on the status board.

"I guess they're cautious," DeCarde said after scanning the brief missive. "As I would be in their place." She frowned. "Something is bugging me about the message identifier tags."

Major Salmin gave her a grim look. "The Navy is in the habit of putting the initials ISS in front of their ship names. But this one didn't. We checked for a *Vanquish* in our database, and she's a fast attack cruiser attached to the 197th Battle Group, which is assigned to the Shield Sector."

"Are you saying her crew joined the rebellion, Piotr?"

"Could be. However, the 197th wasn't on the list of formations that switched to Admiral Loren. But our copy is three months out of date, and much will have changed since we lost our subspace radio capability."

"Perhaps this *Vanquish* defected and is now prowling the sector's outer systems on Loren's behalf." DeCarde mentally reviewed her options, then shrugged. "We have nothing to lose by being candid. Let me draft a quick situation report, and we'll see if that makes them want to help us or the baying mob outside."

"Shall we tell the countess and Colonel Verkur?"

"Under no circumstances! This doesn't leave the room. It's bad enough Verkur got wind of my attempt to negotiate with the rebels."

"Maybe the Guards somehow tapped into our ground comms," Haller replied. "I'll run a trace and make sure the link to *Vanquish* is clear of unwanted ears before we send your sitrep, sir."

—8—

"Fascinating." Morane indicated the lines of text on his day cabin's main display when Mikkel joined him. "The 6th Battalion, 21st Pathfinder Regiment, commanded by a Lieutenant Colonel Brigid DeCarde, arrived on Coraline three months ago to help the 14th Guards Regiment crush a rebellion against the Crown led by the 118th Marines. And not coincidentally help protect Governor General the Countess Jessamyn Klim, who happens to be a childhood friend of Empress Dendera."

"Which explains how elite troops ended up on this backwater. Nepotism."

"Things didn't go well for them. DeCarde's battalion, what's left of the 14th Guards and Countess Klim, along with her closest staff, are holed up in one of those indestructible, hundred thousand year-old alien fortresses carved into a mountain range. Apparently, the countess and her Guards ran a very inept, bloody and criminal counterinsurgency campaign before the Pathfinders landed.

"DeCarde claims her unit didn't take part in the atrocities or the scorched earth policy imposed by Klim, but the rebels lumped them in with the Guards. As a result, anybody wearing the imperial crown is on the rebels' summary execution list. Surrender apparently means instant death for the Pathfinders and a more protracted agony for the Guards via what DeCarde figures are extermination camps set up to deal with loyalists. But failing that, the rebels intend to let them starve inside the fortress rather than waste more blood, since they're now in full control of Coraline."

"So the rebellion is in control, but not in contact with the wider uprising."

"Aye." Morane nodded. "Subspace communications facilities are gone, destroyed, and we're the first starships to pass through in three months. Since this place isn't a major wormhole junction and has no strategic value for Admiral Loren or the empire, I expect Coraline will be among the first human worlds to wither away. They've already wiped out their satellite constellation and shot down a lot of the atmospheric fliers to blind each other. I would imagine this sort of scenario is occurring everywhere in human space."

"What's the Pathfinders' strength?"

"DeCarde's battalion consists of five hundred and fifty-two, two dozen of them injured; the 14th Guards number just over fifteen hundred, with several dozen injured; Countess Klim's staff numbers sixty-five, she included."

A look of alarm spread across Mikkel's face. "We can't take over two thousand people aboard our three ships, sir."

"I know, Iona. I'll let you read DeCarde's situation report at your leisure, so you understand what I'm about to propose and why."

Mikkel grunted. "You intend to take only the Pathfinders and leave the others to their fate? Harsh."

"But necessary."

"What if DeCarde is lying about her involvement in the counterinsurgency?"

"Read her report and tell me what you believe. It's surprisingly candid, and she attached a copy of her unit's war diary. She doesn't explicitly come out and say it, but I sense she'll gladly renounce the empire if it helps her battalion escape Coraline, where they face certain death."

"And the Guards or the governor general?"

"I doubt she gives a damn about their fate. Again, I'm reading between the lines, but the Imperial Marine Corps has always considered the Guards an unconstitutional abomination."

"Then we face a real challenge getting her unit out of that fortress. She's hemmed in by rebels on one side, and a desperate Guards Regiment seeking escape on the other. We have to avoid letting the latter swamp our shuttles."

"I know, Iona. But first, let's bring the battle group into Coraline orbit so DeCarde and I can speak without a time lag. I'm sure she'll tell us how we might best extract them. They're trained for situations such as this one."

"After you satisfy yourself we're not bringing rabid wolves into the fold, sir."

Morane dipped his head to acknowledge the first officer's caution. "Of course. I shall have a very candid conversation with Lieutenant Colonel DeCarde to make sure she's not a war criminal lying to save her skin. You may recall that I'm a reasonably good judge of people." He pointed at the display. "Now read."

Fifteen minutes later, Mikkel turned back to her captain and grimaced. "What a fucked-up situation. How did we ever reach this point?"

"That is a question best debated in the wardroom, drink in hand. And there's no time for philosophical discussions until we've safely left the empire in our wake."

"The Lyonesse system is still an imperial possession."

"Until we arrive. Now, what do you think of DeCarde's candor?"

"If what she sent us is the unvarnished truth, then I agree. Let's see what we can do."

"I'm glad you agree." He touched the screen embedded in his desk. "Captain to the bridge."

"Officer of the watch here."

"Take the battle group to Coraline and place us in a geosynchronous orbit above the Talera Mountains."

**

Dagon Verkur barged into DeCarde's office unbidden and took a seat across from her.

"Are you talking to someone up there?" He waved his hand at the gray granite ceiling. "Because my command post just intercepted a message that appeared to originate from above the planet's surface. We couldn't decrypt it since the Fleet isn't inclined to give us Guards a copy of your algorithms. Tell me, has the Navy suddenly reappeared? And if so, are they loyalists or rebels?"

"Please come in, Dagon. Take a seat, Dagon. What can I do for the 14th Guards, Dagon?" DeCarde smirked at him. "Now what's this about mysterious messages from the ether?"

"Please, Brigid. Cut the crap. If my people received that transmission, yours will have too. Is help on the way, or are the insurgents getting fire support from orbit so they can turn the Talera Range to rubble instead of waiting until we starve?"

DeCarde climbed to her feet and stuck her head into the command post next door. She caught Centurion Haller's eye and gave her a 'play along' stare. "The Guards intercepted an encrypted message in the last hour. Did we as well?"

"Yes, Colonel. I was trying to find its origin and encryption protocol before telling you. So far, no luck with either."

"Thank you." DeCarde turned back toward Verkur. "There you go, Dagon. We're in the dark too. Maybe they're talking to the rebels, in which case we can expect a deluge of fire and brimstone momentarily. Klim Castle might be the toughest thing on Coraline. But I should think even it can't resist a few dozen penetrator rounds slamming into the mountain at terminal velocity, in spite of the alien magic that kept this place more or less intact for a hundred millennia."

"So we die a little sooner." Verkur stood. "You'll let me and the countess know if you discover anything of interest, won't you, Brigid?"

DeCarde nodded. "Of course."

The Guards officer must have thought her expressionless face hid secrets because his eyes hardened with skepticism. "Make sure you do so."

Once he was gone, she exhaled noisily and turned her eyes to the map projection in one corner of the makeshift office, a cube-like space burned out of the rock with the same uncanny precision as everything else deep inside the mountain range.

Between them, the rebels and the 14th Guards Regiment might make sure any escape becomes a dicey proposition — if this *Vanquish* actually had room for her battalion and was willing to take them off Coraline. There were precious few safe landing zones with the rebels controlling the surrounding countryside, save for a flat, clear space above the main fortifications, where its builders had sliced off a mountaintop. But it was covered by the last of the imperial aerospace defense guns.

And now that the Guards knew someone out there was talking to Coraline, they'd be listening intently to intercept any further communications, as would the insurgents, no doubt. They might be vicious in their hatred for the empire and its representatives, but they weren't stupid.

—9—

Lieutenant Vietti let out a low whistle when a bird's-eye view of the ancient fortress appeared on the bridge's main display after *Vanquish* settled into geosynchronous orbit above Coraline.

"That is seriously impressive."

"And seriously old." Morane ran his hand, fingers splayed, through his short, stiff hair. "They say the ancestors of the Shrehari built it during a previous civilization cycle when our ancestors still hunted animals with stone-tipped spears."

"I bet future humans won't find anything like that left over from our era. Just look at the thing. It's what? Two-and-a-half kilometers long at the top and goes who knows how deep."

"Those ancients were more advanced than we are." Morane studied the dark gray, almost black fortifications rising from steep slopes in precise blocks hundreds of meters to a side as if birthed by the mountains themselves. "Apparently, those shiny walls are impervious to lasers, plasma and chemical explosives, which is probably why the loyalists chose it as their last redoubt."

"Nukes should do the job," Vietti replied, eyes narrowed in thought, "but this close to Alexandretta, the rebels would be pissing in their own soup."

"They've done enough of that already," Chief Lettis' disembodied voice said over the live connection between the bridge and the CIC. "There's not a single intact satellite left in orbit, only junk. It's a good thing Coraline had no inhabited orbital platforms. Otherwise, we'd be picking up frozen stiffs."

Morane and his first officer exchanged glances. "And so it begins," the latter murmured.

"Indeed." Then, in a louder voice, "Signals, please ping our Marine friends on the same frequency as before, using the same encryption. But make it a narrow beam transmission, so we don't alert the rebels besieging..." He turned to Mikkel. "What did DeCarde call the fortress again?"

"Klim Castle, though its official name is the Talera Fortress."

"Right. So we don't alert the rebels besieging Klim Castle. Once they reply, we can narrow the beam down to its point of origin and make sure even the 14th Guards can't overhear."

"Unless their command posts overlap from our angle," the signals petty officer warned. A few minutes passed while Morane and his officers studied the rebel dispositions, then, "They responded and are standing by. We can open a video link whenever you want."

"Do it."

The fortress shimmered away, replaced by a blonde woman wearing Marine Corps rifle green battledress. Her sharp, angular features were tight with fatigue and worry, though a spark of hope seemed to shine in those deep blue eyes.

"I'm Lieutenant Colonel Brigid DeCarde, commanding the 6th Battalion, 21st Pathfinder Regiment, sir." Morane briefly thought she wanted to say more, but deliberately held back.

"Jonas Morane, captain of the fast attack cruiser *Vanquish* and commanding officer of the 197th Battle Group's remains. Your sitrep and war diary are interesting, to say the least, Colonel."

"I wouldn't call our situation interesting, sir. Desperate seems a more appropriate term. Although it might become of interest to future historians as a case study in how to fuck everything up."

"If there are future historians."

DeCarde frowned. "Sir?"

"We — *Vanquish*, a replenishment ship by the name *Narwhal* and the frigate *Myrtale* — are all that's left of the 197th save for another frigate. It is now on the way to Aramis and Admiral Loren's forces with those who didn't want to join us. Four ships out of eighteen. The others were destroyed by rebel Navy units who didn't even give them a chance to surrender.

"I doubt there will be much left of the empire by this time next year, Colonel. Loren isn't the only sector commander to mutiny against the Crown and set himself up as a warlord hoping to take the throne for himself. Civil wars often spiral out of control until there's nothing left."

DeCarde's tired face took on a knowing look, and she nodded. "You mean we might finally face the long night of barbarism that's been predicted for so long, sir."

Morane gave her an appreciative smile.

"You've studied Arnold Toynbee's modern disciples, I take it? Good. Then this will be easier to explain. I do indeed think we might face a civilization-level collapse and after seeing what both rebels and loyalists did to Coraline in a few short months, I'm more convinced than ever. Without a resumption of shipping and trade, Coraline won't be able to rebuild and will begin to lose its technological base. Imagine the same scenario repeated on every human world, and you can easily see we're committing civilizational suicide.

"I'm taking our three ships to a colony established at the far end of a wormhole cul-de-sac which I hope might escape destruction. With a bit of planning and some luck, we might be able to turn this colony into a human knowledge vault and preserve what we can. That way, our descendants might short-circuit the long night and allow for an earlier dawn."

DeCarde didn't immediately reply though Morane could see thoughts chasing each other across those intense eyes. Then, she seemed to shake herself. "Permanent exile, in other words, correct?"

"Very much so. The people who left on the other frigate wanted to go home, although I'm not sure about their chances."

"If you have only three ships and you're quitting the empire, why are we talking, sir?"

"We picked up your distress signal, and it occurred to me that our human knowledge vault would benefit from experienced ground troops to set the basis for strong defenses."

"Only if you can lift my entire battalion. We Marines aren't in the habit of leaving our own behind."

Morane smiled again. "I'm aware of the Corps' ethos, Colonel. We can take your five hundred and fifty-two. Barely. Half would go aboard the transport *Narwhal* and live in makeshift accommodations, but we can accommodate the other half in *Vanquish*'s Marine barracks if you don't mind doubling up. It could become a strain on the environmental systems, and rations might become short before we reach our destination unless you bring your own."

DeCarde's burst of laughter was as bitter as it was brief. "There's not much, sir, and most of that is controlled by the 14th Guards at Klim's orders. Neither trusts us. We didn't bloody our hands in the name of Empress Dendera or soil our colors by committing acts that violate the Aldebaran Conventions."

"So I read in your report."

"It's accurate to a fault, sir. Even if you had room for the 14th Guards and Klim's people, I'd recommend against even speaking with them. The Guards are conditioned for loyalty to the Crown and wouldn't take kindly to Armed Services units fleeing the empire."

"While you Marines aren't."

DeCarde shook her head. "Even a sociopath such as Dendera wouldn't dare take that step because it would entail mass mutiny. Although I suppose that ship has already sailed."

"It has." Morane let out a dry chuckle. "From what little we've been able to gather, most of the Corps mutinied. I imagine elite regiments such as the 21st Pathfinders are finding their loyalties severely tested. However, we noticed you didn't use your full title in the distress signal."

"That was in case units answering to Admiral Loren, or any other rebellious sector commander picked it up. I wanted a chance to talk before kinetic strikes from orbit finished us off."

"Do you still consider yourselves loyal, Colonel?"

A grim smile tugged at DeCarde's thin, bloodless lips. "To who, sir? The empress whose orders put us in a situation where we either die of starvation or are shot by rebels intent on avenging themselves? Certainly not to Governor General the Countess Klim and the 14th Guards Regiment. If I'd known upon landing here that this would be our end, I'd have considered joining the 118th Marines there and then. Now we've been tainted by association, it's too late. The truth, Captain, is that my troopers and I didn't become Pathfinders for the sole purpose of finding the most useless, stupid death possible. So no, I do not consider myself loyal to Crown and empire anymore.

"My sole remaining loyalty is to my people, and I will do whatever is necessary to save their lives. I don't mind the idea of dying for a noble cause, but I refuse to die for no damn reason. At least not without trying my best to avoid it. Take my battalion off this shit hole of a planet, and we'll follow you into permanent exile with enthusiasm. It beats any other alternative open to us, especially since the Fleet seems intent on self-destructing. The 21st may not even exist as a unit anymore, and few of us can claim close family ties." DeCarde came to attention. "I place myself and the 6th Battalion under your command, sir."

Her vehemence and the determination he read in her steely gaze convinced Morane that DeCarde was the real deal. He glanced at Mikkel who was standing beyond video pickup range. She gave him a quick nod of approval and mouthed 'take them.'

"In that case, Colonel, perhaps we can explore how we'll lift your five hundred and fifty-two Marines and their gear while incurring no further casualties, from either the rebels or the 14th Guards. Between *Vanquish*, *Narwhal*, and *Myrtale*, we should be able to do so in one go, provided we disregard every single safety limitation placed on shuttle operations."

"Respecting safety limits in a war zone is vastly overrated, sir. However, I'm sure my folks can come up with a few ideas about how we might carry this off."

"That's what I was hoping, Colonel. I'm not particularly experienced in mass troop lifts under enemy fire, nor are my officers."

— 10 —

DeCarde dropped into her chair once Morane's image vanished. She felt lightheaded and not a little giddy at the prospect of rescue even if it entailed the end of everything she and her troops knew and loved. The end of their careers as members of the Imperial Marine Corps' elite Pathfinders. However, if Morane was correct, it could also mean the beginning of something even more important. She gazed around the command post at her staff and saw her own mixed emotions reflected in their eyes. They might survive but at the price of heading into the unknown.

"Well, I'll be darned," Piotr Salmin whispered, "salvation comes from the most unexpected direction. I'll miss the fleshpots of Aramis, but life in the back of beyond beats death here."

"Then we'll just create our own fleshpots when we get there, sir," Centurion Haller said with a smile born as much of mischief as it was of relief.

DeCarde raised a hand to forestall any more banter.

"My biggest concern is to make sure the Guards don't suspect we're leaving. Otherwise we'll be stuck fighting our way through them. Even if Verkur and his officers are ready and willing to die for the Crown, many of the soldiers aren't. Only Guards officers receive deep conditioning apt to produce fanatical devotion, and that means a lot of the junior ranks might look for seats on our rescue flight if they find out. Besides, Verkur could decide we should perish alongside the 14th simply on general principles. He's that kind of an imperial asshole. Therefore, we can't tell our own troops until the last moment, lest word filters out. I don't want one more Pathfinder paying for this madness because we didn't keep operational security as tight as possible."

"And the rebels?"

"Morane strikes me as a man who will find a way to handle them, if only to protect the battle group's shuttles, Piotr."

"We kill the off-duty Guards in their sleep an hour before the rescue flotilla lands," Sergeant Major Bayn suggested, "then toss grenades into the sentry and firing positions to sort out the rest."

DeCarde shook her head. "Tempting, but no. We need to make a clean break, not withdraw under fire, and as much as I find the entire Imperial Guards Corps objectionable, a cold-blooded massacre isn't on."

Piotr Salmin shrugged. "Easy. Ask *Vanquish* to make a big sound and light show outside, so the 14th is fully focused on what's happening beneath the battlements. Then we climb to the roof, sabotage the guns, and shut every staircase behind us with whatever means we can devise. Booby-trap them, even. The moment we're ready, let the shuttles land and load up. That means they should already be circling somewhere beyond sensor range."

"Simple and straightforward. I like it." She glanced at Haller. "Eve, tell Hanni I want the pioneers to run a survey of our withdrawal routes to the roof and plan how they might interdict them — merely as a contingency, of course. If she becomes curious, tell her I'm trying to come up with a harebrained scheme for a last-ditch defense."

The Marines who formed Pioneer Troop, part of Major Hanni Waske's Combat Support Squadron, were the 6th Battalion's in-house combat engineers and experts at setting booby traps.

"Roger that, sir."

"Piotr, I believe you're our most experienced embarkation officer, so that job becomes yours. When we contact *Vanquish* again, ask for a list of their shuttles so you can put together the embarkation scheme. In the interests of time, we absolutely need to make sure they land in the right order based on how we'll form up our folks. Also, find out which of the ships will receive our wounded."

"You got it, Colonel."

"Sergeant Major, see what rations we can scavenge from the central stocks without the Guards getting wise."

"With pleasure. May I also suggest we raid the governor general's piggy bank? Those precious metals might come in handy."

"You may. Just make sure your thieves strike at the last minute." DeCarde stood. "It's presently ten-hundred hours. I'd like to lift off by oh-four-hundred tomorrow morning at the latest, before first light. The longer we delay, the greater the chances someone will realize what we're planning. And now, I suppose I'd better head off to her nibs' daily waste of time."

"Try to keep your own excitement under tight control, Colonel, otherwise Verkur will smell a rat. He's already wondering whether we're in contact with something out there. The 14th's executive officer buttonholed me earlier this morning. He seems to believe we're up to no good."

"I'll do my best, Piotr."

"If Verkur gets too nosy, lead the fucker to a quiet spot and kill him. We'll dispose of the body for you."

"And that's even more tempting, Sergeant Major. If Dagon goes from annoying pest to something more dangerous, you can be sure I won't hesitate."

"One last thing, sir."

"Yes, Piotr?"

"We really should run at least one rehearsal. If we do it by squadron, we can pretend it's to practice repelling a possible airborne rebel attack. My embarkation plan will be built around squadron chalks anyhow."

"Good idea. Do it. Hopefully, the troops won't react negatively once they find out I'm leading them into permanent exile, away from the empire, the regiment and the life we knew."

Salmin shrugged. "They'll react like Pathfinders, Colonel. Adapt and overcome. A few might suffer depression from excessive nostalgia, but until we're settled wherever Captain Morane is taking us, it'll be just another day in the Corps."

Bayn nodded. "The major is right. I'll keep an eye on those with close family back home, but at least we're leaving this shit hole as a battalion, and we'll start our new lives at the other end as a battalion. Being with your mates counts for more than anything else in this business."

**

"I presume you picked up another radio transmission from above this morning?" Dagon Verkur asked by way of greeting when he intercepted her on the way to Klim's conference room. "Brief, but still with the same encryption."

"We did. And we still don't know what that was about. You can always ask the rebels if it's their buddies from Admiral Loren's private navy."

Verkur stopped and examined her with hooded eyes that oozed skepticism. "Why is it I think you're lying, Brigid?"

"Because you spent your entire life surrounded by liars and can't fathom the concept of honesty? Or honor and integrity. Or any other attribute of a good officer."

He shook his head. "No. You're up to something. I can see it in your face. Spending one's life surrounded by liars helps develop finely-tuned bullshit detectors."

DeCarde shrugged dismissively and resumed walking down the cold, bare passage. "Think whatever you want, Dagon. I neither care nor am I inclined to play games. As long as we're alive, I'll turn my energies to finding a way out, and I suggest you do the same."

"There is no way out except by air. Or didn't you notice? And even that's dicey since the rebels still have weapons capable of downing anything that flies."

"Which makes me wonder why you didn't arrange for a backdoor to your bolt hole. That seems rather careless."

"We checked but couldn't find anything. When we tried to create our own, the rock resisted every tool we own. Those aliens were solid builders. Trust me on this."

"Perhaps." DeCarde stepped into the conference room and took her usual seat. "But where there's life, there's hope. We Pathfinders have this curious habit of fighting until the very end."

"An admirable sentiment, to be sure." Verkur sat across from her. "But if I discover you're holding back on me, you may find the end coming sooner than expected. We still outnumber you by almost three to one, and this fortress is part of *our* garrison."

"Why the sudden threats?" DeCarde gave him a puzzled frown.

"Because I trust no one who didn't swear an oath of allegiance to the empress."

"And look where that sentiment got you, my friend. Surrounded by those who reject Dendera and want to rend you limb from limb. I'd suggest you reconsider your prejudices. But since we're not getting out of here alive, there's really no point."

"Oh, yeah." Verkur nodded. "You're planning something. I haven't seen you this chipper since we set up shop inside Klim Castle."

"Just trying to keep my spirits up with a positive attitude. You should try it someday, Dagon."

"You're an example to us, I'm sure, Colonel DeCarde." Klim's disapproving voice washed over them as she entered the room. "If only you could turn that positive spirit to tactical matters, we might all feel a lot chipper."

"Sorry, Countess. We're still hemmed in by the rebels with no end in sight."

Verkur gave DeCarde a deadly stare. "Or maybe not. It's become clear there are one or more ships above the planet, and they're talking to someone on the surface. We intercepted two communications so far, one yesterday, one this morning, but we weren't able to decrypt them. Colonel DeCarde claims she doesn't have the right algorithms either."

Klim cocked an elegant eyebrow. "Curious. So it'll be rebels, then?"

"That's what we believe." Since it was true in the sense that Morane and his battle group renounced their allegiance to the empire, neither Verkur nor the governor general could sense any falsehood on DeCarde's part. But the former didn't seem to buy it.

When the meeting broke up after thirty minutes of desultory conversation punctuated now and then by unreasonable demands from the countess, Verkur's cold eyes followed DeCarde as she left him and Klim to discuss private matters. The Marine knew he wouldn't let the matter rest and thought about Sergeant Major Bayn's suggestion. A stab through the ear with the dagger strapped to her left forearm would kill Verkur instantly and leave very little blood for his soldiers to find. It was an ancient blade but still deadly. And it had taken many lives over the generations.

"Another fun conference?" Salmin looked up from his field tablet when DeCarde entered the command post.

"Hopefully my last. Klim doesn't live in the real universe anymore. I don't know whether it's the booze, drugs she's taking on the sly or a weak character. Not that it matters. But Dagon Verkur is less of a fool than I thought and might become dangerous. His people picked up *Vanquish*'s opening ping, but fortunately not the subsequent link once we were on a narrow beam."

"And he thinks we're plotting something with unidentified naval units in orbit."

"Pretty much. I may be forced to take him out before we trigger our exodus."

"Or I can give the job to one of our experts."

"No, Piotr. If it becomes necessary, I'll do the deed myself."

Salmin saw the determination in his commanding officer's eyes and knew she was thinking of more than merely stilling a suspicious if not yet outright hostile mind. DeCarde still felt anger and shame at not stopping the 14th Guards Regiment before they took out their frustrations against the rebellion on unarmed civilians a few weeks earlier. Never mind Verkur's regiment still mustered almost four times the 6th battalion's strength at the time and could inflict heavy casualties. Or that the extent of the Guards' savagery surprised everyone.

"Fair enough, Colonel. While you were contemplating Countess Klim's descent into irrelevance, I obtained the shuttle specifications from *Vanquish*. It'll be tight — at least half of their atmospheric craft are configured for cargo only — but doable, so long as no one shoots at us. Pioneer Troop is working the escape routes to the roof, and we should see the preliminary estimate within the hour. I've taken the liberty of quietly alerting the squadron commanders as to the real purpose of our repel boarders drill on the roof, but they'll not spread the word any further down their chain of command."

DeCarde nodded with approval. "Probably best they know earlier rather than later. Anything else?"

"Besides the wounded and two squadrons, Captain Morane wants you and battalion HQ aboard *Vanquish*. I'm mentioning that in case you thought about roughing it in one of *Narwhal*'s cargo holds with the other squadrons."

"Not particularly unexpected, I suppose, considering his ship has purpose-built Marine barracks, and will probably have a station for the Marine commander in his CIC. In case we're needed for raiding action en route to this human knowledge vault he mentioned. How about distracting the rebels?"

"Morane's still working on that. We need to complete the plans for what we'll do if this turns into a withdrawal under contact, Colonel."

—11—

"Bridge to the captain."

Morane, sitting at the head of a long, narrow table, held up his hand to forestall Commander Lori Ryzkov's remarks. *Narwhal*'s captain, along with her colleague Nate Sirak from *Myrtale* had joined *Vanquish*'s department heads in the cruiser's conference room via holographic projection over a secure comlink to discuss the rescue operation.

"Captain, here."

"We received a signal from Alexandretta on a narrow beam, sir, someone claiming to be the Provisional Free Government of Coraline. They're demanding we identify ourselves."

Many eyebrows shot up at the unexpected news.

"Meaning they picked up our initial signal, before we switched to narrow beam ourselves, and scanned the orbitals, Captain. We've not done much to keep our presence hidden from prying eyes on the surface."

"No doubt, Iona. A mistake on my part not placing us under silent running."

"At least we shut off our transponders."

"Which is probably why they're demanding identification, rather than merely making it a polite request. We could be marauders. Let's hope the 14th Guards no longer possesses sensors powerful enough to reach geosynchronous, or our Pathfinder friends might find their way out of the fortress blocked." He climbed to his feet. "If you'll continue the discussion among yourselves for a few minutes, I'll take this call from the bridge. It might give me the chance to convince the insurgents that letting the 6th of the 21st go would be beneficial for everyone involved since they didn't take part in the Guards' atrocities. Considering the alternative is us bombarding rebel positions near the fortress to clear the way for our shuttles..."

"Good luck."

Morane smiled at his first officer. "It's not luck I need, but the skills of a silver-tongued rogue."

"Which you seem to possess, Skipper."

Once on the bridge, he nodded at the officer of the watch. "Open a link."

After almost one minute, the image of a middle-aged man in Marine Corps green with a general's stars at his collar materialized. He had the square features, firm chin and the determined gaze of a born fighter. Hooded eyes stared at Morane with undisguised suspicion.

"State your identity and purpose." The unfriendly tone in his voice matched his expression.

"I'm Jonas Morane, captain of the cruiser *Vanquish* and acting commodore of the 197th Battle Group."

"One of Dendera's bootlickers?"

"Not anymore. And you are?"

"The name's Tymak. I run Coraline now."

Morane mentally winced. Warlordism was already taking hold here. "Do you recognize Admiral Loren as regent of the Shield Sector, General?"

"If he makes me the right offer, sure. We certainly don't want the damned empire to come back. Once we've exterminated the last remaining little bits, Coraline will be an empire-free world."

The officer of the watch, standing beyond video pickup range, pointed at a screen next to Tymak's image. It now displayed information on the man culled from *Vanquish*'s data banks. Former major, 118th Marine Regiment, last known assignment was as regimental S-3, running operations. Interesting. From imperial staff officer to warlord in the space of a few months.

"I can help with that if you'd like."

Tymak's expression oozed skepticism. "Oh?"

"Admiral Loren has directed we recover the Pathfinders sent here by mistake before he could countermand illegal orders from Wyvern. The 6th Battalion of the 21st Pathfinder Regiment. They're needed on Aramis. Once we evacuate them, you can deal more easily with the 14th Guards Regiment, or whatever is left."

Tymak gave Morane a thoughtful stare.

"I was going to watch the Guards fight your Pathfinders for the last rations, then see who comes out of that fortress to embrace a quick death instead of a lengthy starvation. You don't know what the damned Guards did to Coraline and her people. They deserve an agonizing end, and if DeCarde's people don't do it for us, we'll gladly send their souls to hell ourselves, along with those of the other filthy loyalists we rounded up."

"Highly commendable, I'm sure," Morane muttered. Then, in a louder tone. "Will you let us evacuate the 6th of the 21st, General? I promise not a single Guard, nor any of the governor general's staff will be allowed to board my shuttles. The admiral doesn't care what you do. He just doesn't want any of them roaming free in his sector."

"They won't be roaming, I can guarantee that." Tymak rubbed his chin with a calloused hand. "What if I decide to keep your Pathfinders? They were collaborating with the Guards and therefore are just as guilty."

"You intended to execute them if they fell into your hands?"

Tymak nodded. "For sure. Except we planned on shooting the Pathfinders by the side of the road while any surviving Guards will answer to the people of Coraline before we put them to death. And it won't be pretty. The empress' bastards will wish they'd merely been shot."

"I understand your desire for vengeance, but let me pick up the Pathfinders. You can save your ammunition and please Admiral Loren at the same time. He'd not thank you for killing troops he needs to fight Dendera."

"And if I don't?"

"Then I'll neutralize everything you own within range of the fortress before sending my shuttles down. You know what an orbital bombardment can do, right, General?"

Tymak's face showed surprise at Morane's matter-of-fact tone. "You'd strike at fellow members of the rebellion?"

"My orders are to retrieve the Pathfinders, and I'll do what I must to carry them out. The choice of how I proceed is yours. If your troops don't target my shuttles, we'll be parting as friends. If they do, Admiral Loren might find it necessary to change Coraline's government, and he won't be gentle, I can assure you."

"You'll leave us the Guards and the governor general?"

"Yes, we will. You can do what you want with them. The admiral has outlawed the Imperial Guards Corps in the entirety of the Shield Sector, and proscribed imperial viceroys, governors-general and governors."

Tymak held Morane's eye for what seemed like an eternity before giving a grudging nod.

"Take the Pathfinders whenever you like. I'll make sure no one opens fire."

"Thank you, General. We intend to do so in the next twelve hours."

"One more thing, Morane."

"Yes?"

"I'd like a full situation report on what's happening elsewhere. We've been cut off for months."

"Of course. I'll also mention you need a new subspace relay once I return to Aramis. Your cooperation today will certainly help convince the admiral and his staff to hasten its replacement."

When Morane saw Tymak's eyes tighten, he was afraid he might have overdone it, but then the self-proclaimed general said, "That'll be a fair consideration. Just make sure you take none of the fucking Guards. They're mine."

"Promised. Thank you, General."

Morane returned to the conference room and updated the others on his conversation with Tymak. When he fell silent, Mikkel grimaced.

"Do you think we can trust him?"

"Probably not. But I don't see how he might profit by firing on our shuttles. If anything, Tymak will want to capture them intact, which is beyond his ability."

"Unless he forces our pilots to land behind his lines under threat of aerospace defense fire," Commander Ryzkov said.

"At which point, we will bombard his troops, Lori. Tymak was an Imperial Marine officer. He knows a Navy ship in orbit always holds the high ground. But just in case, let's plan on the shuttles coming down on the Talera mountain range's far side. From there, they'll fly nap of the earth to the fortress. That'll keep them off rebel sensors until the last minute. Once the shuttles are on final approach, we'll paint the rebel positions with active fire control as a warning."

"That takes care of our part. How about the 14th Guards? They might take exception to our evacuating the Pathfinders and open fire."

Morane glanced at his combat systems officer. "I understand DeCarde plans on blocking and booby-trapping every egress to the fortress roof, Annalise, but we've yet to hear how they intend to deal with the Guards should their delaying tactics fail."

Vanquish's coxswain, Chief Petty Officer First Class Arnon Shaney, shrugged. "Fight. What else is there?"

"CIC to the captain."

Morane swallowed a brief surge of irritation. "Yes?"

"Seven ships dropped out of FTL at the hyperlimit."

All eyes in the conference room turned to Morane. "Transponders?"

"Aye, sir. The 191st Battle Group."

Mikkel swore. "It mutinied and went over to Admiral Loren eighteen months ago."

"If they're broadcasting, they don't expect to find loyalist units, or in our case, neutrals in this system. The bunch Admiral Greth blundered into near Toboso were nice and quiet, even after triggering the ambush."

"Meaning the 191st's arrival isn't due to them hunting us."

Morane made a face. "I sure hope not, Lori. Because it would mean our clean break wasn't really clean. Be that as it may, their arrival forces us to move up the evacuation."

"For more reasons than one, Captain," Mikkel said. "If Tymak finds out a second rebel battle group has entered the system and they somehow spoke with each other, he'll have a lot less incentive to let us pick up the Pathfinders unmolested. As far as the 191st knows, our 197th remains loyal to the Crown."

"Bridge, all ships to go silent immediately. Once that's done, open a link with Colonel DeCarde and pipe it to the conference room."

— 12 —

"Colonel." Centurion Haller stuck her head into DeCarde's office. "Captain Morane wants to speak with you. Apparently, complications just dropped out of FTL at the hyperlimit."

"Shit." DeCarde followed Haller back into the command post, where the hologram of a seated Morane was waiting. "Sir, my centurion said something about new arrivals."

"Correct. The 191st Battle Group, which was among the earliest formations to mutiny. Or at least a portion of it, since we spotted only seven ships instead of the usual eighteen or more. We need to move up the timetable dramatically. The will arrive in a few hours, perhaps as little as five, and if they somehow speak with this General Tymak who seems in charge of the Coraline rebellion, we could face difficulties flying our shuttles in."

"Sir?"

"I told Tymak we were one of Admiral Loren's units here to pick you up at his orders, so he won't shoot at my shuttles, or force me to bombard his units from orbit. Coraline's already suffered enough damage as it is."

"Admirable, I'm sure, sir, but Tymak and his troops aren't much different from the Guards for respecting the Aldebaran Conventions. However, I understand that's neither here nor there. How soon would you like to execute the evacuation?"

"Within the next two hours, if that's possible on your end. My shuttles are ready, and the pilots only need a final briefing from your embarkation officer so they know how to stagger the landings."

A pained expression twisted DeCarde's face. "Leaving in broad daylight means most of the 14th Guards will be up and about, not to mention alert."

"I'm afraid it can't be helped."

"Understood, so long as your pilots realize the last of my troops to embark will probably do so while exchanging shots with the Guards."

"The shuttles' armor can handle most small arms fire, Colonel, and they're equipped with close-in defense calliopes capable of covering your rearguard."

"Two hours?" DeCarde glanced at the time display on the operations board.

"Two hours. Try to keep a constant link with us from now on, so we stay aware of your status."

"Yes, sir."

"*Vanquish*, out."

When DeCarde's eyes slipped to the operations board again, she saw Haller had triggered a countdown timer. "Where are Major Salmin and Sergeant Major Bayn?"

Haller nodded toward a closed door to her right. "In there, discussing the embarkation plan with the squadron commanders."

"Good. I can announce the change in plans to everyone at once."

When she entered the command post's improvised briefing room, Salmin fell silent, and all eyes turned toward her. DeCarde wasn't one for intruding on a subordinate's show, and her unannounced arrival could only mean new developments.

"I just spoke with Captain Morane. A rebel battle group came through one of the wormholes. Our evacuation can't wait until after nightfall. Operation Bug Out is a go in," she glanced at her time display, "one hundred and seventeen minutes."

She saw several eyes widen, but none of her officers made so much as a sound, nor did their expressions change in any other way.

"If it's time to go," Salmin finally said, "it's time to go. We'll be ready."

Major Bowdoin Pohlitz, the officer commanding B Squadron, which would embark last, squared his shoulders and nodded. "That means our chances of withdrawing under fire just increased fivefold if the Guards decide they don't want us to leave or figure on swamping the last flight out."

"The shuttles can offer covering fire."

"As long as their pilots aren't trigger happy and wait until we're clear of the stairwells."

"What about the rebels outside?" Salmin asked.

"Morane bluffed them into holding fire by pretending his ships belonged to Loren, who wants the 6th of the 21st to join him on Aramis. Once this new bunch comes within radio range and contacts Coraline's new rulers, his bluff is over, which is the other reason we're leaving in less than three hours."

"I need another ten minutes, Colonel, then we can start the drawdown. I assume we're still bringing everything we own with us?"

"Absolutely. Where we're headed, we might never see another quartermaster depot again. Besides, I don't want to leave anything useful for the Guards. They don't deserve it."

At that moment, DeCarde's communicator vibrated. "Yes."

"Haller, sir. Colonel Verkur is demanding to enter our unit lines."

"Demanding?"

"He sounds pretty peeved at the new security measures."

"Coming." She gave Salmin a meaningful look. "Trust Dagon to show up at the most inconvenient time."

**

"Now I know you're up to something, DeCarde," the Guards officer said when she joined him at the sentry post. "Why the increased security and why are your people crawling all over the castle's upper levels and rooftop?"

She gestured toward her unit lines. "Why don't we talk in my office?" As he fell into step beside her, she continued, "Troopers become bored during a siege, Dagon. So I'm shaking things up by changing alert levels and running exercises to defend against an enemy attack from above."

"The rebels can't cough up enough aircraft for a raid."

"As far as we know. But you may remember we lost most of our aerospace defense ordnance during the withdrawal from Alexandretta. What's left up top can be taken out in a bold strike to prepare a forced entry. Perhaps it's not the most plausible scenario, but I'd rather my troops keep moving and thinking. Sitting in the fortifications all day long, watching the rebels watch us, dulls the mind. Of course, I should think Guards are used to dull minds, so maybe your folks don't need periodic shakeups."

By the time they passed through the command post on the way to DeCarde's office, Haller had hidden any traces of Operation Bug Out, but DeCarde knew the centurion was anxious to pack.

"In fact," she pointed at a chair, inviting Verkur to sit, "we'll be conducting rapid reaction exercises to repel an enemy landing later this afternoon. You're welcome to watch. Perhaps you might learn something."

The Guards officer studied her as if she were a particularly suspicious coprolite specimen. "What are you *really* doing, DeCarde? We intercept encrypted transmissions from off-planet, and suddenly, your behavior gets even stranger than usual. I have half a mind to remove you from command."

"You even owning half a mind is debatable, Dagon. And you can't remove me from command, even if you claim seniority in rank. We belong to legally separate services."

"Then perhaps I should put a halt to your nonsense by occupying the stairs and roof until you come clean." A slow smile crept across his chinless face. "That would displease you, yes? Then I shall do it."

When he made to stand, DeCarde pulled her blaster from its holster and pointed it at Verkur's face. "Why is it you dumb fucking Guards always end up writing your own death warrants?"

Verkur didn't seem able to decide whether she was joking or in earnest and he smiled. "Come now, Brigid. There's no call to point a weapon at a comrade."

"You were never my comrade. And you're neither a Marine nor a soldier. Marines and soldiers protect civilians. They don't murder them." She stroked the trigger, and a smoking hole appeared where Verkur's flat nose once sat. He crumpled to the stone floor in silence, flash-broiled brain matter oozing from the larger hole in the back of his skull.

"Centurion Haller?"

"Sir." Haller's head appeared in the doorway. Then, she looked down and made a face. "Oops. Clean up in aisle four. I'll get a couple of troopers to hide the body."

"And make sure you erase any evidence he entered our unit lines. Knowing the Guards, they'll run themselves stupid trying to find him before the next in line decides this is his or her big chance at commanding the mighty 14th. Hopefully, that'll further degrade their ability to stop us from leaving."

"Will do, Colonel. And then I can finally pack."

—13—

Morane strode across the hangar deck toward *Vanquish*'s command shuttle, piloted by Lieutenant Commander Creswell who would lead the rescue flight.

"Ready, Annalise?"

"Everyone here is good to go, sir. I'm waiting for *Narwhal* and *Myrtale* to confirm." She tilted her helmeted head to one side. "And they're ready."

"Godspeed and good luck. Bring everyone home safely."

"Aye, aye, sir." Creswell snapped to attention and saluted. "With your permission."

"Launch."

Creswell raised her left hand and made a whirling motion. Almost immediately, a siren began it lugubrious chant while the hangar deck lights dimmed. Large space doors, framed by the shimmering curtain of a force field, slowly drew aside to reveal a carpet of stars above Coraline's curvature. And though Morane knew the force field would keep the deck pressurized, he nonetheless retreated to the control room. From there, he watched as

Vanquish's shuttles lifted off one after the other in a continuous stream until the hanger was empty.

Shortly after that, Creswell's voice came over the control room speaker. "Mercy Flight is assembled and heading for the target."

Morane touched his communicator. "Bridge this is the captain."

"Bridge."

"Warn the 6th that we've launched our side of Operation Bug Out. I'm heading for the CIC."

"Aye, aye, sir."

"Captain, out."

**

"Mercy Flight is on its way, sir."

Centurion Haller slung the surface to orbit radio over her shoulder where it thumped against the pack containing her worldly goods. Like every other member of the 6th Battalion, 21st Pathfinder Regiment, she wore powered combat armor and carried, besides her own equipment, a share of the common gear and of the rations they stole from the Guards. Heavier crates already sat in the stairwells, waiting to be hoisted up by A Squadron, the first in line and headed for *Narwhal*.

"Right on time." DeCarde grinned at her operations officer through an open helmet visor.

Though as commanding officer, she wasn't expected to hump her share of the command post, she still carried the backup radio and the tactical AI that served as scribe, controller, dispatcher, and assistant to Haller and Piotr Salmin. The latter was already on the roof with Sergeant Major Bayn, preparing to marshal the shuttles and direct the embarkation.

So far, the 14th Guards were keeping quiet. Those few who noticed the Pathfinders mustering in full marching order seemed to shy away as if unnerved by the sight of the elite troopers in their powered armor. And no inquiries about Verkur's whereabouts so far. DeCarde figured he probably disappeared for several hours at a time regularly. Everyone knew of his playmate on the governor general's staff.

DeCarde took a last look around the bare room, to make sure neither of them had forgotten anything. "I guess that's it. Time to join the rest of HQ Squadron."

"Aye. If I never see this place again, I'll die happy."

"Me too, Centurion. Me too." But the moment they stepped into the corridor, DeCarde's radio came to life on the priority command circuit. Governor General the Countess Klim wished to see her and Lieutenant Colonel Verkur. "Crap."

"What is it, sir?"

"The countess is feeling lonely. She's convening an impromptu command conference."

Haller snorted. "I doubt she has enough gin to drown the sorrow that will come from finding out both of her military commanders are gone."

"Speaking of which, what's become of Verkur?"

"Best you don't think about it, sir. But his remains will never be found."

"Couldn't have happened to a nicer guy." Their powered armor propelled them up a set of polished stairs and then another, before passing through a hasty defensive position thrown up by B Squadron on the fortress' penultimate level, one of four established to cover the battalion's withdrawal.

Soon afterward, the chase teams passed through them and confirmed that not only was the entire battalion waiting just below the roof, but the obstacles and booby traps were active, sealing them off from the rest of Klim Castle.

Unexpectedly, the countess' grating voice filtered through her ear bug. "Lieutenant Colonel DeCarde, this is Governor General the Countess Klim. Please respond."

"DeCarde here."

"Why didn't you present yourself to the conference room? And where is Lieutenant Colonel Verkur? His people tell me they can't find him, nor can they track his movements. It's as if he vanished off the face of the planet."

"I don't know where Dagon might be, Countess. Did you check with your deputy chief of staff? I understand she's quite close to him."

"Of course I bloody well checked with Azurine, Colonel. I'm not a stupid old woman unaware of what goes on around her."

DeCarde forcefully suppressed the urge to laugh with derision.

"Then I can't help you. Dagon is his own man."

"And when will you show up?"

"My unit is in the middle of a training exercise, Countess. Perhaps afterward."

"You are a very vexing person, Colonel. Did someone ever mention that?"

"I've heard it mentioned once or twice, mostly by those unaware of what goes on around them. But it's fair that I point out you don't yet understand how vexing I can be when I put my mind to it. Now was that everything? I am running a tactical exercise."

"We shall discuss your flippant, disrespectful attitude later, Colonel." Klim abruptly broke the link.

"I think not," DeCarde muttered. "You soused, useless old bat."

"Beg pardon, sir?" Haller gave her a quizzical look.

"Just saying my farewells to our beloved governor general."

Haller's head tilted to one side. "Lieutenant Colonel Gaillard, who I suppose is now the Guards' new commanding officer, though he knows it not, wishes for a moment of your time, Colonel."

"Patch him through."

Moments later, Gaillard's nasal tones erupted from her ear bug. "What the hell are you playing at, DeCarde? My people tell me you've blocked off access to the top level, and now I find our aerospace defense guns are inoperative. Or at least they're no longer talking to us. We're effectively blind topside." DeCarde smiled. Her sabotage experts from the Pioneer Troop were performing their usual magic.

"Hello, Manvil. How are you, Manvil? I'm quite well, thanks. As to what we're playing at, why don't you ask your commanding officer? I warned him we would practice repelling airborne assaults this afternoon."

"No one's seen or heard from Dagon for several hours."

"Did you check under the lovely Azurine's bed, Manvil? I hear she likes to play at repelling assaults as well. Or was that Dagon's role? There are rumors about him..."

"No dice, DeCarde. His absence is as complete as it is unexpected. How about wrapping up your war games and restoring the fortress to what it should be? Dagon was careless to have allowed those shenanigans in the first place."

Did Gaillard sound nervous?

"The 14th Guards might claim ownership of Klim Castle, Manvil, but in matters of training my unit to defend the countess, I needn't ask anyone's permission. We will finish when I say we're done. Now was there something else? I'm rather busy, and keeping tabs on Dagon is your business, not mine."

"Just get on with it, DeCarde."

"I most certainly intend to do so. Goodbye, Manvil." She cut the link. "And enjoy your final days in this life, you prancing ninny."

Then, she glanced at the holographic status projection hovering a few centimeters in front of her left eye. Not long now.

—14—

"I have visual IDs on those seven ships from the 191st, sir." Chief Lettis said the moment Morane entered the CIC. He pointed at a side display. "Two Conqueror class heavies, two Triumph class fast attack cruisers and three Kalinka class frigates."

Morane studied the video feed. Even one of the Conquerors could fight his ship to a standstill, never mind two of them along with a pair of *Vanquish*'s sisters. In other words, enough to wipe out the 197th Battle Group's pitiful remains.

"They don't seem to be in a hurry," Lettis continued. "So there's at least that in our favor."

"Estimated time of arrival in Coraline orbit?"

"At current velocity, and if they remain within normal safety parameters, it'll take them approximately four hours and forty-five minutes. Which gives us just enough time to recover the shuttles and run."

The signals petty officer raised his hand. "They're attempting to contact the Coraline government in clear, identifying themselves as the 191st Battle Group, here at

Admiral Loren's orders to assess the situation. Whoever controls Coraline is to respond and state their allegiance."

"Which means they haven't picked us up yet, but they will once we turn active targeting on the rebel positions around the fortress. I'll be interested to see 'General' Tymak's reaction."

Lettis grunted. "Bugger won't know what to think."

"That's my hope, Chief. Confusion will help us. It's one of the few advantages of a civil war where both sides wear the same uniform and operate the same starships."

A few minutes passed. Then, "Tymak's hailing us. He wants someone to tell him, and I quote, what the fuck is happening."

"Tell him we weren't aware our friends from the 191st were coming. Call it a typical headquarters screw-up."

"He's demanding to speak with you."

"Put him on." When Tymak's thick features materialized, Morane asked, "What can I do for you?"

"What's this new bunch on about? Don't you Navy folks speak with each other?"

Morane shrugged. "You know how it is, General. The left hand rarely tells the right hand what it's doing. We haven't run across the 191st in a few months, so it's quite possible they aren't aware of our mission."

Tymak's eyes narrowed beneath a suspicious frown.

"Yeah? Maybe I should wait until they're here before letting you pick up those Pathfinders. I'd like to make sure we're fighting for the same side."

"My shuttles are already on the way."

"You're early. Is it because of these new arrivals?"

"No. The Pathfinders indicated they were both ready and anxious to leave. Something about being tired of breathing the same air as a Guards regiment. And since there's no time to waste, I advanced the schedule."

"Throttle it back. Your shuttles aren't to land until we can have a three-way conversation with the commander of the 191st Battle Group."

"It's too late for that, General."

"My planet, my rules."

A cold smile played on Morane's lips. "But I own the high orbitals." He glanced at Lieutenant Vietti. "Go active."

"Going active, aye."

"General, the moment you target my shuttles, your entire siege force will vanish. I'll give you a moment to ask your field commanders if their threat detectors are screaming, but as of now, I can launch precision strikes that'll wipe them out."

Tymak's eyes slipped to one side as his lips moved silently. A minute passed, then he stared back at Morane.

"How dare you target fellow anti-imperialists?"

"Call it an insurance policy, General. The deal is my Pathfinders for the entirety of your troops. It remains a profitable exchange for everyone, but I will strike if necessary." Chief Lettis pointed at a side display that read 'Mercy Flight on final approach.'

"My shuttles are almost at the fortress. Make sure your commanders don't target them. I won't give you another warning. One ping from a targeting sensor, and your troops will die. *Vanquish*, out."

**

"Pegasus, this is Mercy Niner, over." A woman's voice broke the lengthy radio silence, startling DeCarde.

"Pegasus Niner Alpha here," Major Salmin replied. His head instinctively turned toward the Talera Range's jagged peaks, eyes looking for the first visual sign of the approaching shuttles.

"Confirm LZ clear and ready."

"We hold the LZ; defensive ordnance has been disabled, and egress points are blocked. LZ is marked, and there are two, repeat two controllers. Myself and Pegasus Niner Charlie. You are cleared to land."

"Acknowledged. We are five, repeat five minutes from LZ. Look to your east. We are flying nap of the earth. Be advised that Mercy Higher is targeting the forces surrounding your location. There may be fireworks if they take aim at Mercy Flight."

"Understood. We are not in a position to observe or engage hostiles other than the ones inside our location, and so far, they're quiet."

"That's what we figured. Mercy Niner, out."

Seconds after Lieutenant Commander Creswell signed off, the voice of Major Pohlitz, the officer commanding B Squadron, came over the battalion net.

"Niner Alpha, this is Bravo Niner, the Guards *were* quiet. We're picking up readings of at least one company, armored and armed, probing the base of the north staircase." DeCarde swallowed a curse. Manvil Gaillard decided the rat he'd smelled was real. "And another company is moving in on the west stairs."

DeCarde nudged Haller. "Patch me into the Guards' network."

"Patching." Then, "You're in."

"Colonel DeCarde for Colonel Gaillard."

Seconds passed, then that irritating, nasal voice came on. "What do you want?"

"Would you like to tell me what you're playing at, Manvil? Two of your companies, in full fighting order, are snooping around my training exercise. Surely even a Guards officer understands how quickly accidents happen when troops are carrying live ammo."

"My guardsmen report you blocked and booby-trapped the north and west stairwells, DeCarde. Additionally, the governor's secretary is up in arms about the precious metals reserve, which went missing after a few of yours were seen in the vicinity. I should be the one asking questions here."

"Stand down, Manvil, before someone gets hurt. The stairwells are blocked, in the interests of making my scenario realistic. Call your people back. We'll be done with our rehearsals in another five or ten minutes, then we'll clear out the stairwells."

Gaillard chuckled. "Before someone gets hurt? In case you didn't notice, we seem to be on the losing side of a civil war. I doubt any of us will live long enough to celebrate the empress' next birthday."

"Shame. It's my favorite holiday of the year, when I devote a whole evening to getting drunk and cursing the Ruggero name. But don't say I didn't warn you if someone's fingers are accidentally blown off. My pioneers are experts at the art of improvised field amputation. Now leave us alone, Manvil, otherwise you and I will have words in private. When you find Dagon, ask him how that usually works out for the Guards. DeCarde, out."

Major Salmin's voice rang out over the battalion radio net once more. "Alpha Squadron, move out and take position."

**

"The 191st finally spotted us, sir. We're being hailed on the emergency Navy subspace channel. In clear."

Morane grimaced. Staying deaf and dumb wouldn't help under these circumstances. Any FTL capable starship has a working subspace transmitter and not answering would confirm something wasn't right in Coraline orbit. And that, in turn, might convince the 191st's commander to pursue once *Vanquish* and its consorts broke away for Wormhole Coraline Four.

He took a quick glance around the CIC, to make sure no stray imperial crown remained to betray them, then nodded at the signals petty officer. "Open a link."

The image of a narrow-faced, silver-haired woman in Navy blue with a single five-pointed star at the collar appeared on the main display. She examined him with pale, suspicious eyes beneath arched, dark eyebrows.

"I'm Commodore Lana Kischak, flag officer commanding Task Force A of the 191st Battle Group. Who the hell are you and why are you navigating without transponders?"

"Captain Jonas Morane of the cruiser *Vanquish*, sir. I'm also in command of the 197th Battle Group's remains."

"Isn't the 197th loyal to the empress?"

"Not anymore, sir. Admiral Greth was, but he and most of our former comrades are dead, destroyed by rebel forces in the Cervantes system. We — my surviving fellow captains and our crews — forswore the Crown."

"Then why aren't you broadcasting a signal identifying yourselves as belonging to Admiral Loren's fleet?"

"We don't belong to anyone's fleet, sir. As soon as we've retrieved our friends from Coraline, we're leaving the Shield Sector."

"You'll do no such thing, Captain. Stay in Coraline orbit and await our arrival." Her gaze slipped to one side as the audio feed died. When she turned back to Morane, her stare became, if anything, even colder. "A General Tymak has apparently taken control of Coraline and claims you're evacuating a battalion of Pathfinders at Admiral Loren's orders. Doesn't that contradict your assertion you've renounced any allegiance?"

"We're rescuing friends from certain death at the hands of the Coraline rebellion. Tymak belonged to the 118th Marine Regiment which rose against Governor General Klim in the early days of the rebellion. I don't know how he became the local warlord, but before our arrival, he intended to massacre those Pathfinders. They landed here three months ago and committed no war crimes. But because they fought alongside the 14th Guards Regiment, who did and deserve execution, they've been condemned to die. The Marines we're rescuing — for the record, they belong to the 21st Pathfinder Regiment — also forswore the Crown."

"And then?"

"We leave, never to return, let alone take up arms against Admiral Loren or any other sector commander who stands against Dendera."

"This Tymak says you threatened to annihilate his troops from orbit should he prevent you from carrying out the evacuation."

Morane nodded. "I did. You'll find the Coraline rebels aren't much better than the Imperial Guards in respecting human rights and the rule of law, and will therefore only bow to superior firepower. It would chagrin me to carry out my threat since I'd rather retrieve my friends and leave without firing a shot, but if forced to do so, I will act. Considering the destruction both sides already wrought on Coraline's infrastructure, any bombardment on my part won't significantly degrade the planet any further."

Kischak made a face. "Yes, we noticed the absence of satellites in Coraline orbit and that the wormhole traffic control buoys and the system subspace relay are missing."

"According to the commanding officer of the Pathfinder battalion, little if any air or spacecraft remain operational. Consider it the wages of unbridled warlordism, if you like. Admiral Loren might be wise to heed the lessons of Coraline if he wants to prevent the entire sector from following its example."

"The problem hardly lies with the admiral, Captain Morane. You can blame Dendera and her adherents for turning political discontent into civil war."

"Perhaps, sir. Nevertheless, I shall recover the Pathfinders, whether or not Tymak opposes me, and then we will leave. If you want to curtail further bloodshed on a planet already drenched in it, you might be well advised to counsel restraint on his part. Although," Morane glanced at the Mercy Flight status display, "since my shuttles are about to start landing, it might be too late. Let's hope for the sake of Tymak's troops he took my warnings seriously."

— 15 —

"I have them on my sensors." Sergeant Major Bayn raised his handheld unit and pointed at a narrow valley beyond Klim Castle. "About twenty kilometers out. No visual contact yet. The lead ships are breaking off from the rest."

Salmin raised an arm to acknowledge the update, then ran a critical eye over the men and women of A Squadron, kneeling on the smooth, black stone by teams as per their shuttle assignments, weapons at the ready. Wearing powered armor and weighed down by both personal equipment and their share of the collective gear, the Pathfinders resembled monstrous, exoskeletal insects, alien creatures that seemed to blend with the background thanks to the armor's chameleon-like exterior. An observer more than a few hundred meters distant would see nothing but an empty roof, and his sensors wouldn't pick up much more since the Marines were under electronic silence.

This wouldn't be their first extraction from hostile territory. Not by a long shot. But once aboard the small, lightly armored craft, they were at the mercy of the pilots and any enemy gun or missile batteries tempted to open fire.

The Pathfinders' usual gunships would be safer since they were purpose-built to land and take off in the middle of a shooting match. But those were light years away. No starship capable of carrying enough to lift a battalion was available when they were ordered to Coraline. By then, many of the precious naval transports had either gone over to the rebels or been destroyed.

DeCarde, watching from the shelter of the south stairwell, heard the soft whine of the approaching craft before she could see them as anything more than an eerie blur against the brilliant blue sky, thanks to their hulls' stealth coating. Then, her helmet's audio pickups registered a faint thump. Moments later, the radio came to life.

"Niner, this is Bravo Niner, the Guards set off a booby trap in the west stairwell. Judging by the confusion we're picking up, no one told them to stay away."

Haller nudged DeCarde. "Colonel Gaillard is calling. He wants to know what the hell is happening."

"Let him eat static, Centurion. Bravo Niner, you are now weapons free."

Seconds after Pohlitz acknowledged her order, the first set of shuttles landed on Klim Castle's flat roof in a staggered line, sending swirls of dust to dance in the chilly afternoon air, and dropped their aft ramps.

At Salmin's signal, the one hundred and ten Marine Pathfinders of A Squadron stood in unison and jogged aboard. Then, the ramps closed again. The ships lifted off one after the other and turned back toward the east, flying low. They quickly vanished from sight. C Squadron, next in line, emerged from its stairwell and split into orderly rows, taking the spots their A Squadron comrades occupied seconds earlier.

The second row of shuttles landed shortly after that. Another explosion, this one closer, reached DeCarde's ears.

"Niner, this is Bravo Niner. The Guards are trying to break through the obstacles we set at the base of the west stairwell. That was their demolition charge."

DeCarde watched C Squadron board with the same speed and vigor as A Squadron, then followed the rest of HQ and Combat Support Squadrons up onto the roof seconds after the second row shuttles lifted. She took her place in line with Haller and knelt.

"Toss a few demolition charges of your own at them, Bravo Niner, and whatever other explosives you still have. HQ and Combat Support are about to board, which means you'll break clean in a moment anyway."

The next line of shuttles landed. A few of them were markedly different from the larger craft of the earlier two sets — smaller, sleeker and more heavily armed. They were *Vanquish*'s where the others had been *Narwhal*'s cargo lifters. As soon as the ramp in front of her dropped, DeCarde stood and, after a last glance at Klim Castle and the towering Talera Range, ran aboard and squeezed onto the bench beside Haller. With what seemed like lightning speed, the passenger compartment filled, the ramp closed again, cutting off her view, and she felt the craft lift off under full military power, banking to port as it did so.

Shortly after that, Salmin's voice came over the radio. "Bravo Niner, this is Niner Alpha, D Squadron is ready to embark. Break clean, I repeat, break clean."

"Bravo Niner, roger. Out."

This would be the critical moment when no one was left to watch the last squadron's back. Surprising DeCarde, the command push came to life with Klim's strident voice.

"Colonel DeCarde, what in the name of everything that's holy is happening? Colonel Gaillard tells me shuttles are landing on top of the fortress, and your troops are fighting with the Guards. Did you go over to the rebellion?"

Salmin cut through on the battalion net. "Bravo Niner, this is Niner Alpha. D Squadron is away. Blow the remaining demolitions and take your positions."

DeCarde smiled with barely suppressed glee as she switched to the command push. "No Countess, the 6th of the 21st hasn't gone over to the rebellion. We've merely gone. Gone from Coraline and once our rides break out of orbit, gone from what's left of this rotten fucking empire. I hope you and the Guards enjoy a long, lingering death for everything you've done to this planet. And I most sincerely hope that depraved sociopath you call an empress gets her just desserts for how she so cavalierly destroyed something that lasted a thousand years."

"Niner, this is Niner Alpha, B Squadron and the LZ team are away, I repeat, B Squadron and the LZ team are away. All of Pegasus Six is airborne."

A subdued cheer erupted around DeCarde, and her smile became almost manic.

"You've obviously gone mad, Colonel."

"No, Countess. For the first time since we landed on this godforsaken world, I feel sane again. Oh, and if you're wondering what happened to Dagon Verkur, I shot him. He was becoming insufferable, just like you. Farewell, Countess. I hope the manner of your death will at least in part make up for the havoc you caused."

DeCarde cut the link and settled back. With any luck, her battalion wasn't merely jumping out of one deadly trap to land in another. But as her most celebrated ancestor apparently enjoyed saying, at least according to family lore, where there's life, there's hope.

**

"*Vanquish* this is Mercy Flight. We have them. All of them."

Pleased grins appeared, and more than one arm shot up in a celebratory fist pump.

"Weapons, cease targeting Tymak's positions. Signals, see if you can get me a link with Commodore Kischak."

A few minutes passed before the latter's icy features materialized on the CIC's primary display. "What is it, Morane?"

"I wanted to let you know my shuttles lifted off with the Pathfinders. Once we've recovered them, the 197th will break out of orbit and head for one of Coraline's wormholes. Not Coraline Two, of course, where you've no doubt left your rearguard. With us gone, you're free to do as you wish with the remaining imperial forces on the planet. They're no longer our concern. But I would ask that you don't pursue us. We're no threat to anyone and will only fight to defend ourselves."

"And you still won't say where you're headed?"

Morane shook his head. "No, sir. We're leaving the empire, or what was once an empire, I suppose, to strike out for ourselves. I fear humanity is on an irrevocable path to self-destruction, and by the time it's over, I doubt there will be much left. We, my crews and the Pathfinders, don't want to be around when the final curtain falls and darkness cloaks this part of our galaxy."

Kischak stared at him in silence for a long time. Then, she nodded.

"Very well, Captain. In that case, good luck, though I would be remiss in my duties if I didn't ask you to reconsider and join us, now that you've turned against the Crown."

"Sorry, Commodore. I see no future that isn't filled with strife and no end that isn't bleak. We need to find our own way out of this mess and perhaps set the foundations for a brighter future."

A wry smile twisted Kischak's lips. "That was a sibylline statement if I ever heard one."

"It's better if nobody knows our heading and destination."

"In that case, Godspeed. I won't come after you if only because I'm not allowed to leave the sector unless in hot pursuit of units still loyal to Dendera."

"Which we are not."

"Indeed. Was there anything else?"

"No, sir."

"Farewell, Captain. Kischak, out."

Morane stared at the blank display, lost in thought, parsing his plans one last time before he committed everyone in his depleted formation to an uncertain future. A future based solely on his conviction humanity was staring into the abyss. But try as he might, Morane still saw no other choice.

He finally shook himself and called the bridge.

"Once the shuttles have been recovered and offloaded, we'll break the 197th out of orbit and head for the hyperlimit at best speed, followed by a coordinated jump for Wormhole Coraline Four. If the Marines want to shift personnel around between ships, we'll do that after we've left the Coraline system. Commodore Kischak might not want to pursue us now, but nothing says she won't change her mind in the next few hours."

"I assume we'll want to let *Myrtale* recover her shuttles after they deliver their load of Marines to *Vanquish*?" Mikkel asked.

"Yes, of course. There is no point in overcrowding our hangar deck for the sake of saving a few minutes. Speaking of which, I'll head there momentarily and welcome Colonel DeCarde aboard."

"That's what I figured. I'll ensure everything is set for us to leave."

"If I'm busy with DeCarde and the other ships report ready, execute without waiting for my order."

—16—

Morane watched from the hangar control room as *Myrtale*'s shuttles disgorged their portion of the Imperial Marine Corps' elite, then launched back into space. Then his own craft crossed the force barrier one by one and landed on their designated spots before releasing the Pathfinders aboard. As Morane expected, they formed up in orderly ranks, powered suits shut in case the hangar deck decompressed and waited until the space doors closed.

With the deck's atmospheric integrity now assured, the inner doors opened, and Morane stepped through, eyes searching for Colonel DeCarde, but in vain. The Pathfinders' chameleon armor blended so well with their surroundings that his eyes immediately felt the strain. Behind him, a stream of petty officers came through another door, lined up with *Vanquish*'s bosun and waited for the Marines' senior non-commissioned officer to make him or herself known.

A tall Pathfinder eventually spotted Morane and came over. When the armored figure removed her helmet, he saw it was DeCarde, her features creased by fatigue though her eyes seemed to sparkle with barely suppressed glee. She stomped to attention and raised her right hand to her brow in salute.

"Lieutenant Colonel Brigid DeCarde, commanding the 6th Battalion, 21st Pathfinder Regiment, sir. Permission to come aboard?"

"Granted, Colonel, and welcome. To you and every single Marine in your unit." Morane returned the salute, then made to hold out his hand before remembering she wore powered armor and might inadvertently crush his bones. He nodded toward the line of petty officers. "Our bosun, Chief Petty Officer Second Class Rossello, and his mates will guide your people to our Marine barracks and see that they take your wounded to our sickbay for medical treatment."

DeCarde nodded. "One moment, sir." She switched to the battalion push. "Squadron first sergeants, report to the chief petty officer standing on my left for barracks assignments." Turning back to Morane, DeCarde said, "HQ, B and D Squadrons, and my wounded are here with me. A, C and Combat Support Squadrons are supposed to be aboard *Narwhal*."

"They are. I received confirmation moments ago. Once *Myrtale* secures her shuttles, we're breaking out of orbit."

"And heading for this mysterious sanctuary."

A faint smile appeared on Morane's lips. "Indeed. You and I have much to discuss, Colonel, but first I shall let you settle in, get out of your armor and enjoy what little amenities we can offer. The senior Marine officer is entitled to private quarters, but I'm afraid it's shared cabins for your officers and command noncoms, and squad bays for your enlisted ranks. We turned a few of the adjacent compartments into makeshift squad bays to take care of the overflow. As I said earlier, it'll be cramped quarters, but at least you're alive."

"Anything is better than Klim Castle, Captain. For instance, here we won't worry about treacherous Guards knifing us in the back. Or insurgents itching for revenge. Or one of Admiral Loren's strike groups appearing above us, ready to turn our hundred thousand year-old final redoubt into rubble."

"No, but we'll have other matters to worry about."

"Such as the rebel battle group approaching Coraline?"

"Yes, but I think I've convinced its commanding officer to let us leave unmolested. In any case, they're still several hours out, so by the time they reach the planet we'll be almost at the hyperlimit. From there, it's an eleven hour FTL jump, followed by a drop into our target wormhole, which will, in turn, take us out of the Shield Sector altogether. After that, we face several weeks, if not months traveling through the wormhole network's lesser used nodes, the ones connecting uninhabited and sterile systems, before reaching Arietis in the Coalsack Sector. From there, we will transit through three more wormholes before finally arriving at our destination."

DeCarde cocked an eyebrow. "Which is?"

"Did you ever hear of the Lyonesse system?"

The Marine searched her memory, then shook her head. "The name doesn't ring a bell."

Morane's smile returned. "That's actually quite comforting, Colonel. If an elite Marine hasn't heard of this particular, and somewhat peculiar wormhole cul-de-sac, I daresay my choice was correct."

"A cul-de-sac?"

"Yes. One single mapped wormhole, which leads to a sterile system with two mapped wormholes, which leads to another one with two termini and thence to Arietis. I'm pinning my hopes on the coming civil war and collapse to bypass the system entirely, so some kernel of advanced technology survives."

"Cutting the long night down to centuries instead of it lasting for millennia."

"Just so."

**

Centurion Haller poked her head into DeCarde's cabin. Already stripped of her armor and gear, she wore Marine rifle green battledress with the regiment's winged dagger insignia on one side of the collar and a centurion's three silver diamonds on the other. Haller looked around the compartment, barely big enough for a bunk, desk, and chair, but with a tiny private heads and nodded.

"Nice."

"It sure beats Klim Castle."

"By a parsec, Colonel. Even squad bays full up with troopers seem luxurious. I'm sharing a six-bunk with the first sergeants and squadron centurions. It'll do us fine. I'm here for the command post gear. We found an empty broom closet at the end of the hallway, so there's no point in it cluttering up what little space you have. Klim's treasure chest is already there."

DeCarde, who was halfway through the process of dismantling her power suit for easy storage, nodded at the bunk.

"Help yourself."

Haller picked up the operations AI, a featureless cube, and stared at its shock-proof case.

"I wonder whether we will ever wake Archie from his sleep again. He served us loyally."

"Should I worry that you're anthropomorphizing an incredibly complex machine again?"

"No." She picked up the remaining gear. "At least not until I take Archie to the officers' mess for a beer."

"I think the Navy calls it a wardroom, Eve."

"They can call it what they want, sir, just as long as they don't call me late for chow."

"Do you think I need to post orders restricting the troops to barracks, so they don't wander all over the ship and scare our Navy friends?"

Haller shook her head. "No. The first sergeants already passed the word. Besides, after the excitement of the last few weeks and today's freedom flight, they'll be happy to sleep in a clean bunk or hang around the barracks mess and shoot the shit."

"In that case, I'll make a stab at relaxing as well."

The centurion snorted. "That'll be the day, Colonel. But try to enjoy the showers. They're a luxury unheard of since the day Countess Klim decided to scorch Coraline."

"And may the devil take her for it, along with the entire 14th Guards Regiment."

"From your lips to the Almighty's ear."

"I don't think the Almighty has a say when it comes to the devil's social calendar. But if you want to do something nice, find out where I can snag a cup of coffee. My guts processed enough tea to last a lifetime."

— 17 —

"Kudos to your housekeeping droids," DeCarde said the moment she entered Morane's day cabin. "Finding my way here from the barracks was easy with their help."

Vanquish's captain waved her toward a chair. "Please sit. With a small crew, the more automation, the better. Your two squadrons and battalion HQ double the number of souls aboard my cruiser. In fact, your battalion as a whole has increased the size of our contingent by over half, that's how automated our ships are nowadays. In the words of an old joke perpetuated by Fleet engineers, given enough automation, two lesser primates and one Academy cadet should suffice to sail *Vanquish*." He nodded at the silver samovar sitting on a sideboard. "Can I offer you tea?"

DeCarde pulled a face. "I've imbibed enough tea in the last few weeks to tan my insides, sir. I'll pass, thanks."

Morane chuckled. "Coffee drinker, eh? My apologies. I have none on hand, but I'm sure the wardroom could organize a cup. We're more partial to tea aboard

Vanquish and like most in the Navy, consider coffee a ground pounder's brew."

"It doesn't matter, sir." She shrugged. "As a caffeine vector, tea will serve the purpose." DeCarde tried to fight back an unexpected yawn and lost. "I accept your offer."

He made a wry face. "Not to put a negative spin on things, Colonel, but tea travels better than coffee, and adapts more easily to other worlds. We may see coffee become one of those things that turn into legend and then myth."

DeCarde considered his words for a few seconds before grimacing as she sat. "I sincerely hope you're wrong, sir, but fear you might be right."

"Unfortunately. And when we're in private, please call me Jonas. At the end of this journey, I think we will find ourselves working as equals for the common good."

"And I'm Brigid. Though I didn't know Navy officers could break protocol, even if they wanted to." She gave him a friendly smile. "We Marines always figured you lot for a bunch of stuck-up prigs. No doubt you consider us uncouth peasants in return."

Morane smiled back. "If not worse things, Brigid, but meant in jest. We, just like you no doubt, save our real venom for the Imperial Guards."

"Which we'll hopefully never see again. You know, if Stichus hadn't replaced the Army with his Guards, things might not be as bad. At least not on Coraline, for example."

"Perhaps, but without Guards Regiments loyal to the sovereign's person rather than the constitution, there could not be a Ruggero dynasty, so it's a bit of a chicken and egg thing."

"And without a Ruggero dynasty, I might not be losing access to coffee. Next, you'll tell me distilling will also become a thing of the past, and I won't ever drink decent whiskey again."

"It won't be that dire. Wherever humanity can grow something that produces sugar, we'll find the basis for booze. Remember, distilled spirits predate the industrial revolution by centuries. We may live long enough to find out whether it will be decent. Coffee on the other hand needs specific conditions to grow. Otherwise it might taste like something that passed through the digestive tract of a Parthian werecat."

DeCarde made a face. "Speaking of places I won't miss."

"You've been to Parth?"

She nodded. "Once, to help the Correctional Service in quelling a revolt by political prisoners. That particular population grew exponentially under Dendera's rule without commensurate growth by the penal system. It was ugly, and probably one of those harbingers of today's situation, except nobody cared to notice. Calling Parth the empire's largest open-air prison doesn't do the place justice. Open-air sewer is a more apt description."

"Wasn't there a Marine regiment stationed on Parth?"

"You mean the Marine Light Infantry? Yes, at one time. Stichus ordered the Corps to disband it when he formed the Imperial Guards. He thought a regiment composed of convicts was unbecoming to the Imperial Armed Services."

"Really? And the Corps accepted that?"

A sly grin appeared on DeCarde's face. "It merely paid lip service to the order. They withdrew the MLI from Parth and renamed it though the regiment was officially struck from the order of battle. Would you like to know what it became?" Mischief twinkled in her eyes. When Morane nodded, she said, "The 21st Imperial Pathfinder Regiment."

A bark of laughter escaped Morane's throat. "Priceless. Is your regiment still composed of convicts?"

"No.   Only the original draft graduated from that program. Ever since, we've filled our ranks in the normal way."

"How about the rehabilitation through retraining idea?"

"It never really vanished. After the Fleet moved the military prisons from Parth to Caledonia, the Corps stood up an Imperial Marine Rifle Regiment to fill the MLI's role. Officially its job was providing field commanders with battalion-sized light infantry units for specialized combat duties. We just never told Stichus and his successors where the rifle battalions recruited their troops. The only difference is we no longer recruit among the civilian convict population, which is a shame. Many of the political prisoners we fought on Parth had the makings of good Marines. Unfortunately, most didn't survive."

"I didn't hear of that particular revolt."

"Not surprising. After ordering us to suppress it, the government made sure knowledge of what happened was also suppressed. Thousands died, and the government never told their families how or why. A number of my troopers quit or took early retirement in disgust at what Dendera forced us to do."

"But not you?"

"My family has served in the Corps since before there was an empire, mostly as Pathfinders. That's where our loyalties lie, which means I couldn't simply walk away from my duties, no matter how I felt about our ruler."

"And yet you're walking away from the Corps now." Morane stood and went to the sideboard.

DeCarde gave him a so-so gesture with her right hand. "Yes and no. By agreeing to follow you, I've done my duty to my battalion in saving their lives. And if you're right about where the empire is headed, the Corps to which my family was pledged for over a thousand years may vanish in my lifetime. But by leaving the empire, I'm also leaving the Corps."

"Or you're setting the foundations for the Marine Corps' rebirth by storing the proper seeds in my human knowledge vault on Lyonesse." Morane drew two cups of tea from his samovar and handed one to DeCarde.

"Thank you. Now would you mind telling me how you came up with the notion of a knowledge vault?"

— 18 —

He sat again and gazed at her over the rim of his mug.

"I'm an avid and lifelong student of history. As such, I learned two vital and inevitable things. First, empires don't last, and at a thousand years, ours entered fatal senility after Stichus Ruggero's uncontested subversion of the succession rules. There have been rumblings of discontent and revolt ever since. And second, the higher a civilization's level of sophistication, the worse its fall and the longer its path to rebirth. You can find countless examples throughout history, not only ours but the Shrehari Empire's as well. You know that their distant ancestors built that fortress you call Klim Castle, right?"

"I thought those were tall tales."

"We don't know much about the proto-Shrehari, but their descendants are once more facing collapse even though they never regained the sophisticated knowledge that produced nearly indestructible buildings. I suppose our empire might have lasted longer if our galactic neighbors were still a threat.

"In any case, once those two notions crystallized in my mind, I set about to gauge where our empire stood on the path to decline. I found that with Dendera's accession to the throne, the decay accelerated so much, collapse wasn't centuries away, but only decades, if that. As a result, I wondered whether finding a sanctuary, a safe haven where advanced knowledge and technology might survive, if it escaped the ravages of civil war, might help humanity reclaim the stars much faster than if it were left to a natural rebirth.

"I eventually decided on Lyonesse with its particular place in our interstellar system. When most of the 197th Battle Group was destroyed by rebellious naval units, I figured the end was rapidly coming. Maybe not that of the empire just yet, but my own end and that of my crews. If we were to try and make the human knowledge vault a reality, escaping from the disaster in the Toboso system was our one chance. The people with us are those who voluntarily followed me into exile. Those who didn't left aboard our other surviving frigate, though no matter whose navy they join, their chances of surviving long enough for a natural death don't seem good."

"Do the people of Lyonesse know we're coming and why?" She took a sip and smiled. "This is much better than the swill we drank on Coraline. There may be hope for the future."

"Enjoy this blend while it lasts. As for Lyonesse, the answer is no. For obvious reasons, I've kept my plans close-held until deciding it was time to strike out on our own. They'll find out once we enter into orbit."

"And what if the colonists don't want to be saddled with fifteen hundred stray Armed Services personnel who, for all intents and purposes, are deserters?"

"We'll cross that wormhole's event horizon when we reach it. But with civil war heating up in every corner of human space, the people of Lyonesse are likely to be grateful for a permanent garrison that supplements whatever defense force they might have. There's also something else, a Fleet supply depot on Lyonesse, established there by persons unknown with greater interest in lining their pockets than helping the Fleet. It will not only help us keep our current technology working long enough to establish new fabrication facilities, but gives us a legitimate foothold on the planet."

DeCarde inclined her head in a gesture of respect. "You thought of everything."

"No. I didn't think about the usefulness of experienced ground troops until I heard your distress signal. There are bound to be more realizations along those lines, if not during our voyage to Lyonesse, then soon after settling there."

"It's probably inevitable." She took another sip and let her eyes wander over the star map covering most of a bulkhead behind Morane. "I haven't yet told my troops about our quitting the Corps and the empire. Telling anyone other than my closest senior staff about the evacuation in advance would have been too risky. But I really should address them before we go FTL. Might it be possible for me to speak with the senior of my squadron commanders aboard *Narwhal*?"

"Certainly. Now?"

DeCarde nodded. "Please, if it's not an inconvenience."

"Captain to the bridge."

"Officer of the watch."

"Open a link with *Narwhal* and pipe it to my day cabin. Colonel DeCarde wants to speak with—" He glanced at her.

"Major Hanni Waske, who commands the Combat Support Squadron."

"Did you catch the major's name?" Morane asked.

"Aye, aye, sir. Wait one."

They passed the next few minutes savoring their tea in companionable silence before the day cabin's display came to life with the solemn countenance of a middle-aged woman whose leathery face spoke of long service.

"How are things over there, Hanni?"

"Good, sir. *Narwhal*'s crew went above and beyond the call of duty to build Marine barracks from virtually nothing. It's not the Aramis Grand Hotel, but it sure beats Klim Castle. Plus, no damn Guards or rebels to ruin a good night's sleep. The boys and girls are smiling. It'll be our first vacation in months. I gather from the radio traffic that B Squadron's extraction was a complete success."

A wry smile turned up the corners of DeCarde's mouth.

"Apparently it wasn't as clean a break as you might think. B Squadron has a few armored suits in need of repair, but beyond bruises, nothing worthy of discussion. The Guards on the other hand probably suffered at least one or two platoons' worth of dead and injured. Bowdoin triggered the booby traps and expended plenty of ammo to keep the bastards from rushing his troopers."

"Couldn't have happened to nicer people."

"Listen, Hanni, there's something everyone needs to know now that we're out of immediate danger." DeCarde quickly relayed her earlier conversation with Morane almost verbatim.

"Lyonesse, eh?" Waske rubbed her chin. "Not a familiar name. I hope you intend to speak with the battalion soon. The rumor machine is already powering up over here, thanks to a few friendly crew members, and it'll come better straight from you rather than me."

"If our Navy friends can rig something that'll allow me to talk to the folks in *Narwhal* over a comlink while I'm speaking to the folks here, then I'd say as soon as possible. Definitely before our FTL jump to the wormhole."

The officer commanding Combat Support Squadron, and by dint of seniority, third in the battalion's chain of command, nodded with approval.

"Good, provided the folks with us will be able to ask you questions right there and then."

DeCarde glanced at Morane who said, "You can assemble your folks in *Vanquish* on the hangar deck, and I'll ask Captain Ryzkov to arrange the same on *Narwhal*. Then we'll set up an audio and video link allowing you to see and hear your assembled troops over there while they can see and hear you from here. The hangar deck traffic control display should suit the purpose."

"Does that work for you? Or should I do this in two parts? Once here and then transfer over to *Narwhal* for a repeat?"

Waske shook her head. "Remotely works, Colonel. The troops understand we need to haul ass and leave this place."

DeCarde turned to Morane again. "Can we do this in one hour?"

"I don't see why not."

"One hour then. Anything else?"

"Nothing that can't wait. Clean bunks, clean heads and real food will work their usual miracle on morale."

"A day or two of rest, then I'm invoking shipboard routine. If our respective captains allow it, I'd like to see everyone do daily parkour runs to stay in shape."

When Morane gave her a strange look, she said, "I'll explain afterward, Jonas. Hanni, you may wish to have the same conversation with Captain Ryzkov."

"Of course. So far, Lori's been more than accommodating."

DeCarde's eyebrows crept up to her hairline. Lori? "Glad to see you're already on first-name terms with *Narwhal*'s captain."

"Since we'll be living in each other's pocket for the next few weeks, getting acquainted seemed like the right thing to do."

"Indeed. Until later, then."

"Until later, Colonel."

— 19 —

After speaking extemporaneously to the tightly massed troops standing before her on the hangar deck and their comrades visible on the wide screen affixed to the far bulkhead for almost fifteen minutes, DeCarde fell silent. She let her gaze roam over the serried ranks, meeting the eyes of her Pathfinders to gauge their feelings and reactions.

"Are there any questions or does anyone wish to comment on my decision? Consider this a battalion commander's hour, meaning anything goes, within the normal parameters, of course. And don't worry. If you think of something later on, the folks in *Vanquish* can always ask me, Major Salmin or Sergeant Major Bayn and those in *Narwhal* can ask Major Waske. They know as much as I do."

A hard-faced Pathfinder from D Squadron stomped to attention and raised his right fist. "Sir."

"Yes, Trooper Maartens?"

"What if we'd rather not settle on Lyonesse and instead want to make our way home?"

"Should we touch port somewhere before reaching Lyonesse, I can release you from the Service, but Captain Morane doesn't plan to stop anywhere. In fact, we're not even scheduled to cross any major inhabited system except Arietis. This entire scheme depends on slipping away unseen, so no one knows we're establishing a human knowledge vault on Lyonesse.

"But once there, if a ship heading into the empire comes by, I'll certainly release you on demand. Or, if you prefer, I'll ask Captain Morane if we can send you back to Klim Castle before we go FTL." She waited for the expected chuckles to die down before continuing. "I can understand not wanting to leave everything behind, but I needed to decide. It was either join Captain Morane's exodus or die with the 14th Guards on Coraline. I chose life in exile instead of death."

Maartens nodded once. "Understood, sir."

"I'm aware not everyone agrees or is happy with my decision and would rather we return to our previous existence, but as long as we're alive, we remain the 6th of the 21st. We'll help each other through this. Besides, who knows what the future holds for us. It's not only our fates that are changing. The empire itself faces a bleak tomorrow."

"But we have a chance at something better," Maartens said.

"Precisely." She smiled at him because it suddenly dawned on her that Maartens wasn't the one with reservations. Instead, he voiced them for those who didn't want to speak out in public. His question was designed to lance what might become a festering boil on the unit's morale. She made a mental note to discuss Maartens with Bayn and see whether it was time to return the corporal's stripes he'd lost to a lack of discretion during shore leave the previous year.

That first question seemed to burst a dam. DeCarde spent another hour discussing everything from mundane matters such as pay — for which she had no answers — to the more philosophical issues such as the future of the empire and what might happen to their extended families. But she was strangely elated after answering the last question, and the troops were dismissed to their barracks.

The general mood seemed better than she expected, and it wasn't just the afterglow of escaping certain death. DeCarde fancied she could almost see a renewed sense of adventure stirring in the ranks, one propelled by a cause larger than themselves. Young men and women joined the Marines precisely for those reasons and then applied to become Pathfinders because they wanted even more.

As she walked back to her quarters, lost in thought, Centurion Haller caught up with DeCarde. "Good session, Colonel, though I figure once they've digested what you said and understand what it means, you might want to hold another one."

DeCarde gave Haller a tired smile. "And I will, Eve. If only to reinforce the idea we are still a unified battalion, one of the Marine Corps' elite, and will stay so forever, because we are now our only remaining family."

"Aye. I guess I should dig up what the Navy has on Lyonesse and prepare briefing packages for the troops, so they can get used to the idea of our new home."

**

When the door to the bridge opened at DeCarde's approach the next morning, she took a deep breath and stopped on the threshold, even though Morane had invited her to join him at oh-nine-hundred.

"Permission to enter?"

Morane swiveled his chair around and smiled. "As commanding officer of the embarked Marine contingent, you enjoy automatic access to the bridge and the CIC, Colonel. I thought you might enjoy watching us fall into Wormhole Coraline Four and leave this benighted system behind forever. I trust your night was restful."

"Best sleep in months, sir. The surroundings and the company are more congenial here than inside Klim Castle, or elsewhere on Coraline."

"No doubt." He pointed at a vacant console. "Consider that yours for the rest of the journey. If we call battle stations, I'll expect you in the CIC. Did you meet some of the ship's officers at breakfast?"

"Yes, sir. Commander Mikkel — Iona — introduced me to several. Compliments to your galley on the food, by the way. We haven't eaten this well since landing on Coraline." DeCarde sat in the form-fitting chair and studied her surroundings, eyes bright with curiosity. "And washing off the filth we picked up serving alongside the 14th Guards did wonders for our spirits."

"Your troopers seemed to be in fine fettle once you finished the session with them yesterday."

"Knowing all of us made it out alive counts for a lot in a tightly knit outfit like the Pathfinders. As I told my operations officer yesterday, the battalion is now our only family."

"We squids feel the same. Perhaps in time, we can merge our two families. By the way, Commodore Kischak seems to be keeping her word. There's no sign of pursuit, and with our next three wormhole transits taking us through unoccupied systems with multiple termini we should be able to make a cleaner break than your own rearguard. No criticism intended."

"None taken, Captain. Breaking clean while withdrawing under contact is one of the hardest tactical moves for us ground pounders. We're lucky to have suffered only mechanical damage to a few powered suits, and no human casualties. Of course, I can't comment on what the Navy does."

"We enjoy the advantage of speed and distance." He nodded at a side display. "Speaking of distance, that bright dot is Coraline, where Governor General the Countess Klim might even now be begging Commodore Kischak for her life."

"Let's hope this Kischak is not a soft touch."

"I doubt she is, Colonel and because of that, I think the empire's last hours on Coraline are nigh."

"And without your arrival, my battalion would likely be dying alongside the Guards just about now. I'm not sure if I can adequately express my gratitude."

"Helping me succeed in my quixotic quest will be thanks enough."

"We will do our best. I give you my word as a Marine."

Morane acknowledged her vow with a solemn nod. Then, he said, "Changing the subject ever so slightly, did you ever witness what crossing a wormhole's event horizon actually looks like?"

"No. I've only been a passenger aboard starships and never served with an embarked Marine detachment."

"The perhaps I should give you the experience."

"Sir." Lieutenant Hak, *Vanquish*'s navigator, turned toward the command chair. "All ships are aligned with the event horizon, synced, and report ready for wormhole transit."

"Take us into the wormhole, Mister Hak."

Nothing happened for what seemed like a long time, even though the tactical projection showed three small icons rapidly approaching a hole in the fabric of space, one invisible to the human eye. Then, the familiar, eerie sensation that everything was being pulled out of shape and distorted overcame her, along with the usual swarm of butterflies trying to escape her stomach.

But that sensation was nothing compared to the spectacle on the bridge's primary display. Where moments before she saw the usual dense speckling of stars against the black velvet of space, something from the fevered hallucinations of dying madman writhed with pulsating colors and shapes, distorting the very fabric of the universe.

"Wow." The word came out as a hoarse whisper. DeCarde couldn't tear her eyes away even though nausea was taking hold of her. It was, in a word, mesmerizing.

"Quite something, isn't it? I never tire of watching the spectacle though I understand many sentient beings become violently ill from the visual overload."

DeCarde tried to stifle a burp and failed. "I seem to be one of them, sir."

Morane gave her an alarmed look and nodded at Hak. The display went dark. Almost immediately, the pain behind DeCarde eyes and in her gut evaporated.

"Better, Colonel?"

She nodded. "Better. That was, um, a once in a lifetime experience, I think, sir."

"Some among my crew would agree with you. We'll be in transit for about six hours, but it sure beats a week traveling FTL to reach the next star system on this branch of the network. And that's even though we can push through hyperspace at over one hundred and eighty times the speed of light outside a star's heliosphere, as opposed to only twice the speed of light within a star system."

"And what's our destination?"

"ISC119041-5, according to the Imperial Star Catalog of 2592, which, as the year might tell you, was published under the empire's first ruler. The last digit was added after the discovery of stable wormholes since it has five termini. But because it has no habitable planets, no one bothered to give it a name, even if it sees a fair amount of traffic. I'm hoping this time none of that traffic is naval, no matter from which side." Morane stood and stretched. "Could I interest you in a tour of the ship?"

"With pleasure, Captain."

"Along the way, we can discuss how to use your Marines as part of the ship's company while we do so. From now on, I can only assume every star system we enter is hostile."

— 20 —

After an uneventful day, DeCarde joined Morane in the CIC for their exit from the wormhole. Mercifully, the video feed turned on only after the strange stretching and distorting sensation passed. Out of precaution, Morane placed his ship at battle stations, in case trouble awaited them on the other side.

Since they were now part of the crew, DeCarde's Marines had donned their armor and taken station around *Vanquish* according to the ship's original standing orders that included the use of any embarked infantry element. Pathfinders were nothing if not adaptable, and after a few quick practice runs, they were ready when the actual call sounded.

"Scanning," Chief Lettis said the moment their universe stabilized again. "*Narwhal* and *Myrtale* are still keeping station and are in silent mode. If I didn't know they were there, I wouldn't see them."

"Both report a successful transit," the signals petty officer added.

Morane turned to DeCarde. "And now we wait and watch for activity in this system. The wormhole ejected us with a decent sublight velocity, meaning we need not light our drives just yet."

No more than an hour passed before Chief Lettis said, "The sensors picked up three hyperspace signatures headed in our direction. Two in close formation some distance behind the third."

"Not quite as deserted as we hoped. No matter. They're unlikely to spot us."

Half an hour later, Lettis spoke again. "Three emergence signatures just over six hundred thousand kilometers off our starboard quarter." A video feed appeared on the main display while the tactical projection gave birth to three red icons. "Two Rancor class frigates and one freighter. Looking for identifying marks on the freighter."

As they studied the unknown ships racing toward Wormhole Four, one of the frigates fired at the civilian ship and scored a direct hit on its aft shields, creating a blue-green aurora that spiked into the purple.

"Judging by that flare, the freighter's aft generators are about to overload. I don't think it has the hull strength to resist for long without shields."

Morane nodded. "Aye."

"Sir, they're broadcasting at the freighter. In clear."

"Put it on speakers."

"*Dawn Trader*, this is *Retribution*. By order of Viceroy Santana, you will decelerate and prepare for boarding. If you do not comply, we will destroy you."

"You're nothing but damned pirates pretending to be part of a navy," an irate man's voice replied, "and your poxed viceroy is no more than a jumped up, sociopathic clerk with delusions of grandeur. Besides, if we surrender, we'll be executed at Santana's orders, so fuck off."

Creswell raised her hand to attract Morane's attention. "*Dawn Trader* belongs to the Galactic Dawn Corporation, headquartered on Yotai. The frigate *Retribution* is listed as part of the 16th Fleet, 168th Battle Group, stationed in the Ariel system."

"Last warning, *Dawn Trader*. Surrender and live. Resist and die."

"And I said fuck off."

"There's a Santana listed as governor general of Ariel. A minor baronet of no great accomplishments or family. He could have declared himself independent of Viceroy Joback, who runs the Coalsack. Or at least Joback did when we received our last update. The admiral commanding 16th Fleet might be in control now if he followed Loren's example in the Shield Sector."

"Maybe this Santana suborned the 168th's flag officer or convinced a subordinate to mutiny in return for a quick promotion, so he could set up his own fiefdom. But I didn't think parts of the empire were already so far down the road to chaos."

"*Things fall apart; the center cannot hold; Mere anarchy is loosed upon the world*," DeCarde quoted in a soft voice.

"Beg pardon?"

"William Butler Yeats, Captain. A twentieth-century poet. The combination of a quasi-eidetic memory and a propensity for collecting pre-imperial and even pre-diaspora historical trivia is a family curse that has afflicted us for centuries. Some say Yeats' poem was meant to underscore the dissolution of a stable political order in the aftermath of a great war."

"Your family curse could be a boon to our project, Colonel. We'll need to consider how best we can tap that particular fount of knowledge."

"I draw the line at anything resembling a mind probe."

"Nothing of the sort, though I do expect you to talk freely and share." Morane's eyes slipped back to the display just in time to catch the frigate *Retribution* firing again. This time, *Dawn Trader*'s aft shields gave birth to a bright purple aurora which collapsed with terrifying suddenness.

"Captain," Mikkel's hologram said, "whatever the reasons for the pursuit we're witnessing, it doesn't feel right watching a pair of Navy frigates — it doesn't matter whose navy — attacking an unarmed civilian ship with who knows how many souls on board."

Chief Petty Officer Lettis glanced over his shoulder. "According to my scans, approximately two hundred."

Morane let out a heartfelt sigh. "You are correct once more, Iona. *Vanquish* will go 'up systems' and target both frigates. Fire at my orders. Signals, open a link with *Retribution*. *Narwhal* and *Myrtale* to stay silent."

DeCarde let out a grim chuckle. "I'd love to see the face of that frigate captain when a fast attack cruiser suddenly appears on his sensors."

When the signals petty officer nodded, Morane said, "You're about to get that chance just now. Open the connection."

An angry, dark-haired woman with a miser's mean features swam into focus on the CIC's secondary display. "Who the hell are you and what do you want?"

"I'm Captain Jonas Morane, 197th Battle Group. Why are you shooting at a civilian freighter?"

"None of your business. And if you're 19th Fleet, you don't belong in this sector." She glanced to one side and frowned. "Where are the rest of your ships?"

"They're here, running silent but watching you, ready to come 'up systems' and open fire. You may have noticed that my ship is targeting you, and as I carry a battlecruiser's weight of guns and missiles, I can easily shred a pair of frigates. And I'm not in a mood to be charitable when I catch Navy ships trying to destroy an unarmed vessel with two hundred innocent people aboard. Therefore, please refrain from firing on *Dawn Trader* again. Oh, and I believe it's common courtesy to name yourself when a senior officer calls, especially when said senior officer is giving you an order."

"I'm Commander Garbina Qoli, of the frigate *Retribution*. And that freighter you seem so keen to protect, Captain, is carrying traitors, dangerous subversives who attempted to overthrow Viceroy Santana."

"Ah, yes." Morane settled back in his chair and gazed at Qoli with hard eyes. "Viceroy Santana. And what would his allegiance be? The Coalsack Sector comes under Viceroy Joback, no?"

"Joback's dead, killed by Admiral Zahar, who usurped the viceregal chair and denounced Empress Dendera. As a governor general loyal to Her Majesty, Guillermo Santana assumed Viceroy Joback's mantle and ordered loyal units of the 16th Fleet to arrest rebels, such as the traitors fleeing in *Dawn Trader*. And what are your loyalties, *sir*?"

"My loyalties are neither here nor there, Commander, but I won't allow you to massacre civilians. The Aldebaran Conventions still apply to any human armed services, no matter to whom they pledge allegiance."

"You'd open fire on us to protect traitors?"

"To protect civilians against rogue naval units carrying out illegal acts? Of course. Now break off pursuit and let them go through the wormhole." When Qoli didn't immediately reply, Morane glanced at Creswell. "A warning salvo across *Retribution*'s bow, if you please. Let's see what color we can get from her forward shields."

"You wouldn't dare."

"Fire."

A half-dozen large caliber plasma rounds erupted from *Vanquish*'s guns and streaked across the void. They grazed *Retribution*'s bow shields close enough to raise a bluish aurora as competing energies clashed.

"Turn around and leave," Morane said. "Your chase is over. Going after *Dawn Trader* through that wormhole to Coraline won't do you much good. The system has fallen to Admiral Loren's rebel forces and is presently occupied by Commodore Kischak's 191st Battle Group."

Qoli sneered. "Meaning you're traitors as well."

"You may believe whatever you choose. However, take note I have not actually fired at you, even though my battle group could destroy your two ships in a matter of minutes. And I will let you leave unharmed once that freighter vanishes without further harm."

Lettis raised a hand and pointed at a side display. *Dawn Trader* was about to cross the wormhole's event horizon.

Morane nodded. "Something that will occur in a matter of minutes."

They saw Qoli's lips move soundlessly as she gave orders after cutting the audio portion of the link.

"They're changing course, Captain."

The audio came back on. "Viceroy Santana will hear of this. There will be no safe haven for you anywhere in the Coalsack Sector."

"Not even in systems held by Admiral Zahar?"

"He miscalculated how much of the 16th Fleet was willing to rebel and will find himself trapped in the Yotai system soon enough. We will meet again, Captain, and under circumstances that will make you regret helping enemies of the Crown escape." The link abruptly went dark.

"Not one for courtesy," Mikkel murmured.

"Apparently not. We will stay at the current velocity until Commander Qoli and her colleague initiate a wormhole transit, to make sure they can't track us."

"What if they leave through Wormhole Three? That's the one you want to use."

"Then I shall be forced to plot a new route, Iona. It's a given they'll be waiting on the other end for a day or two in case we come through. If not to ambush us, then at the very least to find out what we supposed rebels from the Shield Sector are doing in their part of the empire. Though I fear our new path might lead through more inhabited systems than planned, with the risk it entails."

DeCarde gave Morane a wry grin. "No plan survives contact with the enemy, right?"

"Correct. And I fear we now face nothing but enemies. The loyalists consider us rebels, and the rebels believe we're loyalists."

Chief Lettis snorted. "And that means we've reached peak FUBAR, sir."

—21—

"There's no hiding from the fact our options are shrinking." Morane's eyes went around the conference room table. "Since the ships from the 168th took the wormhole I intended us to use, our next best route means eventually crossing the Parth system. Thankfully, it's the only major populated junction before Arietis. The other inhabited systems shouldn't present any problems since they're unlikely to have a naval presence from either side."

"Famous last words?" Mikkel's eyes twinkled with mischief.

"More like a pious hope, Iona. As our Marine reminded me yesterday, no plan survives contact with the enemy. My first one didn't, and this new one probably won't either."

"Adapt and overcome."

Morane nodded at DeCarde. "Precisely."

"Is there still time to quit this caravan of the damned?" Lori Ryzkov, present via holographic projection once more, asked in a joking tone.

"I think *Dawn Trader* was your last chance," Mikkel replied.

"And head back to where Admiral Loren started this fun? Pass."

Morane raised one hand to stop any further banter. "If there are no more points up for discussion, I intend to stay on our current heading for another eighteen hours while we run silent and see if Qoli and her ilk show up again. Then we will get underway for Wormhole Two." When no one spoke, he stood. "Thank you. Dismissed."

He intercepted DeCarde at the door. "Buy you a cup of tea?"

"Certainly."

Morane ushered her into his day cabin and then filled two mugs from the samovar. After handing her one, he settled into the chair behind his desk. "You know, I can't help but wonder who the people aboard *Dawn Trader* were and what their fate will be."

DeCarde gave him a quizzical glance. "You considered asking them to join us?"

"If they're people with nowhere else to go."

"Do you intend to collect every stray who is neither loyalist nor rebel?"

"Sure, if they own a starship and buy into my plans."

"Then we might really become Lori Ryzkov's caravan of the damned. Didn't I once read an ancient tale with a similar theme? A fellowship formed to redeem a fallen world?"

"You may well have. That story is as archetypal as they come. People fleeing collapse and banding together for a trek to some Promised Land."

"Perhaps the next shipload of subversives fleeing naval units turned warlord enforcers will stick around long enough to hear your sales pitch."

Morane cocked an eyebrow. "Warlord enforcers?"

"You didn't seriously buy this so-called Commander Qoli's contention a self-proclaimed viceroy, Santana, became the Crown's legal representative in the Coalsack Sector after Admiral Zahar killed Viceroy Joback?"

"Clearly you're not a believer."

"Empress Dendera is infamous for nepotism. Far more so than her father, who was no slouch himself. Viceregal appointments are her sole preserve, and she only hands them out to her close family and cronies. She'd never countenance a governor general, a minor baronet at that, practicing self-promotion on such a scale. Santana might call himself viceroy now, but he'll not be a loyalist, and he may not rule over anything more than the Ariel system."

"You seem well versed in these matters."

DeCarde smiled ruefully and tapped the side of her head with an extended index finger. "It's that hereditary talent for trivia."

"Then I suppose Qoli decided we were loyalists and spun her tale accordingly."

"I'd wager your restraint toward her was the giveaway. Rebels don't play the noblesse oblige game from what I've seen since the uprising began, which is probably why the loyalist factions in the Armed Services are losing badly. They're not ruthless or hungry enough."

"Or care about Dendera enough."

DeCarde inclined her head. "That too."

**

DeCarde was at lunch with her officers the next day when the battle stations siren sounded. The Marines swallowed a last bite and rushed back to the barracks where she grabbed her emergency gear and headed for the CIC. Once there, she studied the tactical projection and saw a single icon near the wormhole terminus leading to Coraline.

"One of Commodore Kischak's ships?"

Chief Lettis shook his head. "The power curve is that of a civilian vessel, and I do believe it's our old friend *Dawn Trader*."

DeCarde and Morane exchanged glances. "They didn't stay long on the other side," the latter said. "We last saw them what, eighteen hours ago?"

"About that, sir."

"Not long enough to reach Coraline." Morane turned to the signals petty officer. "Try to raise them on subspace."

The voice that finally replied was the same irate one telling Commander Qoli where to go the previous day.

"What do you want?"

"I'm Jonas Morane of the cruiser *Vanquish*. We held up your pursuers yesterday and forced them to break off the chase. I'm curious why you came back here so quickly."

"Shit's hitting the impeller over by Coraline. Who knows how many warships are pounding each other into scrap metal. I figured I'd never make it to my target wormhole without being intercepted by someone, and any other terminus would spit me out where my passengers don't want to go. So I'm looking for another way around." A pause. "I suppose we owe you our thanks for stopping that bastard Santana's minions. The name is Rinne, by the way. I'm *Dawn Trader*'s master."

"A pleasure, Captain Rinne. Let's just say I'm averse to naval officers attacking unarmed civilians."

The man snorted with derision. "They might have been naval officers once upon a time, but now they serve only the highest bidder, which is Santana, who saw the opportunity to seize control of Ariel and the adjoining systems for himself."

"And Admiral Zahar?"

"Bah. He's an idiot. After murdering the legal viceroy, Zahar tried to tighten his grip on the Coalsack Sector, but the harder he squeezes, the more star systems break off and proclaim independence. May I ask to whom you owe allegiance, Captain Morane? You evidently came from Coraline where it seems rebels and loyalists are fighting to the death right now. Yesterday, you behaved like a proper Imperial Navy officer in shielding me from Qoli and her mercenaries but didn't identify yourself as such. I'll confess to being puzzled by your intentions."

"When we left Coraline, the only other ships we could detect in the system belonged to Admiral Loren's rebellious 19th Fleet, and they were heading for the planet itself where a small loyalist contingent is still holding out. Who might be fighting them now is a question I can't answer. As for our allegiances, we belong to neither Loren, nor the empress, nor anyone else."

"Mercenaries, then." Rinne's tone held barely suppressed scorn. "Like Qoli and her ilk."

"No. We don't intend to hire ourselves out for pay or fight for anyone."

"What then?"

"My ships and crews, as well as the Marines we carry are quitting the empire. We're leaving the madness to play itself out while we settle in a place where we can preserve enough knowledge and technology to rebuild once the fighting's over."

Rinne cackled. "An idealist — nay, a dreamer — commanding a damned cruiser? May the Almighty take me now because I've heard of everything."

"It's that, or die fighting for one side or the other, and we've had a taste of where such a soul-destroying alternative leads. The empire is finished, but we're not going down with it, and if we can't do anything to change the present, perhaps we can influence the future. Now I've told you about us, how about you tell me why Santana and his minions want your ship so badly? Maybe we can help each other."

Dawn Trader's captain didn't immediately respond, and Morane knew better than to prod. Finally, Rinne said, "I can always judge someone by their face, Dreamer. Open a video link and let's see if you're an honest man or another Qoli."

—22—

Morane gestured at the signals petty officer, and one of the side displays came alive. To DeCarde's eyes, Rinne's appearance matched his voice and his words. He had the narrow, seamed face of a lifelong spacer, framed by a wild, snow-white beard and equally unkempt white hair. His dark, hooded eyes glowed with an almost religious fervor beneath bushy brows.

He nodded once. "Morane."

"Captain Rinne."

"You don't seem like the sort of over-bred prig I expect in command of a flashy imperial fast attack cruiser. Nor are your eyes those of a born mercenary, or of a dreamer for that matter. Interesting." Rinne hummed to himself for a few seconds. "And before you say it, I am aware I look like a half-crazed frontier preacher, full of fire and brimstone, ready to rant against the unholy depravity of our empress and her familiars. But I reserve my ill temper for the imperial nobility, venal politicians and the servants of evil who do their bidding."

DeCarde successfully repressed an urge to chuckle at the man's words. He even sounded like a half-crazed frontier preacher.

Morane, however, kept a straight face. "And why were you fleeing these particular servants of evil, Captain?"

Rinne scratched his beard. "Well, since we're beyond the reach of your weapons, and can escape if you have a mind to turn on us, I guess there's no harm in speaking. Especially since we're in your debt. I carry what's left of the Order of the Void's Yotai Abbey. Ninety-five sisters and one hundred and two friars, my crew and I included."

A stunned silence descended on the CIC.

"What's left, Captain?"

"The Yotai Abbey was the largest in the Coalsack Sector, and the hub of our network in these parts, connecting the minor abbeys and houses. Over seven hundred of us called it home. *Dawn Trader* carries what is left after Admiral Zahar proscribed our Order and set his troops upon us. We don't know what happened to our Brethren in outlying star systems, but I fear the worst." A fleeting expression of sorrow aged him beyond his years. "And merely because Empress Dendera once proclaimed her support of our work. That tainted us as imperial loyalists in Zahar's eyes, and therefore the enemy of a godless creature such as him. My ship arrived in Yotai orbit while this was happening, and I saved what survivors we could find."

"If you don't mind, Captain — of should I address you as friar?"

Rinne grim expression softened, and it transformed his face from that of a mad preacher into something less intense. "Since I'm speaking with you as *Dawn Trader*'s master, captain is fine."

"How is a monastic also the master of a freighter belonging to the Galactic Dawn Corporation?"

"Galactic Dawn is wholly owned and operated by the Order of the Void. My crew members, what little I have, are also of our congregation. Good, honest interstellar trade is one way in which we earn money to fund our various works and support our houses. Zahar might believe we're Dendera's pets, but the Order never took a single mark from her or her coterie. We stopped accepting donations from the high and mighty long ago to avoid any hint we might bow to political interference, or worse, use our standing as spiritual and worldly counselors to influence people."

Morane shook his head and smiled. "I learn something new every day. The empire's most mystical and reclusive religious institution runs its own shipping line."

"And more. Or at least, it did. Only the Almighty knows what the truth might be nowadays. It seems those of us who live apart from the mainstream of humanity are becoming the enemies of all sides and friends to none."

"What is Santana's involvement?"

"I made the mistake of passing through Ariel and inquiring about sanctuary for my brothers and sisters. In contrast to Zahar, Santana welcomed us with open arms, on the condition we settle on Ariel and pledge obedience to his vice regal throne."

A puzzled frown creased Morane's forehead. "Why?"

"He labors under the mistaken belief we wield mystical powers capable of helping a ruler consolidate his grip. Arrant nonsense, of course. Our Order is thirteen hundred years old. You'd think it would be obvious by now if we were more than just humble servants of the Almighty. Dendera thought the same, from what I was told, hence her support of our good works. Which, I suppose was a better approach than Santana's. When I refused and ran, he sent his mercenaries after us. The rest, you know."

"I see." Morane nodded slowly, unaware that DeCarde's face wore a worried expression since Rinne confessed he belonged to the Order of the Void. "You were traveling where, if I may ask?"

"The Brethren aboard *Dawn Trader* voted to head for our abbey on Lindisfarne, where the Order established its own colony under imperial charter. There, our brothers and sisters live independent from oversight by the Shield Sector viceroy, or ruling warlord nowadays if I understand the situation correctly. We hope it is isolated enough to survive the madness sweeping across human space."

"Lindisfarne?" Morane glanced to one side where a wormhole network projection, courtesy of Lieutenant Commander Creswell's unbeatable sense of timing, marked the long, convoluted route between ISC119041-5 and the Lindisfarne system. Almost half of the wormhole junctions glowed the red of rebellion, many the purple of the unknown, while the rest showed loyalist blue. "You'd be hard-pressed to find a lengthier or more perilous route, Captain Rinne. I'll transmit what we know of the situation so you can see for yourself. Wait one." He nodded at Creswell.

Moments later Rinne's eyes slipped to one side, and his frown deepened. "I see."

"Our intelligence is a few weeks out of date, but any changes since then would likely be for the worse. Even your destination might not be safe. It has three wormhole termini, which makes it a not inconsiderable crossing point."

"But it is our spiritual home."

"Until the reivers come. They'll not waste riches on fuel to cross the stars in hyperspace. Instead, they'll visit every marked and undefended wormhole junction to look for plunder now that the empire can no longer police its own systems. Lindisfarne will be a prime target, considering it sits in a region of the galaxy known for aggressive, hostile species, not least among them human renegades."

A pinched expression hardened the friar-captain's face. He nodded. "There is truth to your words, Morane. In my years as master of *Dawn Trader*, I've fled from many a pirate, which is why I managed to evade Qoli for so long. They are as cunning as they are brutal, a trait the damned bastards share with Dendera's Guards Regiments. But Lindisfarne is the Brethren's choice. If the Almighty's will is that we not reach sanctuary, then so be it. The Void giveth and the Void taketh away, by the will of the Almighty."

Morane met Rinne's eyes. "What if the Almighty wants you to find another sanctuary? One where you could lay the foundation for a rebirth? Another Lindisfarne, but less vulnerable?"

"You want us to enter your dream, Morane?"

"I am offering an alternative. Our voyage does not take us through four dozen star systems sinking into utter chaos. What if Santana isn't the only one who believes in the Order of the Void's mystical abilities? You evaded evil twice, the second time only because we made ourselves your protectors. Can you do it again and again, with no guarantee other former Imperial Navy ships might protect your passage? I doubt many out there would respect neutrality in a civil war pitting human against human. You're either for one side or against it, with no shades of gray in the middle. And things will become worse. Much worse."

"Hence your dream." Rinne stared at Morane with eyes that betrayed no emotions. Then, he shook his head. "But I agree. The odds are against us, much as I wish things were different."

"We're likely the only neutrals you'll encounter."

Rinne seemed lost in thought for a moment. Then he asked, "Where does your dream take you, Morane?"

"I can't reveal our destination until you commit to joining our little caravan, lest word gets out and we find undesirables invading what we hope will be a sanctuary."

"Understood." He gazed at Morane for a while longer then nodded once. "I will put it to the Brethren. It may take time. We love debating the smallest matters."

"You have until we reach Wormhole Two, Captain. We will go FTL shortly to jump across the system. Once on the other side, I will listen on this subspace frequency for your reply. Should you wish to join us, we will wait." Morane glanced at the navigation plot to one side of the CIC. "But only a day. After that, we cross the event horizon to continue on our journey."

"Fair enough. Until later, Captain."

When the display went dark, Morane turned to Mikkel's hologram. "Get us underway for Wormhole Two."

"Since we're synced and ready, stand by for the jump klaxon."

— 23 —

"Could we speak in private, Captain?" DeCarde asked once the customary transition nausea faded and *Vanquish* stood down from jump stations.

"Certainly. Join me in my day cabin. Commander Creswell, the CIC is yours."

Once there, he drew two mugs of tea, handed one to DeCarde and sat. "What's on your mind, Brigid?"

"The Order of the Void." She made a face. "I don't quite know how to put this, but I'm not sure it's a good idea to invite them along. Rinne claims they're nothing other than humble servants of the Almighty, but our family lore holds them to be more than that, something not entirely benign. Well, not everyone, but the sisters."

"Oh? Your family believes in the sort of mysticism that drove Governor General Santana to try and capture Rinne's ship?"

"One of my distant ancestors, we call him the Ancestor with a capital A, was a general of Imperial Marines under the first emperor. Family lore says he had something like a sixth sense capable of detecting anyone who touched his mind via empathic or telepathic means. After an ordeal fully woke this talent, he discovered the Sisters of the Void were empaths who could taste the emotions of others.

"Some supposedly even developed the ability to influence unwitting victims by, in the Ancestor's words, mind-meddling, though these were rare and under tight control by their Order. Rogue sisters weren't tolerated. The Order's female branch was created to take women with the ability out of the mainstream and train them, so they didn't either go insane by being bombarded with the emotions of others or use the talent to cause evil."

A frown creased Morane's brow. "That's quite a fantastic claim."

"Agreed, but family lore has always proved to be correct, and has been passed through the generations with no deviation from the original wording, although each generation added its own new bits of knowledge. And it says do not trust the Sisters of the Void. Ever."

"Do only the sisters have this ability, or the friars too?"

"I don't know. Family lore does not speak of the friars, or mendicant priests as they were known back in the early days of the empire. The Ancestor's ability was apparently a male version, but his was a wild mutation triggered by the ordeal I mentioned. Perhaps the friars developed something similar over the last ten centuries. Consider that Rinne made a quick judgment about your character the moment he saw your face. Empath and subject are supposed to be within line of sight of each other, but no one knows if there's a distance limit."

"Or he could simply be equipped with good bullshit detectors. Some of us are, you know." He gave her a crooked grin. "I took you with us on the strength of your word. Remember, the Order of the Void produces notable psychologists, among other medical specialties, and historically, clerics were trained to observe and influence people."

"But if I'm right, it might explain Admiral Zahar's desire to exterminate them, especially if Rinne was lying and Dendera does, in fact, enjoy the services of mind-meddlers. The advantages for a ruler would be incalculable, as Santana seems to think."

"And yet the empire is slipping from her grasping, diseased fingers one star system at a time."

"True. Maybe the sisters around Dendera, if any, drove her mad, either by accident or on purpose."

"I've not heard the Order of the Void having apocalyptic aspirations." He shrugged. "We'll never know. But as a student of history, surely you remember the vital role of monastics in preserving knowledge when the Western Roman Empire fell?"

"And you hope the ones aboard *Dawn Trader* would assume such a role on Lyonesse to prepare for the fall of the Human Empire? Wouldn't that be a case of forcing history to repeat itself?"

A rueful smile replaced Morane's earlier grin. "Perhaps. But my point is valid, and they do come with many skills that might be useful if our sanctuary slides down the technological ladder."

"If or when?"

"We'll likely lose the ability to do many things. But so long as we don't lose the knowledge of how they're done, or worse even, the idea that they *can* be done... Which is the whole point. Besides, Rinne's Brethren might well decline our offer and attempt the perilous trek to the Lindisfarne system, making this conversation rather moot. Though it would be disappointing."

"And what about them perhaps being more than they admit? Couldn't they be a danger to your sanctuary plans?"

"If you're right, then they've lived and worked peacefully among us for centuries without imperiling humanity. Why should that change when we might become humanity's best hope of recovery after the wars stop? If they wish to follow us, I will welcome them with open arms."

DeCarde inclined her head, acknowledging the discussion was over.

**

"Anything?" Morane dropped into the bridge command chair, eyes scanning the various displays out of sheer habit. One readout held his attention for more than a few seconds. The countdown to their planned wormhole transit was now showing under an hour remained.

"No, sir. The relevant subspace frequency has been quiet," Lieutenant Hak replied. "Though the CIC reports they can't detect *Dawn Trader* in the area we last saw her. They might be rigged for silent running to avoid detection in case someone comes through the Coraline wormhole."

"Perhaps," Morane murmured as he felt disappointment replace his earlier sense of anticipation, even though DeCarde thought the notion of monastics reclaiming their ancient role as keepers of knowledge a bit too fanciful. "Are the ships ready and synced?"

"Ready and synced, sir." Hak nodded toward the navigation display, which showed three blue icons almost touching the edge of a wormhole that remained stubbornly invisible to the naked eye. "We're just waiting for the word to accelerate, but it must be within the hour. Otherwise, we'll miss and be forced to come around."

Mikkel breezed onto the bridge. "No sign of our mysterious monastic mind benders?"

Morane smiled at his first officer. "You've been listening to Colonel DeCarde, Iona?"

"She makes compelling points."

He chuckled. "Not you too?"

"I strive to keep my mind open, sir. And I've always found the Order of the Void to be a bit — fey, I suppose is the best word."

"And yet they have their uses, not least in bringing succor to the most disfavored in the empire."

"True." Mikkel took her station. "But we're not disfavored, nor are we part of the empire anymore. But it seems what you or I think on the subject won't matter, Captain."

"Probably not."

She smiled at him. "Don't sound so crestfallen."

"CIC to the bridge."

"Officer of the watch here," Hak replied.

"Sensors are picking up a hyperspace trail coming in our direction. Judging by the size, it might be *Dawn Trader*."

A big grin appeared on Morane's face. "Perhaps the subject *will* matter, Iona."

"Possibly, but we should go to battle stations nonetheless, sir. In case that trail is someone hostile and not our mystic friends."

"At this point, everybody might be hostile to the likes of us, I suppose." Morane nodded at the officer of the watch. "Make it so, Mister Hak."

Once *Vanquish* and her consorts were ready for any eventuality, they settled in to wait. Morane repeatedly fought off the temptation to glance at the countdown timer every few seconds and see how much remained before they were forced to accelerate toward the wormhole's event horizon. Finally, the CIC called again.

"We detected an emergence signature one hundred and fifty thousand kilometers aft. It's *Dawn Trader*."

"Open a link." Moments later, Rinne's craggy features materialized on the main display. Morane gave him a genial smile. "In the nick of time, Captain. We're minutes from having to accelerate if we wish to make the wormhole on this heading. I gather you've opted to join us?"

"It was a debate for the ages, and before you ask, I can't share what happens in chapter with outsiders," Rinne replied. "But in the end, more than two-thirds of the Brethren agreed to follow you to your sanctuary instead of facing an uncertain and potentially impassable road to Lindisfarne. That network map you sent me was rather convincing for many."

"And what will happen with those who voted against this decision? The reason I ask is that I released the ones in the 197th Battle Group unwilling to come with us and let them leave aboard our second surviving frigate to a fate we'll likely never know."

"They will follow willingly, fear not. Obedience is one of the vows we take when we join the Order of the Void."

"May I ask what your opinion was?"

Rinne grinned. "You may, but since I expressed my views in chapter, I cannot divulge them. However, I am placing my ship and myself under your command. We are ready to receive and execute navigation orders."

"Welcome to the 197th, Captain, though I never figured we'd recruit a religious auxiliary. Fleet command wouldn't be amused if they knew. Please take station between *Narwhal* and *Myrtale* and match our velocity. Then we can synchronize you with the others and accelerate toward the wormhole together."

"Certainly. What is our destination?"

"Ever heard of a little wormhole cul-de-sac system called Lyonesse?"

Rinne squinted as if searching his memory. "I can't recall having visited the place, but this is not the first time

I hear that name. Wormhole dead-end, eh? Not a bad idea. It'll mean less unwanted guests passing through."

"Would you believe it's supposed to host a Fleet supply depot?"

The friar-captain laughed uproariously. "Trust the imperial government to set up a logistics base in a cul-de-sac, where it's convenient to no one. The bribes must have been enormous."

"But it could be very convenient for us."

"Indeed. So long as the locals didn't help themselves or the depot staff hasn't sold off the stock for fun and profit."

—24—

"All ships made a successful transit and are in silent running mode," Chief Lettis reported after their third wormhole crossing since *Dawn Trader* joined *Vanquish* and her consorts. Coraline and the Shield Sector were now dozens of light years away.

"I still can't believe how good our friendly neighborhood clerics are at this," Creswell commented. "Their ship is once again as undetectable as the others. Are we sure the Void Congregation doesn't have a military arm we never heard of?"

Morane shrugged. "Anything is possible. I'm just happy they're able to follow along almost as well as any naval transport."

"History is replete with military orders, Annalise," DeCarde said. "Templars, Teutonic Knights, Hospitallers, and the list goes on."

"A good subject for discussion during the wardroom's next dining-in, I should think."

"Yes, sir." The Marine now knew enough about Morane's mannerisms to understand his tone and choice of words were meant to forestall any further discussion of historical trivia. With the ship at battle stations, minds needed to focus on potential threats. And this system, named after the sole habitable planet, Palmyra, was their first with a known human presence since leaving Coraline.

The minutes passed in silence while sensors reached out into the night, looking for non-natural energy emissions that might betray the presence of starships. Then, the signals petty officer raised a hand.

"Sir, nothing on any of the subspace bands, which isn't surprising, since Palmyra doesn't have a system subspace relay, but the normal sublight radio frequencies are being flooded by a distress signal."

Morane glanced over his shoulder at DeCarde. "Another Pathfinder battalion facing a last stand against enraged rebels?"

She grimaced. "Doubtful, since I've never even heard of this system before you mentioned it."

"Palmyra, despite the sumptuous name, is only marginally habitable," Creswell said. "The latest entry in our database lists just under a thousand colonists, members of a fringe political movement that settled there eighteen years ago after its members were expelled from Mykonos because of alleged subversive activities. There are no further details."

Morane turned to the signals console. "What's the nature of the distress signal?"

"Text only. They claim to be under sustained attack by reivers."

"It didn't take long for vermin to come out and sniff at the outer systems now that the Navy is busy fighting itself instead of patrolling. How old is the broadcast?"

"According to the universal date stamp, it started forty-one hours ago, sir."

"Any evidence of ships around Palmyra, Chief?"

Lettis shook his head. "None we can pick up right now, but the time lag is over twenty hours."

Morane studied the navigation plot, a three-dimensional projection of the Palmyra system with its three wormholes clearly marked.

"I recognize that look," Mikkel, once again present in the CIC via hologram, said. "You're wondering whether to investigate instead of simply jumping across the system for Wormhole Palmyra One. We're no longer part of the Imperial Navy, or did you forget?"

"But we are still part of humanity and owe a duty of care to others, no? Diverting to Palmyra for a peek won't lengthen our crossing of this system by more than a day. Besides the reiver who can take on a warship like *Vanquish* hasn't been built yet."

Mikkel sighed. "I'll ask Lieutenant Hak to recalculate our course. May I suggest we think how to best protect the two non-combatants in our little fleet should this mission of mercy involve shooting?"

"That consideration was high in my mind, Iona. Which is why I intend to send *Myrtale* ahead of the rest, to be our screen. Her hyperlimit is closer to Palmyra than ours or *Narwhal*'s. She can approach the planet and see what, if anything, we can do to help."

Mikkel seemed to consider the idea, then nodded. "The difference between our hyperlimit and hers would be a sufficient buffer, in case something is going on that might threaten *Narwhal* or *Dawn Trader*."

"Done. Signals, set up a conference call with the other captains."

**

"Comments or questions?"

Ryzkov of *Narwhal* shook her head, as did Sirak of *Myrtale*.

The latter said, "My sensors will get a clear picture the moment we emerge, and after what happened around Toboso, you can be damn sure I won't take any chances."

"And you, Captain Rinne? Any qualms about sailing into potential danger with us?"

"I would be a poor servant of the Almighty if I showed any hesitation at offering those poor colonists succor against heathen reivers, no matter the risks. I've seen what that ugly lot can do to defenseless people. I'll trust in Him and your guns to keep the Brethren safe, Captain."

Morane inclined his head. "Thank you. In that case, Lieutenant Hak has prepared the new navigation plan, which he will transmit shortly. *Vanquish*, *Narwhal* and *Dawn Trader* will synchronize and jump as one. *Myrtale* will jump on her own. The countdown timer is set and running. We will speak again after the jump. Carry on." The images of the three captains faded.

"Feeling better now, skipper?" Mikkel asked.

"Simply passing by was never an option, Iona. I'd not forgive myself. Until *Vanquish* is in Lyonesse orbit, we stay on call to protect the innocent."

"I know. Let's hope we reach Palmyra in time to save lives, but if the reivers started their attack almost two days ago..."

The signals petty officer raised a hand. "*Myrtale* reports ready to leave. She requests permission to go 'up systems,' sir."

Mikkel's right eyebrow shot up. "That was quick."

"Indeed. Sirak runs a tight ship. Permission granted. The sooner she gets there, the better."

The first officer's holographic head turned to one side. Then, she said, "Hak reports *Vanquish*, *Narwhal* and *Dawn Trader* linked and synced. We can also leave whenever you give the word, sir."

"As soon as *Myrtale* goes FTL, we can change course and accelerate."

**

"Subspace link with *Myrtale* is live," Chief Lettis announced shortly after *Vanquish* and the rest of the 197th dropped out of FTL. "No contacts to report. No satellites in orbit. *Myrtale* is three hundred thousand kilometers out and closing."

A visual feed of the planet shimmered to life on a side display.

"Lovely name, but it doesn't seem pretty, does it?"

Morane glanced at the Marine. "A hard-scrabble sort of place, according to the Encyclopedia Galactica. Atmospheric pressure at sea level — what little seas there are — is half of the standard one hundred and one kilopascal. Oxygen levels are lower as well. And if the planetologists are right, its best days are long past, as in billions of years ago, hence the rather unlovely, worn-out looks."

"I prefer my planets with a bit of vibrant color rather than unrelieved gray and beige. Is anything native still living there?"

"Some. It boasts hardy plant and animal life that adapted to a declining ecosystem, but no one's ever found traces that sentient life evolved on Palmyra."

DeCarde grunted. "Not a place I'd choose to raise my kids."

"Desperate people will take whatever they can and adapt to the most marginal environments. The first human colonies beyond Earth's moon were on Mars, which was much less hospitable than Palmyra by several orders of magnitude."

Chief Lettis forestalled DeCarde's reply. "*Myrtale* found the source of the distress beacon. She's scanning the area now."

Several more minutes went by in silence before the image of Palmyra from high altitude was replaced by that of a small settlement on the shores of an inland sea.

DeCarde winced. "Ouch. Whoever hit them left nothing but ruins. Unless they built their village to appear pre-distressed, or they weren't much good as builders to begin with."

"Standard instant colony, it looks like," Creswell said. "Containers dropped from orbit and once emptied of their contents, turned into housing, storage and the like."

"And now turned into smoking wreckage."

"*Myrtale* is picking up life signs in the settlement's vicinity, but only three dozen."

"Three dozen out of almost a thousand?" The Marine sounded incredulous. "That's not a reiver attack, it's a damned massacre."

"Or a slaver's raid," Morane replied in a soft voice. "Or most of the original colonists died from natural causes before this. I'll let *Myrtale* finish her reconnaissance, but we will send one of your squadrons to the settlement, Colonel. Nate Sirak just doesn't have enough crew members left to form a useful landing party."

"Of course. If you'd rather only bring *Vanquish* into Palmyra orbit, it'll be one of the squadrons here. Probably D Squadron since B Squadron enjoyed most of the action when we evacuated Klim Castle."

"I would. As soon as *Myrtale* is done, we will switch places with her, so that *Narwhal* and *Dawn Trader* aren't unprotected."

"In that case, I'll brief Cosimo Ossott and his command team. With your permission?" DeCarde stood.

"Go ahead, Colonel."

— 25 —

A scene of utter devastation greeted Major Ossott's Pathfinders as they cautiously climbed out of *Vanquish*'s shuttles on the outskirts of the settlement. Corpses, most of them mutilated in one way or the other, were strewn haphazardly everywhere. The officer commanding D Squadron, a stocky, middle-aged veteran who climbed up the ranks from private, cursed without caring that the live audio and video link to the cruiser's CIC made his sharp words audible to everyone, including his commanding officer.

"I second the sentiment," DeCarde said. "Those who did this are inhuman. Clever but vicious animals."

"Do you want us to tally up the corpses?"

"No. Send out search parties to recover the living and record everything. We can analyze the recordings later if we want to do a head count. Find the distress beacon as well. I'd like to understand how it survived this rampage."

"Roger that."

The armored Pathfinders spread out by troops and teams, each intent on its mission, each one of them feeding raw video and telemetry data to the ship above. DeCarde, Morane, and the others saw what the Marines on the ground saw. And what they witnessed was a story of merciless brutality perpetrated by beings without a shred of conscience or compassion.

The close-up view of the first corpse showed a woman barely in her twenties. Someone had beaten her to death with a hard object, perhaps the butt of a plasma rifle, after she suffered unspeakable violations. Near her lay the body of a child, vaguely recognizable as having once been human. More heartfelt curses erupted from Ossott's mouth, and DeCarde could only imagine what the troopers were saying among themselves, off the battalion radio net. She stopped counting after fifty murdered colonists and instead fought to restrain her rising fury.

It must have shown on her face because Morane turned to her and said, "I'm afraid this scenario is already being repeated on the empire's crumbling fringes, Brigid. Those unfortunate colonists are merely among the first to die at the hands of scavengers sniffing around the corpse of Dendera's rapidly shrinking realm. All we can do is rescue the survivors and move on. But it gives us an idea against what we'll be defending our sanctuary."

"A shame we can't go after the assholes who did this," she replied through clenched teeth. "Before they hit another colony left defenseless because admirals want to play warlord and overthrow the empress."

"Even if they left a trail we could follow, our purpose in making this journey must come first."

Major Ossott's voice came over the live link once more. "We found two of the survivors. Kids only twelve years old. They've been hiding in native thickets, terrified out of their minds. At least the poor bairns can still recognize Marines when they see them. Otherwise, they'd be running even deeper into the woods. They'll need medical care and a good psychologist. I know they watched those fucking animals rape and murder their own parents. If you're not following any of the video feeds from my troopers, then my recommendation is don't. You'll not be able to sleep soundly for a while. There's not a single body that hasn't been grievously abused in some way. More than one of mine lost their breakfasts already."

"Any idea yet how many colonists lived in the settlement?"

"No. But I'll wager the dead represent only a fraction of the total, judging by the number of houses that appear occupied versus the body count."

"Slavers."

"Aye." Ossott sounded like a man losing his fight against an outbreak of murderous rage. "There's a pattern to the dead. My guess is they either resisted during the initial attack or were considered unfit to serve as human chattel and became flesh dolls, to be abused and killed for sport. Judging by the condition of the bodies, they've been dead for almost two days, which means the bastards wasted no time. Should we figure out a way to bury them? It seems obscene to leave these poor folks lying around like this. And Palmyra being an alien ecosystem, they might take forever to decay."

"Find the survivors and come home, Cosimo. I'm sure Captain Morane won't mind using his ship's weaponry to cremate the entire site from orbit." She glanced at Morane, who nodded.

"Will do."

DeCarde sighed. "I think it won't just be the survivors who'll need counseling. Where will we put them?"

Morane held up a finger. "I believe I know the answer. Signals, connect us with *Dawn Trader*."

**

"Of course we'll take the survivors," a grim-faced Rinne said after Morane apprised him of the situation. "Our sickbay is well equipped, and we'll do our best to help them overcome what they experienced. It will take time. Some might never recover, but we'll try. A few of the sisters aboard are specialists and worked with children before."

"Do you have sufficient food for additional passengers? If not, we can shift a few crates of the hard rations Colonel DeCarde's Marines brought with them from Coraline."

"Don't worry, there's more than enough to go around. *Dawn Trader* has her own hydroponics farm."

"Thank you, Captain. It means a lot. We're not equipped to deal with this situation. At least not beyond immediate aid."

"As I said before, I'd be a piss-poor servant of the Almighty if I didn't extend a helping hand to those in dire need. Send your shuttles directly to *Dawn Trader*. I'll join you in Palmyra orbit and make sure our hangar deck is ready to receive them."

"Major Ossett will split the survivors up between two shuttles, Captain Rinne," DeCarde said.

The friar nodded. "Duly noted. Please let us know when they're on final approach. *Dawn Trader*, out."

"My folks just said they found the distress beacon. It was sitting out in the open, inside what might be the town hall." DeCarde pointed at the feed from Major Ossett's helmet video pickup.

"Strange. You'd think a transmitter that powerful would interest reivers."

"Only if they knew how to disarm that very obvious booby trap Cosimo is pointing at. I'm sure they weren't inclined to linger around trying to figure it out, in case a Navy ship showed up unexpectedly."

"Aye. But those savages will soon learn they can rape, pillage and plunder at their leisure."

"Until local militias spring up to fight back."

"Which is why I'm glad I stumbled across a battalion of Marine Pathfinders looking to escape certain death."

Ossett's voice came over the CIC speakers. "We rounded up thirteen survivors so far, children. Their parents sent them to hide the moment alien ships landed. Not all did."

"Sadly. Otherwise, more would have survived."

"Indeed. We found over thirty slaughtered kids, from babies to teens. The stuff of nightmares, Colonel. I've never seen the like, nor have my troopers. May I suggest we borrow a few counselors from the Order? I know you don't trust them, but some of those here with me will need a sympathetic ear, one that can help them shake the worst off. If we can avoid an outbreak of post-traumatic stress..."

"I'll make the necessary arrangements, Cosimo. They can shift to *Vanquish* after you've delivered the children."

"Thank you, Colonel. I don't think there's enough booze in our little fleet to help us forget what we've seen today." A pause. "The kid who spoke with us is helping draw the others out of hiding. It won't be long now. Thank Heavens."

When Morane gave DeCarde a questioning glance at Ossett's tone, one of man on the verge of breaking, she said, "It must be terrible. I've not known Cosimo to react so strongly at seeing dead bodies. The sight of butchered children must be breaking through his hardened shell. Could you please see whether Captain Rinne might send us a few counselors by return of shuttle, sir? If Cosimo is asking, they're most assuredly needed, no matter what I think of the Void. He's the longest-serving in the 6th of the 21st and has seen things most of us would never encounter in our worst nightmares."

Morane, no stranger to the ugliness of war, courtesy of Empress Dendera's destructive reign, merely nodded.

"Of course. I'll do so right away. I'm sure it will please them to help."

— 26 —

DeCarde watched the last of her Pathfinders silently exit the shuttles, helmet visors open. As with the first group which landed on *Vanquish*'s hangar deck earlier while two shuttles stopped off at *Dawn Trader*, the usual post-mission banter was noticeable for its absence. Instead, she greeted another column of grim-faced men and women who were itching for a chance to kill as many reivers as possible.

Two women exited on their heels. One was tall and dark-haired, her hatchet face dominated by intense lilac eyes framing an aquiline nose. Though the sister's features were still smooth, DeCarde easily gave her sixty or sixty-five years of age. The other, shorter and younger, seemed soft, almost sensual where her companion was ascetic. Long, dark red hair crowned a round face noticeable for its full lips, green eyes, and a snub nose.

Instead of the robes DeCarde expected, both wore unadorned black, loose-fitting one-piece garments like the coveralls preferred by starship engineers, the legs tucked into sturdy work boots. Each carried a small bag slung over one shoulder, and neither wore the slightest bit of jewelry, not even discreet religious symbols.

The Marine inclined her head in a polite greeting. "Sisters Gwenneth and Katarin, I presume? I'm Lieutenant Colonel Brigid DeCarde, commanding officer of the 6th Battalion, 21st Pathfinder Regiment, formerly of the Imperial Marine Corps. On behalf of Captain Morane, his crew and my unit, welcome aboard. Captain Morane would be pleased to offer you tea in his day cabin once I've shown you to your quarters."

"Thank you for your courtesy, Colonel, and we'd be honored to share a cup with Captain Morane. I'm Gwenneth," the older one said. "Rinne told us of your need for counselors. Katarin and I are both experienced psychologists and worked with military personnel before."

The younger sister, who'd been watching DeCarde intently since emerging from the shuttle, smiled, revealing bright white teeth that seemed almost too perfect for a product of nature. "I think the good colonel isn't a fan of our Order, Gwenneth."

"Oh?" The elder tilted her head to one side and studied DeCarde. "I suppose she isn't. But calling on our aid shows commendable self-awareness."

DeCarde bit back the first reply that came to mind and merely shrugged instead.

Gwenneth chuckled. "No, Colonel, we're not mind readers, but we are well versed in interpreting the smallest bits of body language and hearing the most subtle intonations. I think my colleague noticed a change in your demeanor when we exited the shuttle. A reaction you might think well-hidden, but not to eyes that see what others can't, or don't want to. It's part of our professional arsenal when treating people."

"Speaking of which," Katarin added, "the orphans your Marines rescued from Palmyra will be well cared for by the Brethren. Several pediatric psychologists from the Yotai Abbey survived Zahar's purge and made it aboard *Dawn Trader*. Rest assured there will be no religious indoctrination involved. We help anyone, regardless of faith or creed, and only discuss our beliefs if a patient asks."

"Good of you to say so, Sister, but I wasn't worried. The Order of the Void is known for not proselytizing." DeCarde gestured toward the inner door. "If you'll follow me. We prepared a two bunk cabin near the Marine barracks."

"Thank you for not putting us with the ship's officers, Colonel," Gwenneth said as she fell into step beside DeCarde. "It's important that we live among your troops, just like any chaplain would, so that those in need of counseling can approach us without hesitation. Many would rather not broadcast they're seeking help. I gather you no longer have chaplains in the Marine Corps?"

A bitter laugh escaped DeCarde's throat. "Emperor Karlus, Dendera's father, discontinued the practice, Sister. He didn't like clerics infecting troops with the belief there is a higher power than the Crown."

"Might we also impose on you for another compartment, so that both of us can counsel simultaneously? A cubbyhole with two chairs would be sufficient."

"I'll see to it, Sister."

"Once again, my thanks. And Colonel, you're most welcome to bend our ears if you feel the need to chat with someone not in your chain of command." Gwenneth's tone was almost hypnotically soft. "We're remarkably non-judgmental, even toward those who don't much like our Order," she added in a voice that seemed to ring with gentle laughter.

**

DeCarde ushered her, for want of better words, new battalion chaplains into Morane's day cabin and said, "Captain Jonas Morane, may I introduce Sister Gwenneth and Sister Katarin."

He stepped out from behind his desk, smiling and stretched out his hand. "Welcome aboard, Sisters. I trust you found the accommodations to your satisfaction."

Gwenneth nodded by way of greeting. "The cabin you've given us is luxurious compared to our accommodations aboard *Dawn Trader*. She was never designed to carry two hundred of us, and now another thirty-six children, but needs must when the devil drives."

The customary handshakes over, he gestured toward the chairs. "Please sit. Would you like a cup of tea? There's black in the samovar, but if you'd like something else, I can ask the wardroom to bring a tray."

"Black is fine. No need for additives."

"Sister Katarin?"

"The same please, Captain."

Both women examined the day cabin with inquisitive eyes while Morane served, and DeCarde knew right away they were taking the measure of their host. He distributed steaming mugs and sat.

"We'll be breaking out of orbit soon to resume our trek. But you arrived in time to witness our incinerating the settlement, and thereby the mortal remains since we could hardly ask Major Ossott's Marines to bury hundreds of bodies." He pointed at the main display. "If you like, I can ask the CIC give us a live feed."

"Please do, Captain. Katarin and I will say a prayer for the dead."

"Captain to the CIC."

"Creswell, sir."

"Are we ready to incinerate the settlement?"

"Yes, sir. Our window of opportunity is opening in one minute."

"Please feed the visual to my day cabin."

"Right away."

"And then you may open fire as soon as you wish."

Both sisters put their teas down and composed themselves. An aerial view of the tiny colonial village appeared on the primary display, clear enough to see the wrack and ruin left by the reivers. And to see the small smudges of bodies lying in the streets. Sister Katarin gasped at the sight, then joined her colleague in a softly spoken prayer, imploring the Almighty to receive the souls of those who so cruelly died in this faraway place.

Moments after they fell silent, a bright light washed out the details, followed by an ever-expanding cloud with a hellish glow at its center. When it, in turn, faded away, nothing remained, but a crater surrounded by cinders.

Morane cleared his throat. "May they rest in peace. In a year or two, once the native flora grows over the scar in the landscape, there will be no sign humans ever inhabited Palmyra." He exhaled. "We likely witnessed the first of many human worlds to be entirely depopulated. Captain to the bridge."

"Officer of the watch here, sir."

"We're leaving. Reassemble the 197th and put us on a heading to the wormhole."

"Aye, aye, sir."

He picked up his tea and took a sip. "The next system is uninhabited, but the one after that also has a small colony. Bigger than Palmyra's to be sure, but still relatively defenseless. I shudder to think what we might find there."

"Hopefully nothing," DeCarde replied. "But wishing we could save everyone we meet is a short path to madness, Jonas."

Morane gave her a rueful shrug. "In that case, it's good two specialists on the subject joined us."

Gwenneth tilted her head to one side and smiled. "We would be more than happy to help any of your crew, Captain, you included, of course. A man in your position faces added stresses, not least thanks to his isolation at the top of the military pyramid. More so now you've broken away from the Navy."

"Brigid is kind enough to endure my occasional rants at the universe, Sister."

DeCarde grinned at him. "As any good friend would, even though we haven't known each other for long. My unit was his first rescue project, so to speak. Without his fortuitous arrival and willingness to brave rebel guns, we'd likely be dead by now."

Katarin nodded. "As would we, I should think. And that can become a burden, Captain, even though you might not realize it."

"Another cup of tea?" He asked, as a way to change the subject.

Both sisters nodded, but this time DeCarde did the honors.

After the Marine served them, Morane settled back in his chair. "Would you be willing to discuss the events on Yotai that led to your abbey's destruction?"

Gwenneth hesitated before replying. "I suppose so, even though it is a painful memory for us. What would you like to know?"

"We've heard almost nothing about Admiral Zahar's revolt because we were part of the 19th Fleet out in the Shield Sector. And even there we know little of how Admiral Loren overthrew the viceroy and started this fetid mess. How did the rebellion start on Yotai?"

"In the most prosaic manner possible, Captain. We understand Zahar refused to carry out Dendera's orders. What they were, I don't know. Viceroy Joback tried to dismiss Zahar, but the admiral, backed by his immediate subordinates, at least those on Yotai, refused. Once news of Admiral Loren's rebellion reached this sector, Zahar imitated him and removed Joback, who died under uncertain circumstances shortly afterward. Then, Zahar set about to consolidate his power in the Yotai system even as he dealt with more junior admirals in other parts of the sector either declaring for the Crown or themselves.

"Part of that consolidation was to proscribe anyone who might show the slightest bit of loyalty to the empire, or who might not wholeheartedly embrace the new reality. Since we monastics try to stay out of temporal matters, the rebels deemed our support for Zahar lacking, and so he tried to make us vanish." Gwenneth gave a fatalistic shrug. "Our Order wasn't the only entity targeted by him and our Brethren weren't the only humans on Yotai to die violently at the hands of Zahar's troops. Katarin and I found hiding places until Rinne sent out the call to assemble survivors. Most weren't so lucky.

"The Yotai Abbey is now nothing more than ruins. In my entire life, I've never seen such a display of hatred. I suppose if we were worldlier, we might have seen the social fractures long before they starting oozing blood because this eruption of violence can only stem from long-simmering resentments." She paused, eyes averted. Then, she said, "And now, if you'll excuse us, Katarin and I would like to rest."

Morane stood. "Certainly. Let me summon a guide."

Both sisters imitated him. "No need, Captain. We can find our way back to the Marine barracks without difficulties. A good memory is something we also cultivate."

"Enjoy your rest, Sisters. And once again, welcome aboard *Vanquish*."

—27—

"All ships made a clean wormhole transit, sir," Chief Lettis said a few minutes after *Vanquish* emerged from Wormhole Parth Two. "And came through the terminus in silent running mode."

"As did we," Mikkel added. "But chances are the wormhole traffic control buoy saw us anyway. Or at least noted something came through."

"Thank you." Morane, a worried frown creasing his forehead, studied the tactical projection of the empire's notorious prison star system. It would be the first tricky crossing since they left Coraline.

Unlike Palmyra, and the Yawin system they just left, it was not only inhabited, but it boasted a permanently stationed Navy task force. Yawin was, to his relief, unharmed, as proved by a message exchange between the small colony and his cruiser during that system's crossing. Unable to do more than warn them about Palmyra's fate, he tried to push Yawin's bleak future from his thoughts, although it remained a struggle.

"No subspace relay carrier wave," the signals petty officer said. "And no subspace traces from Parth itself."

"Radio waves?"

"Plenty, sir. I'm running them through the AI filter."

Lettis raised his hand. "Captain, sensors are picking up a mass of debris approximately one million kilometers from our current position. The debris field's velocity approximates that of ships approaching Wormhole Parth Two for a transit."

Morane sat up in his command chair. "Beacons?"

"Aye," the signals petty officer replied. "Five distinct beacon signals, each reporting the complete destruction of a naval unit belonging to the 12th Battle Group."

"Ships from the 1st Fleet?" Mikkel's ever-present hologram asked. "They're far from home. What are they doing in this sector?"

"Escorting a prisoner ship, perhaps," DeCarde proposed.

Morane nodded slowly. "Could be. If we're talking about political prisoners, having their transport watched by ships from the most loyal part of the Navy would fit with Dendera's paranoid modus operandi." He turned to the signals station. "Any non-naval beacons, PO?"

"No."

"Maybe the 12th fell afoul of a rebel strike force after delivering a prison ship."

"Could be, though Wormhole Parth Two isn't where I would enter the network if I were heading for the Wyvern Sector, Colonel. Traveling through the Yawin junction means an extra two or three transits before reaching a junction that connects to the heart of the empire. Although, if they were fleeing rebels, I suppose taking a less obvious escape route might make sense." He paused, eyes on the tactical projection before continuing. "Be that as it may, the fate of the 12th Battle Group or any prison ship it escorted to Parth isn't our concern. Avoiding a similar fate is."

"That would be nice." Lettis nodded. "And my sensors are looking, sir. But anything running silent will perforce escape passive scans. Unless you'd like me to go active…"

Morane waved off the suggestion. "Not yet. Let's give it a few hours and see what we can pick up from further afield. But keep an eye on the debris. I'd like to know what happened to those ships."

"Aye, Capt—" The sensor chief's voice faded, then he let out a low grunt. "Huh. The sensors caught something previously masked by the debris field. Looks like a somewhat intact ship. Or at least one that wasn't blown to smithereens. But no beacon. Merely low-level emissions proving its systems are still running, albeit at a reduced rate."

"Life signs?"

"We're too far to pick them up on passive, sir. I've taken a visual scan and am running it against the starship database." More minutes ticked by as they waited for information to trickle in and Morane fought his usual battle to mask any signs of impatience. Then, Lettis said, "That seemingly intact starship is the Imperial Prison Service ship *Tanith*."

"Oh?" Morane turned a surprised gaze on DeCarde. "Interesting."

"It is."

Mikkel's hologram shrugged. "Perhaps the 12th was ambushed somewhere between the wormhole they came through and Parth, and they tried to escape via this one rather than retrace their steps. Or someone ambushed them on their way out after delivering prisoners."

A quizzical expression creased DeCarde's face. "If *Tanith* landed any prisoners she carried, I see no reason she wouldn't share the warships' fate. If she didn't land prisoners why abandon her? Wouldn't the rebels welcome politicals with open arms?"

"I'm afraid we won't know the answer until we subject her to active scans, Colonel." Morane's eyes turned to the side display showing a live video feed of *Tanith*.

"And right now, you're wondering if she still carries a load of political prisoners the rebels didn't want or didn't have time to rescue," Mikkel said. "I know you, Skipper. You're wondering about the wisdom of investigating rather than finding the safest route to our exit wormhole."

A rueful grin tugged at Morane's lips. He ran a hand through his short, dark hair, the unmistakable sign of an internal struggle, and nodded. "If there are human beings aboard that ship, not investigating means we — I — condemn them to almost certain death. My conscience won't allow me to do that."

"And what if it's a lure? Bait for a foolish starship commander?"

"How could the rebels know we or anyone else would come to Parth via the Yawin system, Iona? As lures go, it's rather random, no? Unless there's a disabled Prison Service ship near each wormhole, a notion that stretches the laws of probability."

"At least wait until we know what's going on in this system before lighting up active sensors, let alone drives. That debris field proves there's a strong naval force somewhere nearby, and they might either take us for loyalists or decide we aren't allowed to decline participation in their rebellion. Chief Lettis, how long before we pass *Tanith*?"

"We'll pass her at the closest range in about twenty hours, if we maintain present course and speed, Commander."

"Considering the time it'll take to change course and match velocities, should we want to near the ship close enough for boarding, how about we decide in twelve hours whether to light up and maneuver, Skipper?"

"A reasonable proposition, Iona. Let's make it so. In the meantime, we stay on our current heading and stick to silent running while we watch and wait."

"I thought you'd see it that way, Captain."

"I am the soul of caution, as you might remember. Chief, tell me we have a full data pack on *Tanith*."

"Aye, sir. Including a full interior schematic."

**

"Decision time, Skipper," Mikkel said by way of greeting as she entered Morane's day cabin the following morning. She found him sharing a tea with DeCarde and Sister Gwenneth. "If you want a boarding party to check out *Tanith*, it must launch within the next two hours. Otherwise, we either miss our chance or break silent running to maneuver *Vanquish*."

Morane gave the Marine and Gwenneth sideways glances. Both kept diplomatically neutral expressions, their way of telling him it was his choice and his only. But he wasn't about to let them shirk their responsibilities as his advisers, people who weren't naval officers like his second in command, and therefore brought a different sensibility to problems involving ethical considerations. Such as whether to risk notice from aggressive rebel forces by checking if *Tanith* still carried human beings who might or might not be worthy of salvation. What if she carried criminal sociopaths instead of political dissidents?

Gwenneth must have seen the thoughts reflected in his eyes because she gave him a commiserating smile. "There are no guarantees in this life, Jonas. Go with your conscience. I cannot speak to the safety of our little convoy, but I can worry about your soul. And to my unworldly eyes, it is the force propelling us to a safe haven."

"And you, Brigid?"

"What's life without a little risk, a little adventure? My folks will compete to join the boarding party if only to stretch their legs and see something other than the same bulkheads day after day. Tell me how many Marines you want, and they'll be on the hangar deck in a matter of minutes."

Morane seemed lost in thought for almost a minute, his jaw muscles working as he chewed on the decision. Then he nodded. "For the sake of my soul and the morale of Brigid's Marines, please prepare three shuttles, Iona. Two for the boarding party, one to provide top cover."

"Meaning you want two of my troops?"

He inclined his head. "I do. Departure in one hour."

DeCarde stood and joined Mikkel by the door. As one, they came to attention and said, "Aye, aye, sir," before vanishing into the corridor.

— 28 —

Centurion Adrienne Barca, executive officer, B Squadron, 6th Battalion, 21st Pathfinder Regiment finished briefing the command sergeants leading the two troops she was taking to board *Tanith* when DeCarde entered the hangar deck. Olive-skinned, with an aquiline nose, watchful dark eyes and dark hair, her angular features seemed frozen into a perpetual frown of suspicion that matched her low-pitched, almost husky voice.

"Ready, Adri?"

Barca snapped to attention. "Ready and eager, Colonel. It'll make a nice break from the usual."

Lieutenant Peg Vietti, *Vanquish*'s gunnery officer, whom Morane appointed to lead the boarding party, approached the Marines, saluting DeCarde as she came to a precise halt three paces away. Vietti, like Barca and her troopers, was clad in powered armor, able to withstand small arms fire and the deadly cold of space.

"Care to join us, Colonel?"

DeCarde returned Vietti's smile. "As much as I'd like to, this is a Marine centurion's command, not a colonel's, and Adrienne won't thank me for breathing down her neck. Bad enough I'll be monitoring her battle suit's sensor feed in real time from the CIC."

Barca chuckled. "Ain't it the truth? Good thing basic training purges us of any inhibitions."

"Any?" Vietti asked with the hint of a smirk on her thin lips.

Barca gave the pale, freckled redhead with watery green eyes a knowing wink. "Buy me a drink after this mission, and I'll give you chapter and verse."

"Is Bowdoin not seeing you off?" DeCarde asked, to forestall any further bantering.

"He imparted his wisdom in the barracks and left me to it, Colonel." Barca's grin softened her harsh features. "I think he's miffed at this being a centurion's mission rather than a major's."

DeCarde snorted in disbelief. Major Bowdoin Pohlitz was well known for giving his officers and command noncoms plenty of independent operations to develop their tactical abilities and allow them to shine.

"Take care, Adri. You too, Lieutenant." Both junior officers saluted. DeCarde returned the compliment and then left the hangar deck. She lingered in the control room and watched Vietti lead her flight of three armed shuttles through the energy barrier keeping the compartment pressurized until they vanished from sight. Then she returned to Morane's day cabin.

Upon entering DeCarde found *Vanquish*'s captain and Sister Gwenneth engaged in a discussion that trailed off while she served herself another cup of tea and joined them.

"I was just telling Jonas that it would be unwise to take the crew's equanimous acceptance of our fate for a sign they're reconciled to the idea of permanent exile, Brigid. The same goes for your Marines. Military personnel are trained to keep a stoic facade in the face of adversity. But as Katarin and I discovered since joining you aboard *Vanquish*, many of your people are dealing with considerable inner turmoil, the sort that builds until it trips an emotional overpressure valve. Sadly their training and the social conditioning of military service prevents most from releasing some of the buildup before it goes critical and leaves permanent scars. Katarin and I are discussing how we can best help, but it is as much a leadership problem for you and yours as it is a counseling challenge for us."

DeCarde nodded. "I'm not surprised. But thankfully so far I've seen none of the signs pointing to morale issues. At least not the usual ones — like arguments over trivial matters, silent insolence toward superiors, or withdrawal from the group, to mention the more prominent indicators."

"They will no doubt appear in due course. The more we near our destination and therefore the further we get from the life they've known, the more overt their turmoil will become. Consider that unlike the Navy personnel, your troopers were not given a choice whether to follow Jonas' quest for sanctuary or find their way home through the flames of civil war, no matter the risks involved. A few may come to resent the decision you made on their behalf even though it saved their lives. We will try to ease the distress of those we can identify as suffering and who are willing to accept our help. Not everyone welcomes our presence as you well know. And before you ask, any intervention we make comes under the seal of confidentiality so we cannot discuss individual cases. Except if the person involved presents an imminent danger to him or herself, or to others."

"Then at least let me know who you think is struggling but unwilling to speak with you. Sergeant Major Bayn may not be a psychologist or a Friar of the Void, but there's little he doesn't know about Marines and their problems."

Gwenneth inclined her head. "Of course. I've spoken with Cazimir already and know he will prove an invaluable ally. But the issues we're seeing won't be confined to *Vanquish*." She turned to Morane. "May I suggest you ask Rinne that a few of us be sent to *Narwhal* and *Myrtale*, Jonas? Now that I have an appreciation of the situation, I think making counselors available on every one of your vessels would be salutary for both Marines and crew."

"Of course. There will be plenty of time for inter-ship transfers while the boarding party investigates *Tanith*." He climbed to his feet. "Let me arrange it right away."

**

"Fascinating." Lieutenant Vietti stared at the shuttle's sensor readout as her flight neared *Tanith*. "Are you getting this, *Vanquish*?"

"Aye," Chief Lettis replied over the tight-beam comlink joining Vietti's craft to its mother ship.

"She's on a stable trajectory. No tumbling or yawing. Her power emissions are minimal, congruent with a ship running silent. Sensors show she's still pressurized and seems undamaged."

"Except for this." Centurion Barca pointed an armored finger at the visual display. *Tanith*'s sleek black hull, framed by long, narrow hyperdrive nacelles, showed signs of many atmospheric re-entries but, with her gun turrets retracted, little else other than a small divot that escaped Vietti's attention until now.

"Someone's boarded her. They forced the outer airlock door and didn't bother shutting it. Since there's still internal pressure, they must have turned the adjacent compartment into an inner airlock. I'll bet we'll see the same on her starboard side. We Marines like to come at our targets from several directions."

"Any life signs?" Morane asked over the comlink.

"None we can detect so far, sir. But the Prison Service usually puts prisoners in stasis during transport, meaning we wouldn't pick them up anyway."

"If there are any," Barca said. "It doesn't look like the ship's crew or the Prison Service bulls are aboard."

Vietti nodded. "Or they're aboard but no longer alive."

"Possibly. I can't see rebels greeting bulls with open arms. On the contrary. Especially bulls guarding politicals."

"What would you prefer, Adri?"

"Make one low-level pass around the ship, scan every part of the hull and check if the boarders forced any other airlocks. When we're happy, we choose an airlock and match velocities a few dozen meters away. Then, I send an EVA team across to give it the once-over and make sure no one left little presents behind to blow up unwary scavengers. If it's clean, we board. One shuttle, one troop. If there's no one awake or even alive, we don't need more. The others can stay in reserve."

"You want our shuttle to be the one that docks?"

Barca gave the Navy officer a hungry smile. "Of course." Then she glanced over her shoulder at Command Sergeant Rand Tejko, riding behind her with the rest of B Squadron's Number Five Troop. "Am I right, Sergeant Tejko?"

He nodded. "Abso-fucking-lutely, sir."

"All right, then. How about we button up our suits so I can depressurize the shuttle while we run a low-level survey?"

"It's your spacecraft, Peg." Barca slammed her helmet shut and motioned for the others to follow her example. When Tejko gave her the okay signal after verifying that everyone's armor was airtight, she nudged the lieutenant. "Clear."

"Here we go."

— 29 —

"Nothing," the EVA team sergeant reported. "Someone forced the hatch, but there's no sign of booby traps or other uglies." He and his four troopers had jumped across the void between Vietti's shuttle and *Tanith*'s hull several minutes earlier, landing near the open port. They now stood around the gaping hole, magnetic soles affixed to the hull. "I figure you can still mate airlocks. Just let us climb inside before you do so."

Barca glanced at Vietti. "We good, Peg? My troopers don't make mistakes with spotting nasty stuff."

The Navy officer glanced at the open airlock through the shuttle's thick cockpit window one last time, then nodded. "I'm good. Move your team out of the way."

"In you go, Sergeant. But stay within the depressurized zone. I'd rather we tackle the first functioning airlock at the troop level."

"Acknowledged. We'll keep checking for presents inside." Moments later, the five Pathfinders swung through the opening, landing on their feet as they entered the artificial gravity envelope and disappeared.

Shortly after that, Vietti mated the shuttle to the prison ship with a muffled clang. "Final stop, the Imperial Prison transport *Tanith*. All Marines off my ship."

"You're not coming?"

"Someone needs to mind your ride and keep an eye on the rest of the expedition. Enjoy." The shuttle's aft airlock iris reopened to reveal the darkened inside of *Tanith*'s entry port. The advance team was gone.

Barca let Sergeant Tejko's troopers lead the way. Though she could exercise her privilege and be part of a reduced boarding party, she knew better than to interfere. Her place was behind the lead troop, not on point.

The Pathfinders fanned out, one half under Tejko which joined the advance team by a set of airtight doors that led forward, where the ship's bridge could be found. The rest moved aft under the orders of Sergeant First Class Eddy Craddoc, Tejko's troop sergeant, toward another set of airtight doors. Their job was checking out engineering and the compartments where prisoners if any still remained, would be held in individual stasis pods.

Careful scans confirmed the presence of an almost perfect one hundred and one kilopascal of atmospheric pressure on the other side of both sets of airtight doors. And they indicated the absence of anything dangerous. Therefore, Barca gave permission for the first teams to pass through the small secondary airlocks separating the ship into sections. Seconds after the point trooper passed through into the pressurized compartment, he swore volubly in several human languages.

"It's a fucking charnel house in here, and the environmental systems haven't been keeping up if you know what I mean. The stiffs are days old."

Barca followed the last of Tejko's Pathfinders through the inner airlock and was immediately grateful she wore fully pressurized battle armor. The stench of decomposing bodies must be horrific, based on the state of the half-dozen Prison Service bulls who were slaughtered by what was presumably a rebel boarding party.

Thankfully, the clinical detachment afforded by her helmet's visor with its heads-up display allowed her to study the scene with little more than mild disgust. It quickly became clear, based on their poses in death, that the boarders massacred them after they surrendered.

"Whoever killed those men and women did so with a deep hatred rather than a soldier's clinical detachment," an unfamiliar voice said over the comlink joining Barca to *Vanquish*'s CIC. "It's as if something unleashed a great evil aboard that ship."

"Merely part and parcel of the evil washing over Dendera's dying empire, I should think, Sister," Morane replied. Barca nodded to herself. Gwenneth. The Sister of the Void enjoyed CIC privileges.

"Perhaps, Captain. But even though we may be at a distance and seeing it second hand through Centurion Barca's eyes, I can sense darkness in *Tanith*. Something that transcends the wickedness of civil war."

Barca mentally shook her head at the sister's mysticism, but she couldn't fault her verdict that opponents who took pleasure in their handiwork slew the bulls.

Sergeant Tejko's voice pulled Barca from her morose contemplation of the scene. "We've secured the bridge and found eight dead crew members. They also look like they were executed by psychopaths intent on causing exquisite agony."

"Same in engineering," Sergeant Craddoc reported. "Five bodies. Their own mothers wouldn't recognize them."

Morane's voice came over the comlink again. "See if you can access the ship's log, Centurion Barca. Perhaps we'll find out what happened here, and why."

"Will do. Sergeant Tejko, keep your troop moving. I'm coming to the bridge."

Barca felt a brief stab of nausea born from disgust when she entered *Tanith*'s command center. The duty watch had been killed at its stations. Black crusts of congealed blood surrounded the base of each chair. Some were barely identifiable as humanoid, let alone human. She found an unoccupied console and began to interrogate the ship's AI.

"The attack happened five days ago," she finally said aloud. "I'll send you a copy of their database for further analysis, but someone ambushed them as they come out of Wormhole Parth One."

"Makes sense," Morane replied. "It leads to the most direct set of junctions to and from the Wyvern Sector."

"A rebel task force numbering more than twenty starships destroyed half of the 12th Battle Group. The rest fled across the system in FTL, hoping to make for Wormhole Parth Two and a series of transits through unoccupied systems. Unfortunately, the rebels caught up with them shortly after they dropped out of hyperspace and put paid to the remaining warships. They ordered *Tanith* to stand down and let herself be boarded. Her captain was disinclined to obey, but the rebels knocked out his shields with, and I quote, incredible precision. The last log entry states that rebel Marines forced their way through four of the main airlocks and weren't taking any captives."

"Those weren't Marines." DeCarde's voice held a depth of anger the likes of which Barca had never heard before. "Imperial Guards who changed sides, perhaps, but not Marines."

"Imperial Guards going over to the rebellion?" Morane sounded skeptical. "I suppose in this topsy-turvy universe, everything is possible. The real question is why they bothered to board *Tanith* when they showed no hesitation in destroying the battle group."

"I think I can answer that, sir," Sergeant Craddoc said. "I'm in the main prisoner transport compartment. Eight of the stasis pods are hanging open as if they'd been decanted recently. The rest are shut, with someone inside, except for a few that were shot up. Maybe they boarded to take someone important off."

"Could well be," Barca said. "Standby while I find the prisoner manifest. We can run it against the empty and shot-up pods." The minutes passed, then, "No need to run it. The ship's AI has kept a tally. Whoever boarded *Tanith* and massacred the crew decanted a political prisoner by the name Devy Custis."

"*Grand Duke* Devy Custis?" DeCarde sounded incredulous. "He's one of Dendera's many cousins. Last I heard, she wasn't thinning out the family ranks."

"One and the same, Colonel," Barca replied. "Decanted along with him was one Isobel Custis, the grand duchess, and six Custis children aged between six and seventeen."

Morane made a pensive sound. "So the rebels boarded *Tanith* to rescue a member of the imperial household. He contacted Zahar's faction somehow and set himself up as one of the rebellion's putative leaders."

"Grand Duke Custis always had a reputation for overweening ambition," DeCarde said. "I guess Dendera couldn't bring herself to kill them, so it was to be exile on Parth instead, but Zahar's people heard about the prison convoy and set an ambush. And the shot-up pods, Adrienne?"

"The ship's AI reports those also held former members of the imperial court, including Grand Chamberlain Nelly Asher."

A low whistle escaped DeCarde's lips. "Looks like Dendera's paranoia went into overdrive in recent months. Asher's been chamberlain for decades. Her name has always been a byword for loyalty to the Crown."

"I suppose Custis ordered his rescuers to kill them," Morane said. "Perhaps he saw his fellow courtiers as potential competition for supremacy inside the rebel command structure. But why leave the rest of the convict draft to live on in their pods?"

"I'm not sure to live on is the right expression, sir," Barca replied. "Without maintenance, the ship's power plant will eventually fail, no? When that happens, the remaining five hundred and sixteen convicts will die."

"True."

"The bastards didn't want to waste ammo." DeCarde's tone dripped with disgust. "Except on those few Custis needed to see dead with his own eyes, I guess. More of your great evil, Sister Gwenneth?"

"Indeed, Colonel. You may not know this, but when a stasis pod's life support fails before the occupant has been properly decanted, he or she regains enough consciousness for the mind to realize his or her body is shutting off permanently. Although the victim feels no physical pain, I can only imagine a soul's agony at understanding it is dead already and merely experiencing the brain's last few electrical impulses. Apparently, the experience is quite similar to the last few seconds of awareness in a person who's been decapitated."

Barca shivered more at the sister's otherworldly, almost ethereal tone than at her words.

"I'm not sure I want to find out how you came by that information, Sister."

"Merely one of the more esoteric bits of medical knowledge humans discovered many centuries ago. However, your reaction shows why practitioners don't care to discuss the subject with lay people." A pause. "As much as it pains me to say this, Captain Morane, your options are limited. Leaving *Tanith* in its current state, with the prisoners condemned to die when their stasis pods fail, is surely not something you'll countenance."

Morane sighed. "No. Of course not, Sister."

"It would be kinder to destroy the ship in such a manner that their minds won't awaken before the final moment of death."

"Either we decant a few so they can take control of the ship and bring it to a safe port," DeCarde said. "Or we plant a few nuclear demolition devices around the antimatter containment bottles and pray for their souls."

"I cannot order what would be, in everything but name, the execution of five hundred and sixteen humans in cold blood, Colonel. They weren't found guilty of capital crimes. Otherwise, they wouldn't be aboard *Tanith*."

"You want us to go through the prisoner manifest and find a couple of likely candidates to decant?" Barca asked. "The list shows mostly political prisoners, but there are common criminals among them. I wouldn't recommend setting the odd murderer and rapist free to roam even if he or she has experience as starship crew."

"Why don't you transmit the manifest and we'll take a look as well, Adrienne."

"Will do, Colonel. Stand by."

— 30 —

"Is there anyone left running the empire?" Morane studied the manifest displayed on a side screen with an air of astonishment on his face as he ran a hand through his hair. "Dendera seems to have purged half of her court and the upper levels of the imperial bureaucracy."

"With so many high-born names, it doesn't surprise me the rebels could wait in ambush. I wonder how many figured someone might rescue them if their friends leaked *Tanith*'s sailing schedule to the right ears. Other than Custis, I mean." A wry grin twisted DeCarde's lips. "Mind you, the imperial government is probably working a bit more efficiently with several of these grandees no longer able to gum up the works with incompetence, venality, and corruption. Who are the common criminals again? And how do we differentiate them from the nobility?"

Morane snorted. "I'll have you know the broader Morane lineage includes barons and baronets, most of them lauded for their honesty and integrity. Although there are none in my immediate and almost extinct branch of the family."

"Not among the DeCardes. Family lore says the Ancestor forbade any of his descendants from accepting a title, on pain of having his or her name stricken from the family tree."

"Not even a hint of nobility in your lineage? I find that hard to swallow, Colonel."

"Ever noticed the dearth of titled officers in the Marine Corps?"

"As opposed to the Imperial Guards? Sure. I always attributed it to the Ruggero dynasty's deep dislike for you jarheads."

"Distrust would be a more apt term, though the dynasty hasn't showered us with honors and awards either."

Sister Gwenneth discreetly cleared her throat. "I see a member of my Order among the convicts, Captain Morane. Friar Locarno. His presence aboard among those courtiers could indicate he was one of Dendera's confessors."

"Should we ask Centurion Barca to decant him, Sister?"

Gwenneth nodded. "If you would."

"Very well. Friar Locarno is on the decanting list. But we still should identify individuals capable of sailing *Tanith* to safety."

Mikkel, or at least her hologram, since she was still occupying the bridge command chair and not physically in the CIC, exhaled noisily. "I hate to say this, Skipper, but judging by the prisoner manifest, we're the only people within reach capable of sailing a starship. There's not a single spacer among them. No doubt the smarter ones might be able, with help from the ship's AI, to carry out a successful wormhole transit, but making it home to Wyvern, let alone evading hostile forces of any kind, is probably beyond them. Perhaps it would be kinder to set nuclear demolition devices around her antimatter containment vessels and be done with the problem. After we remove the wayward friar."

"Or we take them with us."

"You want to pollute our sanctuary with useless nobles, government drones, and hardened criminals?" Mikkel's voice rose by an octave. "I thought the whole point was to preserve the best of humanity so our descendants might hasten a rebirth, not to saddle us with specimens of the very people who helped push a thousand year empire toward collapse."

"Isn't respecting the sanctity of life in the midst of a murderous madness an example of the best our flawed species can muster?" Morane asked in a gentle voice.

"Let them sail to Parth under our guidance and hope they find salvation there."

"Salvation? Or death? We don't know who is in charge. But if it's the people who destroyed the 12th Battle Group and murdered *Tanith*'s crew, we'd once again find that the more humane answer is executing them with due care right now."

"Did I ever mention you're a stubborn specimen, Skipper?"

"Not in so many words. If we were to take *Tanith* along—"

"Provided she can travel FTL and make wormhole transits. She still needs a complete survey by our engineers. Colonel DeCarde's people are highly competent, but they're Marines, not spacers."

"Of course. If we were to take *Tanith* along, who would you consider as prize crew? No need for an immediate answer, but by the end of the watch. *Vanquish* is best placed to spare a few officers and ratings."

"Provided most, if not all convicts stay in stasis."

"That goes without saying, Iona."

"Let me give the matter some thought, Skipper," Mikkel replied in a grudging tone. "Meanwhile, might I suggest we stick to decanting Sister Gwenneth's colleague and leave it at that?"

"Sir?"

Morane turned to Lettis. "What is it, Chief?"

"The long-range sensors aimed at Parth just picked up several energy spikes congruent with six or seven starships lighting up to break out of orbit."

"What's the time lag?"

"Just under twenty hours, Captain."

"Meaning they could be FTL by now and almost here."

Creswell grimaced. "Maybe the traffic control buoy saw something, and they finally decided it was worth investigating. Mind you, since this system has five wormhole termini, there's a good chance those starships are headed elsewhere."

"Nonetheless," Mikkel said, "I suggest we act as if they're headed here, just in case. The debris field that used to be the 12th Imperial Battle Group is proof whoever owns this system isn't playing tiddlywinks."

"Meaning we need to be FTL in the direction of Wormhole Parth Four as soon as possible."

"Not without a survey, and if there's more wrong than a few outer airlock hatches torn open, we will not have time for repairs. We don't even know if we can quickly restore hull integrity by fixing those hatches or sealing the airlocks off. I wouldn't want to risk multiple FTL jumps and wormhole transits with compromised integrity." Mikkel paused. "And before anyone suggests we decant five hundred and sixteen humans right now and take them aboard our three — sorry, four ships, think again. *Narwhal* and *Vanquish* are at their maximum already, at least for anything more than a short jump, and I doubt *Myrtale* and *Dawn Trader* have space or environmental systems capacity between them for over five hundred added passengers."

Morane allowed himself a few well-chosen words but kept his voice to a whisper. "Then Lieutenant Vietti better survey *Tanith* right away. Ask Roman Pavlich to assemble a team and get them over there as soon as possible."

"Apologies for barging in," Commander Lori Ryzkov, *Narwhal*'s captain said over the battle group command link. "But I may have a solution."

—31—

"Go ahead, Lori."

Commander Ryzkov's sharp features materialized on a side display. "I'm not sure if any of you know this, but they designed Monokeros class replenishment ships like *Narwhal, Licorne, Oryx* and the rest to mate with a large transport pod, effectively tripling the ship's carrying capacity. It's why she has that unusual concave underside and a gull-wing shaped hyperdrive pylon and nacelle configuration. When they designed the Monokeros class, the theory was to build a transport that could become anything a strike force commander needed by simply adding a pod. Add a shuttle carrier pod, and we become an assault ship; plug in a personnel pod, and we can become an orbiting battle station; give us a pod carrying orbit to surface containers, and we can seed any planet with the wherewithal to build Marine ground bases. That was the theory. Unfortunately, the Admiralty never really put it into practice. Money to build a fleet of pods was diverted to other projects, and the Monokeroses were turned into regular replenishment vessels."

"And you're proposing to haul *Tanith* as if she were a pod."

"Aye, sir. She's wider, longer and has more mass, and there's no way we can mate her to *Narwhal* as cleanly as a purpose-built pod. However, I'm sure that between my grappling arms and tractor beams, I can hold her in place long enough to escape this system while she's surveyed and repaired. The only issue is my hyperspace bubble. It will essentially be twice as big, meaning I won't be able to push into the higher hyperspace bands, and of course, I will leave a more easily detected trace. Wormhole transit shouldn't be an issue. My shields were not only designed to envelop a pod but also given a healthy margin in case the Admiralty came up with bigger pods."

Morane studied Ryzkov for a few moments. "It can't be that easy, Lori. What aren't you telling me?"

A faint gleam of embarrassment leavened with annoyance briefly crossed her limpid blue eyes. "There's a tiny, really tiny chance we won't be able to balance out the combination of *Narwhal* and *Tanith* sufficiently for a safe transition to hyperspace. That's because we can't mate with her as closely as with a purpose-built pod and we're stuck estimating the effect she'll have on our total mass to power ratio."

"Meaning?"

"An attempt to go FTL might, in the worst of circumstances, fail. Perhaps even spectacularly."

"I see." Morane ran his hand through his hair as he processed the implications of her admission. "Am I right to assume you're proposing this course of action because you feel the risk of failure can be managed?"

"I believe so, sir."

DeCarde cleared her throat. "If I may interject, *Narwhal* is carrying half of my battalion, more people than her entire crew. As their commanding officer, I think I deserve a say in risking their lives for the sake of an equal number of convicts, some of whom actually deserve a long stay in a penal colony."

Everyone in the CIC, plus Ryzkov and Mikkel stared at DeCarde. *Narwhal*'s captain was the first to react. She inclined her head in acknowledgment.

"Point taken, Colonel. But I would not propose this course of action if I thought the risk to your Marines as well as my own crew was unacceptable. My people and I are confident we can pull this off with minimal problems."

"Because of your extensive experience hauling pods and other assorted naval implements?"

A tiny smile tugged at Ryzkov's lips. "As a matter of fact, my coxswain is one of the few still serving who've worked with pods. Not in *Narwhal*, but in her sister ship *Eland*. I've never suspected him of minimizing risks. On the contrary. If he believes it's workable, then so do I."

DeCarde gave her a grudging nod.

"Very well then. As a fellow beneficiary of advice from noncoms with more experience than I'll ever accumulate, you have my agreement. And before Sister Gwenneth joins this debating society, I'll say it. What happens, happens. The Void giveth and the Void taketh. Blessed be the Void."

"Indeed." Gwenneth gave DeCarde an amused glance. "And the Almighty blesses those who put humanity before self."

Morane clapped his hands once. "Then we're in agreement. *Narwhal* may go up systems and maneuver to close the distance with *Tanith*. Lieutenant Vietti?"

The gunnery officer's disembodied voice echoed from the CIC's speakers. "Sir."

"Do you think you can bring *Tanith*'s thrusters online, flip her end for end and reverse or at least kill her momentum without overstraining the inertial dampeners? Otherwise, *Narwhal* will be forced to circle around, and there's not enough time."

"If her systems are still working, sure. I'll know in a few minutes."

"Go."

"Barca here, Captain. Do you still want us to wake the friar?"

Morane glanced at Gwenneth who shook her head. "Your people have more pressing things to do. Locarno can wait."

**

Barca heard dry retching over the boarding party's radio frequency and turned to see Vietti leaning against the bridge's open doorway.

"You okay, Peg?"

Vietti waved feebly, then said in a reedy voice, "I wasn't expecting this — this butchery." She retched again. "Sorry about that, and don't worry, my breakfast hasn't made a run for it yet."

"I suppose we should dispose of the remains if we're to bring this tub with us to the Promised Land. Sergeant Tejko?"

"Sir?"

"If you've been monitoring the command frequency, you'll know we're taking *Tanith*. That means disposing of the bodies and sanitizing the ship."

"Roger that, sir. May I suggest we bring Anno Leung's troop aboard via the port side main airlock? Extra hands will make lighter work."

Vietti, who'd found an unoccupied console and was now sitting with her back to the remains raised her arm. "I can do one better. The bastards didn't waste time sabotaging the ship's systems. I'll open the hangar deck doors for the other two shuttles. It won't be pressurized, but people can cycle through the inner airlocks. I'll need all the Navy folks I can get to help me right this tub."

"Acknowledged," both shuttle pilots said almost simultaneously and without prompting.

"And I suppose someone should bring my shuttle in as well. It won't do to leave it sitting on the hull like a damned carbuncle when *Narwhal* swoops in to make sweet starship love. Besides, we have to somehow close the hatches that were forced. I'll need a few of your Marines for that, Adri."

"Whatever you need, Peg. And it just so happens I'm qualified as a Marine dropship pilot. It's been a few years since I sat in the hot seat, but if you want, I can bring your shuttle in. I promise not to scratch its pristine paint job."

Vietti snorted. "That thing hasn't been pristine since before I entered the Imperial Academy. Go for it. There's more than enough for three of me to do here if we want to be ready when *Narwhal* shows up. And if you could put a priority on getting the stiffs off my bridge, I'd be ever so grateful."

At that moment, one of Tejko's teams showed up and, after swallowing a surge of revulsion, Barca grabbed what had been *Tanith*'s captain by the shoulders while one of the Pathfinders took him by the feet. She gave the trooper a nod, then they lifted the remains and shuffled through the door, heading for the nearest airlock. Barca was damned if she would assign a dirty job like burial detail for decomposing corpses to her Marines and not do her share of the work.

**

"I wouldn't open my helmet visor just yet," Vietti said several hours later, "but the environmental systems are finally working properly, so the stench should subside. Tell your people well done from me." The gunnery officer and temporary prize captain turned away from the engineering panel to glance around a bridge that no longer looked like a slaughterhouse. "A hell of a job. How many bodies did you toss out the airlocks?"

"Seventy-five in total. Forty-one crew, fifteen bulls, and nineteen prisoners. It wasn't the most dignified set of burials in space, but our choices are limited and I made sure someone said a few words for each one before turning them into corpsicles. How's the ship doing?"

Vietti nodded at the two senior petty officers manning bridge consoles since they brought their shuttles aboard. "We flipped her end for end, so at least our bow is pointing the right way even though we're still moving in the wrong direction. Now it's just a matter of killing that momentum without blowing out the inertial dampeners. If they fail, we turn into pink goo. Next up is closing the damned airlocks."

"Sergeants Tejko and Leung are already working on the outer hatches. They found the engineering section's tool locker, but whatever they end up doing might not be elegant or even Navy fashion."

"So long as we restore hull integrity, I don't care how it's done or how it looks. This is a bloody prison scow, not a warship."

Barca grinned at her. "Not so bloody anymore, thanks to your favorite neighborhood Marines. How long before *Narwhal* takes us into her tender embrace?"

"Not until we've reversed course and can match velocities with her, which will be few more hours, but she is closing the distance. So far the other ships are still under silent running, and no sign of any approaching bad guys. But the sensors *Tanith* carries aren't naval grade, so we'll be the last to know."

"Speaking of naval grade, we found the galley and took an inventory. The Imperial Prison Service lives better than we Fleet pukes do. Once the air clears, we can sample a bit of the high life."

"You still have an appetite after hauling stiffs?"

"A woman has to eat, Peg. Otherwise, she's no good to man or beast."

"I'm not even going to ask what that piece of jarhead weirdness is supposed to mean."

Barca winked at Vietti. "Stick around, Squid. You might learn something."

— 32 —

"CIC to the captain."

Morane, half-dressed and sprawled out on the bed in his private quarters rolled to one side. He blinked several times, shaking off the strange dream that haunted his twilight state.

"Morane."

"Creswell, sir. Sensors picked up hyperspace traces headed in this direction. If they're aimed at Wormhole Parth Two, I estimate emergence will occur within thirty minutes."

"What is *Tanith*'s status?"

"She's almost done shedding reverse momentum. *Narwhal* is standing by, but estimates put them at least forty-five minutes apart."

Vanquish's commanding officer bit back choice words. Instead, he said, "All ships will go to battle stations, but *Vanquish*, *Myrtale*, and *Dawn Trader* are to remain under silent running. Inform *Tanith* of the reduced timeline and ask if she can finish decelerating sooner and still stay within acceptable risk limits. At this point, it doesn't matter if she incurs structural stress by pushing the inertial dampeners into the red, provided she keeps hull integrity."

"Aye, aye, sir."

"I'm on my way. Morane, out."

He sprang to his feet and pulled on the battledress tunic that lay crumpled on a nearby chair as the battle stations siren echoed throughout the fast attack cruiser.

"Ask me for anything but time," Morane intoned. Then he paused, head tilted to one side and muttered. "Who said that again?"

No doubt DeCarde could dig the answer out of her vast historical repository. He made his way to the CIC with long strides, a confident expression pasted on his craggy features as he greeted crew members hurrying to their stations. The moment he entered, Creswell rose from the command chair and stepped aside.

"Peg Vietti says she is, and I quote, already flirting with the fine art of turning humans into jam. It will take the time it takes."

Morane sat and scowled at the tactical projection, now showing the hyperspace traces in pale red.

"I was hoping to make my way across to Wormhole Four unseen, but if those ships emerge nearby before we can go FTL, they can't fail to spot us and realize we're taking *Tanith*. Should they be the same people who destroyed the 12th and freed Grand Duke Custis, I don't doubt they'll come about and try to cut us off from our escape route. Or chase us through the wormhole network. And with *Narwhal* hauling twice her mass, we won't be able to push past the in-system FTL limits and gain an edge over a strike force that'll probably be long on heavy cruisers, if the remains of the 12th Battle Group are any indication."

"We could always recover our boarding party and bugger off without *Tanith*," Mikkel, present once more via hologram from her normal station on the bridge, suggested in an arch tone. When she saw her jest fall flat, Mikkel shrugged. "Or not."

Morane ran a hand across his chin, lost in thought. Then an air of determination replaced his earlier scowl. "I doubt they'll chase us through Wormhole Parth Five."

"I'm not sure I like the way you said that, Skipper."

A wicked grin briefly creased Morane's face. "Look it up in the catalog, Iona."

Mikkel fell silent, and during that pause, Colonel DeCarde took her station in the CIC, wondering about the discussion she'd just interrupted.

"Surely you jest, sir," the first officer finally said.

"Not in the least. Few commanders would follow us through Wormhole Five. At least not for the pleasure of destroying *Tanith* and the unknown starships that salvaged her."

"No sane commander would go down Wormhole Five, period."

"Which is a good reason to do it." Morane caught DeCarde's quizzical look out of the corner of his eyes and turned to face her. "Iona thinks making a transit to a quadruple star system is a dangerous idea."

"I'm not sure I understand, Captain."

"Stable wormholes are tied to stars, or so the theory goes — the astrophysicists could never prove it conclusively, let alone figure out why. Most seem to exist within ten to twenty-five light hours from a star's core. Rogue wormholes, on the other hand, come and go in interstellar space, seemingly without the anchor of a primary, and they're the ones theorized to connect different points in time as well. However, most believe what we call stable wormholes are only stable over a limited time span. Since wormhole travel only began two centuries ago, we've not seen many mapped termini vanish. Or at least not in star systems we occupy or use as junctions. With one exception."

"Multiple star systems — binaries, triples and so forth. The more stars, the greater the exception," Mikkel interjected. "Like the one at the other end of Wormhole Parth Five, which is a quadruple. *If* that's where the terminus lies."

"Indeed. Wormholes hooked into systems with more than one star appear to have an unfortunate tendency to shift position unexpectedly, vanish or go rogue by connecting to a different system from the one previously mapped. Something about the stars interfering with each other's tied-in wormholes. We're taught to avoid any junctions in systems with more than two stars except in case of absolute emergency. But that's mostly by way of ensuring a ship won't spend months, if not years finding its way home if a previously mapped route disappears or has shifted and now leads to an unmapped star system. In my opinion, the fear of passing through multiples stems from apocryphal stories about starships wandering through the galaxy for ages because wormholes went rogue and cut off the way back. And since modern starships no longer carry enough antimatter fuel to travel FTL for long interstellar crossings, getting lost in the network has become a bogeyman."

"In your opinion, Skipper."

"Name me one ship that was lost due to using a multiple star junction. Sure, we hear tales of misadventures, but every ship made it back."

Mikkel snorted. "You know I can't because we never find out what happened to ships that vanished."

"ISC37800-24 was last mapped ten years ago. Only three of its twenty-four wormhole termini had changed since the previous survey fifteen years earlier."

"So the Navy does send ships into multiples?" DeCarde asked.

"Aye." Morane nodded. "Survey cruisers. But they carry enough fuel to cross several hundred light years through interstellar space in case they have wormhole misadventures."

"Survey cruisers don't leave the vicinity of the terminus they emerged from either," Mikkel pointed out. "They send probes to verify that the other termini still connect to the previously mapped systems."

"If you come up with a better alternative to give our approaching friends the slip within the next hour, I'll consider it. In the meantime, please ask Tupo Hak to plot a jump for Wormhole Parth Five and share it with the rest of the battle group."

"Will do, Skipper. But be prepared to hear an earful from the others."

"In fact, I won't wait. Signals, set up a conference link with *Myrtale*, *Narwhal* and *Dawn Trader*."

**

"You appear remarkably sanguine about my plan, Captain Rinne." In contrast to Commanders Ryzkov and Sirak, who voiced pointed objections against traveling through a quadruple star system, the Friar of the Void seemed eerily serene thanks to a mysterious smile creasing his weathered features.

"I crossed many strange star systems in my forty years as a spacefarer, including quadruples such as your ISC37800-24. The Almighty provided for me then and I'm sure he'll provide for us now, especially since we're risking ourselves to save those unfortunate souls in stasis aboard *Tanith*."

Morane could see Lori Ryzkov restraining an eye-roll at the friar's words, but with limited success. Whether it was because he casually dismissed risks drummed into a Navy officer's head from the first day of astrogation training or because he insisted on trusting a deity for their safety remained open to question.

Rinne smiled. "You may not believe in a Supreme Being, Captain Ryzkov, but the evidence of his existence is around us."

To Ryzkov's credit, she inclined her head in silent acknowledgment of their differing views.

Sirak's dark-complexioned face took on a thoughtful mien. "I suppose it's immaterial whether we end up taking a more circuitous route to our destination thanks to a wormhole or two going rogue, so long as they don't shift us in time as well as space. For all intents and purposes, we are fugitives — deserters from the Imperial Armed Services who are fleeing every rebel force we meet. Being able to go home again is no longer necessary because our eyes are firmly fixed on the road ahead. And even if we get lost, evidence so far shows wormholes cover limited distances. I doubt we'll suddenly find ourselves on the other side of the galaxy."

Rinne nodded sagely. "Well spoken, Captain Sirak."

"I guess I'm outvoted," Ryzkov said with a wry grimace. "If there was nothing else, sir, I must prepare to take *Tanith* under *Narwhal*'s wing. After what happened in the last few hours, it would be a shame if we screwed up the rescue that'll see us traipse through one of the wormhole network's more adventurous sections."

— 33 —

"Captain, the sensors just picked up seven emergence signatures approximately three hundred thousand kilometers ahead."

"Almost exactly thirty minutes since you detected the hyperspace trails. Excellent estimate, Chief."

Lettis dipped his head in acknowledgment. "Thank you, sir. I make four heavy cruisers and three frigates. No transponders, no other broadcasts."

"They should only see *Narwhal* and *Tanith*, even at that range," Creswell said. "Since we, *Myrtale* and *Dawn Trader* are still under tight emissions control. And may I say once more that I'm impressed by *Dawn Trader*'s emcon. It makes me wonder what else the Order of the Void can do just as well as the Navy. And why they should be so proficient."

"Best not to dwell on it, Annalise."

The signals petty officer raised his hand. "The unknowns are hailing *Narwhal*, though she's being called unknown vessel, ironically enough. It's a warning to stay clear of *Tanith* and prepare for inspection."

"Put it on speakers."

"I repeat, unknown vessel approaching the Imperial Prison Ship *Tanith*, stay clear, heave to, and prepare for boarding. You are not authorized to engage in salvage operations in this star system."

"Since I don't know who the fuck you are," Ryzkov's tone came across as an aggressive growl, "tell me why I should give a damn. I claim this wreck under imperial salvage laws, and if you try to interfere, I will make you kiss your ancestor's rancid ass in whatever hell they send terminally brain-damaged morons. Now sod off and let me work in peace."

The usually staid Chief Petty Officer Third Class Karlo Lettis barely repressed a guffaw, and even Morane cracked a smile at Ryzkov's impudence.

"I had no idea Lori could be so — pungent," Mikkel said.

"I am Rear Admiral Sir Rayder Ostrow, of Viceroy the Grand Duke Devy Custis' naval forces, and you are conducting salvage in the Coalsack Vice-royalty without a permit."

"How d'you know I don't hold a fucking permit from her fucking Imperial Majesty Dendera, poxed be her name. And other parts of her body."

Silence ensued while those in *Vanquish*'s CIC watched *Narwhal* swoop toward *Tanith*, ready to take the prison ship into her embrace.

"I'm afraid Dendera the usurper no longer has authority to issue salvage permits in the Coalsack Sector. And now that I've identified myself, who are you, pray tell?"

"Me? I'm the Dread Pirate Lori, come to scavenge pod people for the Trans-Coalsack slave markets. Imperial dandies fetch a good price, enough to make shooting my entire load at you worthwhile. I'd offer a profit-sharing scheme, but where I'm headed, you ain't about to follow. So like I said before, sod off, you little twit. Everyone will be happier that way, and you won't be meeting the Lord of the Underworld before your time."

DeCarde chuckled under her breath. "Impressive. I didn't know Lori Ryzkov was such an accomplished loudmouth."

"Neither did I. Just think of her bridge crew trying hard not to die laughing right now, in the middle of what's probably the most delicate maneuver they've ever tried."

"Perhaps we should light up and enjoy a glimpse of your ability to distract the rebel commander with salty language."

"That's not a bad idea. Give them something else to worry about while *Narwhal* snags *Tanith* and goes FTL ahead of us."

DeCarde laughed. "And here I thought you Imperial Navy stiffs didn't know humor from a black hole."

"Wait a minute," Rear Admiral Ostrow said, "you're a damned Monokeros class naval transport, aren't you?"

"Excellent starship identification skills, Rayder. That ought to help with the next promotion boards. But so what?"

"It means you're Navy. To whom do you pledge allegiance? Dendera or Viceroy Custis?"

Ryzkov didn't immediately answer, and for an excellent reason. Morane and everyone else in *Vanquish*'s CIC held their breath as they watched *Narwhal* close the last few hundred meters separating her from *Tanith*. Then, Ryzkov's voice sounded again, but on the battle group frequency this time.

"*Tanith*, this is your ride, I'm about to grapple you with my tractor beams. Please do not, repeat, do not fire any thrusters, drives or toss any garbage through the airlock. The next few minutes will decide whether we become best buddies or rebel fodder."

"Roger," Vietti replied. "We're almost afraid to breathe over here."

"Don't worry, we'll be gentle."

"Unknown vessel, you still didn't answer my question." The rebel admiral seemed both impatient and more than a bit vexed. "To whom do you pledge allegiance?"

"To Admiral the Viceroy Hedwig Wafflegab, Knight of the Black Nova. Now fuck off, Rayder. I'm busy." Then, on the battle group channel. "My tractor beams are on you, *Tanith*. Stand by for grappling arms."

"Standing by."

A pregnant pause enveloped the CIC before *Vanquish*'s captain said, "Time to go up systems, Iona. Signals, as soon as we show up on their sensors, I'd like a link. *Myrtale* and *Dawn Trader* to stay silent for a little longer."

"Aye, aye, Skipper."

Morane's eyes returned to the primary display, where the distance between *Narwhal*'s keel and *Tanith*'s upper hull was now measured in single meters.

"Grappling arms away," a rough male voice said. Morane presumed it was that of *Narwhal*'s coxswain, the man with experience hauling pods slung beneath Monokeros class transports. "And locked. Wait while we confirm mating integrity."

"What the..." Rear Admiral Rayder Ostrow's voice trailed off into stunned silence.

"I guess we just popped up on their sensor screens." A wry grin twisted Morane's lips. "Let me speak with him, audio only."

"You're good to go, sir."

"Ah, rebel force threatening my transport, this is Admiral the Viceroy Hedwig Wafflegab, Knight of the Black Nova. Stand off, and nobody gets hurt. You took your turn at getting folks off *Tanith* since it seems that congenital idiot Custis has decided he was the Coalsack Sector's ruler. By the way, is Admiral Zahar aware? A courtier with more ambition than ability might not impress him by usurping the vice-royalty he usurped with such butchery."

"What in the name of everything that's holy are you talking about, Wafflegab? If that's your name. Admiral isn't your rank. I've never heard of a flag officer called Wafflegab. In fact, I've never heard of anyone with such a ridiculous name. And what is this vice-royalty you claim? It isn't the Coalsack Sector, which means your presence here is questionable. And salvaging an Imperial Prison Service vessel without permission in Viceroy Custis' dominion is definitely not legal."

"Tell you what — Rainer was it?"

"Rayder, but to you, I'm Rear Admiral Ostrow."

"Whatever floats your starship, Rayder. We're almost done here. Once my transport confirms she's secured *Tanith* and is ready to go, we'll leave former Grand Duke Devy's domain. Let us go and no one gets hurt. If my battle group doesn't open fire, your ships will be able to keep on scaring off uninvited guests. Cross me, and I'll do more than merely scratch your flagship's paint job."

"Battle group? I see one fast attack cruiser whose transponder seems to be offline, one transport, ditto on the transponder, and that's it. How, pray tell, do you intend to scratch my flagship's paint job?"

"With the rest of my ships, which are still running silent, but have their targeting sensors pointed straight at your throat, Rayder. Considering what's happening in the empire these days, you can't afford to lose a few cruisers. Between limited repair yard capacity in the Coalsack Sector and no new shipbuilding for the foreseeable future, every one of your units is irreplaceable."

"So are yours."

"Of course, but I'm a desperate man. Are you?"

"What are you talking about? Desperate? Whatever for?"

Creswell raised her hand to attract Morane's attention. He made a cutting gesture, and when the signals petty officer nodded, he asked, "What?"

"*Narwhal* confirms she has *Tanith* and is ready to go FTL for Wormhole Parth Five."

"Is Commander Ryzkov sure?"

"She says they docked with *Tanith* as cleanly as possible under the circumstances and that squeezing the last few percentages of certainty would take longer than we have."

"*Narwhal* is authorized to proceed. Iona, once she's transitioned to hyperspace, *Myrtale* and *Dawn Trader* can go up systems and hook into our navigation plot. The moment Tupo confirms we're linked, you can take us FTL as well."

He nodded at the signals petty officer to reopen the link with Rear Admiral Ostrow.

"You still there, Rayder? My transport is about to leave. I suggest you don't waste ammunition or any of my goodwill by obstructing her departure. Once she's FTL, I'll take the rest of my battle group away from here."

"Now wait a moment!"

Creswell pointed at the port side status display. *Narwhal* and her cargo shimmered out of existence and headed across the Parth system in hyperspace, albeit in one of the lower bands. Moments later, the frigate and *Dawn Trader* appeared on sensors, and Iona Mikkel's hologram nodded. "Ready."

"Sorry, Rayder. I'd love to stay and hurl insults at you a little longer, but it's time to go. Enjoy your life and please restrain your atavistic instinct to chase intruders. We'll be wormholing out of here as quickly as we can." He nodded at his executive officer. "Go."

Transition nausea gripped him instantly, but it faded within moments, and he felt his tense shoulder muscles relax.

Creswell pumped a fist in the air. "We did it!"

"I never figured you to be such a talented bullshitter, as well, Skipper."

"It surprised me too if truth be known, but when Lori Ryzkov began taunting Ostrow, it reminded me of something I read during my misspent youth at the Imperial Academy. *De l'audace, encore de l'audace, toujours de l'audace.*"

"Meaning?"

Morane glanced at DeCarde. "Does your vast fund of trivia include that quote, Colonel?"

She grinned at him. "Audacity, yet more audacity, and always audacity. Though I believe the man who coined the expression didn't have a good end. He lost his head, so to speak."

Mikkel groaned. "And then, there were two."

— 34 —

"Yee-haw." Lieutenant Vietti's heartfelt shout echoed through *Tanith*'s bridge the moment jump nausea faded, drawing smiles from her companions. "In case you were wondering, that wasn't me making you want to puke, but *Narwhal.* We went FTL without breaking a sweat."

"Meaning we can sit back, enjoy life and pretend we're on a cruise, right?" Barca's playful tone was a sign she didn't think it would be that easy. The Marine, like everyone else aboard, had opened her helmet visor once the environmental systems finished taking care of any lingering odors from the massacre.

Vietti shook her head. "Sadly, no. But we can strip off our tin suits, now that we're no longer under threat of rebel fire. Then, it's survey time. Since there are only three of us Navy types, I'll want you Marines to crawl through every space. Report anything that seems abnormal or out of place even if you don't know what it is."

Barca grinned. "A tall order for people short on technical knowledge."

The naval officer grimaced. "Rancid pun, Adri. Just for that, I'll make you check the environmental filtration system personally. But kidding aside, if it looks cracked, bent, strained or out of alignment, your folks should take a picture and log it with the ship's AI while we spacers survey the systems both here and in engineering."

One of the petty officers, Leo Atreus, said, "Perhaps Vlad can take engineering while you do the bridge and I ride herd on our ground pounder friends, Lieutenant."

Vietti considered the suggestion for a moment, then nodded. "I guess it makes sense. Petty Officer Harkness has the most experience of us three with engineering."

"And you being an officer would know about bridge matters," Atreus said, grinning. "Leaving little old me with the rest."

"If we find no issues, does that mean *Narwhal* lets us go once we drop out of FTL?" Barca asked.

"No. This is just a preliminary survey. We'll need a qualified engineering officer to sign off on a full survey that'll allow us to go FTL or transit a wormhole under our own power. I doubt Captain Morane will allow that before we're well away from any threats."

"As long as *Narwhal* doesn't experience problems hauling twice her mass," Petty Officer Harkness said. "She isn't fresh out of the builder's yard and won't have carried a pod in more years than I've served her Imperial Majesty."

"Hello, passengers," Commander Ryzkov's voice unexpectedly boomed through the bridge speakers. "This is your cruise director."

Barca's right eyebrow shot up. "Radio? In hyperspace?"

A peal of gentle laughter followed the question. "No, not radio. Since you're physically mated to my ship with grappling arms, we can talk as though we were in separate parts of the same entity. With more time to prepare, we might even have set up an airlock to airlock connection allowing free movement between ships."

"Which would let your engineer carry out a survey, sir. This is Vietti, by the way. Centurion Barca of the Marines and Petty Officers Harkness and Atreus are with me on the bridge."

"When we drop out of FTL on our approach to Wormhole Parth Five, maybe we can jury-rig an airlock connection. If there's enough time. Meanwhile, I suggest you do a preliminary survey."

"Already planned and about to start, sir."

"In that case, carry on. Call us if you need to talk. Reassurance and information is pretty much all we can offer right now."

**

The sound of footsteps echoing through the prisoner transport compartment pulled Adrienne Barca from her examination of yet one more apparently functioning stasis pod. After more than a hundred, her eyes were getting blurry.

"There you are." A smiling Peg Vietti came around the corner.

"Here I am." Barca lowered her tablet and exhaled. "I figured I'd best take the duty of checking on our sleeping beauties, in case the ship's AI forgot to tell us about impending or actual malfunctions. None of us can face tossing another dead body out the airlock so soon after cleaning up the Imperial Starship *Slaughterhouse*."

"And?"

"So far, so good. One hundred and five down, four hundred and eleven to go."

Vietti examined the closest pods, five to a stack with enough space for a human between each stack. The semi-transparent sides let her make out vaguely human silhouettes flat on their backs, unmoving. The hatches, which doubled as front panels, boasted small displays showing the health of each pod's systems and that of the inmates. Green lights, which would no doubt turn amber or red if problems arose, gave the casual observer an instant glimpse that everything was well. And in this section of the stasis compartment, all the lights, as far as Vietti could see, were green.

"I wonder what it's like to be inside one of those," she said in a contemplative tone. "Do you dream? Or is your existence a void from the moment they turn on the stasis field to the moment they decant you?"

"Apparently, from what they told me, it's a void. You remember nothing. What I wonder is how the last moments feel before entering the pod, knowing you'll wake up on Parth, exiled to a prison colony forever, never to reunite with friends and family again."

Vietti chuckled. "Other than the stasis part, isn't that our fate? Exiled to a faraway colony, with no chance of seeing friends and family again?"

"Touché." Barca ran calloused fingers over one of the hatches. "I wonder how they'll react when they wake up and find we've rescued them from an ugly fate on Parth for a different place of exile."

"I should imagine that those who with a limited sentence, or the hope of buying their way out won't be pleased."

"More reason to leave them in stasis until we reach wherever we're going. Dealing with a bunch of pissed-off courtiers isn't my idea of fun. And it's beyond my pay grade. Not that we're getting paid anymore."

"Agreed. Dealing with courtiers is for Captain Morane."

"I've meant to ask, but how did a nice girl like you end up in this mess? We Marines didn't have a choice, or we did but preferred not to die alongside the thrice-damned Imperial Guards. But I understand Morane let one of the

197th's ships leave with those unwilling to follow him. Why this and not that?"

Vietti shrugged. "It seemed the right thing to do. Staying with my shipmates, I mean. I left home fourteen years ago to enter the Academy and haven't seen my family since then. They weren't happy with my choice, and I couldn't be bothered staying in contact. So my only real family is the people aboard *Vanquish*. It's the same story for a lot of us. The ones who left were those few with spouses or children waiting at some forlorn naval base. Might I regret it one day? Perhaps, but living long enough for regrets means getting to the captain's sanctuary and making a new life for ourselves. What about you?"

"The Marine Corps is my mother and my father. My fellow Marines are my brothers and sisters. I've not set foot on my homeworld since enlisting twenty-five years ago." When she noticed the surprise in Vietti's eyes, Barca chuckled. "No, I'm not a product of the Imperial Academy. I enlisted as a private, worked my way up to command sergeant and took a commission as a centurion."

"You don't look old enough."

Barca winked at her. "Why thank you for the compliment, honey. But I spent more than half of my life in uniform and can't quite remember what being a civilian puke was like, so I don't mind following Colonel DeCarde to a new home. Besides, if your captain is right, the Corps I used to know won't live for much longer and fighting for a jumped up admiral or viceroy would stick in my craw. My oath was to defend the Imperial Constitution, not whichever warlord might end up owning the 6th."

The two women studied each other in silence for a few moments, then Barca cleared her throat. "Did you want something, or is this a social call?"

Vietti gave her a sly grin. "Just practicing something I learned from Captain Morane — leading by walking around the ship."

The Marine gave her a knowing nod. "It also helps keep an eye on any miscreants."

Before Vietti could answer, the ship's public address system came to life. "Harkness to Vietti. I found something in engineering you'd better look at yourself."

"Vietti here. What is it?"

"The crew or the rebels left a little present behind, one that, if I'm right, would have ensured none of the stasis stiffs ever felt sunshine on their faces again, along with whoever salvaged this tub."

— 35 —

Both officers made their way aft to engineering at what was almost a running pace. When they entered the compartment, Petty Officer Harkness waved them over to where the hyperdrive controller housing sat like a hulking elephant.

"Keep in mind I'm a bosun's mate, not an engineer, Lieutenant, but I spent enough time getting cross-trained, and my eyes are telling me this doesn't seem right." He pointed at a holographic projection of the antimatter injectors. "As far as I can tell, it looks like someone's buggered up the magnetic valve system and made it so the AI doesn't know. I figure the moment you charge up the hyperdrives by drawing antimatter from the magnetic containment units, everything goes kaboom."

Vietti shook her head. "I wouldn't know, PO. We'll need to wait until a proper engineering team comes aboard. But what made you check this out?"

Harkness' chuckle was grim. "Healthy paranoia, Lieutenant. A bosun's version thereof. Fucking with the antimatter fuel system is the one thing that can turn a starship into cosmic dust, and that means it's the best thing to sabotage if you're aiming to screw over any salvagers or scavengers. Since the Navy routinely does it to fuck with reivers and they with us, and bosun's mates are front and center in boarding parties when there are no Marines around, they taught me how to spot this crap. Fixing the damn thing? That's for a real engineer."

"Which we won't be able to bring aboard for a while. Are you sure this won't go off for other reasons? Once I make my report to Commander Ryzkov, she'll wonder whether it would be best to drop out of FTL, set *Tanith* loose and wish us good luck."

"Like I said, Lieutenant. I'm a bosun's mate who knows a trick or two. The only thing I can tell you is someone messed with the antimatter fuel feeds. If we don't use the hyperdrives, we don't need antimatter fuel. Therefore, no kaboom. I might find more presents but if they rigged something as powerful as this, why bother, right?"

Vietti slowly nodded. "I suppose." Then, she sighed. "Time to head for the bridge and let *Narwhal* know she's carrying an antimatter bomb cleverly disguised as an Imperial Prison Service starship. Feed me a copy of that hologram, and I'll pass it on to Commander Ryzkov. Perhaps her chief engineer can tell us whether we're the walking dead or it's something they can disarm once we drop out of FTL."

**

"Nasty trick." Ryzkov's tone was sour, and Vietti could almost picture her pinched face. "A good thing Captain Morane didn't tell you to light up and instead, let us be your bearer. I'll ask my people to look at what you found, but if I understand Petty Officer Harkness' explanation correctly, we're in no immediate danger. If the saboteurs used something more sophisticated, such as a detonator capable of sensing the transition to and from hyperspace, we might not be speaking right now, but they're notoriously hard to build and calibrate. Much easier to mess with the antimatter flow regulation system. However, I'd rather not tempt fate and do a wormhole transit before we disarm that little trap and an engineer looks over the rest of the fuel, reactor and power systems."

"So you won't jettison us?"

Ryzkov's chuckle wasn't entirely reassuring. "Not yet, Lieutenant. But once we drop out of FTL by Wormhole Parth Five, that may become not just an option but a necessity, though I'll send over a team to assess your situation first. In the meantime, my people will study that hologram your petty officer helpfully provided and work toward a solution. Keep going with that survey."

"We will, sir. That's all I wanted to pass on."

"In that case, *Narwhal*, out."

Vietti glanced at Barca, who grimaced. "I feel no better than I did before you spoke with Ryzkov, Peg."

The Navy officer gave her friend a half-shrug. "If it helps, keep in mind she doesn't appear to think there's an imminent danger. Otherwise, we'd be watching *Narwhal* go back into hyperspace without us. Since we can't do anything else, we might as well return to work. It'll keep our minds off this matter."

"So long as no one finds any other poisoned presents."

**

"*Myrtale* and *Dawn Trader* kept perfect station on us," Chief Lettis announced shortly after *Vanquish* dropped out of FTL near Wormhole Parth Five's event horizon. "No sign of *Narwhal* just yet."

Morane nodded. "I'm not surprised. We traveled the higher bands. She'll be stuck in the lower ones thanks to *Tanith*'s added mass. So long as Rear Admiral Ostrow and his merry band of rebels don't try to chase us, everything will be good."

"No evidence of that, sir. Yet."

Creswell grinned. "Always the optimist, eh, Chief?"

"I'm rarely disappointed if I expect the worst, Commander. Especially with the human species."

"You and every other chief petty officer throughout the course of history."

"Comes with the starbursts." Lettis paused, then raised a hand. "I see a hyperspace trail. A fat one. Must be *Narwhal*."

"Making good time." Morane studied the updated tactical display. "She'll meet up with us well before we reach Wormhole Five and that means no extra loitering. If Ostrow is serious about chasing us, he'll catch up within a few hours. It doesn't take that long to turn a flock of heavy cruisers around and jump."

"If he divined we intend to take Parth Five, contrary to common sense," the holographic Mikkel at Morane's elbow said.

"Ostrow will have calculated our trajectory when we went FTL and extrapolated. He's known since shortly after we jumped that this is our destination and that unless he pushes his ships into the highest hyperspace bands, we can transit through the wormhole before he reaches the terminus. Then, if his orders allow him to leave the Parth system, it becomes a question of whether he thinks following us is prudent."

"His orders may be to prevent *Tanith* from falling into the wrong hands, Skipper."

"Possibly. But if so, why not destroy her right after freeing Grand Duke Custis and his retinue?"

"Perhaps Custis changed his mind once someone showed him a passenger manifest? Or they meant it as a trap for someone specific, and we buggered it up for them? We'll probably never know for sure."

"Saving several hundred lives will suffice."

"In a galaxy where billions will die prematurely in the next few decades because humanity simply can't play nice with itself, I'm not sure that counts as a great victory."

Morane gave his second in command a sad smile. "I'll take my victories when and where I can. It may not matter in the grand scheme of things, but perhaps the ancestor of whoever is destined to reunite a fractured humanity is even now in one of *Tanith*'s stasis pods. Think about that."

"I'd rather think about a way to avoid transiting a wormhole that went rogue shortly before our arrival and no longer connects to the destination we want."

"Turning one of our shuttles into a drone and sending it ahead to reconnoiter the other end would work. If you're willing to risk losing it, considering we may not be able to obtain a replacement in our lifetimes."

Mikkel sighed. "Now why didn't I think of that?"

"You're too worried about preserving what's still ours."

"One of us has to be, Skipper. But now that you mention it, wasting a wee little shuttle to preserve a battle group, even one as tiny and unusual as what's left of the 197th is one of those trade-offs even I can contemplate with perfect equanimity. I'll have two of them configured just in case while we wait for *Narwhal*."

"Excellent idea."

"If you'll excuse me."

Her hologram vanished, leaving Morane to stare once more at the tactical projection showing his pitifully small caravan slowly approach Wormhole Five. Around him, the small CIC crew worked quietly and efficiently, including the petty officer who transferred over from

Nicias before the frigate left the 197th to find its way home, replacing a noncom who wanted to see his family again. Time ticked by until Chief Lettis raised his hand again.

"*Narwhal* just dropped out of FTL."

"Finally. Signals, please set up a link with—"

"Commander Ryzkov is calling, sir."

— 36 —

When Ryzkov's face appeared on a side display, Morane smiled. "Glad to see you made it, Lori."

But instead of responding in kind, she grimaced. "We have a problem, sir. Your folks in *Tanith* found a doomsday machine. Someone rigged the antimatter fuel system to blow when the hyperdrives draw power. Thankfully, that's the only thing they found, but I'd like to send a team of engineers aboard to disarm the booby trap and do a complete survey before we transit through the wormhole." She paused. "I transmitted the holo scan Lieutenant Vietti provided. You may want to ask your chief engineer for an opinion."

Silence cloaked the CIC at Ryzkov's announcement. Morane briefly thanked the Almighty that he'd accepted the suggestion *Narwhal* carry *Tanith* until they could survey her. Otherwise, he'd have condemned hundreds to death, including a half squadron of DeCarde's Pathfinders and three of his own crew members.

"How long will it take to put a team aboard?"

"A few minutes. I'll simply shift them with a shuttle."

"Do it."

"How long until we cross the event horizon?"

Morane glanced at the status display. "At the current velocity, a bit over three hours."

"Hopefully, it'll be enough. Was there anything else?"

"No."

"*Narwhal*, out."

Morane touched his command chair's arm. "Engineering, this is the captain."

"Pavlich here, sir. Signals sent me a holo from *Tanith*'s antimatter fuel system. I presume you'd like an analysis."

"I do. Someone appears to have rigged a booby trap. *Narwhal* is sending a team aboard to examine it."

The chief engineer grunted. "There's no appears about it, Captain. The moment someone lights the hyperdrives, it's farewell cruel universe. But I doubt the rebels did it. The degree of access you'd need to set that trap? There's no doubt this is the crew's handiwork. Boarding parties looking for a smash and grab won't have the time or the expertise. *Tanith*'s own chief engineer on the other hand? And I bet he showed the boarding party what they did, as a final, desperate attempt to prevent piracy. It's what I'd do. There's no point in sabotaging your own ship to immobilize it if the enemy doesn't know what you've done."

"Which explains why they decanted Custis and his family, then left *Tanith* as a derelict instead of bringing her to Parth. And why they massacred the crew no doubt, by way of revenge or to vent their rage."

"And came back to look once they spotted us nosing around," Creswell said. "They must be unhappy we found a way to recover and move the ship."

"Which makes me wonder who else of value is in the stasis pods. One or more people of interest to the rebellion, hence the unwillingness to destroy *Tanith*. But the rebels either didn't know who or didn't want to decant them yet."

A grimace briefly twisted Creswell's face. "Meaning Ostrow is on our tail right now."

"Be that as it may, Captain," Pavlich said. "Even though I'm not seeing it in person, I'd say there's a strong probability *Tanith*'s chief engineer made sure only he or one of his could unlock the booby trap. That's what I would do. If disarming the trap was easy, the rebels would have tried already, but something caused them to hesitate, hence their leaving the ship until they found an answer or a transport. I'd recommend *Narwhal*'s folks don't even try. At least not while the ships are mated. It would be easier to install a failsafe device to prevent any antimatter from flowing through the system in the event someone or something accidentally spools up the hyperdrives. That, or vent the damned fuel. And check for other problems. If *Narwhal* hasn't suffered from carrying the load so far, she'll do the wormhole transit fine. In fact, why don't you let me speak with whoever's leading the engineering team aboard *Tanith*?"

Morane glanced at the signals petty officer, who nodded. "We're patching you in."

**

A pressure-suited man stepped out of *Narwhal*'s shuttle and gazed around the prison ship's narrow hangar deck until he saw Lieutenant Vietti standing by the control room door. Raising his helmet visor, the man walked over to her, trailed by two more pressure-suited spacers.

"Peg Vietti?"

She nodded.

"I'm Kyle Wen, assistant chief engineer aboard your taxi. I understand you found an explosive problem in your fuel lines."

"We're not the only ones with that problem, Kyle. Not so long as we're dangling off your keel."

Wen grinned. "Ain't that the truth? I was speaking to your ship's chief engineer on the way over here. He seems to think we should let the booby trap be and simply make sure no fuel passes through it, either by accident or by design. He suggested a few ways."

"Why?"

"So long as we can carry your ship, there's no need to risk tampering with what is probably a very tamper-proof trap. Or so your chief engineer thinks because he'd design it that way himself."

Vietti shrugged. "In that case, take his advice. Roman Pavlich is no slouch in figuring out things that stump everyone else. But what does Commander Ryzkov think?"

"So far, so good. *Narwhal* came through the FTL jump without strain, and Pavlich figures it's proof enough she'll have no problems with the wormhole transit. My own boss and our captain agree with this, by the way, so that's what we'll do. Once I've shut off the antimatter fuel system, we'll do a complete survey of engineering to make sure *Tanith*'s previous crew didn't also install something triggered by a wormhole transit."

"Is such a thing even possible?" Vietti gestured toward the corridor, inviting the team to follow.

Wen fell into step beside her. "Commander Pavlich seems to think there might be an outside chance. He told me what to look for. I also wouldn't mind taking a peek at the stasis stiffs. I've never seen the inside of a prison transport."

"It's not terribly interesting. If you wanted excitement, you should have been with us when we pushed seventy-five real stiffs out the airlocks."

"What's this 'we' shit, Peg?" Barca asked with a broad grin as she came around a corner. "According to my recollection, that cleanup job was Marines only, while you squids lounged on the bridge. And you must be the technical wizard sent by our mothership. I'm Adrienne Barca, B Squadron."

"Kyle Wen. And before you ask, yes I play cards and no, I don't play against Marines anymore. You people take it way too seriously, almost like it was a blood sport."

"You've come to disarm our bomb?"

"Render it safe by cutting off the flow of antimatter fuel. This ship won't be traveling FTL under its own power for a while yet, if ever."

"Too bad." Barca winked at Vietti. "Peg was looking forward to calling herself captain."

**

"Ah, Iona." Morane smiled at *Vanquish*'s executive officer as she entered his day cabin. "I was discussing the *Tanith* situation with Sister Gwenneth and Colonel DeCarde, and we were speculating about why the rebels left the ship more or less intact instead of destroying it after freeing Custis and family."

Gwenneth nodded politely at Mikkel while DeCarde gave her a wink. "As I was telling Jonas, our brother, Friar Locarno, could well give us the answer to that question, but it might still be prudent to wait until we're no longer in danger of pursuit before waking him."

"Peg Vietti called to report that *Narwhal*'s engineers disabled the antimatter fuel cycler. *Tanith* can no longer go FTL, but she won't accidentally turn into a tiny supernova either. They're still looking for other potential problems, however."

Morane glanced at the time readout. "One hour before we cross the event horizon. Otherwise we're stuck making a full turn. But you didn't come here to tell me something the CIC would have reported in due course."

Mikkel made a face.

"The cox'n caught two of the crew going at it bare-handed in one of the storage compartments. Frayed tempers, he thinks. It could be due to the reality of our situation finally sinking in. We've always figured some of the crew might have been better off leaving aboard *Nicias.* The two in question aren't known for disciplinary problems. Quite the contrary, but neither will say why the fisticuffs happened, and both will take bosun's punishment without demur. However, the cox'n figures it's the beginning, and we will see more such incidents as we head deeper into the unknown."

Gwenneth gave Morane a knowing look. "This is much as I expected. Katarin and I both sensed that the crew's morale was a bit more brittle than the Marines', so it's unsurprising that the first reported disturbance involved spacers. If you would like us to seek out those two crew members and offer spiritual solace, let me know who they are."

The first officer shook her head. "Not yet, Sister. I'd rather let the chiefs and petty officers deal with minor disciplinary and morale matters for now. Giving ratings experiencing tough times a shoulder to lean on comes with the job. In that way, we're much like our Marine Corps siblings. But it couldn't hurt for you to speak with Chief Shaney since he'll be watching over the crew like a worried father now that problems might surface."

"I shall do so."

Mikkel headed for the samovar, intent on a fresh cup of tea when Morane's communicator buzzed.

"CIC to the captain."

"Yes, Annalise."

"Sensors picked up seven hyperspace trails headed in our direction. They'll arrive in about thirty minutes. Chief Lettis thinks whoever that is must be pushing the upper bands, based on the trail's visibility."

"Ostrow. Either someone has ordered him to recover *Tanith* come what may, or he doesn't believe we'll actually use Wormhole Five. Tell Commander Ryzkov time's up for her engineering team. She has fifteen minutes to recover them, no more. Otherwise, they temporarily become part of *Tanith*'s crew. As soon as that's done, the battle group will accelerate toward the event horizon. I'd like to be in transit when Ostrow comes out of FTL."

"Yes, sir. CIC, out."

Mikkel returned the unused cup she held in her hand to the sideboard and sighed. "No rest for anyone, wicked or not. I'll be on the bridge to supervise preparations, Skipper."

"And I should resume my stroll through the ship," Gwenneth said, standing. "Katarin and I find counseling by walking more effective than waiting for those in need to knock at our door."

Morane grinned. "Proving once again that certain common sense leadership precepts apply across a broad range of disciplines."

— 37 —

"Commander Ryzkov will leave the engineering team in *Tanith*," Creswell announced the moment Morane entered the CIC and dropped into his command chair. "That way they can complete the internal survey during the wormhole transit."

"Excellent. Did she think there was still a risk to *Narwhal*?"

Creswell shook her head. "Not that I could tell. But then, I've always found her to be all business all the time."

He turned to Mikkel's hologram at his elbow. "Is everyone else good?"

"Everyone is synced and waiting for the word to accelerate so we can hit the wormhole before Ostrow and company show up to stop us."

"The word is given, Iona. Engage drives. We're out of here, probably for good. Hopefully, for good."

Morane called up a view of Parth as seen from high orbit, courtesy of *Vanquish*'s long-range sensors, wondering if this was the last time he would set eyes on the world that served the empire and the Commonwealth before it as a planet-sized prison.

Would the tens, if not hundreds of thousands of political prisoners marooned there by successive Ruggero dynasty emperors fare any better under the rebels, or was it different boss, same garbage? And what about Custis, the self-declared sector viceroy? Would he set up his capital on Parth, surrounded by the worst humanity offered, save for those condemned to death and executed instead of exiled? Or was Custis already on his way to Yotai? Questions to which Morane would likely never find an answer.

The countdown timer in the display's lower right-hand corner was approaching zero when Chief Lettis let out a muffled curse.

"Those buggers forced the upper hyperspace bands. They just dropped out of FTL and can't help but see us enter the wormhole terminus."

Morane bit back a curse of his own. "Thank you, Chief. It is what it is. We can only hope Ostrow gets cold feet at the thought of transiting to a quadruple star system."

"And if he doesn't?" Mikkel asked.

"He's still subject to wormhole physics, meaning he'll be several hours behind us at the very least. While we're in transit, I'll sit down with Tupo and figure out our navigation plot when we reach the other side."

"And hope the latest survey still reflects reality, lest we become permanent wanderers."

He smirked at her. "Always the optimist, Iona."

"One of us has to be, Skipper. Contrary to the learned sisters, I believe the universe, or the Almighty as they would say, is less about rewarding compassionate behavior than messing with mere mortals for fun and games."

"Cynic."

"Where I hail from, we see cynicism as a virtue. Time to say farewell. We cross the event horizon in thirty seconds."

The signals petty officer raised his hand. "Admiral Ostrow wishes to speak with you, sir."

"He's a bit late for that. No reply."

"They're accelerating," Lettis said.

At that moment the tactical projection went blank as *Vanquish* crossed the event horizon. "And we are gone."

**

"I'm underwhelmed." DeCarde gave Morane a disappointed grimace. With the ship at battle stations in case hostile forces waited for them at the wormhole's other end, she was back at her station in the CIC, along with the rest of the command crew. "From your discussions with Iona and the other captains, I was expecting a hellish part of space where our survival would be iffy. But I can't even make out four suns."

"There's nothing wrong with this system, other than the fact it's devoid of habitable planets. The wormhole junction, is something of a mess, however. Twenty-four termini at last survey in what is, relative to galactic distances, a fairly restricted area makes for unpredictable interactions. That's why the network goes through single star systems, although we'll use binaries if necessary since there's so many of them."

"But quadruples are a gamble, especially when they're young," Mikkel's hologram said. "And we lost this one. The reason you only see two suns is that we're not in ISC37800-24. Something kicked the terminus from Parth out of that system."

"Oops." Creswell's eyebrows rose. "And you're sure we didn't simply misplace a pair of stars?"

Mikkel's chuckle was as grim as death.

"Oops indeed. ISC37800-24 A, the system's dominant star is spectral type B7V, which neither of those two out there is, so it's clear we're somewhere else. We don't know yet where, but Tupo is running that binary's spectral type against the catalog. Hopefully, we'll find a match and an entry that includes a wormhole survey. Otherwise, in technical terms, we're fucked." She didn't add the expected 'I told you so,' but Morane heard it nonetheless.

"We're likely still within the sphere claimed by the empire, Iona. There's an upper limit to the distances stable wormholes can connect."

"Stable, Skipper. Perhaps the one that spit us out turned rogue while we were in transit."

"But the transit still took roughly the right length of time. It means we're not much further from Parth than ISC37800-24. I'm more concerned about Ostrow and his ships. If they decide to pursue, we'll be playing hide and seek while trying to figure out where we are and how we re-enter the mapped network."

"And won't he be surprised?" She paused, head turned to one side. "According to the catalog, we landed in ISC254130-9, which is unclaimed and therefore not within the empire. But you're right, it's only a few light years further from Parth than our original destination, but much closer to the Coalsack Nebula."

"Tell me they surveyed it."

"Over twenty-five years ago, Skipper. Even though it's only a binary, that survey will probably be out of date. Still, we were lucky. It could have been much worse." A pause. "Here we go. It lists nine wormholes, but only four with identified connecting star systems. Hang on, Tupo is setting up a visual."

A network schematic took the tactical projection's place. Four yellow lines radiated out from ISC254130-9, connecting to yellow nodes tagged with Imperial Star

Catalog numbers. They, in turn, sprouted more yellow lines. However, scattered among the four charted wormholes, another five were marked in red with no identified node at the other end, except for one, which was also red but had an ISC number.

"Presumably, we can now add a tenth connection, the new one to Parth punted here from 37800-24."

"But tagged in deep red as a known rogue."

"No arguments here. What is ISC377242-15?"

"It's a triple star system inside the Coalsack Nebula. Apparently, it was home to Tortuga Station, a hollowed out asteroid turned pirate's nest. Legend has it that when wormhole transits became the primary means of interstellar travel, Tortuga lost most of its charm as a meeting place for scum of every known oxygen breathing species. And without ill-gotten gains to fund the place..."

"Because of a triple system's flaky wormhole junction problem," DeCarde said.

"Correct." Mikkel's hologram looked up at Morane's face. "No, Skipper. Don't you dare."

"Dare what?"

"Transit through 377242-15. One rogue wormhole terminus is enough."

A faint smile creased Morane's face. "Did you check where the four surveyed wormholes lead?"

Mikkel didn't immediately reply. Then, "One is a direct connection to Yotai."

"Which, as the sector capital, will have a defensive array covering every terminus. I'm sure Admiral Zahar won't be kind enough to simply wave us through."

"How about the one linking to Peralka? It takes us closer to the Coalsack, but from there, we can travel back through four uninhabited systems to where we would have gone from Parth if we weren't running away."

"Peralka is home to the 162nd Battle Group, and since it's the last imperial star system before the Coalsack

Badlands, it also has defensive arrays guarding the wormhole termini. Less risky than Yotai, perhaps, but still too much for the likes of us. The third surveyed wormhole leads to a part of the network that'll force us through a triple before we're back on course to Arietis and our ultimate destination while avoiding inhabited systems. Then there's the fourth, which will make us cross the Parth system again unless we want to backtrack so far we'll almost end up in the Shield Sector again. Our food supplies won't last that long."

DeCarde let out a low whistle. "And here I thought finding and mapping the wormhole network made interstellar travel easier."

"It did, unless you're like us, trying to make your way undetected, and in this case, there are no easy answers."

"There's at least one easy answer," Mikkel said. "Since there's no survey of 377242-15's wormhole junction, I'd say a side trip into the Coalsack Nebula to see if the mythical Tortuga Station still exists makes it option five out of four possibles."

"Then we take Wormhole Three, and hope *that* triple won't send us sideways."

Mikkel snorted. "At least it's deep enough within the empire's sphere that another shifting transit won't send us so far we end up contemplating alternate feeding methods."

"Alternate feeding methods?" DeCarde put on a puzzled face.

"Old naval tradition for shipwreck survivors. The one who draws the short straw becomes alternate food."

An expression of disgust crossed the Marine's face.

"And here I thought I was the only one interested in unappetizing historical trivia."

"I blame my upbringing."

"You were born to a parent in the Navy?"

"My father was a historian with a warped sense of humor. I'm actually the first in my family to wear a naval uniform, and look where that got me." Holographic Mikkel turned to Morane again. "My recommendation is Wormhole Three, not Wormhole Nine. We know where Three supposedly ends. Nine's far terminus might no longer even be anywhere near Tortuga Station."

"So be it. Ask Tupo to plot a course and sync the ships. If Ostrow is following us, he'll be here in less than two hours."

— 38 —

"Anything?"   Morane, after shaking off the usual emergence nausea, looked at the tactical projection. It showed four ships — five, but two were really one — heading toward Wormhole Three as if pulled by a common thread.   They were running silent, as per Morane's standing orders to do so whenever they came out of FTL, or through a wormhole terminus. And they were at battle stations.

"No, sir," Lettis replied, shaking his head. "But the rebels could have entered the system and gone FTL while we were still in hyperspace. We're seeing what's near that terminus as it was ten hours ago."

"If they've gone FTL, the question is where," Creswell said. "By the time they completed their transit we were too far for detection, and I doubt Ostrow has enough information about us and our intentions to come up with the same conclusion as you, Captain, and chosen Wormhole Three.   Not to mention the amount of disorientation caused by finding oneself in the wrong star system."

"Nor would he have enjoyed the gentle nudging of a first officer uninterested in seeing if the legendary Tortuga Station still existed. Let's hope he turned around the moment he realized that not only did we manage to break clean, but this wasn't the right star system, as per the most recent survey. Some admirals aren't fond of straying too far from the comforts of home."

Mikkel's hologram smirked. "Unlike some captains who call themselves desperate."

"Mock me if you want, Iona. But the idea of no longer being fettered by the chains of an increasingly despotic Fleet command, while simultaneously seeking a way to escape the madness Dendera created, changes your outlook on life. In the meantime, please tell me everything is well."

"Everything is well, Skipper. The other ships report no issues, and we're already synced for the next wormhole transit."

"Even Lori?"

"*Narwhal* has yet to show any strain at carrying *Tanith.*"

"They built those old Monokeros class transports to last, didn't they?"

"Thankfully for the stasis stiffs."

"Captain." Lettis glanced over his shoulder at Morane. "Something just came out of Wormhole Three. Four somethings, to be precise. No transponders." Red icons appeared on the tactical projection.

Creswell snorted softly. "I'd be shocked to meet a starship actually broadcasting its identity nowadays."

The minutes ticked by in silence as they neared Wormhole Three's event horizon. The newcomers showed no sign of having spotted the 197th Battle Group's remains and stayed on a course aimed at Wormhole One, which led to Yotai, the sector capital.

"I make them as three Kalinka class frigates and one civilian liner," Lettis finally said.

"Protecting a regular run against pirates?" DeCarde asked.

Morane shook his head. "They wouldn't deliberately go through an uninhabited binary system, especially not one with so many unsurveyed termini. There are safer routes leading to Yotai from just about anywhere in this part of the empire."

"The liner looks like it has superficial hull damage." Lettis pointed at a side screen showing the image of a graceful interstellar greyhound, one of a breed that combined speed and luxury. "And it's the kind you'd get from a stern chase after your shields collapse."

"So a rescuee, then."

Mikkel grunted. "Or a victim. And no, Skipper, we shouldn't investigate even though *Vanquish* can take on three old Kalinkas."

Sister Gwenneth, who'd become a fixture in the CIC during battle stations, albeit a silent one, unexpectedly spoke. "I sense evil in those ships, Captain Morane. Something isn't right."

That sibylline statement earned her dumbfounded stares from captain and crew. It wasn't her first since coming aboard, but it was her most astonishing so far.

"I beg your pardon, Sister."

"You were wondering whether they rescued that liner from malefactors or whether it is their victim. I would say the latter."

"Are you counseling me to intercept them?"

Gwenneth shook her head. "The time for rescue has likely passed already."

"That's for sure, Sister," Lettis said. "They went FTL."

"More Navy vessels turned pirate or privateer in service to rebellious viceroys and governors?" DeCarde asked.

The Sister of the Void nodded once. "Chaos always nurtures the seven deadly sins. And it always inevitably dissolves the painfully thin veneer of civilization that keeps humanity's baser instincts in check, despite the technological prowess that has allowed our species to colonize hundreds of worlds."

"And how did you figure those frigates pirated the liner, Sister?" Creswell asked. "With respect."

Gwenneth gave her a thin smile. "I didn't say pirated. I merely said it likely fell victim to the frigates. But to answer your question, we of the Order are attuned to the Void, Commander. Some more than others and a strong enough evil disturbs the Void."

Creswell frowned, trying to find meaning in what seemed very much like a non-answer. Then, she shook her head and shrugged. "I suppose I won't hear a more useful answer no matter how I phrase my question."

"Yet, my answer is clear to one who can see. But to see, you must also believe."

Morane raised both hands to forestall a religious debate in the CIC.

"It's academic at this point since that trio is now out of our immediate reach and on a course too perilous for us. We will go ahead with the Wormhole Three transit."

"Thank you for that, Skipper," Mikkel said. "I wasn't thrilled with the idea of another debate about our duty to save those already among us versus helping more strangers at the risk of not achieving our goal."

"However, Sister Gwenneth's most recent intervention brings my thoughts back to the friar currently held in stasis aboard *Tanith*." He turned to her. "Would now be a good time to decant him? We might determine if he knows who among the remaining prisoners could interest the rebels? You said he might give us answers. If I recall correctly, the procedure with this sort of deep stasis takes several hours. Peg Vietti could do it while we transit through the wormhole and when we emerge in what will hopefully be an empty star system, you can speak with your colleague."

**

Lieutenant Vietti stuck her head into *Tanith*'s saloon where Adrienne Barca and Command Sergeant Tejko were enjoying a cup of the prison ship's excellent coffee.

"Hey Peg. Want one?" Barca raised the mug in her hand. "We might as well enjoy our fill before your captain finds out and has you send every last roasted bean over to the flagship."

"No. I'm a tea drinker, through and through, like any proper spacer. Captain Morane wants us to decant a prisoner while we're in transit. A Friar Locarno."

"Did he say why?"

"Locarno might be able to tell us which among the remaining stasis stiffs is of such importance that the rebels who rescued Grand Duke Custis didn't destroy *Tanith* or decant other bodies. And why this Admiral Ostrow was and might still be on our ass."

Barca made a face. "Let me guess. You want us Marines to do it."

"My hands are full monitoring *Tanith*'s systems, now that Kyle Wen and his team are back in *Narwhal*. She might be our carrier, but there's still plenty to track, so we and our human cargo stay alive."

The Marine snorted. "Human cargo, eh? That sounds no better than stasis stiffs or sleeping uglies as my troopers like to call them. I'll read up on the procedures. It can't be difficult if they let Imperial Prison Service bulls do it. They're not known for shining intellects. Otherwise, they'd be in the Corps."

"You can start the moment we've entered the wormhole."

"Which is when?"

"Thirty minutes, give or take."

"That should be enough time to read the manual. I bet it's mostly pictures anyway." Barca drained her mug and stood. "We'll set this Friar Locarno up in one of the crew cabins, Sergeant, with a troop medic standing watch."

"I'll sort it out, sir. Have fun learning how to decant."

**

"Another good transit." Morane climbed to his feet and stretched. "Let's hope we can cross this system without making any unfortunate encounters. As soon as sensors report the all-clear, we can go light up and accelerate away on the new course. Signals, call *Tanith*. Let's see if we have a Friar Locarno up and about."

"No need. *Tanith* is calling us, sir."

"Put it on."

Lieutenant Vietti swam into focus on the port side secondary display. "Good day, Captain. We that is, Centurion Barca and her Marines decanted Friar Locarno as ordered during the transit. He woke two hours ago. Once he regained his faculties, we told him about events since finding *Tanith* in the Parth system. He requests to speak with a representative of his Order."

"As it happens, Sister Gwenneth is in the CIC." Morane glanced over his shoulder and with a nod of the head, invited her to join him by the command chair.

A new face appeared beside Vietti's. Crowned by a shock of silver hair and framed by an equally silver beard, it was deeply lined by the travails of age and disappointment at an imperfect universe. His deep-set dark eyes beneath woolen brows seemed to hold secrets from before the dawn of time. He could easily be over a hundred years old. Someone who saw most of the Ruggero dynasty at work as it eroded the compact between the Crown on one hand and the Senate, Fleet and Sovereign Star Systems on the other. And all purely in a quest for absolute power.

"I am Gwenneth, late of the now-defunct Yotai Abbey."

"Defunct?"

"Admiral Zahar and his rebels razed it. They murdered most of the Brethren. And you are Locarno, late of the Order's delegation at the imperial palace?"

"I am he." Locarno inclined his head. "Pardon my rudeness in not naming myself first."

Gwenneth made a dismissive gesture. "It is of no import, Friar. Why were you in a prisoner draft, destined for exile on Parth?"

"The empress turned against the Order when we refused to involve ourselves in secular matters such as helping her find anyone who might become disloyal, so she could purge them. I am the last surviving member of the delegation at the imperial palace and was spared only because of my age and length of service to the throne. And that only at the behest of Dendera's closest confidante, the one person she still trusts. Death squads from the 1st Imperial Guards Regiment murdered the others." A spasm of pain seemed to deepen the lines etched in his tired features. "I was told by Centurion Barca and Lieutenant Vietti you think another prisoner aboard this ship might greatly interest Grand Duke Custis. But that you could not identify the individual and suspect Custis couldn't either."

Morane nodded. "Indeed. Otherwise, I'm sure the rebels would have gladly destroyed *Tanith*. It has to be the only logical reason they left her intact where we found her, considering they couldn't move her in FTL and needed to find a solution such as ours."

"And your logic is sound, Captain Morane. There is indeed an individual of interest aboard, hidden among the surviving prisoners under a false identity, one only I know. And I suspect my knowing is somehow related to surviving Dendera's purge, or at least being exiled to Parth instead of murdered."

— 39 —

"Who?"

Morane's single word question hung in the air for what seemed like an eternity before Locarno shook his head. "My most sincere apologies, Captain, especially in light of your safeguarding my life and that of the others condemned with me, whether it be justly or unjustly. But the answer to your question is a matter the Brethren must consider. Lieutenant Vietti tells me a ship carrying the Yotai Abbey survivors is under your care. I would speak to a plenary session aboard her so that our Order may debate the matter."

A sideways glance at Gwenneth confirmed she would support Locarno should Morane argue the point. It was written all over her angular features, and almost certainly by design as if she knew he would take her unspoken objection into account.

"Very well. I will let the matter rest. For now. We will transfer you from *Tanith* to *Dawn Trader*, but please consider this, Friar Locarno. If what you know has a bearing on our collective welfare, let alone survival, I believe your moral obligation is to share it with us."

The man inclined his head.

"Of course. And if I may provide a modicum of explanation. I fear there might be a chance that my revealing the identity of the person in question could prove fatal in present company. But since I come from the poisonous atmosphere of the imperial palace on Wyvern and know nothing of you, your followers and your quest, a jaundiced view of everyone wearing the imperial uniform might unjustly contaminate my views."

"I understand. But if only for precision's sake, please keep in mind the uniform we wear is no longer that of those who pledge allegiance to the empire. Or of those who've thrown their lot in with one of the many warlords claiming suzerainty over various parts of the frontier."

"I got that from your officers safeguarding *Tanith*, Captain. They were refreshingly truthful and candid. Quite a change after a lifetime at court, watching the Ruggero dynasty chip away at the consensus that has allowed our species a millennium of peace. My compliments. I forgot that such still exist away from the miasma of the imperial capital."

Vietti raised a hand as if asking for permission to speak. "I'll fly Friar Locarno to *Dawn Trader* aboard one of my shuttles, sir. If you'll delay our going FTL for a bit."

"Very well. Make it so." He turned to the signals petty officer. "Please warn Captain Rinne he's about to receive a shuttle from *Tanith* with one of his Order aboard."

"Aye, aye, sir."

"Rinne?" Locarno asked.

Morane nodded. "Yes."

The smile on Locarno's face went a long way to softening his severe mien. "It's been a long time, but when both of us were younger, we troubled our superiors in the Order regularly. Until they separated us by sending him to apprentice as a starship officer and me as counselor to the noble born. That was a long time ago, Captain. Before you were born."

"Then you'll be in familiar hands, Friar."

**

With the 197th once more in FTL and headed for the next wormhole terminus, Mikkel found DeCarde and Morane in the latter's day cabin. For once, Sister Gwenneth wasn't there with that eerily unnerving, watchful gaze.

"Everything clear, Iona?"

"The ship is secure, Skipper."

"In that case, join us. What do you think about this Friar Locarno business?"

"Another perplexing development brought to us by an Order best defined as a riddle wrapped in a mystery inside an enigma," the first officer said, heading for the samovar and a cup of Morane's tea. "But I'll venture a guess we're dealing with a prisoner who was once close to the throne. Closer than Grand Duke Custis or the Imperial Chamberlain. Another victim of Dendera's growing madness."

"That'll be a very limited number of individuals, I should think," DeCarde said. "Surely we can figure this out ourselves if the Brethren don't feel inclined to share."

Morane made a face. "While speculating is fun, I don't intend to press the point. Rinne, Gwenneth and the rest know their survival depends on ours. If they believe keeping this prisoner's identity under wraps for now is necessary and doesn't imperil us, I'm willing to let matters lie."

"You're more tolerant than I when it comes to the Order of the Void playing games," DeCarde said. "But you're also in command."

"Being tolerant does not equate to being happy, Brigid. Since I've taken up the responsibility to see us reach a safe harbor, everything about the people and ships in our caravan concerns me. Especially if we carry a politically sensitive person whose escape might trigger interest from various parties that could do us harm. By now, the rebel forces in Parth will have passed the word to their allies that a Monokeros class transport escorted by a small battle group is carrying an Imperial Prison Service starship with a person or persons of interest aboard. Anyone we meet in the Coalsack Sector could well be on the lookout and try to arraign us if they're of sufficient strength."

"Even more reason to take the network's less traveled routes."

A mocking smile twisted Morane's lips. "Even though we'll be passing through a triple star system?"

"Better than a quadruple. But it'll still take us through Lorien and Mentari, two systems with minor colonies, before we reach the biggest obstacle, Arietis. Thankfully, neither boast a permanent naval presence."

"True."

Mikkel's communicator chirped for attention. "Yes?"

"Cox'n here, sir. The bosun just broke up another fight. Both are in sickbay, though it doesn't appear serious."

"I'm with the captain, Chief. Will this be another case of bosun's punishment or is it time for a captain's mast?"

"Let us chiefs and petty officers deal with it, sir. A captain's mast won't cure the *cafard* or help ease homesickness. Hard work has a better chance of success."

Mikkel glanced at Morane who nodded, then said, "It's in your hands, Chief."

"Aye, aye, sir. Cox'n, out."

"Let's hope this was not the symptom of a coming epidemic." Morane glanced at DeCarde. "Any incidents in your battalion so far?"

She shook her head. "None that were brought to my notice, which doesn't mean my troopers aren't feeling a touch of the old *cafard* as well. However, Marine noncoms know how to stop fights before they start and are even better at finding mind-numbing physical activities to prevent wandering spirits from going mentally absent without leave. And, as much as it pains the DeCarde in me who believes in family lore to make this admission, Sisters Gwenneth and Katarin are proving useful in helping my less stoic Marines aboard *Vanquish* keep the megrims at bay, as are the sisters aboard *Narwhal*. Or so I've been told."

"Surprise, surprise." Morane smiled at her.

"But I still don't trust their motives."

**

"Are we sure this damned system is still inhabited?" Chief Lettis asked under his breath once the first sensor scans of Lorien came back. Then, in a louder tone, "Nothing to report, Captain."

"Any wormhole traffic control buoys?"

"Not here."

"No subspace carrier waves to indicate there are working buoys at the other termini," the signals petty officer added. "No system relay and I'm not picking up any radio waves. If someone's alive on Lorien, they're not broadcasting, period."

Morane studied the tactical projection, then called up a navigation plot showing their course between this wormhole terminus and the one through which they planned to exit the Lorien system.

"Iona, I'd like to pass within sensor range of the planet and find out what happened to the colony. The last census update, only two years old, showed over twenty thousand colonists. We need to dogleg it with two jumps on this crossing anyway. Our ingress and egress wormholes are in direct opposition. Jumping inward and cruising by the planet before the outward leg won't cost us much in terms of time. Only a day."

When Creswell saw DeCarde's quizzical look, she whispered, "A single jump would take us smack dab through the star, and you can't do that, even in hyperspace."

"Ah, of course. Thanks."

"As you wish, Skipper, but there's no room for more strays."

"I merely want to see what happened to Lorien. No radio waves whatsoever coming from that planet bodes ill."

"You're thinking another Palmyra?" DeCarde asked.

Morane's face twisted into a sad grimace. "That is my fear, Brigid. And if Lorien suffered the same fate, it is only right someone should bear witness to the colony's disappearance."

"Course is laid in, and ships are synced, Skipper."

"Thank you, Iona. You may start the countdown to FTL jump at your leisure."

Mikkel's leisure proved to be short. The five-minute warning klaxon sounded almost before Morane finished speaking.

— 40 —

"Still nothing. Not even satellites in orbit, or at least none that are active." Lorien, a violently green orb mottled with dark patches, was glowing malevolently on the CIC's main display as *Vanquish* and her consorts neared their closest point of approach.

"No radio waves either."

"Doesn't seem welcoming," DeCarde remarked. "There's something about the colors that is giving me the faintest bit of unease."

"Perhaps it's not the colors," Gwenneth said in a quiet voice.

The Marine swallowed a sigh. "What do you mean, Sister?"

"Over twenty thousand souls called Lorien home two years ago, yet we seem unable to find any evidence they still live."

"Perhaps the colonists moved to a safer place."

Gwenneth turned her eyes on DeCarde. "You don't believe that, do you?"

The latter hesitated, then finally said, "No."

"And therein lies the source of your unease."

Almost an hour passed before Chief Lettis spoke again. "I found the main settlement, Captain. Or what's left of it. The sensors aren't detecting any human life signs though there's plenty alive down there."

"Put it on the main display."

"Are you sure, sir? It's pretty grisly."

"We're here to bear witness, Chief. To remember the twenty thousand who suffered because empresses, viceroys, admirals and other assorted power-seekers couldn't remember that their first duty was to the empire's common citizens and not their own self-aggrandizement."

When the first image of ravaged houses and dismembered corpses fill the screen, Sister Gwenneth began to pray, softly, but with deep feeling.

"Looks like this happened a while ago," Creswell said. "Judging by the degree of decomposition." She winced as a new image appeared. "Are those decapitated children?"

A pale-faced Lettis nodded. "There's worse to come, Commander."

DeCarde swallowed the bile rising in her throat with difficulty before speaking. "What manner of being does this?"

"The sort that considers any life but their own, or that of their clan to be inferior and unworthy of respect, Colonel. Humans have a long history of inhumanity. I fear those who fled beyond the pale centuries ago bred a progeny no longer possessing the inhibitions we take for granted."

"And that progeny is returning to take what the empire denied their forebears. A cheerful thought, Sister. But at least we won't face any moral quandaries when we kill them." DeCarde half expected Gwenneth to mumble something about the Almighty and the sanctity of life, yet she nodded in agreement.

"We should not kill wantonly, Colonel. However, the Almighty will not condemn those who kill beings intent on destroying what is good."

"Nice to know. Because watching that horror show is making my trigger finger itch something fierce."

Image after image from the sensor feed crossed the CIC's display, each with fresh horrors until everyone was numb. Finally, even Morane could no longer bear witness.

"Enough, Chief. Annalise, target the settlement with a nuclear warhead. We can't leave them like that."

"Aye, aye, sir." Creswell sounded hoarse with suppressed rage.

"Once the missile is on its way, Iona, we can accelerate back toward the hyperlimit. The Lorien system has slipped into the badlands, perhaps forever."

**

"So far, so good," Mikkel said after Chief Lettis reported all-clear. "Even though we passed through a triple system, this is indeed Mentari, our last low-risk crossing before Arietis. I'd say we've been extraordinarily lucky since shaking off our little rebel-induced misstep when we fled Parth. Maybe waking that ancient friar brought us good fortune."

"We'll need that and more once we transit through Wormhole Mentari Three. I'll wager the admiral in charge on the Arietis side will have left something guarding his termini, even the one leading to a minor colonized system like Mentari. Especially now that it's clear marauders are creeping out of the badlands and testing the Coalsack Sector's defenses."

Holographic Mikkel made a face. "And there's no way but through Arietis. I know. Our supplies are insufficient for another long, roundabout run. Nor will *Narwhal* last for more than perhaps a dozen wormhole transits before the strain of carrying *Tanith* finally turns her into another derelict needing a ride. Lori Ryzkov just reported more microscopic stress fractures in her outer hull. She didn't sound worried yet, but once these things start, they'll keep coming unless the cause of the stress goes away."

"And we can't cut *Tanith* loose."

DeCarde smirked at Gwenneth. "At least not without knowing which personage of high importance is hiding among the stasis stiffs."

"The Brethren deemed it prudent to wait until we reach our destination," the sister replied in a tone suffused with such indulgent patience that the Marine wanted to scream. The knowing expression on her face when she gazed at DeCarde just made matters worse.

But then, everyone's tempers were fraying. The 6th of the 21st experienced its first disciplinary incident aboard *Narwhal* three days earlier when two privates from A Squadron pushed a friendly bout of wrestling into a violent release of pent-up anger. Neither could explain why he turned into a berserker and DeCarde let the squadron commander apply informal punishment.

"Might I suggest you consider subterfuge to aid in traversing the Arietis system, Captain?"

Morane swiveled his command chair to look at Gwenneth. "What do you mean?"

"On balance of probabilities, the local commander will be one of Admiral Zahar's officers. Enter the system as if you were under orders from the admiral. You can project utter confidence when you so wish."

"Ah. You mean bluff?"

"I think the sister means bullshit our way through, Skipper. I can think of worse plans."

"You may call it what you wish, but it is a practical option, one that could see us pass through without a fight. And you can do so with ease, Captain."

Gwenneth's eyes held a spark of something undefinable as she gazed back at Morane and he felt strangely inspired by her calm certainty. He wondered once more about DeCarde's family lore concerning the Sisters of the Void.

"We will enter the Arietis system in our accustomed manner, by going silent so we can see what if anything might be lurking. Once the situation is clear, I shall decide on our best course of action. But first, the 197th must cross this system."

"Did you want to pass near the colony, Skipper?"

"Are sensors and signals picking up any anomalies?"

"No," Lettis and the signals petty officer replied in unison.

"Everything appears normal, sir," the latter said. "Plenty of radio waves from Mentari itself, and there's a subspace carrier wave from a system relay."

"No starship traffic, but Mentari's satellite constellation is operational."

"In that case, we'll cross to Wormhole Mentari Three in one jump and avoid broadcasting our presence." He sighed. "Funnily enough, it still pains me to say it. There was a day when patrolling Navy ships visited every inhabited world on their route to check with the colonists, discuss any problems or concerns. Offer a little help."

"That day might come back."

Morane gave DeCarde a sad smile. "I hope so, but it will happen long after we're gone."

"I agree. Which means as I read somewhere, the only thing we can do is figure out how best to live the life we've been given."

"You're turning philosophical, Colonel. Congratulations."

"Perhaps condolences would be more appropriate. I used to be a simple Marine before I threw my lot in with you. Perhaps I will regret letting that person slip away."

"Regrets are a futile human affectation," Gwenneth said. "The past is gone, and nothing can change what was."

"And our future, death, is the undiscovered country from which no visitor returns." DeCarde made a face. "On a certain level, I envy you and Captain Morane, Sister. You both seem to follow a guiding light, something drawing you forward, a belief that the rest of us mere mortals lack. Call it faith, a vision or whatever you wish. Those of us who don't share in that belief need to find a reason elsewhere, otherwise it becomes difficult to see why we should continue on the path we're shown."

"I never thought you for a doubter, Colonel."

A sardonic grin met Morane's words.

"I doubt everything, sir. But I also try to find meaning in everything and hope for a balance. Right now, my meaning is survival. That of my troopers and my own. The rebirth of a new empire, long after we're dust, is of little importance by comparison."

Gwenneth, uncharacteristically, laid a hand on DeCarde's arm. "Your sentiments are not only understandable, they're also human. Few are able to see beyond a mortal lifetime."

"But you can?"

"My Order has existed since long before the birth of the empire, and it will exist long after the empire's current incarnation is dust. We are among the few whose duty is to see beyond a mortal lifetime, and it has been so since our creation. Even then, not all Brethren can accept the idea with equanimity. Many struggle with the concept we exist to serve a cause that transcends our brief lifespans." Gwenneth nodded at Morane. "Though it appears our shepherd has a firm grasp of what the long view means."

"Then I'm glad one of us does, Sister. As I keep reminding myself, we Marines are not on this voyage by choice but by chance."

Gwenneth's lips twisted into that mysterious smile DeCarde found so infuriating. "The Almighty leaves little to chance, Colonel. You and your battalion are on this journey for a purpose, though it might not become plain any time soon, if ever."

"This is one of those moments when I wish I possessed your faith, Sister."

"Each of us follows his or her our own path to the Almighty, and we all eventually pass through the Void, even hardened skeptics from the DeCarde lineage." Gwenneth stood. "If you'll excuse me, our conversation is a reminder of my duty to those in *Vanquish*."

Morane and DeCarde watched her leave the CIC while the rest of the crew pretended they didn't overhear the conversation. Then, the Marine said, "As much as I try to ignore her mysterious statements, I really wouldn't mind knowing what she meant by hardened skeptics from the DeCarde lineage."

"Perhaps she has a copy of your family lore in her travel bag." Morane chuckled. "Come to think of it, isn't your family lore something that transcends a mortal lifetime and connects you to your forebears since before the birth of the empire? A bit like the Order of the Void's teachings isn't it?"

She gave him a dirty glance and muttered, "Please, Captain, don't compare us DeCardes to those mind-meddlers. Not even in jest."

Morane raised his hands in surrender. "Hey, you heard the sister. I'm just a shepherd, not a philosopher. But I am good at pointing out the obvious."

DeCarde gave him a dirty look and growled, "Obviously."

—41—

"We're in the Arietis system. All ships present," Lettis reported, "and they came through the terminus in silent running mode."

"Now the real fun begins," Mikkel murmured. "Bullshitting our way through a rebel-held system on the longest path between termini this junction has to offer."

"Have a little faith, Iona. I hear it can move mountains." Morane glanced over his shoulder at Gwenneth, who gave him a solemn nod. "Besides, Arietis is not a strategic node. It's merely one gateway to the peripheral imperial systems, far from the turmoil surrounding the sector capital. The local commander won't be expecting trouble, nor will he or she be up on the latest news. That's the one advantage of operating in a chaotic environment. You often can't tell who is a friend and who is a foe until the shooting starts."

"But whichever flag officer runs this place will be puzzled by our heading for a wormhole cul-de-sac."

"Perhaps, but I can't see the Arietis Task Force chasing us into a dead-end."

A few minutes passed, then the signals petty officer turned toward Morane. "Sir, I'm not picking up a subspace carrier wave from the system relay. Either it's dormant or gone."

"How about normal radio waves?"

"The usual coming from Arietis. But nothing from the system relay. And no starship beacons. However, I am picking up the wormhole terminus traffic control buoys' subspace carrier waves. They seem to be the only extra-atmospheric transmitters in operation."

"Strange. Where is the Arietis Task Force?" Morane ran a hand, fingers splayed, through his hair as he studied the tactical projection with a puzzled expression on his face. "Hook us into the traffic control buoys. At least we'll know if something comes or goes without waiting for visuals to catch up a day later."

They spent the next hour in almost total silence as the 197th's sensors probed for human activity while its receivers kept listening to both the subspace and normal radio bands.

"Nothing," Lettis finally said. "No evidence of activity in this system either, but the planet's satellite constellation appears functional, just like Mentari's."

"Could it be a trap?" DeCarde asked. "Custis somehow spread the word about us stealing *Tanith* and they're waiting in ambush?"

"Possible but not probable," Morane replied. "There's no way for Admiral Ostrow to figure out our destination and I can't see Custis ordering every system under his control to go silent in case a rag-tag battle group shows up. Besides, if the Arietis Task Force is setting a trap, would they leave the traffic control buoys active? Or at least would they leave them so any naval unit can connect, including us? Perhaps the Arietis Task Force left the system in response to a call for reinforcements closer to the badlands. In Peralka for example."

"Or the rebel Navy buggered off and abandoned this system. Arietis isn't exactly an economic or political powerhouse. On the contrary."

"That could very well be, Annalise. And since this system has six wormhole termini, it's just a matter of time before—"

"Before reivers start probing? I think time's up, sir." Lettis pointed at a side display. "According to the Wormhole Arietis Three traffic control buoy, four ships just came through the terminus, inbound from Peralka. And they don't look like naval units to me."

Morane and Creswell studied the buoy's data stream.

"Not Navy and not merchant. A wolf pack," the latter said. "Reivers, no doubt about it. Look at those power curves."

Morane made a sound of agreement.

"Which means Peralka is no longer under Navy control. Either Admiral Zahar withdrew the 162nd to reinforce another, more important part of the sector, or its commander remained loyal to the Crown and decided to head for Wyvern or one of the core sectors."

"Our last update from HQ shows the Arietis Task Force as coming from the 162nd Battle Group. If the one-six-two abandoned its home system, then that might explain why there are no naval units here either."

"Indeed, Annalise. And now the barbarians are probing the next junction in the network."

"They might know the Arietis Task Force bugged out along with the 162nd."

"Could well be. If they're paying attention, they'll soon realize that Arietis is no longer defended either. And then they'll strike."

"Sir?" Morane turned to the signals petty officer. "The traffic control buoy's carrier wave just vanished."

"Meaning they're aware Arietis is no longer defended and destroyed it. If we head for the planet straight off, we might arrive simultaneously or shortly after they do. Four of them shouldn't prove a problem for *Vanquish*, let alone *Vanquish* and *Myrtale* together."

Creswell nodded in agreement. "We need to cross the system from side to side anyway. A brief stop shouldn't delay us much, and so far we haven't expended ammunition since leaving Cervantes."

Mikkel reacted at once.

"You want us to head for Arietis and beat off reivers? What about our mission? Sail to Lyonesse. Saving Arietis isn't our fight."

"I don't doubt that wolf pack is headed for the planet, Iona. The least we can do is intercept it and give the colonists a chance since they seem to be totally unprotected." Morane's voice was calm, his tone soft and measured. "Providence put us in a position to help, and I think we should do so. Plot a course to the Arietis hyperlimit. When ready, sync the ships and engage. Once we're there, *Vanquish* and *Myrtale* will continue on to Arietis at best speed, while *Narwhal* and *Dawn Trader* go silent and loiter until we're done."

Iona Mikkel knew any argument would be futile. "Aye, aye, sir."

**

"They beat us by a nose," Chief Lettis growled once he, and the rest of the CIC crew, recovered from the usual FTL emergence nausea ten hours later.

Morane swallowed a few times to settle his stomach as he studied the tactical projection showing four red icons nearing Arietis. "Smaller ships, closer hyperlimit, Chief."

"Is there a point in running silent?" Mikkel asked. "Which *Narwhal* and *Dawn Trader* already are, by the way."

"No. Pour on as much acceleration as we can handle. Pass the word to *Myrtale*."

"Done."

"Signals, see if you can raise anyone on Arietis. Traffic control, for example. If their satellites are still up, they should be able to hear our subspace transmission. They may not see the reivers yet."

Several minutes passed in silence, then, "I have Arietis Traffic Control, sir. Audio only."

"On speakers."

"Who is this?" An irritated voice asked.

"I'm Captain Morane, of the 197th Battle Group. And you are?"

"Biro Jacks, operations manager."

"Are you aware four suspected reiver ships are on course for Arietis, Mister Jacks?"

"Yep. Took the fuckers long enough."

"Why do you say that?"

"Commodore Kajo pulled out with the rest of the Arietis Task Force eight weeks ago. No explanation, no farewells, nothing. The governor, his staff, and the entire colonial office bunch bugged off with them. Took the damned system subspace relay too."

"So you've been both leaderless and defenseless for two months?"

A grim chuckle came over the comlink. "Yep. Although we've set up our own governing council. We also scraped together a few hundred volunteers, pilfered the Navy's storehouse in Cintrea and set up an informal militia."

"Then you're ahead of other frontier systems. We passed through two where the entire population was either kidnapped or massacred. Places that never had a Navy presence to begin with."

"Those animals will find out we shoot back once they land."

"The 197ᵗʰ is inbound, though about an hour behind them. We'll try our best to help."

"Thank you kindly, Captain. Shintaro Keen, our council chief, is about to warn the militia, but anything you can do is much appreciated."

"Then I suggest you deactivate your satellite constellation, so the reivers don't shoot it up, just for fun. What they can't track, they can't target."

"Thanks for the suggestion. We'll do so now. Good hunting. Arietis Traffic Control, out."

Morane exchanged a puzzled glance with DeCarde. "Biro Jacks sounds more annoyed than worried."

"Maybe they built the mother of all reiver traps?"

Sister Gwenneth shook her head. "Many people hide their fear behind irritation. Jacks is deeply concerned."

"At least we can help with the reiver incursion, Sister."

"And your interrupting our journey for this purpose is a good thing, but do not be surprised if the people governing Arietis pressure you to stay and become their protector."

"I know." Morane grimaced. "But much as it will pain me, I understand that staying here would be like trying to hold back the tide of history. Arietis is one of those crossroads doomed to see every barbarian invasion pass through, and that makes it utterly unsuitable for a knowledge vault."

"Can I make a suggestion? Something that might help salve your conscience about leaving the folks behind when we pull out?" DeCarde asked. When Morane nodded, she said, "Jacks mentioned a volunteer militia. Do you think we could stick around for a while after dealing with the reivers? To give the volunteers a hand with their training? And whatever else they need to deal with the next incursion? Send my battalion to the surface for a week or two. Let us stretch our legs, and we'll do what we can."

Morane glanced at Commander Mikkel's hologram, hovering by his elbow as always. "Iona?"

The first officer gave him an irritable shrug. "Why ask me, Skipper. I know you'll do as you see fit no matter what anyone says. Besides, it's taken us this long to reach Arietis. What are a few more weeks before we enter the Promised Land?"

"So it shall be done. Once we clean up the orbitals." Morane settled back in his chair and stared at the tactical projection, willing his two warships to close the distance with Arietis and the approaching reivers.

— 42 —

"They're about to enter orbit."

Morane made a face. "I was afraid we might lose this race, Chief. Although I'd much rather get close enough without being noticed for guaranteed kill shots, letting them enter the atmosphere and land, or worse yet, bombard the colony's command-and-control nodes won't do. Annalise, ping them hard with our targeting sensors. Let's see if that spooks the bastards enough so they veer off and run. They might not quite believe the Arietis Task Force left for good and think we're Commodore Kajo coming back."

"Pinging."

Several minutes passed without the reivers changing course. But as Morane expected, they finally realized something was coming up behind them.

"We're being pinged in return," Chief Lettis said. "They know we're here, armed and hazardous to their health."

"And they're veering off," Creswell added. "Smart little beggars."

Morane studied the ships' relative vectors. "Iona, we will pursue. Cease decelerating and pour on the gees again. Annalise, as soon as we're in effective missile range open fire. Coordinate with *Myrtale* on targeting. Two reivers each."

"Remember," the first officer said, "a stern chase is a long chase. They may well reach their hyperlimit before we can score disabling hits, and you don't sound prepared to follow them in FTL, let alone through the wormhole to Peralka."

"Doesn't matter. If the only thing we do is frighten them into thinking the Navy never left Arietis, then it'll at least buy the colonists more time to prepare." He glanced over his shoulder at DeCarde. "With your help."

The next hour passed in tense silence, but it soon became obvious *Vanquish* and *Myrtale* wouldn't catch all four reivers. The two lead ships had a better rate of acceleration than their comrades and were pulling away, leaving the laggards to their fate.

Creswell startled everyone except Morane when she broke the CIC's silence to announce, "Missiles away." Muted vibrations reached them as the autoloader in the ship's keel rotated to refill the launch tubes. Small blue icons separated from the larger images representing the 197th's two warships. One cluster soon settled behind the rearmost ship and the other behind the second last.

The lead ships suddenly winked out of existence as they jumped into hyperspace. Chief Lettis grunted. "The buggers don't much care about stressing their hulls, because they weren't quite at the hyperlimit yet."

"Needs must when the devil drives," Creswell replied. "And we're an avenging Satan come to life."

Then, a tiny supernova flashed in the tactical display, and one of the two remaining red icons vanished.

"Those were our missiles." Then the remaining red icon dematerialized. "*Myrtale* scored direct hits, but the reiver jumped seconds later, so there's no way of knowing how much damage they caused. If it's catastrophic enough, he'll come out of FTL as a debris field. But we'll never know."

"Better than nothing. Thank you, Annalise." Morane looked at Mikkel's hologram. "Take us back to Arietis and open a link with the man in charge, Iona."

**

"I understand we owe you thanks for chasing off those unknown starships." A wizened man, with craggy features that seemed almost as ancient as Arietis' arid surface, looked out at Morane from the CIC's main display. His eyes gleamed with the stubbornness of someone determined to outlive his contemporaries. "Shame you only destroyed one of them. I'm Shintaro Keen, by the way, the guy who supposedly runs this place since the governor and the Navy buggered off without so much as a goodbye kiss."

"Pleasure, sir. And we winged another who might not survive an FTL jump to the wormhole. But as my first officer keeps reminding me, a stern chase is a long chase, and something of that size can outrun a cruiser like *Vanquish* if it has a head start."

"Does your arrival mean we're no longer alone? That the viceroy, whoever holds that cursed title nowadays, or his admiral figured out this system and its six wormhole termini isn't something you abandon with complete disregard?"

"I'm sorry, sir, but my battle group is merely passing through on another mission. We spotted the reivers and diverted to intercept them."

Keen's face sagged into a crestfallen expression. "So you'll be leaving us too."

"Yes, sir." Morane felt his heart sink at the despair he saw in the chief counselor's eyes. "I can hardly find the words to express how sorry I am, but I have no choice. However, if you like, we can spend a week or two helping you prepare. I carry a Marine Pathfinder battalion. It would please them to land on Arietis and give your volunteers with whatever training, advice and assistance they can before we move on with our mission."

"You know this attempted raid is only the first, right, Captain?"

"I do. Arietis has an unenviable position, especially since it seems Peralka has slipped into the badlands because that's where those four ships originated. If Peralka was still patrolled by the Navy, the reivers wouldn't have dared come here."

"Good thing we own little of interest. Outside of the rift valley, there's nothing. Not even native wildlife. Reivers must be daft to figure they can strike it rich."

"They're not particularly intelligent, sir. Cunning, yes, and definitely cruel. But not smart. Otherwise, they'd engage in honest trade."

"Not smart? Or not quite human anymore? I've heard stories of what goes on in the badlands, Captain." Keen sighed. "We'll gladly take whatever aid you can give, and welcome your Marines with open arms. Arietis doesn't offer much, but if you're looking for a home base, you'll find us more hospitable and more grateful than pretty much anyone in the Coalsack Sector. Keep that in mind."

"Yes, sir. We'll be in orbit shortly. My other two ships will arrive approximately four hours after that. If you don't object, I will land the first half of the 6th Battalion, 21st Pathfinder Regiment the moment we're above Cintrea, with the rest to follow later in the day. Colonel DeCarde will be pleased to meet with whoever you appoint so they can discuss how she might help the Arietis Volunteers."

"That'll be Ramirus Brockway. He's what you might call the commanding officer of our little defense force. Former Marine. Solid man. But there's not much to work with. Mind you, we haven't broken into every Navy warehouse yet. Some of them are tough nuts, and could even be booby-trapped. Ramirus didn't want to push things."

"We can try our codes, sir. And Colonel DeCarde's people know a few tricks. Every last Navy storeroom will be yours before we leave."

"Much appreciated. Tell us when the good colonel is landing, and I'll ask Ramirus to meet her at the Cintrea spaceport. Once again, thank you for stopping by to chase off those thieving scum, and keep in mind you could find a home here if you so wish."

Morane inclined his head. "We were merely doing our duty, sir. And that duty demands our presence elsewhere."

"I understand. Until later."

Keen's image faded away. Morane turned to face DeCarde and Gwenneth. "It's hard not to feel for them. Keen puts on a good poker face, but he knows the future is grim."

"Someone said this to you before," DeCarde replied. "Perhaps me, perhaps Iona, but we can't save everyone."

"That doesn't make it easier to bear." A sad smile briefly crossed Morane's face.

"No. I suppose it doesn't." DeCarde stood. "I'll see that B and D Squadrons prepare. We'll try to do our best to help. Short of settling here, we can't do more, right? And stopping short of our goal is not an option. Not if we're to bring your scheme to life. And if we don't bring your scheme to life, then my battalion might as well have stayed in Klim Castle, fighting to the bitter end."

— 43 —

"This is not good."

"Hmm?" Lieutenant Commander Creswell's head came up, and she turned her eyes on Lettis. "What's not good, Chief?"

"Three ships dropped out of FTL near Wormhole Arietis Six. Not Navy, that's for sure. No beacon either."

"Telemetry?"

"On the main screen."

Creswell studied the data. "You're right. Not good at all. Those aren't honest merchantmen. They have that look. The same look as those four we chased away two weeks ago."

"And those power curves as well, sir." He pointed at a side display.

"Woah. Really, not good." Creswell touched the control screen in the command chair's arm. "They probably came from Peralka through Wormhole Arietis Three, since we didn't see them slip into the system. CIC to the captain."

A few seconds passed, then, "Morane."

"The Wormhole Six traffic control buoy reported three ships, definitely not Navy and likely not merchant coming out of hyperspace on a course to enter the terminus. Emissions signature is consistent with high-powered raiders. We didn't spot them entering the system, which indicates they probably came from Peralka, like the others."

Morane's muffled reply sounded suspiciously like a half-swallowed curse. "Meaning they could be the three we chased off the other day. Or members of the same clan. And since Arietis is now defended, perhaps they thought it would be a good idea to probe Lyonesse."

A pause, then a sigh. He mentally damned himself for tarrying in this system, trying to help the stranded colonists prepare their defenses. But leaving them to an uncertain fate without at least doing something would grievously wound his conscience.

"Captain to the bridge."

"Officer of the watch."

"Order our and *Narwhal*'s shuttles to evacuate everyone on the surface and warn the battle group we're leaving the moment the Marines are aboard." He thought for a few moments. "Raise *Myrtale*."

Sirak answered with commendable speed. Morane told him about the three suspicious ships spotted by the wormhole terminus leading to Lyonesse's dead-end branch.

"I must recover the Marines, which might take two or three hours, if not more, and with *Narwhal* so sluggish, I fear they might reach Lyonesse and commit mischief before we can stop them."

"And you'd like me to head out right away."

"Push *Myrtale*, Nate and never mind the Fleet's safety regulations. Every hour you can save by jumping before you reach the hyperlimit and by pushing into the upper

FTL bands could mean lives saved. Track those ships and if they're what we fear, destroy them."

"In other words, you'd like me to act like a typical frigate captain." A sly grin appeared on Sirak's swarthy features. "Done and done. Just don't take too long. Otherwise, I might leave nothing for *Vanquish* to dine on. With your permission?"

"Go. Godspeed and good luck."

Sirak's face faded away. Morane, sitting at the desk in his day cabin, tapped its surface with his fingertips as his mind feverishly spun through a long list of scenarios, none of them with a happy ending for Lyonesse. Three ships might not seem like much, but they could devastate a colony of less than a million inhabitants, whose settlements were concentrated along one strip of shoreline in a matter of hours.

So much for hoping no one would venture into that particular wormhole branch while more accessible systems lay wide open. And what about Arietis? Once they left, its colonists would quickly find themselves in an existential struggle with barbarians seeping in from beyond the empire's old borders. However, even with the best will in the galaxy, there was nothing Morane could do besides sacrifice his dream. Arietis might not count as a strategic wormhole junction, yet its termini would make sure the system became part of a vital incursion route for any invaders, and therefore indefensible by two warships and a naval transport.

The comm system chimed again. He glanced at the screen embedded in his desk. A call from the surface. DeCarde. Morane accepted the link.

"Why the sudden evacuation, sir? We're not done yet."

"Sensors picked up what looks like reivers near Wormhole Six. They'll be on their way down the Lyonesse branch within a few hours."

"Shit."

"*Myrtale* is on her way as we speak, but I'm afraid the worst might happen, so there's no time to lose. We shouldn't have stayed this long in the first place. With the 16th Fleet gone, Arietis is doomed anyhow."

DeCarde snorted. "Doomed, perhaps. But I think we helped them buy a little more time."

"For what?"

"I don't know. For a warlord from the badlands to adopt Arietis as his or her fief instead of pillaging everything. You're usually more upbeat and hopeful, Captain. Perhaps you need to spend more time with Sister Gwenneth and search for your waning faith."

Morane bit back a curt reply and tried to shove his anxiety about reivers reaching Lyonesse before the 197th Battle Group to one side.

"Just get up here, Brigid. We must leave."

"What do I tell the colonists? Goodbye and good luck? Sounds a little harsh."

"Tell them the star system next door needs rescuing from death by reiver, just like we saved Arietis."

A sardonic grin appeared on the Marine's face. "My, my, you *are* testy today. Warm up those drives, Captain Savior. We're coming home."

Her face faded away, and Morane found himself tapping his fingers on the desktop again. He successfully resisted the urge to visit either the CIC or the bridge, knowing his presence in either wouldn't speed up their departure, though it would ensure his impatience and anxiety became contagious. No one would thank him for that.

**

DeCarde tucked her communicator away and turned back to where D Squadron's Pathfinders were putting another batch of Arietis Volunteer Force members through basic small unit tactics. They were willing enough after living in fear since the Arietis Task Force bugged out weeks earlier, leaving them with nothing more than abandoned naval stores at the Cintrea spaceport. Yet DeCarde didn't think most would live long enough to become even semi-capable fighters.

But the planet was ancient. It saw other species settle, thrive and vanish long before humanity showed up to re-occupy the towns and villages strung along the bottom of its continent-sized rift valley. That valley was the only place left where temperature, air pressure, and shelter combined to allow large-scale agriculture capable of supporting millions. But Arietis never supported millions. At least not during the centuries of human tenure. No one knew quite how many colonists remained, but Cintrea, Hauk, Lomis and Mezza, the four major settlements where she'd deployed her squadrons to train locals, seemed capable of housing much larger populations.

She found the head of the Arietis Volunteer Force, an old Marine veteran who somehow ended here after retiring and slumming his way across the empire, talking to D Squadron's first sergeant by the side of the road. Ramirus Brockway was one of the few left behind who knew what the business end of a plasma rifle looked like, let alone how to hit a reiver at five hundred meters, when the rebels bugged out. But at least Arietis wouldn't die off like Palmyra, Lorien and who knew how many other outlying colonies that didn't realize soon enough the empire no longer protected them.

At her approach, Brockway and the first sergeant came to attention. The retired Marine saw the expression on DeCarde's face and grimaced. "You look like someone who just swallowed a lump of antimatter fuel, Colonel."

"I'm afraid we have to leave, Sergeant Brockway. Our sensors spotted a reiver wolf pack heading into the

Lyonesse branch, and if we don't go after them, the people at the other end won't be as fortunate as Arietis."

"Now?"

"Within the hour."

Brockway spat on the dusty road. "Satan take the reivers and their spawn." His eyes met hers with unabashed frankness. "I'll confess I'd hoped you might settle here, Colonel, or at least stay for a while, but I understand. You and your Captain Morane are what's left in these parts to fight the scum." He stuck out his hand. "Still, I'm glad to have met you, and so are the others. Maybe they've learned enough to make the next raiding party that lands think twice. On behalf of the Volunteers, thanks and may the Almighty watch over you."

"Good luck, Sergeant Brockway."

DeCarde briefly thought about offering the veteran a berth in *Vanquish* but understood her intimation he might abandon Arietis to its fate would insult him. This was now his home, something worth fighting for after a life of fighting for an empire that stopped caring long ago. She stepped onto the road and looked up at where the Cintrea spaceport sat high above the rift valley.

"All Pegasus call signs, this is Niner. Wrap up activities, prepare for immediate departure, and activate beacons. Shuttles are inbound. *Vanquish* spotted tangos near our destination wormhole. They could threaten our future home. Acknowledge."

Five squadron commanders promptly replied, and moments later, she saw D Squadron break away from the Volunteer Force's Cintrea Company to form in three ranks. The non-plussed colonists simply stopped in mid-stride and watched them leave until Brockway shouted an order to carry on. He gave DeCarde a final salute before joining his troops. She knew then they would never meet again.

Half an hour later, after a forced march, DeCarde and D Squadron climbed aboard the creaky funicular connecting Cintrea to its spaceport and watched the rift valley dwindle below them. She found Combat Support Squadron, which was training the Volunteer Force's own support troops, already formed up, ready to climb aboard *Narwhal*'s shuttles when they landed.

The flight from *Vanquish* arrived first, however. A funny sensation settled in the pit of her stomach as she lifted off, leaving Major Waske and her troops on the dusty tarmac. But it passed the moment Waske reported she and hers were also in the air.

During the flight into orbit, she tried to analyze that unexpected reaction and concluded Waske briefly stood in for Brockway and the other frightened but willing volunteers they were leaving to an unknown and probably unhappy fate. But as she'd told Morane several times during their long voyage, they couldn't save everyone.

— 44 —

"The traffic control buoy confirms the three tangos dropped into the wormhole, Captain. They're definitely headed for Lyonesse. They'll enter ISC668231-2 in seven hours."

Though Morane knew it was coming, his fists clenched nonetheless. ISC668231-2 was the first of the two sterile systems in the Lyonesse branch. But *Myrtale*, still boosting out to the hyperlimit at a rate of acceleration that was making her inertial dampeners scream, wouldn't reach Wormhole Six until the reivers were already halfway across the system.

And that was if she jumped upon entering the hyperlimit's red zone instead of waiting to reach a safe distance and pushed her speed beyond what was considered safe within a star's heliosphere. Those additional stresses on top of the battle damage she suffered weeks earlier would cut her remaining service life short indeed, but Morane saw no other way. She was still the fastest ship in his flotilla. The fastest warship that is. *Dawn Trader* might outrace the frigate, but she didn't carry sufficient ordnance to take on three reivers.

Lyonesse would be on its own for the better part of a day before *Myrtale* arrived and face a desperate situation. Unless he could warn the colonists.

Arietis no longer had a system subspace relay, but there was an outside chance *Vanquish*'s subspace transmitter might reach the Lyonesse system relay. It might give them time to prepare. If Lyonesse was listening. And if the listeners were inclined to believe his message.

"Bridge, this is the captain."

"Officer of the watch."

"Aim our subspace transmitter at the Lyonesse system, boost its power as high as possible and send the following. Three suspected reiver ships are on their way to Lyonesse from Arietis. Expected arrival in the Lyonesse system any time after seventy-two hours from this message's date-time stamp. We are following but will be as much as twelve hours behind. Signed, Captain Jonas Morane, Starship *Vanquish*, 197th Battle Group. Put it on repeat until we break out of orbit. And make sure *Myrtale* hears the message as well."

"Aye, aye, sir."

Morane sat back in his chair and let out an exasperated sigh. So close and yet it might be for naught. If only they hadn't lingered around Arietis. Or swung by Lorien to witness its devastation. If, if, if.

No doubt Sister Gwenneth would tell him to trust in the Almighty; that he had a plan in mind; that things were unfolding as they must, and that none of them would ever grasp, let alone see the downstream effects of each decision, each choice and each action. Sometimes such effects don't become apparent for generations if ever.

That was good and well, but it didn't ease his growing anxiety. What would the future look like if Lyonesse, instead of providing sanctuary, met a horrible end because the 197th arrived too late? Where would he take his people and where would he build the knowledge vault that was his sole driving passion? Questions with no answers.

"Bridge to the captain."

"Morane."

"Pegasus flights are in the air."

**

"How did they take it?" Morane asked, not bothering with the usual greeting when DeCarde entered his day cabin to report.

"I took the coward's way out and only spoke with Ramirus Brockway. He wasn't happy, needless to say, but he understood. We gave Arietis the chance to live and fight another day. It's only right we do the same for Lyonesse." She went to the samovar and poured herself a cup without waiting for an invitation. "What are the chances we'll arrive in time to prevent total disaster?"

Morane gave her a disconsolate shrug. "I don't know. If the Almighty is smiling on Lyonesse, they'll hear our warning and prepare. If not, the reivers might get half a day to wreak havoc unopposed before *Myrtale* catches them."

"Three against one aren't the greatest odds, even if *Myrtale* can hit hard and take as good as she gives." DeCarde made a doubtful face as she took a seat across from him.

"Let's hope they're not in a hurry." She paused. "You could always order Lori Ryzkov to drop *Tanith*, so we can push beyond the safety limits and only end up an hour or two behind *Myrtale* instead of what? Half a day or more?"

"And abandon our mysterious prisoner? The one Friar Locarno and his Brethren consider so important they won't even tell us his or her identity until we're well out of reach from both the empire and the rebellion? They wouldn't allow me to do that."

"Why not? You're the supreme commander and shepherd of this convoy."

"Don't ask me why or how. I just know they won't allow me to do so. *Tanith* comes with us. *Myrtale* will hold her own long enough to shield Lyonesse until the reivers either break off or we arrive. Remember, marauders want easy pickings, not something they must fight the Navy for. There's no profit in dying, and they have no cause to die for." He tapped the desktop with his fingers for a few seconds. "I know the Marine Corps pulled its last unit out of the Lyonesse system eight years ago. The 77th, if I recall correctly."

DeCarde nodded. "Also known as the Land Raptors, on account of their regimental crest. It features a Cimmerian pteranodon for some unknown reason."

"Perhaps they were wise enough to raise colonial troops in the interim. Equipping such a force wouldn't be difficult, and as we saw with our friend Brockway and his drinking buddies, Marine Corps veterans pop up in the most unlikely places and organize things."

"If they did, someone forgot to tell Fleet HQ. There's no defense force or colonial militia listed in the official records."

"It wouldn't be the first time a colony did its own thing without notifying the sector government, let alone Wyvern. Once the Ruggero dynasty started squeezing to consolidate its power, more than just the sovereign star systems pushed back. Even those under colonial office administration became balky in recent decades, hence the fractures now splitting wide open with such tragic results."

The ship's public address system came on, cutting off DeCarde's reply.

"Now hear this. Departure stations in five, I repeat, five minutes. That is all."

"Do you think we'll ever see Arietis again?" She asked instead.

"I don't know. Doubtful. *Myrtale* and *Narwhal* will suffer from enough structural stresses by the time we reach Lyonesse to ensure they never leave the system. Ditto for *Tanith*, because I'm not about to risk anyone's life fixing the sabotaged antimatter fuel system. That leaves *Vanquish*, who I expect will finish her years as an orbital defense platform because I don't expect the Lyonesse antimatter fuel cracking station to last without regular maintenance and orbit adjustments."

"And *Dawn Trader*."

"Which is neither a warship nor under my command once we reach our destination. No." He shook his head. "This will be a one-way trip. Would you like to take a last look at Arietis? I can dial up a view."

"Pass. It'll simply remind me we're abandoning good people to a difficult future."

"Humanity's collapsing empire is full of good people, Brigid. They're in the majority. Yet they'll suffer the same fate as those who deserve it. And there's nothing you or I can do, except carry on with our self-imposed mission and see our charges to a safe harbor."

DeCarde snorted with amusement. "For a moment there, I almost heard Gwenneth speaking. You spend too much time with her."

"The Void giveth and the Void taketh away," he solemnly intoned with a small, but mischievous smile relaxing his tense features.

"Blessed be the Void."

PART II - PROMISED LAND

— 45 —

Gaspard 'Gus' Logran, Chief Administrator of Lyonesse and a thirty-five-year veteran of the Imperial Colonial Office, looked up irritably from the monthly expenditure report when his office communicator chimed. Stocky, in his late fifties, the owner of a strong, angular, almost pugnacious face framed by short, gray hair and a longer, gray beard, Logran's hooded eyes narrowed with irritation. Bad enough he was forced to go through every line with a micrometric scanner because the colony's financial administrator took an unaccountably optimistic view of his staff's honesty. Logran knew better, but catching the culprits who engaged in a bit of peculation on the side required meticulous verification. And since the colonial office hadn't sent auditors in almost two years, Gus was it.

An interruption now, after he expressly shut himself away from everyone but Governor Yakin, merely served to send his blood pressure into the stratosphere. He stabbed the screen embedded in his desktop and, suppressing a frustrated snarl, asked, "What?"

"Operations Center, sir. Ulla Buccieri, here. The system's subspace relay captured a message addressed to Lyonesse by someone calling himself Captain Jonas Morane, of the Starship *Vanquish*, 197th Battle Group. He claims to be in the Arietis system, but the message came on a carrier wave so faint it's clear they didn't use the Arietis subspace relay. It came from a ship's transmitter."

"And what does this Captain Morane say?"

"Three suspected reiver ships entered the Lyonesse branch of the wormhole network. We should expect their arrival here any time after seventy-two hours from his message's coordinated universal date-time stamp."

"What? How did reivers get through the Arietis system with no one stopping them? How did they even dare try? Is this a hoax?"

"He says they're pursuing but are at least twelve hours behind the reivers." A pause. "There's a Captain Jonas Morane, commanding the fast attack cruiser *Vanquish*, 197th Battle Group, 19th Fleet."

"19th? Isn't their area of operations way out in the Shield Sector? What the hell is he doing in the Arietis system?"

"The message routing tags appear genuine, sir, and the subspace relay accepted the identifiers as coming from an Imperial Navy unit. Why would a hoaxer warn us of an impending raid?"

"*Imperial* Navy? Didn't those idiots on Yotai declare the Coalsack Sector's independence or some such folly?"

"Sorry, sir. I misspoke. The relay confirmed the message's identifiers were from a Navy unit, allegiance unspecified."

"Route a copy to me right away, then sit on the news until I can confer with the governor and the speaker, and warn the operations duty staff to stay quiet. Anyone who leaks a word before I give permission gets to spend the next six months babysitting the arctic research station."

"Of course, Chief Administrator."

"Logran, out."

He sat back in his chair and exhaled. Reivers. In the Lyonesse branch of the wormhole network. Where was the Arietis Task Force? Did the empire collapse entirely? More importantly, was Lyonesse now alone, with no military protection except a colonial militia that looked splendid on parade but wasn't even battle tested? He called up his assistant.

"Please ask Her Excellency to schedule an emergency meeting of the executive council this afternoon at Government House."

**

An hour later Logran, who preferred to take his exercise when he could, walked down Lannion's shop-lined central boulevard from the colonial administration's offices to Government House. The colony's capital still kept a frontier flavor with its one and two-story buildings, and streets crossing at precise right angles. It was strung out along the banks of the broad, sluggish Haven River where the first colonists settled more than a century earlier.

That river turned into a flat delta several kilometers beyond Lannion before spilling into the Middle Sea, an equatorial ocean separating Lyonesse's only significant landmasses, a northern and southern continent, the former named Tristan and the latter, Isolde.

Isolde was uninhabited, save for temporary prospecting or scientific camps. Almost every human settlement was within a few hundred kilometers of each other on Tristan's subtropical southern edge.

Logran turned off the boulevard and, after satisfying Government House's automated security checkpoint, passed through an open gate piercing a high stone wall. Within the enclosure, a white, red-roofed, two-story mansion surrounded by a broad colonnaded veranda sat on a slight rise by the river's edge.

Three flagpoles lined the curved driveway by the front steps — the silver and blue imperial banner in the middle, Lyonesse's double-headed golden condor on a green background to one side and the gubernatorial standard on the other. Logran looked up at them by force of habit as they flapped in the soft breeze, but this time he wondered whether two of the three weren't superfluous. If both the empire and the rebellion had abandoned the Arietis system, Lyonesse's sole connection to the rest of humanity, then the gold condor was now truly alone.

A pair of Colonial Militia soldiers in dress uniform standing at the head of the stairs shouldered their weapons with crisp, precise movements as he came near. When he was a pace away from the steps, the soldiers silently presented arms and held that position as he passed between them. Logran returned the compliment with a nod and a 'thank you.'

Inside the mansion, a soberly dressed, thin man in his thirties by the name Wickham Sanford, private secretary to Governor the Honorable Elenia Yakin, youngest daughter of Baron Hengist Yakin, Peer of the Empire, greeted him with his usual punctiliousness.

"Her Excellency is waiting for you in the main drawing room with Speaker of the Council Hecht and Major Kayne. If you'll follow me." He led Logran through a set of double doors, then came to a precise, almost military halt on the threshold of a large, airy room with floor to ceiling windows and an oversized portrait of Empress Dendera. "Your Excellency, Chief Administrator Logran."

Sandford stepped aside and ushered Logran into Yakin's presence.

The colonial office veteran dipped his head at the slender, forty-something woman with long dark hair, limpid green eyes, and sharp, high cheekbones. "Your Excellency." Then he turned to the others. "Rorik, Major."

Speaker of the Council Rorik Hecht, the eldest of the three by far, greeted Logran with a curt nod. His wary brown eyes, deeply set in a tanned, leathery face beneath bushy eyebrows watched Logran closely as the chief administrator took his seat.

"You interrupted what promised to be a fine bird-watching session, Gus. I hope your emergency really is one. Am I to deduce that Major Kayne's presence indicates you're about to drop a security problem on our heads?"

Hecht gestured toward the grizzled, whipcord lean fifty-something major with a veteran's leathery features and a thousand light year stare. He wore a Marine's rifle green battledress uniform and sported Marine-style rank insignia. But the unit badge on his collar and field cap featured a double-headed avian, twin to the one on the Lyonesse flag flying in front of Government House. Except this version was clutching a pair of crossed rifles. And unlike Imperial Marine Corps regimental crests, it wasn't topped by a crown. Instead, it bore the word Lyonesse in gold characters.

Logran pulled a data chip from his tunic pocket and glanced at Governor Yakin. "Could I trouble your secretary to project the file on this wafer, Madame?"

At her nod, Sanford took the wafer. Moments later Morane's message appeared on the drawing room's primary display.

A few seconds after that, Yakin, Hecht, and Kayne turned to Logran with disbelief in their eyes.

"Is that for real?" The Speaker of the Council asked. "Or did you decide this would be a great day for a prank?"

"The message tags are genuine, and our subspace relay accepted the identifiers as coming from a naval unit. A Jonas Morane commands the cruiser *Vanquish*, assigned to the 197th Battle Group. Beyond that, I know nothing more."

"But reivers coming through Arietis? How is that possible?" Yakin asked in a husky alto that matched her unconventional, yet patrician features.

"The Navy withdrew its task force and abandoned the system, Madame," Kayne replied. "That's the only answer. If there were still a permanent naval presence, no reivers would dare pass through."

"But this 197th Battle Group seems to be in the Arietis system."

"So it appears, Madame. However, since they're from the 19th Fleet and the Coalsack Sector belongs to the rebellious 16th, we can only guess at what happened, and with little chance of finding the right answer." Kayne's brusque tone didn't quite hide an undercurrent of worry. "It sounds like we're about to find ourselves FUBAR."

When he saw Yakin's quizzical expression, he added, "Sorry, Madame, Marine Corps lingo. Something that doesn't belong here. What I meant is I think we're about to live in interesting times."

Hecht's bark of laughter echoed across the room.

"I'm sure Her Excellency has heard plenty of cuss words at court, Major. Fucked-up beyond all recognition, right? A very apt term if this Captain Morane isn't pulling some elaborate stunt. And why would he? We're nobodies at the far end of nowhere, with respect, Madame."

Yakin waved Hecht's apology away with a languid wave. "If I were a somebody, I'd still be enjoying the constant infighting and backstabbing at court. Or fall victim to Dendera's latest bout of paranoia. Living here as a nobody is preferable." She turned her eyes on Kayne. "You're our military expert, Major. What should we do with this warning?"

"If we ignore it and reivers show up, we're screwed. Begging your pardon again, Madame. If we prepare and reivers don't show up, we're no further behind. Seems like a simple choice."

—46—

"Nothing's showing up on sensors," Chief Lettis reported a few minutes after *Vanquish* dropped out of FTL near Wormhole Arietis Six's event horizon. "*Myrtale* would almost be at the wormhole's far end by now anyway."

"Or so we hope," Creswell added.

"Sir?"

Morane turned to the signals petty officer. "What is it?"

"I'm receiving an encrypted signal. *Myrtale* left a stealth buoy to tell us when they entered the wormhole. Captain Sirak promises to leave more along the way, so we keep abreast of her progress."

"Show me."

Telemetry data filled a side display. Creswell let out a soft whistle. "Well done, Nate Sirak. That's one fast passage from Arietis. The safety boffins at Fleet HQ would suffer a fit of apoplexy if they found out how hard he pushed against the intra-heliosphere FTL limits. If he can cross the next two systems that fast, he'll only be a few hours behind the reivers."

"Except *Myrtale* will shake herself into a wreck. The safety boffins put those limits on in-system FTL travel long ago for a very good reason."

Morane glanced down at the first officer's hologram by his right elbow. "At this point, whether our ships are usable by the time we reach Lyonesse takes second place to ensuring there is a Lyonesse to reach."

"We still must defend it."

"One step at a time, Iona. If we're synced and ready to cross the event horizon, please engage. There's nothing left for us here." He glanced over his shoulder at DeCarde and Gwenneth. "Would you like a last view of Arietis?"

DeCarde shook her head, but Gwenneth said, "Please. I'd like to say a prayer for the souls who live there and will soon confront a time of grave peril."

The Marine made as if to open her mouth and say something that might impugn the Almighty's motives, but Morane gave her a stern glare, and so she remained still until the planet's image faded away. Then, the universe vanished as Wormhole Arietis Six pulled them into its embrace.

Morane climbed to his feet and stretched. "The CIC is yours, Annalise. Sister, Colonel, could I offer you a cup of tea?"

"Certainly."

Once in the captain's day cabin, Gwenneth studied Morane as he served them. She accepted a mug, waited until he took a seat across from her and said, "You hide it well, but you must bleed off the stress you're feeling. Otherwise, you won't be in any condition to lead this battle group against the reivers, Jonas. You did everything in your power so far, but strength of will cannot influence events in the Lyonesse system before we arrive. That is entirely in the hands of the colonists, the reivers, and Captain Sirak's ship. However, I believe the

Almighty would not let us travel this far only to fail. Will there be suffering and destruction? Perhaps. Nothing worthwhile ever comes without challenges."

"Easy to say, Sister. But a lot harder to do." He took a sip. "I don't possess your faith or your training to deal with my human failings. I'm a worrier by nature. Even about things I can't influence. It's a family trait, one bred into us by generations of service, be it political, humanitarian, or military."

"Admirable in its place and probably at the origin of your vision to save humanity's future. But it can also be destructive. Perhaps I might teach you how to meditate while we pass through this wormhole."

A skeptical eyebrow greeted Gwenneth's suggestion. "Meditate? Really?"

"It is an ancient technique to help bleed off stress and learning it would be a better use of your time than fretting until we reach the next system where you can determine whether Captain Sirak is catching up to the reivers. Or not." She turned her impassive gaze on DeCarde. "The invitation is open to you as well, Brigid. There's no mind-meddling involved unless you consider taking control of your own thoughts a form of mind-meddling."

When the Marine saw a sardonic grin twist Morane's lips, she sighed. "Very well. Since his fretting about the situation is contagious, and I'm highly susceptible to catching it just by breathing the same air, teach me O Sister of the Void."

**

Governor The Honorable Elenia Yakin, stood with a graceful movement, followed by the others in quick succession as they tried to avoid being the only one sitting in her presence. It always amused Yakin to see Kayne, the dour former Marine noncom, be first on his feet and

Logran last, while Hecht somehow seemed to rise effortlessly and almost match Kayne for promptness.

Almost, but not entirely, as if the Speaker of the Council carefully timed his gestures to make sure he wasn't first and thereby appear to be the most subservient. Hecht nurtured his own ideas on Lyonesse's power hierarchy.

"Thank you, gentlemen. We will speak again tomorrow after digesting this ill news. If you would please stay behind, Major."

"Certainly, Madame."

They watched the politician and the career bureaucrat leave the main drawing room side-by-side, followed by Sanford who closed the doors behind him, leaving the governor and her colonial militia commander alone.

"You put on a brave face in front of Rorik and Gus, but this is me. What do you really think?" Yakin gestured at the sofa, ordering him to sit again. He obeyed once she took her own seat.

Kayne appeared to carefully choose his words. "We owe this Captain Morane big time."

"So you think it's real. There are three reiver ships headed here."

"Yes. And if not, no harm, no foul. At least we'll be prepared. But without the warning? I doubt we'd be able to call out the militia in time. Hecht and Logran don't want to panic the population and keep this quiet until we know for sure, but folks will figure something's up when I place my soldiers on active duty even though it's not a weekend or the annual training period. And the troops will need to understand why if I'm to put up the best possible defensive measures. Then they'll talk to their families, no matter what I say. Bugger Hecht and Logran. Get on the net and talk to the colonists. Tell them what's coming, what we're doing and how they can best protect themselves."

"And that would be?"

"By packing a few days of food and water, then heading north, into the wilds. There are enough mining, farming and forestry settlements tucked away in the hinterlands that can help the townspeople."

"What about the Harper Caverns?"

Kayne vigorously shook his head.

"No. People need to scatter. If the reivers are looking for flesh, they'll zero in on where the life signs are most concentrated. The Harper Caverns and others like them will become traps, with no way out. At least in the wilds, folks can run. As a matter of fact, that's what I'll tell the troops to do with their families. Send them upcountry so they can concentrate on soldiering."

"What if we offered the reivers booty? Let them take what they want from the naval supply depot unopposed in return for leaving us unmolested?"

"Never." His tone brooked no arguments. "The best way to attract more of their sort is to pay them. The only way to see less of their sort is either kill them or make coming here so painful they'll look for other victims. Right now, they're not aware we can field a thousand troops, plus three dozen Imperial Navy folks at the Lannion Base Supply Depot. We're not Marines or Guards, and only one in ten of mine is full-time, but they're as well trained as any militia. Better equipped than most, thanks to Lieutenant Grimes turning a blind eye, unlike some logistics officers I've known. The bastards will have a shock once they land and find themselves under attack."

"You intend to let them land." Yakin gave Kayne a look of utter disbelief. "Isn't Lannion Base surrounded by aerospace defense pods?"

"Six are operational, but we don't have properly trained crews. The Land Raptors used to man them, but since they left, Grimes' logisticians and my full-timers are the only ones who even know how the pods work, let alone how to ensure a successful first salvo. Because if that first salvo fails to take them out of action, the reivers will drop kinetic strikes from orbit on anything that looks like it can shoot back. Best to let them believe we're helpless until we can see the whites of their eyes. Starships are at their most vulnerable on the ground. In space, they can laugh at us ground pounders as much as they want. Let them land on the strip at Lannion Base." He raised his chin in a defiant gesture. "And they'll see just how vulnerable their ships are to aerospace defense guns firing over open sights. Or at any spaceport once my heavy weapons detachments cover the tarmac."

"Shoot at them while they're landing," Yakin suggested.

"And watch a starship with antimatter fuel aboard crash into the middle of a built-up area? No. Once they're on the ground, we can cause them enough damage to prevent a liftoff without turning the tarmac and everything around it into a crater."

"I hope you know what you're doing, Matti."

Kayne snorted. "So do I. But what I've just said is per the book. Imperial Marine Corps doctrine. Chapter twenty-two of the manual. How to defend a colony against reivers."

A skeptical smile pulled up her lips. "Is it really? Chapter twenty-two, I mean?"

"No. I can't even remember from which manual the plan I described comes. But the part about it being Corps doctrine is a hundred percent true. I've never seen anyone carry out such an operation because the Navy was always around to stop the fuckers before they could even enter orbit. But they usually base Corps doctrine on figuring out how to avoid the sort of screw-up that made developing said doctrine necessary in the first place." He gave her a crooked grin. "As a wise man once said, good judgment comes from experience, and that comes from bad judgment."

— 47 —

"The promised buoy is transmitting. Same sort of telemetry as before."

Morane nodded his thanks at the CIC signals petty officer. "Put it up." He studied the data. "*Myrtale* spotted no trace of the reivers when she emerged from the wormhole terminus. But Captain Sirak was confident they were still in this system when he dropped the buoy. He'll drop another one before taking the next wormhole, to let us know if he managed to reduce their lead a bit more while crossing ISC668231-2."

"How long will we loiter here?" Mikkel's hologram asked.

"No longer than it'll take *Narwhal* and *Dawn Trader* to declare themselves ready for FTL travel. We, *Myrtale* and the reivers are the only ones here *if* the reivers aren't already in transit to the next system, and I don't particularly care if they spot us. In fact, I hope they do. It might give the bastards pause, or even a reason to turn around before easy pickings turn deadly."

Morane studied the tactical display, more as a way to pass the time than anything else and DeCarde, sitting at her station, noticed he was much calmer now, with none of the subtle signs of stress Gwenneth had mentioned. None of the fidgeting or unconscious gestures.

She too felt less on edge and gave the silent sister sitting next to her a grudging mental nod of thanks. Perhaps her sort wasn't as suspect as the Ancestor made them out to be. Much changed in a thousand years, even ancient religious orders.

Then, as if Gwenneth could sense her thoughts, she glanced over at DeCarde and smiled.

"You and the captain both seem much more relaxed," she murmured. "But if you don't practice regularly, the stress will return."

Startled, the Marine could only nod. "As you say, Sister."

Gwenneth turned her eyes back on the CIC's main display.

Damned mind-meddlers.

"Now hear this. Transition to FTL in five, I repeat five minutes. That is all."

**

"I'm not sure that was wise, Your Excellency." Logran, wearing a gargoyle's scowl entered the small conference room next to Government House's main salon, where Yakin, Hecht, and Kayne waited for the tardy chief administrator. He dropped into the sole empty chair with a sound akin to that of a deflating balloon. "Recommending the townspeople head into the wilds, I mean."

"What would you have me do?" Her voice was as cold as the glaciers covering the Yakin family's homeworld, Scandia. Her expression was even icier. "Wait until the reivers appear above us and witness mass panic? The sort that leads to mass confusion and casualties? This way, I gave them time to disperse in reasonably good order. And with their families out of the way, Major Kayne's troops can better concentrate on preparing the defenses."

"We still don't know a raid is coming. Our only evidence is one faint message from someone who shouldn't even be in this sector. In the meantime, your announcement threw everything into turmoil. Our stores are empty and our economy is essentially shuttered. Hell, I just walked along Founder's Boulevard and there's not a soul in sight. Half of my staff didn't report for duty. The other half are glancing at the hinterland with increasingly nervous eyes. I'll be lucky if I can keep the operations center running."

"Nonetheless, it is done. No one will argue being prepared for a non-event is better than being unprepared for a disaster. I called you here to discuss moving the colonial government to Lannion Base. Major Kayne assures me that since the supply depot's warehouse chambers were dug deep into the cliff side, they're impervious to anything short of a direct nuclear strike."

Logran gave her a grudging nod. "If we can use the Lannion Base control center for operations, that would convince more of my people to stick around instead of taking an impromptu wilderness vacation. At this point, the only part of the colonial administration still at one hundred percent strength is the police. I truly wish we'd discussed this before Your Excellency went on the net."

Yakin inclined her head by way of apology. "You are correct. But I felt giving the people more time to evacuate was paramount. Let's consider it a learning experience. If the Navy has abandoned Arietis, this raid could only be the beginning."

"You're free to use the control center and its adjacent offices, Chief Administrator. Neither the Navy nor we use it much anyway," Kayne said. "Lieutenant Grimes and her folks are checking to see how we can connect the Navy's systems with the colonial administration's, so we're not blind should the reivers decide the government precinct makes a nice target."

"Good."

"Then I suggest we shift to Lannion Base in the morning."

"As you wish, Madame. Major, will you please order your militia to carry out regular patrols in every town, just in case a few of our fellow colonists decide to carry out impromptu wealth redistribution? Surely that can be done without compromising your own preparations."

"I've already passed the order. Maybe a proclamation that anyone caught looting will get an all-expenses-paid one year stay in the Windy Isles might help discourage miscreants." The Windy Isles, a vast archipelago at the center of Lyonesse's World Ocean, which covered almost an entire hemisphere, was a place of exile, home to hardened criminals who either couldn't or didn't want to reform their ways.

Logran snorted. "Decreeing punishment before due process? And sentenced to the Windies at that? It's just the thing to get up Justice Dettmar's great beak of a nose. I'll issue the proclamation as soon as we're done here. There's one more order of business I'd like to raise. What about the folks who sent their families upcountry but stayed behind to protect their properties? A lot of the colonists aren't exactly short on guns, and most of them know the business end from a hole in the ground."

Kayne shrugged. "Nothing will convince any die-hard property defenders that it's safer to leave, and when it comes to making reivers pay a price, the more, the merrier. Teach them we're no pushovers. So long as they don't open fire on my troops by mistake, I see no issues."

**

"Right on the nose." *Myrtale*'s jubilant navigation officer grinned over his shoulder at Captain Sirak. "Twenty thousand kilometers from the wormhole's event horizon."

Sirak smiled back at him. "Excellent job." He touched the panel in his command chair's arm. "Engineering, this is the bridge."

"Aye, Captain," the chief engineer's dour voice replied moments later.

"Tell me our little sprint broke nothing."

"Break? No. But half a dozen systems are almost giving me the amber eye, and I won't even mention the microfractures I'll find in her bones."

"So long as those half-dozen systems don't go red yet. We're making our next wormhole transit in fifteen minutes, so there's no time to run a full check."

"I wasn't expecting to, but I can't guarantee what she'll be like after two more wormhole transits and two more FTL jumps at speeds beyond the safety limit, Captain."

"The only thing that matters is getting to Lyonesse and stopping those reivers, Collin. This is the old girl's final chase. Best she arrives broken but on time than too late."

Lieutenant Commander Collin Partlow emitted a sound halfway between a grunt and a sigh. "More's the pity. But we knew that going into this."

"Cheer up, Collin. With any luck, you'll be a prosperous farmer this time next year, just like you've always wanted to do after swallowing the anchor."

"It's one thing to talk about it, Captain. Staring that future in the eye is another." Sirak could hear Partlow scratch his beard. "If there was nothing else, I'd best make sure we don't lose odd parts here and there while crossing the event horizon. Otherwise, I might buy that farm before setting eyes on Lyonesse."

"Always the optimist."

"It's part of my charm, Captain. Engineering, out."

Sirak turned to his second officer. "Helena, please load the next buoy with the latest telemetry and kick it out the door."

— 48 —

Built at the foot of a tall escarpment several kilometers north of Lyonesse's capital, the Imperial Navy's Lannion Base appeared distinctly unimpressive to the casual observer. A fence-topped earthen berm surrounded its centerpiece, a long, wide tarmac. But other than a few defense pods, little else was visible above ground. Though she had never visited the installation, Elenia Yakin knew the warehouses, offices, and everything else were dug into the escarpment.

As her ground car came around the last bend in the road before running straight through the security checkpoint, she got a glimpse of the dull metallic portals at ground level. These were wide and tall enough to admit the largest of orbital transport shuttles. Human-sized doors pierced the reddish-gray granite between them while windows looked out from above.

Up close, Lannion Base seemed well-nigh impregnable, the only place on Lyonesse capable of resisting marauders more interested in plunder than combat. Yet she knew the supply depot was not designed as a fortress.

A determined foe could peel back the layers of defense and plunder what it contained. Which would now include the colonial government's core people. But reivers weren't that sort of determined foe.

Her car, driven by Wickham Sanford, pulled up to one of the smaller doors where a pair of militia soldiers in light armor stood guard. They snapped to attention and saluted as Yakin climbed out. She returned the compliment with her usual nod and smile, then waited as the private secretary retrieved their luggage from the rear compartment.

Another car, this one driven by Gus Logran, screamed across the tarmac and stopped beside hers. The chief administrator jumped out and pulled a stuffed knapsack from the passenger seat.

"Good morning, Your Excellency."

"Good morning, Gus. I trust you're well."

"As well as a colonial chief administrator can be when his colonial administration is in chaos. You shut Government House?"

"The mansion is locked up tight, but if the reivers want my formal silverware, they won't find breaching the defenses a particular challenge. And quite frankly, they're welcome to it. We no longer need a reminder of the feckless empress and her degenerate court. Not when we're about to face a dread enemy thanks to the Navy's self-immolation."

The cliffside door opened and Major Kayne, in battledress minus the light armor his troops wore, stepped out, came to attention and saluted the governor.

"Welcome to Lannion Base, Your Excellency, Chief Administrator. Although I suppose that should be Lieutenant Grimes' line since this is still legally an Imperial Armed Services installation."

Yakin's lips twisted into a moue. "Does it matter? Or should I use my executive powers to declare Lannion

Base a possession of the Lyonesse government and
Lieutenant Grimes an officer of the Lyonesse Colonial
Militia?"

"It doesn't matter. If you'll follow me, we've given you
rooms in the barracks formerly occupied by the 77ᵗʰ
Marine Regiment. They're next to the regiment's old
administrative offices, which I've been using since
Lieutenant Grimes opened her doors to the militia.
We've prepared office space there for you, Madame, the
chief administrator and Speaker Hecht. Then we can visit
the operations center and the workspace set aside for the
rest of your staffs."

Kayne first showed Yakin into quarters that were once
assigned the Land Raptors' commanding officer. She
gazed around the suite while Sanford brought her bags
into the bedroom and said, "Cozy. And I'll certainly sleep
better know I'm surrounded by tons of hard granite
rather than Government House's comparatively flimsy
walls. If I sleep, that is. Considering we're slowly coming
up on Captain Morane's deadline. Why don't you see that
Gus is settled in so we can continue the tour, Major?"

"Certainly. The chief administrator's quarters are next
door. The Land Raptors' second in command used to
occupy them. Speaker Hecht will stay across the hall in
those once occupied by the regimental sergeant major."

Kayne and Yakin exchanged an amused glance when an
air of satisfaction briefly lit up Logran's face at hearing
his quarters were one notch above Hecht's. The Colonial
Militia depended on the chief administrator for funding
and not the council even if Kayne reported directly to the
governor.

Lieutenant Hetty Grimes, overweight and more than a
little overaged for an officer of her rank, came to attention
as Yakin entered the Lannion Base operations room. A

pair of chief petty officers who also seemed slightly gone to seed, the result of too many years serving in a backwater where nothing ever happened, flanked her.

The governor knew Grimes from formal occasions, most notably when the naval logistician first presented herself at Government House as a courtesy upon her arrival. The intervening years had not done her any favors, in large part due to a lifestyle informed by the knowledge her career prospects were dim.

"Your Excellency."

"Lieutenant Grimes. How are you?"

"As well as can be expected under the circumstances, Madame. This is the most excitement I've seen since coming to Lyonesse. I don't know if you've met Chief Petty Officers Beeney and Kopman." Grimes gestured at the noncoms behind her. "Chief Beeney is the Lannion Base coxswain, and Chief Kopman is in charge of the warehouses."

Yakin gave both a polite, quasi-regal nod. "Gentlemen." Then she looked around at what seemed almost like a starship's bridge, or what the Navy called a combat information center if her memory served.

Displays covered three of the four walls. A panoramic window overlooking the tarmac fifteen stories below dominated the fourth. From this height, she could see all of Lannion, including Government House sitting shuttered by the river's edge, and as far as the mist-shrouded shores of the Middle Sea.

Workstations, each with its own terminal, surrounded a large command chair set on a pedestal. Men and women in both Navy blue and militia green occupied several of them.

"Would you like to try the duty officer's chair, Madame?" Kayne asked.

"Why not?" Yakin settled into what seemed like a throne and examined the control surfaces set in each of the wide arms. "I imagine I shouldn't touch any of these."

"No worries, Madame," Grimes replied in her surprisingly high-pitched voice. "They're not active right now."

After pointing out the various functions that could be carried out from the operations center, Grimes caught Chief Administrator Logran's eye.

"If you don't mind me asking, sir, did you consider shutting down the entire satellite constellation, except perhaps for one of the surveillance units? While the satellites are active, any hostile ship approaching Lyonesse can target and destroy them. And if I understand the situation correctly, we may not see replacements for a long time, if ever. But put into dormancy, they might escape attention. I would suggest we do the same to the wormhole traffic control buoy the moment it reports something coming through the terminus, and then the system subspace relay. With any luck, the bad guys might not notice either as they orient themselves."

Logran rubbed his bearded chin, eyes staring sightlessly through the panoramic window. Then he seemed to shake himself as if Grimes' proposal added an unwanted layer of realism to a peril he still felt could be theoretical. When he spoke, Logran's tone was grudging rather than dismissive.

"Not a bad idea, I suppose. If this turns out to be real rather than a drill. Can we do it from here? I mean at the last minute since shutting the orbital constellation now would cause even more chaos when we're still trying to evacuate the towns."

"If you'll allow us to link into the ground control network, sure. But I suggest we put the constellation, save for a surveillance satellite to sleep at least twenty hours before Captain Morane's deadline. A ship with military grade sensors could pick up an active satellite network from the wormhole terminus. And as I said, we turn off the traffic control buoy and subspace relay the moment the former reports an intruder."

A stubborn glint lit up Logran's eyes, but before he could speak, Yakin raised a hand. "Do it, Lieutenant. See that ground control is linked to this operations center, then prepare. I'm sure Chief Administrator Logran will want to disseminate a final notification, so people know they're about to lose communications, global positioning and the other niceties of a peaceful, technologically advanced world. Albeit temporarily."

Logran gave the governor a sour glance but inclined his head. "As you wish, Madame. If Lieutenant Grimes can hook me into the net, I will take care of warning the colony. Then I'll ask ground control to connect to this place and hand authority for extra-atmospheric infrastructure over to the Navy. Lieutenant Grimes can do as she thinks fit after that."

"Thank you."

**

"We'll be fine, sir. The chances of something happening to us while we cross this system are negligible. I'm sure Captain Rinne agrees. One more pair of jumps, one more wormhole transit and then it's Lyonesse. We're almost home. Go."

Morane's eyes went from Commander Ryzkov to the friar-captain who merely nodded, a serene expression on his weathered brow.

"Go," Ryzkov repeated. "Push *Vanquish* so far past heliosphere FTL limits that the universe will sing. Give her an in-system speed record that won't be matched until a new empire is born from the ashes of the old. If those reivers exercise caution when they enter the Lyonesse system and decide to loiter while scanning for potential threats, *Myrtale* might still come out of the terminus on top of them, and she'll be glad for the help. If her drives fail, then you're Lyonesse's last best hope."

The buoy left by Sirak near wormhole exit that spat *Vanquish* and her consorts into the Lyonesse branch's second sterile system warned Morane the frigate was faltering. Her chief engineer, after inspecting the drives during their wormhole transit, advised they could no longer exceed FTL speed limits without causing damage that might immobilize her entirely. What gains she'd made on the reivers in the Arietis system and ISC668231-2 would be lost crossing ISC683422-2. If not worse.

The moment he read Sirak's message, Morane knew there was only one card left to play. He assembled his department heads and linked in the other two starship captains so he could place that card before them. No one demurred. They met Morane's proposal with squared jaws and determined shoulders.

"It's unanimous," Mikkel said after a moment of silence punctuated Ryzkov's passionate entreaty. Everyone, even Roman Pavlich, the cruiser's hard-pressed chief engineer, nodded enthusiastically. "We sail this cruiser as she's never been sailed before and to hell with safety limits. One last hurrah for *Vanquish*."

"*I'll chase him round Good Hope, and round the Horn, and round the Norway Maelstrom, and round perdition's flames before I give him up,*" DeCarde quoted in a soft voice. Morane gave her a curious glance. "A line from an ancient tale about one man's pursuit unto death, Captain. I thought it fit the moment."

Chief Petty Officer Shaney chuckled. "Or as we say back home, Colonel, *yippee-ki-yay, assholes*."

Morane's open hands slammed down on the table and a double clap, like gunfire, echoed through the cruiser's conference room. "We go FTL in five minutes."

— 49 —

Governor Yakin and Major Kayne stepped through the ground floor door and out onto Lannion Base's tarmac, intent on a few breaths of fresh air after suffering a sleepless, anxiety-filled night. They'd met by chance in the corridor and wordlessly left the rest of Lannion Base's complement, except for the duty staff, sleep a bit longer.

Above them, a dense field of stars sparkled against the inky black of space. At its center, the Milky Way, stretching over thirty degrees of sky made for a mesmerizing spectacle, one visible from every human-colonized world. And from deep in the Orion Arm's badlands, where invaders waited for centuries until the day the empire could no longer protect its star systems. Now they were coming to reap what successive emperors and empresses had sown. Yakin shivered at the thought.

"Are you cold? Should we go back inside?"

She turned a sad smile on her militia commander. "It's not the kind of cold central heating or a thick coat can ward off, Matti." She nodded up at the sky. "All that beauty hides so much death."

"We'll come through this, Elenia. Three reiver shiploads don't make an invasion force."

"Perhaps, but they can still destroy what they don't take."

"Not on my watch."

She laid a soft, long-fingered hand on his arm. "I don't doubt that you and your soldiers will do their duty in the best of military traditions. But if we escape devastation this time, what happens the next time? Or the time after that? Who will warn us if the Navy withdrew from Arietis?"

"I don't know. However, we can work to harden Lyonesse, make her into something so tough future marauders will look elsewhere for profit. Become one of those creatures covered in poisonous spines no one dares touch."

"Marine Corps doctrine again?"

A gentle grin softened his grim features. "Matti Kayne's doctrine. And perhaps you can convince this Morane fellow to give us a hand when he shows up. If he's willing to chase reivers into the Lyonesse branch when he could just as well go on his way with the rest of the damned Navy, he might be amenable."

They reached one of the silent, hulking aerospace defense pods and turned to walk back.

"We should know soon enough. Our last night of innocent peace seems to be over." A faint band of light on the eastern horizon heralded the approach of dawn. As it grew before their eyes, the distant clouds took on a red tinge so intense it seemed the sky was bleeding. "Does this new day mark a permanent break with the past and herald the start of a new, dark and dangerous era? A future of barbarian raids, of pillage, plunder, and destruction?"

Yakin's hand tightened around Kayne's arm, and he placed his own hand on top of it.

"Best not to borrow trouble ahead of time, Elenia. Even if they come through the wormhole today, they'll not reach Lyonesse until tomorrow."

"But they'll arrive eventually."

"Perhaps. If that's our fate. Which may or may not be foretold. But whatever that fate is we must still live through it. The Almighty doesn't allow shortcuts."

A warm chuckle escaped her throat. "Military doctrine and religious philosophy in almost the same breath. Why were you only a command sergeant in the Marine Corps while an idiot like my cheating, lying, social climbing husband, who wouldn't know deep thoughts from soiled toilet paper, is an Imperial Guards general dancing attendance at court?"

"I suppose I was lucky."

Her throaty laughter echoed faintly against the cliffside. "And having you here instead of him, on this day of all days, means I'm lucky too."

"We'll see about luck later."

"Isn't it said that faith can stop even the greatest of evils?"

"It's also said that the Void giveth and the Void taketh away."

A warm gust of air from the Middle Sea, carrying the faint but unmistakable tang of salt water, washed over Lannion Base as the sky lightened and the lower atmosphere stirred to life.

"When this is over, I'd like to spend a day at the beach."

Kayne squeezed her hand. "That's the spirit, Your Excellency." Then he released it.

Using her title signaled the end of their brief intimacy, and she withdrew hers.

"Tea?" The former Marine asked. "The samovar in my office should be ready. I set it before heading out."

"Certainly."

"They will serve breakfast in the base mess hall at seven. It won't be up to Government House standards, but tasty nonetheless."

They walked up to the regimental office suite where Kayne ushered her into the one he'd taken after temporarily giving up the commanding officer's space to his commander-in-chief.

Cup in hand, they took chairs around a bare field desk, one no different from those in use elsewhere on Lannion Base. Neither spoke, preferring to let their thoughts wander, eyes staring through the narrow window as night slowly gave way to another sunrise.

Storm clouds were gathering over the Middle Sea. Prominent, gray and towering, their undersides painted the same blood red as those on the eastern horizon. Yakin repressed an involuntary shiver, telling herself there were no such things as omens.

The chirp of Kayne's communicator startled both from their silent contemplation, and Kayne sat up with a jerk, almost spilling tea over his battledress.

"Yes?"

"Lannion Base Control, sir. The wormhole traffic control buoy reports three sloop-sized ships of unknown type and provenance exiting the terminus. None of them are broadcasting on subspace bands. The only thing we can tell is they're definitely not Navy."

"Order the buoy and relay to go dormant. I'm on my way."

Yakin's face tightened. "The enemy is finally at our gates. So much for Gus' fervent wish it was a hoax. Shame we won't know when Morane's ships will show up. Or if. How long do you think before they're in orbit?"

Morane drained the last of his tepid tea and stood with weary resignation. "Based on Hetty Grimes' best guess, if they don't loiter they could reach the Lyonesse hyperlimit this evening, about twelve hours from now. From there, they might reach us before dawn tomorrow."

**

Myrtale dropped out of FTL a hundred thousand kilometers short of the final wormhole terminus before the Lyonesse system, but the force of the transition nausea told Sirak something was very wrong with his ship's hyperdrives. They'd been unable to reach even twice the speed of light during their jumps across the system without triggering every alarm in engineering, but this felt more serious.

He was reaching for the screen embedded in his command chair when the intercom went off. "Chief engineer to the captain."

"Yes, Collin.

"You felt her shudder when we came out of FTL?'

"*I* shuddered quite a bit."

"Same thing, Captain. The drives aren't done for yet, but almost. Without a few weeks in dry-dock, we can do a few more short jumps if we stick to one and a half times cee within the heliosphere, but that's it. And with the drives gone, the captain can reclassify *Myrtale* as a monitor and stick her into orbit around Lyonesse."

Sirak repressed a sigh of annoyance. So close and yet it might still be insufficient. "Can we make a safe wormhole transit?"

"Aye. No question, though it could be our last."

"Helena, please prepare another buoy for *Vanquish*. Let them know about our status."

A mischievous smile crept across Lieutenant Helena Lee's taut features. "Crippled, clobbered and crawling?"

"Something like that, but make sure they understand the condition isn't due to our cleaning out the ship's alcohol stores while in FTL. It may not do much good, but at least the captain will know he could be on his own in the Lyonesse system."

"If it's any consolation," Collin Partlow said, "we wouldn't have lasted much longer even without the battle damage we took before entering the Cervantes system, back when we still worked for her Imperial Majesty and not Jonas Morane's ideals. *Myrtale* is older than I am, and that's a condition beyond even the best starship engineers."

A tired silence enveloped the frigate's bridge. Sirak wasn't the only one wearing a crestfallen expression. But the moment proved short-lived.

"Subspace message from *Narwhal*, sir. They're transmitting on spec, in case we're listening. Because of our growing engine problems, *Vanquish* left *Narwhal* and *Dawn Trader* after transiting into this system and is currently doing what we've done - pushing as far past twice cee as she can without destroying her drives. We're to continue commensurate with the safety of the crew."

Sirak exhaled noisily. "At least that's something. *Vanquish* might be almost double our size, but she's newer and has suffered no damage. Take it as a lesson, folks. Always let the boss know about everything, especially problems, so he can find other ways of getting the mission done. Now let's push across that damned event horizon and see if we can't finish the job before that flashy cruiser robs us of our kill marks."

∗∗

Kayne turned around when he heard the sound of feet by the operations room's doors. A grim-faced Gus Logran stood on the threshold, as if unsure of his welcome.

"Her Excellency told me three unidentified ships came through the wormhole in the last hour."

"That's what the traffic control buoy reported. They're the right size and shape for reivers, and Lieutenant Grimes assures me their power emissions are much too high for honest starships. We won't find out more until they drop out of FTL at the hyperlimit, which could be any time after sundown tonight, depending on how long they loiter by the wormhole. And we won't know because as soon as the buoy reported, it and the subspace relay went dormant, per their programming. Hopefully, they'll still be there when this is over." Kayne waved Logran in and gestured toward an unoccupied workstation.

"Please sit."

Logran almost stumbled as he made for the chair, then dropped into it like a deflated balloon. "When?" His voice sounded like a frog's croak.

"When will they arrive? Lieutenant Grimes figures between midnight and dawn tomorrow."

"And there's no chance they might be friendly?"

Kayne's smile was as thin as a miser's charity. "There's always a chance, Chief Administrator. But plausible does not mean probable. When is the last time we saw two ships travel through that wormhole simultaneously, let alone three? Unless they're in convoy, I've never seen merchantmen travel in packs. Reivers on the other hand..."

Logran seemed to regain control of his emotions. "I suppose I owe you an apology, Major."

"Of course not. You were perfectly within your rights to question the veracity of Morane's message and our assumptions. You may have heard the expression, 'if everyone is thinking alike, then somebody isn't thinking.' I'm sure the governor would like you to keep on thinking even if your conclusions clash with mine or anyone else's. Heck, Gus, we've known each other for years. Too long to apologize for being who we are and doing our jobs as we think best."

A sound like that of an angry bull's snort escaped Logran's full nose. "Don't think this gives you bragging rights, Matti. At least not until you've seen the buggers off with a kick in the pants. Preferably a nuclear-tipped kick."

"That depends on how many of them lift off once we've kicked them in the pants."

"You still intend to go with the ambush option?" Logran raised both hands in a gesture of surrender. "Not that I'm questioning your military decisions."

"Now we've confirmed they're sloop-sized and capable of landing on a standard gee planet with an atmosphere, I'll place my bets on at least two of them coming down. If we convince them we're unaware, unprepared and helpless. The alternative is a bombardment from orbit to soften us up."

"Won't they do that to Lannion Base anyway? Because of your aerospace defense pods?"

"Which won't show up on their scans because they're dormant. Nor will they see them on visual. Chameleon coating. Effective against any optical sensor at more than a few meters distant, and any human eye at more than a hundred meters."

Logran was silent for a few moments. Then, "I'm glad you sound confident, Matti. Because I sure as hell don't *feel* confident."

— 50 —

"*Myrtale* left us another message buoy." A pause, then the signals petty officer said, "The transcript is on the port side display."

Morane read Sirak's message and winced. "At least they haven't lost their sense of humor. Crippled, clobbered and crawling. She won't be able to rise above one and a half cee crossing a star system without time in dry-dock. Nate suggests we turn her into a monitor and put her in Lyonesse orbit once we remove any invasive species and become farmers. At least he didn't word it in the more macabre way."

"You mean he didn't say once we buy the farm?" DeCarde asked in a droll tone. Morane, Creswell and everyone else in the CIC turned to give her the stink eye. She raised her hands. "Okay, okay. Terrible joke, but I figured if *Myrtale* can crack wise about falling apart..."

"The good news is, we're only six hours behind her," Morane said. "She's not out of the wormhole yet."

"And we're about six jumps away from needing the same tender loving dry-dock care." Mikkel's ever-present hologram smirked. "Be glad Roman is cussing at me about the treatment we gave his precious drives and not you, Skipper."

"But even he has to admit we broke Fleet records, Iona."

"Oh, *Vanquish* made the universe sing all right. Except it wasn't the universe singing but her hull integrity screaming. There's a reason we shouldn't try interstellar speeds within a star system. Offer Roman a cup of tea and an hour of your time once we're inside the wormhole. He needs to unburden himself, and I've done my part."

"So long as we can break the rules one last time after this transit."

"Roman says we're good for a final try at improving the record."

"That's what I wanted to know. Now take us over that event horizon."

**

"I'm not picking up any starship traffic," *Myrtale*'s sensor chief said once he completed his first scan of the Lyonesse system. "But with time lag, they could be at the hyperlimit already. Or close to coming out of FTL at any rate."

"Let's hope they went FTL not long before we arrived after loitering a bit." Sirak turned to the signals station. "Anything?"

"No subspace carrier wave. I can't find the wormhole traffic control buoy or system relay, and none of the orbital platforms are broadcasting. It's like Lyonesse is under radio silence."

"Maybe they heard Captain Morane's message and took the system relay and their satellite constellation offline to keep the reivers from shooting it up," *Myrtale*'s first officer suggested. "Meaning they're prepared to resist in one way or another."

"Let's hope that's the case. The alternative would mean Lyonesse already suffered a raid that took out its orbitals and this new one will do little more than bounce the rubble. Who knows how many raiders slipped through Arietis between the time Zahar withdrew his ships and our arrival."

"Should we try sending a message anyway?"

Sirak shook his head. "If their orbitals are dormant or gone, I'm not sure they'll hear anything." He tapped the screen embedded in the command chair's arm. "Engineering, this is the captain. Please tell me we can jump soon."

A few seconds later, Collin Partlow's rough voice replied, "Aye. Whenever the fancy strikes you, but stay at one point five cee. The wormhole transit hasn't done our hull integrity any favors. And the drives themselves aren't doing any better than they did before we crossed over. I tried, but too many parts are suffering premature end-of-life."

"So long as we reach Lyonesse in condition to fight."

"I'll get us there, Captain. Just don't overshoot the regulation hyperlimit by too much. As for fighting, that's in your wheelhouse, not mine."

"Fair enough. Navigation, if you're happy with the plotted jump, let's punch out of here."

**

Major Kayne climbed out of his air car and returned the Trevena District company commander's salute. "How are you, Devin?"

"On edge more than anything else, sir." Centurion Devin Hamm stiffened when he spotted the car's second passenger as she climbed out the other side. "I'm sorry, sir. If I'd known the governor was coming, I'd have organized something more suitable."

"Her Excellency is here as Colonel of the Colonial Militia, Devin, and not as the empress' representative on Lyonesse. Treat her like you would any senior officer."

"Yes, sir." When Yakin came around the car, Hamm saluted again. "Welcome, Your Excellency."

She inclined her head in greeting. "Centurion."

"How are your troops?"

"Equally on edge. Good thing we moved the families out, otherwise half of them would be mad with worry instead of doing their jobs. Did you want to see anything in particular?"

"Nothing specific. The governor and I are making what you could call a morale-boosting tour of the militia companies. The reivers won't be here until the early hours of tomorrow morning at best, so there's time to show the flag."

"Good idea."

Hamm gestured toward the Trevena spaceport, a rammed earth strip bordered by a low-slung passenger terminal, little more than a few old containers knocked together, and a half-dozen high-domed transshipment shelters. Though rudimentary compared to the Lannion civilian spaceport, let alone Lannion Base, it could easily accommodate a sloop-sized starship.

And since Trevena was Lyonesse's second largest settlement, it would almost certainly be a target. "We set up fighting positions surrounding the strip and along the main road leading into town. Those extra platoons from Caffrey and High Bend will come in handy to give the ambush some depth."

Kayne chuckled. "Tyra said almost the same thing when we visited Carhaix."

"We studied under the same teacher."

"Who's about to find out if the lessons stuck. Walk the governor and me through your plan and around the site. We'd like to speak with as many of your people as possible."

**

The angry sun painted Lannion's somber western horizon with an ominous riot of colors when Kayne brought his aircar into the Lannion Base motor pool. It was carved out of the cliff beneath the barracks that housed the 77th Marine Regiment, his old unit, years earlier.

When it left, he and a handful of other noncoms with thirty years of service in the Corps elected to stay on Lyonesse rather than say farewell to a place they considered their adopted home. Not long after, a newly arrived Elenia Yakin asked him to form a militia under her auspices.

Once Kayne turned off the car's power plant, Yakin laid a gentle hand on his right forearm. "Thank you for taking me along, Matti. I feel better now I've seen how determined your soldiers are, how well they hide their fear beneath masks of defiance. We may actually live for another day."

"Our soldiers, Elenia. Remember, you're their colonel. And I could tell it pleased them to see and speak with you. As a morale-boosting tour, it was a success. If it were just me visiting, not so much."

She smiled. "Thank you for saying so. Perhaps later we can discuss ways of turning our militia into a regular defense force. I fear the days of relying on volunteers to deal with whatever the Navy doesn't catch are over for good."

"It'll be a long night. We can talk about it while we wait for the reivers to arrive. Unless you'd rather try sleeping."

Yakin's peal of laughter sounded just a little forced to Kayne's ears. "I doubt I'll be able to lie still, but if you don't mind company, I'll gladly sit with you until the battle is joined."

"That would be lovely." He glanced at the time. "We can expect our unwanted visitors to drop out of FTL at the hyperlimit any time now. Then it will be a matter of how hard they're willing to accelerate and decelerate."

They left Kayne's car sitting alongside those belonging to Yakin, Logran, and Hecht, amidst the two dozen ground vehicles owned by the militia and took a lift to the operations center's aerie high above the tarmac.

Lieutenant Grimes turned the duty officer's chair around at their entry and made to stand until both Kayne and Yakin waved her down.

"No need for formalities, Hetty, not when we're about to call battle stations. Anything new?"

"Nothing, sir. The heavens are as quiet as can be, and with both the subspace relay and the wormhole traffic control buoy dormant, we won't know if help is coming until a day after it arrives in-system."

"By which time we'll have seen the reivers off ourselves," Yakin said with a confident smile that Kayne knew to be just a little counterfeit.

"Absolutely, Your Excellency."

"We'll be in my office, Hetty."

—51—

"Checkmate, I believe." Yakin released her chess piece and looked up at Kayne with a sly expression.

Kayne studied the board, then tipped his king over with an extended index finger. "That gives you five victories out of seven games, and I will gladly concede you're the better player."

His communicator chimed, and he grinned at her. "Saved by the operations center. Kayne."

"Grimes, sir. Three emergence traces at the hyperlimit. Visuals confirm they're the same ones spotted by the wormhole traffic control buoy."

"Finally." An eerie sense of relief washed over the militia commander. "The bastards took their sweet time getting here."

"Probably loitered at the wormhole or dropped out of FTL along the way to make sure no surprises waited for them in Lyonesse orbit."

"How long do you think?"

Grimes didn't immediately reply. Then, "Around dawn, I'd say, but they'll take a few hours to scan the surface before landing, in case we're a tougher nut than we look."

"A good thing we don't look like a nut."

"Not so we could fool a psychiatrist, but reivers? Sure. Would you like to see the visuals?"

"Yes. Pipe them to my office display."

Moments later the elongated shape of a dark, vaguely menacing spacecraft nestled against a sea of stars replaced the Lyonesse Colonial Militia's double-headed condor. "This one is the lead ship. The others are almost exact duplicates."

"Any sense of crew numbers?"

Grimes hesitated before answering. "Based on apparent size, each could easily carry a hundred humans."

"So three hundred in total?" Yakin's tone betrayed puzzlement. "That's not much to threaten a colony of our size."

"It's amply sufficient if the colony has no defenses and doesn't expect a raid, Madame," Kayne replied. "These are people who will use surprise and unrestrained violence to terrorize civilians into submission while they rape, pillage and plunder. I expect them to be well armed and highly aggressive, capable of defeating a population that has only a lightly equipped police force at the ready. Without enough warning, deploying a volunteer militia such as ours takes too long, and it would get chewed up piecemeal as it tried to organize while fighting off the raiders."

"Oh." The puzzlement gave way to an expression of concern. "Unrestrained violence means what, exactly?"

"Reivers will kill anyone they come across unless they're looking for slaves. To them, we're prey, something they kill for sport, nothing more. Three hundred can cause havoc even on a planet with half a million colonists. But we can manage, provided they don't bombard us from orbit."

"Which they shouldn't if they're looking for tech, precious metals and other portable valuables to steal," Grimes said. "And definitely not if they're looking for slave market meat."

Yakin suppressed a shiver. "You make it sound so — clinical."

Instead of replying, Kayne stood, walked over to the narrow window and stared out at a moonless, starless night. Rain-laden clouds had swept in from the Middle Sea during the evening, promising an almost tropical downpour at daybreak. The sort of weather that gave defenders an advantage. Not by much, but little things could tip the balance as he knew from going through a self-study version of the Imperial Marine Corps staff officer course. It was a far from perfect education, but in eight years, Kayne read a lot of manuals, histories, and commentaries. And he spent a lot of time thinking about how to best defend his adopted home.

But at heart, he was still a Marine Corps command sergeant, a non-commissioned platoon leader. And now that his first engagement as head of the Colonial Militia loomed, Kayne longed to be a platoon leader again and do what the infantry does best: find and destroy the enemy.

His outlying company commanders didn't need him now that everything was in place and the final orders were given. They would fight their own battles in Trevena and Carhaix, or if the reivers targeted the smaller settlements: Caffrey, High Bend, Arran or North Wall.

Names that had become achingly familiar over the years. The inhabitants, many of whom served under his orders a few days a month and a few weeks a year, were now almost a part of his extended family.

His fight was here in Lannion, and the idea of leading it from the operations center suddenly felt wrong. Like he was shirking his duty. Oh, sure, the manual said a battalion commander whose unit was dispersed should stay where he could best keep in communications with his subunits. But Lannion Company and most of the Militia Combat Support Company were out there, in the darkness, surrounding the planet's main spaceport. Waiting for the reivers to land and come out of their ship, intent on rapine.

Reivers who wouldn't realize their every move was being watched; that every one of them wore an invisible target marker on their chest or back, and that well-hidden heavy weapons detachments were preparing to damage the grounded ships.

No, he belonged with them, not here. Lannion would be the enemy's focus, his center of gravity — his *schwerpunkt*, as the staff officer manuals called it. This was where the clan chief would land and where they would win or lose the battle. It was why he'd brought in platoons from the outlying companies, from Arran and North Wall, to round out Combat Support Company and put over two hundred soldiers on the ground. He would see the enemy with his own eyes here, in Lannion.

"Hetty, please warn Centurion Greff and Sergeant Major Havel that I'm activating my tactical command post and shifting it to the spaceport." Greff and Havel, another pair of retired Marine noncoms from the 77th, would understand. They would even welcome the idea.

Elenia Yakin's eyes widened when Kayne's words registered. "You're leaving?"

He gave her a confident grin. "Only until I've dealt with the current unpleasantness. Once we've cleared Lyonesse of vermin, I'll be back."

"I warned Greff," Grimes said. "His reply, which he asked I pass on verbatim was, quote, it's about fucking time, unquote. And begging your pardon, Madame."

"No matter, Lieutenant. I've heard worse at court. Much worse."

"Keep an eye on the old homestead, Hetty. Don't power up the pods too early and if one of the buggers decides to land in our front yard, enjoy the fun."

"Good luck, sir."

Kayne grunted. "We don't wish each other luck in the ground pounders. We wish each other good hunting."

**

Driving through Lannion in the dead of night under a heavy sky felt eerie. Kayne saw nothing but unrelieved darkness where in normal times, a few lights would shine. Yet he knew hundreds, if not thousands of die-hards waited in their homes and businesses with hunting weapons or old souvenirs from a tour in the Corps, lovingly maintained and ready to fire.

Kayne, like Centurion Greff, Sergeant Major Havel and the rest of his tactical command post platoon wore militia issue light armor and carried militia issue side arms. Both came from old Fleet stocks shipped to Lyonesse at Yakin's request. Though classified as light, meaning unpowered, their battlesuits had the same chameleon coating as those worn by regular troopers, and similar, if less sophisticated built-in electronics.

The ground car, a civilian truck donated by Speaker Hecht's corporation — or rather that of his children, since he surrendered control so he could stand for elected office — pulled up to the spaceport's main administrative building. Centurion Yao Algava, who commanded the

Combat Support Company, emerged from a darkened doorway and waved them over to where he stood.

"I figure you might want to use the control tower, boss," Algava said the moment Kayne was within earshot. "I've taken the spaceport administrator's suite as my CP. It has a great view of the entire spaceport. But the tower lets you see every egress point and more importantly Tony's company."

"And makes the boss vulnerable to enemy fire," Havel growled.

"Only if the buggers suspect someone's there. I doubt they carry the sort of sensors that can spot a human body wearing a chameleon tin suit if said human sticks to radio silence. I'll take it for now." Kayne turned to Greff. "But the sergeant major is right. Look for an alternate, will you?"

A drop of rain splashed on Kayne's helmet, then another and he reflexively looked up at the sky.

"That's a south-easter," Algava remarked. "It'll dump enough rain on the tarmac that the fucking reivers will be blind from steam when they land."

Sergeant Major Havel's brief outburst of laughter sounded like a wildebeest's dying gasp. "Never thought I'd bless a south-easter. They're the one thing I can't stand about living here. That damned rain when the wind blows off the Middle Sea."

Kayne's helmet radio clicked for attention. "Niner here."

"This is Zero," Hetty Grimes' voice replied, using the Imperial Marine Corps designator for a unit operations center. "Another ship dropped out of FTL at the hyperlimit. A Byzance class frigate. No transponder. She gave herself a massive boost, more than I would think prudent, then shut her systems, so her emissions don't show up on sensors. We only saw her because the surveillance satellite is still looking in the wormhole's direction."

"Hot damn! The cavalry. They're only a few hours behind the reivers. Looks like this Morane fellow who sent the warning was on the level about everything."

"I thought you might enjoy the news."

"And our unwanted visitors?"

"Decelerating hard. They'll pass Gwaelod's orbit within the hour." Gwaelod, the outer of Lyonesse's three moons was overhead tonight and would shine brightly but for thick clouds propelled by the sea-borne gale.

"Pass the word to all units. It'll give them a shot in the arm."

"Will do. Zero, out."

"The Navy is here," Kayne told the others. "Probably not close enough to keep them from landing, but we're no longer alone. Now, where do we hide this thing?" He nodded at the truck.

**

"Three assholes decelerating hard." *Myrtale*'s sensor chief sounded jubilant. "Three hours ahead of us, about to pass the outer moon's orbit."

Sirak's fist slammed his command chair's arm. So close. "Anything from Lyonesse?"

"Nothing. It's like nobody's home. No radio waves, no satellites. Hang on." The sensor chief squinted at his readout. "Correction. One active satellite on low power."

"Hah. The rest of their constellation is dormant. They received Captain Morane's transmission. Let's hope whoever thought of shuttering the orbitals is also smart enough to clear out the likely targets. Nav, give us the hardest boost our strained dampeners can manage. Number One, as soon as the drives shut off, we go silent until it's time to fire the braking thrusters. Maybe we can shave another hour off the buggers' lead without them knowing we're here."

"With any luck, they'll spend a few hours scanning likely target areas before trying to land. If they don't realize the colonists took everything above the atmosphere offline, they might count on the element of surprise and try to pass themselves off as legitimate traders before running rampant."

Sirak grinned at his first officer. "Let's hope their leader is a prudent being and spends at least four hours looking at the target area from on high."

"Indeed. But somehow, I think those people down there aren't going to simply fold in the face of what? Three hundred scum. Or at least they won't fold until we can give the reivers a choice between dying in space and dying on the ground."

— 52 —

Major Matti Kayne, commanding officer of the Lyonesse Colonial Militia, was about to comment on the rain-drenched sky gradually shedding the unrelieved darkness of night when he heard his helmet radio click. With the defense network under radio silence, it could only be important news.

"Niner, this is Zero."

"Niner."

"Another ship dropped out of FTL at the hyperlimit a few minutes ago and is pouring on the gees like something that doesn't care about the laws of physics. I make it as a Triumph class cruiser."

"*Vanquish.*" The name came out in a whisper.

"She's a Triumph class cruiser. According to the specs, she can take out those three reivers without reloading."

"How long until she's here?"

"Not much longer than the frigate, I figure. Triumphs aren't nearly as old as Byzance frigates and have inertial dampeners to match. She can brake a lot harder. Shall I pass the word?"

"No. The reivers might pick up long-range transmissions."

A muffled curse escaped Grimes' lips.

"What?"

"The surveillance satellite is no longer talking to us. I guess they found and destroyed it."

"No matter," Kayne said, eyes staring at the unrelieved gray sky above the Lannion spaceport. "We'll know when they come through the cloud cover."

"In that case, good hunting."

Kayne grinned at his faint reflection in the control tower window. Grimes might come across as a career lieutenant with no ambitions, but she was shaping up well in an emergency.

"Thank you. Niner, out."

**

"This will be one for the books, Skipper," Mikkel said after Chief Lettis reported. "The reivers aren't on the ground yet. We're four hours out, and *Myrtale* has to be somewhere between Lyonesse and us, running silent."

"As is Lyonesse itself, it seems. Unless there's nothing left. In which case the reivers would be leaving by now. No, the colonists are imitating us, hiding from enemy sensors. I wish we could contact them, but this is not yet the time."

"Especially if they've taken measures to defend themselves," DeCarde said. She glanced sideways at Sister Gwenneth. "What does the Void say about Lyonesse's chances?"

That faint yet infuriating smile briefly crossed Gwenneth's lips. "Trust in the Almighty and in the stout hearts of those who stand against the darkness."

"I don't know whether or not that's reassuring, but since we won't get there before those reivers wreak havoc,

I guess trusting in the colonists' stout hearts is as good as it gets for us spectators."

"Pretty much," Morane said. "How did the ship fare from this latest burst, Iona?"

"Roman's still checking, but you might have noticed our transition back to sublight was more violent than usual. That's never a good sign."

"At least we're here and able to fight."

"And still four hours away. We can cheat the laws of hyperspace once or twice, but trying to cheat our inertial dampeners' ability to keep us alive is a lot different."

"Sir." Chief Lettis raised a hand to attract Morane's attention. "I think I've spotted *Myrtale*. She's leaking emissions like a sieve. At least to my sensors. The reivers probably won't notice against the background radiation."

"Open a tight-beam connection and give *Myrtale* an encrypted ping, so she knows we've arrived."

**

A wet, gray dawn blanketed Lannion when the first rumbles of artificial thunder reached Kayne's ears. Where the south-easter brought the occasional ear-splitting drumroll, complete with jagged, piercing bursts of lightning, this rumble was not only sustained but growing. And so far without bright visuals.

He felt Greff and Havel stiffen as the sound reached their ears and suppressed the sudden desire to call his company commanders and see if ships were landing elsewhere. But radio silence remained an essential part of this ambush. Of any ambush, really.

"There." Centurion Greff pointed upward. A black dot riding a column of pure energy was breaking through the low cloud cover.

Eric Thomson

A few minutes passed while the dot grew and lengthened, but it remained stubbornly solitary. Were the other ships landing in Trevena and Carhaix? Or in one of the smaller settlements. Or even, the Almighty forbid, in the hinterland, where most of the townspeople cowered in hiding, beset both by fear and torrential rains?

The reiver's rumbling grew louder, more menacing, but seemed oddly muffled at the same time. Yet the sparkling light of its thrusters lent a deadly beauty to this dull morning.

Kayne, and the other retired Imperial Marine Corps noncoms in the militia last saw shots fired in anger more than a decade ago. For the vast majority of the Lyonesse volunteers, today would be their first time shooting at anything more than a holographic target during training. But they were defending their homes, their families and their communities, everything they and the earlier generations of settlers built since Lyonesse was opened to colonization in the last century.

The black dot, now clearly identifiable as a needle-shaped starship of unusual design, quite unlike the broader, more rounded merchantmen Kayne was used to seeing, slowed its descent until it almost seemed suspended in midair. Gun turrets, retracted for the plunge through Lyonesse's atmosphere, seemed to sprout along both sides and the ship's keel, removing any last doubts this could be an honest visitor.

"They're scanning us," Greff said in a whisper.

This was the moment of greatest peril. Were the militia soldiers still adequately camouflaged? Did their battlesuits still absorb a sensor's pulses without reflecting them? Was everyone still respecting the order to keep weapons unpowered until the last minute? The smallest thing might tip the reivers off and tell them they weren't about to hit an unwitting, defenseless colony. And that could be enough to trigger a massacre thanks to those guns pointing at the spaceport.

It felt as if the entire town was holding its collective breath during the ship's last few minutes of descent. Then, as predicted, its thrusters turned a night's worth of rain puddles into super-heated steam, blanking everything out for a few heart-stopping moments. The reivers had landed.

Little by little, tendril by tendril, the steam clouds dissipated, leaving a lean, black-hulled raider sitting on thick struts in the middle of Lannion spaceport's tarmac. Up close, it looked worn, rough, pitted by too many atmospheric re-entries and too many fights.

But Kayne sensed an almost feral aura of death and destruction emanating from the now silent silhouette. One part of him knew the feeling was only a flight of fancy, but somewhere, deep within, it was almost as if a genetic memory of the first Viking raids on unsuspecting villages three thousand years ago, on a world far away, was resurfacing.

Part of the ship's keel broke loose and dropped, forming a ramp wide enough for five humans to walk abreast. A minute passed, then dark shapes emerged, moving with caution, weapons held at the ready. As they came out of the shadows and into the watery morning light, Kayne saw they were human. But that was where any resemblance to his soldiers ended.

Long-haired, scarred, tattooed and otherwise disfigured, the reivers appeared brutal, almost bestial, as if they were snarling hyenas in human form. They wore what looked like castoff pieces of armor from two dozen sources over leathery black tunics and trousers tucked into knee-high boots. The clothes themselves were covered with a bewildering array of metallic adornments, plates, and spikes, adding to the overall savage appearance.   Their   weapons   appeared   equally heterogeneous, with no discernible, let alone familiar pattern.

More of them poured out as the first few cautiously walked toward the silent terminal building, their heads on a swivel, eyes searching for potential threats. Yet their strutting demeanor screamed of confidence born from overrunning helpless frontier settlements without so much as taking return fire.

A few carried handheld sensors and were sweeping their surroundings, but if the ship's more powerful scanners hadn't noticed the hidden soldiers, these didn't stand a chance. To them, the terminal and every other spaceport building appeared empty, as they would this early.

A few tried to enter the terminal, but upon finding every door locked, they simply followed their comrades around instead of forcing their way inside. By the time Kayne stopped counting, almost a hundred filled the main road leading into Lannion proper. A silent, heavily armed mob. How many more remained aboard the ship was difficult to assess.

He heard three clicks over the battalion radio network. Then, all hell broke loose.

— 53 —

"All three have entered the atmosphere," *Myrtale*'s sensor chief reported.

Sirak gestured at his first officer. "Go up systems, Number One. There's no point in hiding anymore. And put us at battle stations."

"Should we try calling Lyonesse?"

"No. Not just yet. I'd rather we didn't spook the reivers until we're in a position to fire, but since Captain Morane was kind enough to let us know he's here, please set up a subspace link with *Vanquish*."

Moments later, a visibly tired, but steely-eyed Morane appeared on the display. "How is *Myrtale*, Nate?"

"Keeping together thanks to our hopes, our prayers and a chief engineer who doesn't know when to quit. But after this, you might as well put us in permanent orbit around Lyonesse."

A small grin softened Morane's face. "You have one of those mule-headed wrench jockeys too, eh?"

"I think they teach them not to quit at starship engineering school, sir. That, or they select them for extreme stubbornness. But we received an object lesson in why the Fleet limits FTL travel to twice the speed of light within a heliosphere. Above two times cee, hyperspace is like molasses compared to interstellar space."

"We apparently received the same lesson. My chief engineer isn't pounding on my door yet, but Iona Mikkel tells me he's not a happy man. At least we're not leaking emissions like you are. Not yet."

Sirak chuckled. "Are we that bad?"

"A blind sensor chief could find you."

"But not a reiver. They entered the atmosphere like tourists without a single worry in the universe, let alone a Navy ship on their ass. A shame we didn't make it here faster. I'm not looking forward to the aftermath."

"Let's wait before writing Lyonesse's obituary, Nate. I think they received our warning and are prepared to give these roaches a less than friendly welcome."

"I certainly hope so. What's your plan?"

"Once we're sure they've landed, you can call the colony's traffic control center on the Fleet emergency band and see if anyone answers."

"And if there's no reply?"

"The moment you're in geosynchronous orbit over the settled area, find them and figure out what they're doing. When we arrive, I'll send my Marines to the surface in full combat configuration. The reivers probably landed at spaceports, which means we can't open fire willy-nilly."

"Sounds good, and if the buggers come back up, I won't hesitate. When do we expect *Narwhal* and *Dawn Trader*?"

"I think they're already in-system, but they still face a few more hours in FTL."

"Which means they'll miss the show."

"As will half of Colonel DeCarde's battalion. She tells me they'll be inconsolable."

**

The main road leading from the spaceport's passenger terminal erupted in gunfire at the prearranged signal. Militia soldiers hidden in buildings along the thoroughfare poured a continuous stream of plasma into the massed reivers, many of whom fell into smoking heaps before they could even understand what was happening.

Marksmanship wasn't important, not at such close range, not with a dozen squad automatic weapons doing the bulk of the killing. A few of the reivers, with quicker wits than the rest, sprinted for the nearest cover while firing back blindly.

Kayne, mesmerized by the sight of his ambush working as planned, a rare occurrence, jumped when Greff tapped him on the shoulder and pointed back at the tarmac. Combat Support Company's heavy weapons platoon was unmasking its fighting positions and opening up on the grounded ship.

Energy shields were of limited use in an atmosphere, but the reivers were so confident, they hadn't even raised them after disgorging the raiding party. Streams of plasma spat out by six of the battalion's twenty millimeter, four-barrel calliopes were chewing up the exposed gun turrets, turning hardened metal into molten lava.

One of the as yet undamaged aft turrets belatedly came online and destroyed an unoccupied cargo shelter to the terminal building's right, then another, before two calliopes put it permanently out of action.

To Kayne's surprise, the belly ramp rose and slammed shut. Then the roar of thrusters under emergency power filled the air while steam from the freshly accumulated rain puddles shot up in ragged tendrils, and the ship lifted.

Someone finally remembered to switch on the shields. A bluish aurora sprang to life several meters above the hull where streams of plasma splashed off in all directions before dying out. But the Support Company's gunners didn't let up until the reiver vanished into the clouds.

The barbarians who'd survived Lannion Company's initial onslaught seemed to become suicidal at the sight of their ship leaving them behind and began a series of individual berserker attacks against the militia's fortified emplacements. Others, taking advantage of the confusion, ran toward the center of town, intent either on escape or causing as much havoc as possible before dying in turn.

And that's when the die-hards, the armed colonists who stayed behind, came out of their hiding places and picked the remaining reivers off one by one.

Kayne, stunned by the violence and the militia ambush's success could do nothing more than stare until Sergeant Major Havel nudged him.

"Zero is calling, Major."

"What? Oh. Right. Zero this is Niner. What's up?"

"We're receiving a call from the Navy frigate *Myrtale* on the Fleet emergency channel via Lyonesse traffic control. She's in geosynchronous orbit above us."

"Tell them the reiver that landed in Lannion just lifted off without its raiding party, which is now mostly dead. They might try bombarding us from higher up out of spite. Ask if *Myrtale* could deal with it."

"Wilco."

He waited until Grimes passed his instructions to whichever of her chiefs was manning the signals station, then asked, "What's happening elsewhere?"

"No idea. None of the outlying companies have called in yet."

"Break radio silence and try to raise anyone who can hear you. I need to know what the reivers are doing elsewhere. We caught them completely by surprise here, but our success may be a fluke."

"Wilco."

"Niner, out."

Kayne took a last look at the carnage. A few shots still rang out as troopers fired on twitching bodies, to make sure the berserkers were indeed dead. Then he gestured at the stairs leading down from the control tower. "Shall we?"

"If you don't mind me saying so, sir, that ambush was a thing of beauty. Colonel Hertog would have cried with pride."

Kayne gave his sergeant major an ironic grin. Hertog was the 77th Regiment's last commanding officer before it left Lyonesse. "He would have bawled me out at the sheer waste of ammunition, not sobbed with glee."

"Meh." Greff shrugged. "Hertog understood that weekend warriors are more prone to heavy triggers in high-stress situations than hardened Marines. Besides, there's still plenty of ammo in the warehouse."

**

The round-faced logistics lieutenant who called *Myrtale* from the surface might have a manic gleam in her eyes, but Sirak thought her high-pitched voice was commendably calm.

"I'm relieved to hear you say that, Lieutenant. And your commanding officer is right. I wouldn't put it past one of those bastards to toss a few kinetic rounds at your Lannion spaceport just because. If he lifted in a panic, he's written off his landing party. What about the others?"

"I'm trying to reach them, but without our satellite constellation, our communications are limited in range."

"Where did you expect the other two ships to land?"

"Major Kayne figured Trevena and Carhaix, the second and third largest towns after Lannion."

Sirak turned to his navigation officer. "Find their location, then put eyes on them. CIC, you caught that about the reiver heading for orbit?"

"Yes, sir," the frigate's combat systems officer replied. "We're searching for him."

"Once you get a targeting lock and he's high enough that neither the shock wave of his antimatter fuel exploding nor the resulting debris will strike the settled area, take him out. No need to wait for my orders."

"Aye, aye, sir."

The navigation officer raised a hand, then pointed at a side display, which showed an aerial view of a small spaceport labeled Trevena. Because of the thick cloud cover and the rain, it was a reconstruction from sensors picking up infrared and other traces rather than an actual visual.

"Lieutenant Grimes, a reiver ship appears to be on the ground in Trevena. We see a lot of tiny hot spots, which means sustained gunfire. Unfortunately, the reiver is so close to the town, I can't risk shooting from geosynchronous."

"Understood, sir."

"But I'll act as a communications relay if you can't wake your constellation quickly."

"That would be fantastic, sir. It'll take a good hour to rouse every satellite."

"Consider it done. We're aiming a transmitter at Trevena. Your commanding officer will be able to speak with his people. Now for the third bastard." A pause while Sirak studied yet another side display. "Looks like Major Kayne called it, Lieutenant. He's in Carhaix alright. And it looks like he's lifting off, but there's still an awful lot of gunfire being exchanged, some of it seems to be large caliber, from the ship's guns. We'll aim a transmitter at Carhaix as well. CIC, do you see the second ship lifting?"

"Yes."

"Same as for the first. Take him out the moment you can."

—54—

"Two-Niner, this is Niner." Kayne was watching the soldiers from Lannion Company walk among the dead and dying reivers, picking up weapons and other items of interest.

Former Marine noncoms, Sergeant Major Havel and Centurion Greff among them, gave those who were still alive the *coup de grâce* — a quick headshot with a pistol. It was not a job for weekend warriors about to crash from an adrenaline high. The battle was over in Lannion, but according to *Myrtale*, the Trevena Company — designator 'Two' — was still fighting.

"Two-Niner here," an out of breath Centurion Hamm answered. "I was beginning to think we were the only ones left."

"The situation in Lannion is under control. What's your status?"

"A bit of a mess, I'm afraid. A few of the barbs wised up and forced us to spring the ambush early. Casualties on both sides but no dead for us so far. The Trevena spaceport is pretty much in ruins now they've opened up with their ship's guns, and so is the edge of town. We're trying to put the calliopes into action, but they hit two of them already. About a hundred got off, but only fifty made it into the ambush zone. The others are trying to extract their buddies. Any chance of help?"

"It'll take an hour at least to move a company from Lannion to Trevena. But perhaps our Navy friends in orbit might come up with ideas. They're relaying my transmission and no doubt listening."

"We are," a new voice said. "I'm Nate Sirak, captain of the frigate *Myrtale*. We're watching events on the ground, Trevena. I can't fire from here without risking collateral damage. We're too high for that sort of precision, but since the other reivers lifted off, could I suggest you withdraw your forces and simply let them go? Once they're well off the ground, then I can engage. We're already tracking the one that landed in Carhaix and will obtain a lock on the one from Lannion momentarily."

"You hear that, Two-Niner. Sounds like a plan. Try to break free. Abandon the heavy equipment if you need to."

"You mean run."

"I mean move out of the way and let *them* run so the Navy can do its thing. No dishonor involved."

A brief silence ensued, then, "Wilco. We're pulling back now."

"Call when you're clear, and he lifts. Niner, out." Kayne took a deep calming breath. Casualties. Damage to the spaceport and town. Lannion was a fluke. Maybe once they compared timelines, it would show the Lannion ship was first to land and first to be ambushed. Its crew warned the others, if not in time, then fast enough to prevent the other raiding parties' destruction. But no matter. The Navy was here.

"Three-Niner, this is Niner."

He was about to repeat the call when an exhausted voice said, "Three-Niner here."

"What's your status?"

"Bruised, bleeding, burning, you name it. But the bastards lifted."

"Talk to me."

"The ship landed like we expected. Its belly ramp opened, and they poured out. Ugliest fucks you've ever seen. More like animals than people. About fifty of them were spreading out across the tarmac, and more were coming when for some reason they stopped. Looked around like they smelled something bad. Then, one of them opened fire and shot up the terminal building. That was the start of a free-for-all.

"I don't know what set it off, but weren't able to trigger the ambush, so my folks returned fire with everything we own while the reivers pulled back into their ship. Then the damn thing pumped out round after round as it lifted. Carhaix spaceport is a smoking ruin as is a good chunk of the nearby outskirts. We have two dozen wounded, five dead. Could be a few of the citizens who stayed in their homes also took hits. We're checking."

"Sit tight. The Navy's here. They'll take care of the reivers. When the satellite constellation is back up, we'll sort out the casevac."

Kayne didn't hear Centurion Janey's reply. The gray overcast sky to the north suddenly lit up with an eerie glow, like a second sun above the clouds. It only lasted for a few heartbeats, but then, something roiled those same clouds in an ever-expanding circle as a distant thunderclap reached his ears.

"Hello, this is *Myrtale*. If you're wondering what that was, take heart. We took out the reiver that lifted from Carhaix as it crossed fifty thousand meters. The debris should fall somewhere on your arctic icecap."

"Thanks, *Myrtale*."

"Glad to be of service. One down, two to go. Stand by."

"How's everything else," Janey asked.

"Lannion pulled off a successful ambush. A hundred bastards dead. Their ship took a few hits before it bugged out. But Trevena only managed a partial ambush and found itself in a nasty firefight. They're breaking contact now to let that lot lift as well so the Navy can finish them. I guess the Lannion bunch landed first, took a kick in the face and warned the others before they walked into yours and Trevena's kill zone."

"Makes sense."

Another flash lit up the clouds, and another widening eddy roiled them.

"Number two bites the plasma."

"Indeed," the voice from *Myrtale* said. "It was the ship that lifted from Lannion. Two down, one to go. And I see number three is lifting from Trevena. Stand by."

Kayne fought off an irresistible urge to sit, now that his own surge of adrenaline was ebbing. The fighting might be over, save for the Navy taking out that third ship, but the cleanup job still lay before them. Starting with a hundred or so smoking corpses littering the Lannion spaceport road, and wherever armed colonists killed those trying to flee.

"Zero, this is Niner."

"Go ahead."

"Once the Navy kills that third ship, bring up the satellite constellation, then ask Chief Administrator Logran to sound the recall, so people can come out of the soggy wilderness and go home." Except those whose homes in Carhaix and Trevena were smoking ruins. But that's what neighbors were for. "And I'm coming back. Please tell Her Excellency that Lyonesse is once again safe."

Grimes chuckled. "Her Excellency knows. She's been sitting behind me ever since you left for the spaceport."

**

"Seems almost idyllic if you ignore the fact it was the scene of a battle against reivers a few hours ago." DeCarde admired the blue-green orb partially obscured by shreds of white cloud now filling the CIC's main display. "It's a wonder how the bastards knew about Lyonesse. I'd not heard the name before meeting you and listening to your harebrained scheme."

"I don't know. Traders working the frontier most probably. It certainly wasn't through traffic since Lyonesse is an anomaly among G class stars with its single mapped, stable wormhole."

"And you never visited the place before today?"

"Never. My knowledge comes from many sources, but none of it through personal experience. I'm seeing it for the first time. The only reason Lyonesse came to mind once I understood nothing could arrest the empire's death spiral was because of an Academy classmate born here. She enjoyed speaking about her homeworld, and how it differed from the rest of the empire's domains. Isolated and colonized mostly by those seeking to escape the Ruggero dynasty's misrule, though the Lyonesse governor is appointed by Wyvern."

"Maybe you'll meet her again on Lyonesse."

Morane shook his head. "Sadly, no. She was a Marine and died fighting reivers long ago in an unnamed star system no one wanted, and no one remembers."

"Occupational hazard. It was always thus for my kind, even before our ancestors left Earth."

"Ever been there? Earth, I mean?"

DeCarde snorted. "No. I'm not one for museums and definitely not for the planet-sized version. It would give me the creeps. You?"

"Once. As a young lieutenant. It was both interesting and depressing. I saw what was left of the old Commonwealth capital, Geneva, and the monument to the Imperial Marines killed when the last secretary general ordered the city's destruction rather than surrender."

"The Ancestor was there when it happened. He not only saw the antimatter explosion that wiped out over twenty-five hundred years of history along with an entire Marine division under his command, but he also led the forces that seized Earth for the first emperor. They put that monument up at his behest. A last act before leaving Earth, never to return."

"You're talking about the forebear who started the family lore repository?"

DeCarde dipped her head once. "The very same. I wonder what he would make of the empire's slow death and our undertaking to save what knowledge we can."

"He'd probably experience a déjà vu moment."

"And curse in ten languages at the titled idiots tearing up what he'd reluctantly fought to build."

"Why reluctantly?"

"The Ancestor spent most of his career in the Marine Corps fighting to keep power-hungry sociopaths from turning the Commonwealth into a repressive dictatorship only to serve an empire created by the Fleet as the sole solution to another murderous civil war."

"Which broke out nonetheless, though he and his contemporaries bought us a millennium of peace and prosperity. I daresay your ancestor might look upon our mission with approving eyes."

"Approving eyes, perhaps, but most certainly with a pungent comment."

"Sir?"

Morane turned to the signals petty officer. "Yes?"

"Their satellite constellation is up, and we're being hailed. Audio and video. It's coming from Lannion Base, the naval supply depot."

"On the main screen, please."

The image of four people sitting around the end of a conference table swam into view. Three men and one woman. One of the men wore a green battledress uniform and the expression of someone who was fresh from the fight. The woman, a striking, dark-haired aristocrat with a triangular face dominated by cheekbones sharp enough to cut granite, spoke first.

"Captain Morane? I am Elenia Yakin, Governor of Lyonesse. We owe you more than we could ever repay for your warning, and for coming to our aid."

"I am Morane, Your Excellency, captain of the cruiser *Vanquish* and senior surviving officer of the 197th Battle Group." He gestured to his right. "And this is Lieutenant Colonel Brigid DeCarde, commanding officer, 6th Battalion, 21st Marine Pathfinder Regiment."

"A pleasure. With me is Chief Administrator Gaspard Logran." The bearded, pugnacious-looking civilian raised a hand. "Speaker of the Colonial Council Rorik Hecht." The eldest and baldest man nodded gravely. "And finally Major Matti Kayne, commanding officer of the Lyonesse Colonial Militia. Major Kayne is a retired Imperial Marine." Kayne stiffened to attention. "Sirs."

"We four make up the colony's executive committee," Yakin said. "And though we want to express our gratitude, we're also burning with curiosity to know why you're here. Not only did the last Marine regiment withdraw eight years ago, no Navy ship passed through since well before Admiral Zahar rebelled. Lyonesse is what you might call a barely known backwater though being ignored by the empire and now the rebellion suits us."

"It's a rather long story, Your Excellency."

"We have all the time in the world, Captain."

— 55 —

"Consider us refugees from the civil war, Madame. My cruiser, the frigate *Myrtale* who destroyed those reiver ships, and a naval transport by the name *Narwhal*, still inbound from the wormhole, are what's left of an imperial battle group. The 197th was almost completely destroyed weeks ago in the Shield Sector thanks to a boneheaded loyalist admiral looking for a knighthood. We decided it was wiser to leave the empire altogether instead of aligning ourselves with either faction, knowing our lives were about to become nasty, brutish and short.

"Since I figured Lyonesse was one of the places least likely to become a fresh battlefield, we traveled the wormhole network's secondary branches whenever possible to come here unseen by either side. Along the way, I picked up a Marine Pathfinder battalion about to be massacred by rebels; a shipload of monastics fleeing deadly persecution by Admiral Zahar; three dozen children, survivors of a colony wiped out by reivers, and an Imperial Prison Service ship with over five hundred political prisoners condemned to permanent exile and an early death on Parth because of Dendera's paranoia."

Logran's bushy eyebrows crept up his seamed forehead. "Let me see if I understand this. You and the Marines are deserters, correct?"

"If you wish to get technical, perhaps we are. I prefer to consider myself a rational survivor."

"These monastics, they belong to the Order of the Void?" Yakin asked.

"Yes, Madame. Of every discipline. Healers, counselors, agronomists, teachers, and many more. Zahar's troops razed the Yotai Abbey. They massacred most of the friars and sisters. About two hundred survived and traveled here under our protection."

Hecht shook his head. "Void Brethren. That'll put a lot of noses out of joint on Lyonesse."

"Any reason why, sir?"

"Distrust of their motives, mostly, I'd say. But I suppose no one can prevent you from landing them. And if they stay within Lannion Base's perimeter, they're beyond anyone's jurisdiction, since it's still legally Crown land, never mind the empire's outer edges are light years away."

Yakin nodded in agreement with Hecht. "If we are to consider the Crown's writ has any force here. But that's a discussion for another time. And prisoners, you said?"

"A little over five hundred. They're still in stasis, and will stay so until you permit us to decant them."

"Are they all politicals, with no actual criminals among them?" Logran's eyes shone with skepticism.

"A few. We'll vet each one before decanting them."

"What if you find murderers or rapists? No doubt you'll be looking to us for a few prison cells."

"Or we can set up a place of exile on some island group inaccessible save by air and maroon them there. It would have been their fate on Parth."

The chief administrator's glare softened. "There is a place of exile in the Windy Isles, but we can discuss the matter in more detail later. And what is to be the legal status of your naval ships and the Marine battalion? What if the Arietis system commander sends a patrol here?"

"There is no Arietis system commander. The rebellion withdrew, which is how these reivers could sail down the Lyonesse branch. Arietis faces a dismal future since it's a not inconsiderable wormhole junction connecting with the outer frontier and the badlands beyond. Madame, gentlemen, you need to understand the empire is fracturing at an ever faster rate, with warlords proclaiming themselves rulers over individual systems. Before long, they'll fight each other back into the pre-spaceflight age."

The four stared at Morane, surprised and to varying degrees stunned by the news.

"You asked why we're here, Madame. We're here because of Lyonesse's unique place in the wormhole network. I'm hoping it will escape the ravages of war and so become one of the places if not the sole place where human knowledge and human civilization can survive the empire's collapse. A human knowledge vault, if you like. I intend to pledge my ships, crews, and Marines to help your Colonial Militia defend Lyonesse against any invader."

Yakin studied him with dark eyes that betrayed little of her inner thoughts. "Is the situation really that grim, Captain Morane?"

"Grimmer than you can imagine. The Fleet is tearing itself apart, battle group is fighting battle group, Imperial Guards are grappling with Marines who've mutinied, admirals are assassinating viceroys and Dendera is squeezing so hard, everything is slipping through her fingers. Right now the rebellious sector commanders are cooperating, but that will quickly end as they vie to become Dendera's successor. And their sectors are shrinking, or at least the Coalsack Sector is. Arietis wasn't a frontier system by any stretch, but it slipped into the badlands, nonetheless. And because of the wormhole network's vagaries, so has Lyonesse."

"A harsh assessment. But I won't dispute its accuracy. The signs of a looming crisis were there for anyone to see even while I was still at court. But too many of my fellow so-called nobles were busy playing power games instead." Yakin's gaze remained inscrutable, yet Morane fancied it held a spark of interest. "Some would call you strange, Captain, coming here with a dramatic proposal to make this colony the last repository of humanity's greatness as the galaxy burns up. Many colonists will scoff at you, and they'll not be happy with an enlarged, full-time military garrison adding to the strain on our treasury. But I daresay today's events will convince those paying attention that our universe now answers to different rules. That having only one wormhole terminus doesn't prevent reivers from coming if no one is guarding the other end."

"Indeed, Madame. And a few raids later, any unfortunate colony that falls victim to the barbarians will suffer enough losses to face a catastrophic collapse. Many will die off entirely. This is not speculation. We saw two planets shorn of human life in the last few months, and helped two more, Lyonesse included, fend off such an attack. I would be glad to share the scans we took so you might see for yourselves."

"Except with you here, Lyonesse has a few ships and a battalion of Marines."

Morane nodded. "It does. More importantly, it has ships and Marines whose first and only allegiance will be to Lyonesse. The empire and the rebellion can't call us away since we no longer look to either. Of course, without regular overhauls and repairs, the ships will gradually waste away. But if we know how to build more, we can develop the necessary infrastructure and remain capable of space travel. On a lesser scale, perhaps, but still. However, like the Lyonesse Colonial Militia, our Marines can keep replenishing their ranks for countless generations and destroy any reivers foolish enough to land."

"We would be mad to refuse such an increase in our own defense forces. However, unlike the late, unlamented empire, we don't pay lip service to democracy, and as I said, there will be concern about landing hundreds of monastics and political prisoners, never mind increasing military expenditures." She paused, though her eyes kept studying Morane. "You mentioned scans of colonies that were attacked."

"Indeed, Madame."

"Evidence of what happens without a prepared defense will go a long way to convince doubters. We were lucky this time. Without your warning, I shudder to think how many might be dead."

"I'll see that our records are transmitted right away."

Yakin and Logran exchanged glances, then the former nodded. "If you'd be so kind, Captain. You've given me much to think about and discuss with our leading citizens. I shall contact you again once I've done so. In the meantime, please go ahead and land your Marines and the monastics. Major Kayne's troops can use their help to remove reiver bodies and clean up the damage in Trevena and Carhaix. But can I count on your keeping everyone else confined to Lannion Base so as not to spread rumors about what's happening in the wider galaxy? Folks are already traumatized by today's events and need not know right away that our situation has irrevocably changed."

"Of course." Morane glanced to one side and nodded. "You should receive the scan copies about now. May I also land the prison ship? Without decanting the prisoners, of course."

Yakin hesitated. "If you must. Until later, Captain." The CIC's display went dark.

"Bridge to the captain."

"Yes, Iona."

"*Narwhal* and *Dawn Trader* dropped out of FTL and are inbound. When they get here, *Narwhal* would like to release *Tanith* and take the time for a full survey, in case the stresses from the prison ship make entering Lyonesse's gravity well too risky. Captain Ryzkov proposes to land her Marines by shuttlecraft."

"Permission granted for *Narwhal* to separate from *Tanith*, stay in orbit and transfer the Marines by shuttle. *Dawn Trader* is to land first, followed by the Marines, then *Tanith*."

**

Vanquish's shuttles settled one after the other on the Lannion Base tarmac, touching down light as feathers. The whine of their thrusters faded away as the pilots dropped their aft ramps and the squadron's first sergeants ordered their Pathfinders off and into formation.

DeCarde, followed by Sergeant Major Bayn and Centurion Haller, made her way toward the knot of people waiting at the base of the cliff, near one of the people-sized doors. A few wore Navy blue battledress, the others Marine Corps green.

Yet while the latter sported Marine-style rank insignia, the unit badge on their field caps seemed almost garish and distinctly nonstandard. It showed a double-headed avian, perhaps something native to Lyonesse, wings spread and clutching crossed antique rifles. The badge didn't include an imperial crown.

As DeCarde neared, a major — she recognized him as Kayne, the commander of the militia — barked out something in a rough baritone and the delegation snapped to attention. He saluted.

"Welcome, Colonel. I'm Matti Kayne."

She returned the compliment before removing her battlesuit's right gauntlet and extended her hand. "Brigid DeCarde. I understand you're a Marine."

"Thirty years in the Corps. 77th Regiment. The Land Raptors." He returned her grip with a wiry strength that felt effortless.

"I've never worked with the 77th, but it's still considered a good outfit, though it'll likely be part of the rebellion by now. Most of the Marine regiments in the outlying sectors forswore their allegiance to the Crown."

Kayne nodded at the Navy officer standing to his left. "May I introduce Lieutenant Hetty Grimes? She's the supply depot's commanding officer, and therefore in charge of Lannion Base."

DeCarde held out her hand. "A pleasure, Lieutenant."

"Sir."

"You've been here long?"

"Going on six years, sir." Her eyes shifted toward Kayne for a second. "And I expect I'll do like the major. Retire here, I mean. Considering what one hears about the Navy these days."

Kayne cleared his throat. "May I introduce Centurion Greff, my operations officer, and Sergeant Major Havel? Both also served in the Land Raptors. A fair number of us retired here when the regiment left. Governor Yakin pretty much formed the militia around us."

With the remaining introductions out of the way, Kayne glanced at B and D Squadrons, then back at DeCarde. "Is that your entire command, Colonel?"

"No. Only those who traveled in *Vanquish*. The rest is coming from *Narwhal*. We're five hundred and fifty-two in total."

"You'll fit into the old barracks without problems, sir." Kayne pointed at a cluster of small ground floor doors topped by several levels' worth of windows past the last of the big warehouse portals. "That's where the 77th used to live. The Colonial Militia occupies a small part of the installation. Most of my soldiers are part-timers and live across the settlement area."

"What's your strength?"

"Approximately one thousand, with ninety on full-time duty. I have companies in all seven major centers: Trevena, Carhaix, Caffrey, Arran, High Bend, North Wall and here in Lannion. They're good people, dedicated."

"And they can certainly fight. Congratulations. Most colonial militias can barely shoot, let alone set the sort of ambush you carried out."

Kayne shrugged. "We were lucky to hear your warning, sir. Without it, I doubt you and I would be speaking right now."

"Next time and Captain Morane is convinced there will be a next time, we'll be here, fighting right along with you. Now how about we see that this bunch is settled in before the rest land?"

— 56 —

Captain Jonas Morane came down the shuttle's ramp with a spring in his step and a smile on his face. He wore a naval dress uniform, midnight blue with gold bullion rank stripes on the sleeves, several rows of ribbons on his left breast and a starship captain's wreathed star on the right. The insignia on his blue beret still bore the Imperial Navy's starburst and anchor, but the crown that used to top them was gone.

DeCarde and Kayne came to attention and saluted. Morane returned the compliment and asked, "How was your first night ashore, Colonel?"

"Strange. The 77th did a good job sealing the barracks before they left, meaning our new quarters are pristine, but it's astounding how one gets used to a starship's background hum. I'm not used to the silence of a planetary night."

Morane turned to Kayne and stuck out his hand. "A pleasure to meet you in person, Major. The militia's defense of Lyonesse was masterful. I understand you and Colonel DeCarde share a common background. That should make working together so much easier." Then he noticed DeCarde's uniform, the Marine Corps equivalent of the one he wore, except rifle green and trimmed with silver piping and insignia. Her qualification devices and medal ribbons put his to shame.

"You carried your fancy suit all the way here, Brigid?"

DeCarde chuckled. "No. The original is still in a warehouse on Aramis, with the rest of our personal gear, which we'll never see again. The supply depot has fabricators, and when you told me we were to meet the colony's executive council, I asked one of the chiefs to run up a dress uniform. They were doing them for the Colonial Militia, so it wasn't much of a stretch to enter Marine Corps specs, as you can see."

Morane studied Kayne's uniform, cut in the same pattern as DeCarde's but in a lighter shade of green, with blackened insignia and trim. "Interesting regimental badge, Major. What is that double-headed creature?"

"A Vanger's Condor. The real version is not actually double-headed. That's just a bit of fancy from the guy who designed Lyonesse's original coat of arms. The true, single-headed condor is the largest raptor analog on Lyonesse, with a four-meter wingspan. You can find them up north, in the high sierras." Kayne nodded at distant purple peaks stretching across the horizon.

"Sounds like an impressive creature. I'd like to see one someday. I gather the militia is providing our transport?"

"It is," DeCarde said. "Major Kayne and his people are hospitable to a fault. My battalion is settling in comfortably with their help, as are the Brethren."

Morane inclined his head. "Thank you, Major. I'd enjoy taking a grand tour of Lannion Base after the meeting. Where is Sister Gwenneth?"

Kayne pointed at a waiting ground car with Colonial Militia markings behind them.

"Waiting for us, sir. Shall we?"

As they fell into step beside him, DeCarde said, "It surprised me they didn't appoint Rinne as their representative."

"He told me the membership felt she could best explain that which requires explaining. In practically those words."

At their approach, the passenger door opened and Kayne ushered them in. Morane nodded a greeting at the solemn sister. "I trust you're well?"

"Quite, Captain, now that we've reached sanctuary. I understand the environmental systems in *Dawn Trader* were feeling the strain and my Brethren the aroma."

Morane settled in beside Gwenneth while DeCarde and Kayne took the facing seats. At a gesture from the latter, the driver, a militia private, gunned the car's fans.

The Marine gestured toward her seatmate. "Major Kayne has seen our war diary, including the visual record of the fighting and atrocities on Coraline as well as the scans from the Lorien and Palmyra massacres."

Morane gave the militia officer a questioning look. "And?"

Kayne grimaced. "I've not seen anything so nasty in my entire thirty years as a Marine, sir. If that evil is spreading, then the empire is truly fucked. As far as I can remember, reivers never used to do more than the odd hit and run, not commit outright massacres. And taking humans as slaves? I thought we'd stomped that crap out centuries ago." He shook his head. "We really owe you for the warning, and for showing up, sir."

"More marauders will eventually come sniffing at our wormhole terminus. A distant outpost like this one, with no known permanent garrison, looks like low-hanging fruit, wormhole junction or not. If they can find the fuel, some might even come the long way, crossing interstellar space in FTL."

"And a thousand strong militia, dispersed along Tristan's southern shore, won't be enough. I doubt we'll ever get another timely warning such as yours." He shook his head. "I don't know what the leading colonists will say about your arrival, or your knowledge vault plan, let alone Sister Gwenneth's Brethren and the political prisoners. But after yesterday's battle, I for one am glad the militia is no longer alone."

**

The usual pair of Colonial Militia soldiers, now back in dress uniform, stood at the head of Government House's stairs. They shouldered their weapons with crisp, precise movements the moment Kayne's car came to a halt.

Even if DeCarde, normally no fan of planetary forces, didn't know about their performance against the reivers, she would gladly concede they looked anything but sloppy. When Morane climbed out first at Kayne's urging, the soldiers silently presented arms and held that position as the delegation passed between them. Morane returned the compliment with a salute that would please any coxswain in the Fleet.

Inside the mansion, Governor Yakin's private secretary, Wickham Sandford, greeted them with exquisite politeness.

"Her Excellency is waiting for you in the main drawing room with Chief Administrator Logran and Speaker of the Council Hecht. If you'll follow me." He led them to a set of double doors, then came to his customary precise, almost military halt on the threshold. "Your Excellency, Chief Administrator, Speaker of the Council, may I present Captain Jonas Morane of the 197th Battle Group, 19th Fleet, Lieutenant Colonel Brigid DeCarde, Commanding Officer, 6th Battalion, 21st Marine

Pathfinder Regiment and Sister Gwenneth, Order of the Void. Accompanying them is Major Kayne, Lyonesse Colonial Militia."

He stepped aside and ushered them into Yakin's presence. She was taller and more slender than Morane expected. Her features seemed sharper in person though the aristocratic air she'd worn the previous day remained. Logran, on the other hand, was precisely as he appeared on the video link — gruff, with a testing grip and eyes that took nothing at face value. Rorik Hecht, in contrast, greeted him with the handshake of a confident, powerful individual.

Yakin gestured at a settee group. "Please, take your ease. You've certainly given us something to think about, Captain. Since you and I first spoke, we four discussed nothing else. As you can imagine, we're fairly cut off from the mainstream and news comes either via subspace radio or visiting traders. Since the rebellion controlled the nearest subspace arrays and relays, we saw what they wanted us to, and much of that seemed muddled, if not outright confusing. But yesterday's attack and your evidence proves things are even more chaotic than we imagined."

"We've only experienced a small part, Madame. However, it was enough to prove the empire is falling into the inexorable grip of entropy. And faster than even I expected. At last count, most of the outer sectors have effectively seceded from the empire, each becoming its own entity under an admiral or viceroy turned warlord. In the Coalsack Sector, as we discovered, unity is proving elusive, and we know of at least one governor general who declared himself viceroy, but without allegiance to the Crown. Grand Duke Custis' realm is fracturing even while he tries to consolidate his power, as the Navy's abandonment of Arietis shows.

"I don't doubt that the same scenario is repeating itself elsewhere. The empire, at least as we know it, is finished. My concern is what comes next. The chances a new polity uniting humanity will emerge within our lifetimes are virtually nil. The greatest military force in human history and the strongest in the known galaxy is destroying itself through fratricide. With no one and nothing to arrest the slide, this collapse will continue until humanity hits rock bottom. For some, rock bottom means eradication, as with Palmyra and Lorien. Coraline's state, when Colonel DeCarde and her unit left it, wasn't encouraging either. Fighting between loyalists and rebels destroyed vital infrastructure, much of it impossible to replace without off-world technology."

"So Major Kayne told us after viewing Colonel DeCarde's war diary. He called the devastation alarming."

"I would use another word, Madame. Sister Gwenneth can give you an account of what she and her fellow congregants experienced or saw if you wish to hear more about conditions in the Coalsack Sector."

Yakin shook her head. "That will not be necessary. Many of us thought previous reports of unrest and rebellion were exaggerated. But after seeing the evidence you gave us, and our own brush with a barbarian raid, I fear we must face the worst." She glanced at Hecht.

"We obviously don't want to end like either of those unfortunate colonies," the Speaker said in a gruff tone. "But even though we experienced our own peril, many among the Colonial Council believe your presence here endangers us. Grand Duke Custis might return to Arietis and demand Lyonesse pledge allegiance to him. Yet you claim no allegiance whatsoever. The prison ship you brought, and from which Custis escaped, may still hold interest for him or his followers." Morane kept a straight face as Hecht spoke. He hadn't mentioned Friar Locarno's mysterious prisoner.

"Then there are the Void Congregants who attracted Admiral Zahar's undying enmity if he's ordered so many from the Yotai Abbey put to death. All reasons for us to fear undue attention if not outright retaliation from the rebels."

Morane smiled. "I daresay the empress' portrait and two of the three flags out front won't help either."

A rumble of laughter escaped Hecht's chest. "He's got you there, Madame."

"I understand how our arrival might alarm your fellow council members, Speaker. However, with both naval and Marine units dwindling in number thanks to this madness, neither Custis, nor Zahar, nor anyone else will waste scarce resources whipping a distant, unimportant system into line. They'll be much too busy exercising control over more important wormhole junctions, something at which they will fail in due course. On some level you know it as well as I do. Otherwise the portrait and flags would be long gone."

Yakin gave him what he thought of as a regal nod. "Point well taken, Captain. Of course, I share Speaker Hecht's concerns, but after yesterday and after seeing what happened to other worlds left unprotected, I'm inclined to overrule the council should it vote against welcoming you."

"We would welcome the Navy and Marines without qualms," Hecht said. "The Void Congregants and political prisoners are another matter."

"Yet we come as a single entity, Speaker. I'm pledged to make sure Sister Gwenneth's people find sanctuary, and cannot in conscience abandon several hundred human beings, most of whom are guilty of nothing more than opposing Dendera. The Void Brethren are anxious to become self-supporting and serve any citizen of

Lyonesse who seeks their help. I'm sure the political prisoners will be equally desirous of finding a place here, now they've escaped a far worse fate on Parth."

Hecht made a dismissive hand gesture.

"I understand that Captain, and we won't turn away honest folk with nowhere else to go. I merely want to ensure you understand that an important segment of Lyonesse won't see your arrival with complete equanimity, in spite of our recent fright. Indeed, the militia's performance could blind many to the fact that without your warning and intervention, the outcome would have been much worse for us. But I'll do my best to allay their fears."

"Now we've agreed to welcome all of you with open arms," Yakin said, "perhaps we can discuss this human knowledge vault you mentioned yesterday."

—57—

"That went rather well." DeCarde took a seat behind the bare desk in the office portion of her quarters. Carved out of the cliff's granite by mining lasers, it was one of the privileged few with a real window looking out over the landing strip. Most made do with a simulation keyed to outside video pickups. She waved at Morane and Gwenneth to take the chairs across from her. Kayne's driver had driven them back from the governor's mansion, but without the Colonial Militia commander. He'd stayed to discuss yesterday's militia casualties with Yakin and Logran.

"Captain Morane was convincing," Gwenneth said. "And the recorded evidence of reiver depredations, as well as that of fratricidal war, are enough to give any sensible person pause, even without a first-hand taste of chaos. However, I would recommend prudence. There are agendas at work that may not coincide with your intentions, or even be contrary to your ongoing welfare."

DeCarde repressed an exasperated sigh at yet another cryptic warning by a Void cleric. But she knew better than to ask for clarification.

"Did you sense something?" Morane asked.

"I merely observed. Words, intonations, gestures, facial expressions, everything conveys meaning if one knows how to interpret them. Speaker Hecht is a more formidable man than he lets on and could be the true power on Lyonesse, content to let The Honorable Elenia Yakin provide a facade and allow Administrator Logran to care for the minutia of government. You will note the latter said almost nothing."

Morane nodded. "Yes, and I also noticed that Hecht's questions when we discussed the knowledge vault seemed to indicate he was looking at the proposal from the angle of control rather than preservation for the greater good."

A bleak smile briefly softened the sister's ascetic features.

"Knowledge is power and power leads to wealth. The idea Lyonesse might one day be the sole place where humanity's learning still exists, uncorrupted by time, certainly appealed to him for less than altruistic motives."

DeCarde chuckled. "Nice guy."

Gwenneth's shoulders rose in a dismissive gesture. "Human nature. Altruism is a rare quality. Pure altruism is even less common. Some would dispute its existence. Others will tell you baser human motives are more reliable. And since Rorik Hecht is, by his own admission, the wealthiest self-made businessman on Lyonesse..."

"At least they've agreed to explore the notion," Morane said. "In the meantime, we shan't be idle. I'd like to decant the prisoners. If by chance, word gets back to Custis that *Tanith* was seen passing through Wormhole Arietis Six, I'd rather see her hidden on one of Lyonesse's moons, in the name of plausible deniability. I'm sure we'll find enough room here to lodge them until they can be moved out into the community."

DeCarde made a dubious face. "Between my Marines and Gwenneth's colleagues, we've used up three-quarters of the available bunk space. That leaves enough for half the prisoners unless we crowd everyone."

"My colleagues won't mind doubling or tripling up, Colonel. Space in *Dawn Trader* was tight, and we're used to close communal living." A faint smile appeared once more. "Something we share with you Marines. Thankfully, the Lannion crèche will take the Palmyran children into its care tomorrow. And we intend to move out as soon as Governor Yakin grants us land. The climate in this region is temperate year-round, so we need not build permanent structures for our new abbey right away."

"I'm sure we can raid the depot to equip you. Standard containers are easily converted into building parts."

Gwenneth inclined her head. "Thank you."

"There's no point in keeping the depot's holdings stashed away when we can use them."

"You'll break Lieutenant Grimes' heart, Captain," DeCarde said in a droll tone. "Those supply types don't like parting with their stocks. It's almost as if they owned the stuff."

Morane ignored the jest and turned his eyes on Gwenneth again. "That brings me to the next item of mutual interest, Sister. I didn't mention Friar Locarno's special prisoner to the governor, for obvious reasons. But the time has come for you to tell me who that is so I can decide what, if any danger he or she presents for Lyonesse. This place is now, if I need to remind anyone, not only our permanent home but our responsibility to protect."

"Fair enough. However, in return, I need your solemn oath you will extend that responsibility, so it covers this person because I fear many here will not wish to do so if they discovered the identity."

"You have it." He placed his right hand over his heart.

"Among the prisoners, hidden under a false identity, you will find Empress Dendera's younger sister and former heir designate to the throne, Corinne Ruggero."

A shocked silence filled DeCarde's office. The Marine regained her voice first. "What?"

"The story, according to Friar Locarno is that Dendera accused Corinne of plotting her overthrow, with the help of people close to the throne."

"Was she?"

Gwenneth shook her head. "Not personally. Corinne has no interest in wearing the crown. However, a faction at court wanted to use her as their figurehead. Dendera ordered the arrest of anyone she suspected but was convinced by the few confidantes she still trusted to order people such as Custis, the chamberlain and other courtiers exiled rather than call for their summary execution. A bloodbath would have likely triggered a revolt within the nobility.

"Thus it was mercy for everyone. Except when it came to Corinne. As legal heir, she was one heartbeat from the throne. With help from plotters who were still at large, Friar Locarno hid Corinne, gave her a fresh identity and a new look and arranged for her to slip aboard *Tanith* as a common criminal. Those same plotters ensured Locarno survived Dendera's purge of the Order's delegation so he might join Corinne in exile and watch over her. They must also have informed Custis she would travel to Parth on the same ship, but since Locarno kept her cover identity secret, they could not give him a name."

"Why did a Friar of the Void get involved in secular matters, especially imperial household politics?"

Gwenneth's lips pressed together, the first sign of annoyance Morane had witnessed in their weeks of acquaintanceship. "I can only state the Brethren aboard *Dawn Trader* found his reasons valid. Please don't press me for more, Captain. We are forbidden to discuss certain matters with those not of the Order. This is one of them."

Morane sat back and exhaled noisily. "Now I understand why Custis didn't order *Tanith* destroyed. Perhaps he thought Corinne might still make a perfectly legitimate alternative to Dendera, someone behind whom the rebellious sectors could unite. Of course, it's probably too late by now. I doubt the Ruggero name carries any meaning other than corruption, rot, and decay."

"Corinne would not accept in any case." Gwenneth fell silent for a moment, choosing her words. "She possesses the attributes we seek in novices postulating as Sisters of the Void and was studying for admission under Friar Locarno."

"What attributes are those?" DeCarde asked.

"Another matter we cannot discuss, I'm afraid. Please take my word when I said Corinne did not wish the Imperial Crown for herself, nor would she ever cooperate with Custis. She very much wants to become one of us, which was the true bone of contention with Dendera and led to the massacre of my brothers and sisters on Wyvern."

"As Custis must know, a figurehead need not cooperate, Sister. She merely needs to exist and thereby lend his claim legitimacy. We're definitely decanting the prisoners so we can rid ourselves of *Tanith*. As long as that ship is visible to anyone, it remains the grand duke's lodestone and our liability. He may have abandoned Arietis, but that doesn't mean his people won't think of looking here. I was planning to mothball her on one of the moons, but now perhaps the better alternative is destroying her without leaving any traces. Crashing her into the sun, for example, would do nicely."

"After we drain her data banks."

Morane grinned at DeCarde. "Of course, Colonel. I want our descendants to know about the imperial penal system in all of its glory." His face took on a serious expression again. "Sister, since Corinne is to join the Order, I suggest we decant her first and hide her among you. I've committed to having members of the colonial administration present when we awaken the prisoners so we may assure them we're not setting common criminals free along with the politicals. And since Corinne is hiding as one of the former, we must do it now, before Chief Administrator Logran appoints his watchers. Once she's awake, we'll list her as deceased during stasis and close her record. That way, no one needs to know Corinne exists."

"I agree." Gwenneth climbed to her feet. "Let me fetch Friar Locarno. Colonel, perhaps we might borrow Adrienne Barca since she has experience with the decanting process and Friar Locarno speaks well of her."

"Of course. I'll ask Adri to meet you in *Tanith*." Once Gwenneth was gone, and Barca alerted, DeCarde turned her attention back on a pensive Morane. "Do you think Custis might pursue *Tanith* to Lyonesse?"

Morane raised his hands, palms up. "I don't know. But why take chances? Once Corinne is safely among the Brethren, I'll make arrangements with Chief Administrator Logran to take the remaining prisoners out of stasis."

—58—

Hector Lamert, Lyonesse's deputy chief of public safety looked up from the tablet Lieutenant Vietti provided and grimaced.

"Almost nothing but lords and ladies in your stasis pods, Lieutenant. They'll not find a court where they can idle away their lives on Lyonesse. Governor Yakin's no fan of the species, even if she is an 'Honorable' daughter of a baron."

The whipcord thin, mostly bald man looked past Vietti and Adrienne Barca at the stacks and their softly glowing control panels and frowned.

Vietti made a dismissive hand gesture.

"Waking here will still be an improvement on Parth, where they expect to be decanted. I'm sure Captain Morane will inform them they won't be allowed to live off government stipends."

Lamert cackled.

"Stipends? Perish the thought. There's plenty of work for everyone on Lyonesse. Big planet, small population, right? Those able in mind and body will learn quickly that no work means going hungry. Now, what about the common criminals?"

Vietti reached over and tapped the tablet in Lamert's hands. "Forty-eight. There were forty-nine when we took *Tanith*, but one of the pods malfunctioned during our trip here, and the ship's AI didn't pick it up. We only found out during a visual inspection after landing and disposed of her body."

Lamert made a noncommittal sound.

"Probably best for her that way." Vietti and Barca exchanged puzzled glances at the man's comment while he slowly scrolled through the list. "We can't let any of the common criminals loose, obviously. If you decant them, they must be kept in your own stockade until we sort out the legalities."

"We're organizing the stockade right now, sir. What legalities do you mean?" Barca asked.

Lamert squinted up at the tall Marine. "On Lyonesse, those who are found guilty of non-violent crimes deserving relatively short sentences end up in local detention centers. Although they're actually work camps. Don't work, go hungry applies to everyone, including criminals. Violent offenders get a chance to clear new settlements in the Windy Isles. Open-air prisons if you like. Some for a few years, some forever. And then there's the death penalty." He glanced at the tablet again. "We need to sort out where these stiffs deserve to go. A few of your criminal customers actually seem to qualify for the death penalty, but since our courts didn't condemn them under our laws, I suppose we'll take it down a notch and send them to the Windies."

"What are they, if I may ask?"

"You've seen a map of Lyonesse, Lieutenant?" Vietti nodded. "The large archipelago in the middle of the World Ocean, right above the equator, is what we call the

Windy Isles. The only way there and back is by air. Anyone trying to reach either Tristan or Isolde by sea will die well before coming within sight, thanks to frequent cyclones and aggressive oceanic lifeforms. And since there are no settlements on Isolde as yet, let alone anything other than native species, landing there wouldn't do much good anyhow."

"An effective prison, then."

"Not a single successful escape in over sixty years. And let me tell you, those who survive a sentence in the Windies come back thoroughly reformed, ready to do honest work for a living."

"What's the survival rate?" Barca asked.

"About what you might expect on one of Parth's exile islands."

The Marine winced. "That bad, eh?"

"Seems the right place for most of your criminals, though." Lamert gestured toward the nearest stack. "Shall we start the inspection? The chief administrator wants me to confirm identities and how we'll deal with them before he allows any decanting."

**

Two days later, Morane approached *Tanith*'s belly ramp with long strides, impatient to see the prison ship leave Lannion Base and vanish forever. Lieutenant Vietti stood in the shadow of the ship's pockmarked hull, hidden from an early summer sun baking the tarmac, as she waited for his blessing to lift off. She gave him a crisp salute which he returned with equal solemnity.

"Ready, Peg?"

"As ready as I'll ever be, sir. A shame we can't keep her even mothballed on one of the moons, but I suppose since no engineer in this system can figure out a way to disarm the antimatter fuel trap, there's little choice."

"And she's a reminder of a penal system long on misery and short on compassion."

Vietti nodded. "That too. Although I wonder how much compassion the Lyonesse version shows."

"Ask me again once this place rounds up dissenters and conscientious objectors, and sends them to live a nasty, brutish and short life." He nodded at *Narwhal*'s shuttles lifting off one by one, headed halfway around the planet where the Windy Isles sat in isolation at the center of the World Ocean. "Unlike those charming specimens who earned everything they're getting, and more."

"I hear you, sir. Oh well, mine won't have been the shortest command in the Imperial Fleet's history, but its end will certainly be among the more colorful. How long has it been since the Navy scuttled a starship into a sun?"

"Longer than anyone remembers." He stuck out his hand. "Enjoy your last few hours."

"As prize master, or before I swallow the anchor?" Vietti gave him a smile that was half mischief, half nostalgic.

"Both, Peg. Everyone will end up dirtside eventually. At least you get to develop new gunnery skills when you take over the planet's aerospace defense."

"As long as you don't make me ditch Navy blue for Marine Corps green, I'll survive."

"No worries. I've decided that the Lyonesse surface to orbit defense company will be a Navy unit, Peg."

"Thank the Almighty for that."

Morane and Vietti watched the prisoner shuttles climb up into the clear blue sky until they vanished from sight. Then she came to attention. "Permission to lift, sir."

"Granted."

After a further exchange of salutes, Vietti walked up the ramp while Morane headed for the control room, urged along by the warning siren announcing a starship's imminent departure.

A subtle whine blocked out the background noise while almost subliminal vibrations coursed through the cliff side as the prison ship's thrusters spooled up to full power. Then, without warning, half a dozen incredibly brilliant columns of light appeared beneath her hull and she rose. At first with slow deliberation, then with increasing speed until her aft thrusters kicked in and pushed her on a rising arc toward the edge of space.

**

Lieutenant Peg Vietti, soon to be former prize captain of the Imperial Prison Ship *Tanith* touched the helm control screen one last time and sat back with a sigh. "There. Done." She turned to the petty officer at the systems console. "Everything still green?"

"Yes, sir."

"Then we're out of here." She activated the ship-wide public address system. "All hands to the hangar deck, I repeat all hands to the hangar deck." Then Vietti nodded at the petty officer. "You too. Let me know when everyone's aboard the shuttle."

"Aye, aye, sir."

"*Vanquish*, this is *Tanith*."

"*Vanquish*, here."

"I'm about to cast loose. The ship's AI is programmed, and all systems are green."

"We see you and are ready to recover your shuttle. You are cleared to abandon ship."

"*Tanith* confirms."

Vietti checked the AI one more time for mistakes, but everything seemed in order. Once the shuttle left *Tanith*, she would accelerate well beyond safe limits. With no fragile mortals aboard, *Tanith*'s structural integrity became the sole limiting factor, and like most human-built starships, she was sturdy. Once she reached maximum velocity, it would take her a mere fifteen hours to enter the sun's corona.

"Shuttle to Lieutenant Vietti, everyone's aboard except you."

"On my way."

After one last look around the bridge that had been hers for so many weeks, Vietti jogged through empty passageways until she reached the open hangar deck door. The shuttle, one of *Vanquish*'s armed craft, waited for her, aft ramp down, nose pointed at the open space doors where a shimmering energy curtain separated the pressurized compartment from the vacuum outside. She couldn't see the cruiser against the dense field of stars, but she was there, near enough to see them leave the doomed ship.

Vietti strode up the ramp, passed the members of her prize crew and dropped into the left-hand seat beside Petty Officer Harkness. "Button her up. It's time to go home."

"What home would that be, sir?" Harkness asked as he pulled up the ramp. "I heard you're being assigned dirtside."

"You heard right. Lannion Base has a full complement of aerospace defense pods capable of covering the town. We found another two dozen stored away in the depot which will be deployed to cover the other major settlements. Captain Morane is forming a unit responsible for them and asked me to become its first commanding officer."

"I guess there will be a lot of changes in the next while."

"That would be an understatement PO. The captain said our ships are being reduced to two-thirds crewing on account they won't leave this system again any time soon, with the other third assigned to ground units. Or at least those who don't resign and become settlers."

"Yeah. That matches the gossip. Any idea when this will shake out?"

"It depends a lot on the Colonial Council."

"So a few months then?" He asked with a grin, eyes on his controls as the shuttle edged its way through the force field and out of *Tanith*'s hangar.

"I don't think the captain will let them blow hot air for long. He's a man on a mission and tough luck if you stand in his way."

"Yep. And that's why we're here with him."

"I thought we're all here because we're not all there," Vietti said with a wicked gleam in her eyes.

Harkness' laughter filled the small cockpit. "That too."

**

The next morning's command conference was barely starting when the control center interrupted Morane's opening remarks.

"Sir, *Tanith*'s telemetry transmissions stopped a minute ago, shortly after her last visual transmission showing she was still on course to enter the sun's corona. *Vanquish* confirms she's no longer detectable on either sensors or visual."

The duty petty officer didn't need to say the rest. Since the time lag from the sun to Lyonesse was eight minutes, *Tanith* was already gone. Morane felt a faint upwelling of relief that at least one problem was now solved. One of a long list, beginning with the increasingly fractious political prisoners.

"The colonial administration is still dragging its feet with relocating the politicals," he said. "Major Kayne has proposed an interim solution. I'd like us to consider it so we can relieve the pressure on Lannion Base while the courts void their convictions, because it seems none of the social services agencies will help the politicals without that. If we do nothing, Sister Gwenneth might face a mutiny from her long-suffering colleagues. Please go ahead, Matti."

"Yes, sir. The Colonial Militia established a half-dozen camps scattered around the settlement area so that each company has a proper place to assemble and train. They're nothing much. Shipping containers assembled into buildings within fenced off compounds, with the necessary sanitation and power generation. Suitable for part-time soldiers who train four days a month and assemble for a few weeks once a year. Each of the camps is within easy reach of the respective company's garrison town. Easy reach by ground vehicle that is. More arduous on foot."

"And you propose to disperse the politicals to those camps, pending the court's decision?" Commander Ryzkov asked.

"With a guard detail from the 21st Pathfinders for each, and counselors from the Order, sir. Of course, that puts a logistical burden on us because we would need to make sure they're fed, receive medical care and the camps' infrastructure, minimal as it is, keeps functioning."

"Make 'em dig kitchen gardens," DeCarde said. "And do their own housekeeping, so they learn what a settler's life is like. I vote a great big yes for Matti's suggestion. It's not just the Order that's getting fed up with the buggers."

Morane turned to Gwenneth. "Comments, Sister?"

"I would rather see them released into the community at once, where they would be forced to adapt and integrate. Since that's not possible yet, dispersing them into smaller groups would ease the pressures both they and we feel."

"Can you recommend how best to divide them?"

A cold smile appeared on her lean face. "Oh, yes. We know our guests better than they know themselves by now."

— 59 —

"Are you sure it's wise to head back out so soon?"

Rinne made a so-so hand gesture. "Wisdom has nothing to do with it, Captain Morane. I was charged by the Brethren to look for more of ours fleeing from persecution and bring them here to what will soon be the Order's Lyonesse Abbey. And our new leader," he inclined his head toward Gwenneth, "suggested I could leave as soon as my ship was ready."

The friar, Morane, Gwenneth, and DeCarde were in the latter's office after Rinne asked to meet so he could announce *Dawn Trader*'s departure the following day. Corinne, now a nameless novice of the Order, her cover identity declared dead in stasis, had been subsumed by the Brethren.

"How will you pass through what are now the badlands without falling prey to pirates?"

A small, but confident smile split the friar's white beard. "I've not told you everything about *Dawn Trader*, Captain. She's more agile, can reach higher hyperspace bands and hide her electronic signature more easily than your own cruiser. Many tried to catch me over the years, even when I traveled beyond the empire's writ, but none succeeded."

"In that case, I will wish you fair winds and following seas and suggest you top up your antimatter fuel containment units before leaving this system. The automated cracking station still works, but there's no telling how scarce fuel will become once various sides reach the point of imposing scorched earth policies." Morane stood and offered Rinne his hand. "Make sure you return safely."

"The Almighty willing, I shall, and with the latest news of what's transpiring out there."

"And if the Almighty isn't willing?" DeCarde asked.

"Then he will have other plans for my crew and me, Colonel."

"The Void giveth, the Void taketh away, blessed be the Void," the Marine intoned.

Rinne, refusing to be baited merely smiled beatifically. "Just so. I know you mean to be ironic, but someone reconciled to his or her fate inevitably finds a more fulfilling path through life."

"Such as accepting I'm marooned in a star system few ever heard of, let alone visited."

"Marooned is such a harsh word, Colonel," Gwenneth said. "You and your Marines escaped certain death on Coraline because you're needed here, be it to help Lyonesse in the present, or to lay the foundations of something that will help Lyonesse and perhaps even humanity in the future."

Her calm certitude gave the Marine pause, and when she repeated, "Blessed be the Void," in a soft murmur, it was with less asperity.

"Do you need any supplies?" Morane asked in an attempt at steering the conversation onto a more practical track. "Whatever you need from the depot is yours. It hasn't been pilfered nearly as much as I feared and Speaker Hecht's family business replenishes preserved food stocks regularly."

"Rations, and perhaps my chief engineer can go through the parts inventory and see what might be useful. I'd like to lift within the next day."

"Of course. Colonel, might I impose on you to warn Lieutenant Grimes?"

"Certainly, sir." DeCarde gestured toward Rinne. "Perhaps we should obtain a copy of *Dawn Trader*'s databanks before she leaves, just in case."

"Already taken care of," Gwenneth said. "You will receive what we consider general knowledge in due course."

"Once you strip out the secrets of the Order."

"Just so, Colonel."

**

"Do you think we'll ever see her again?"

DeCarde, Morane, and Gwenneth stood by the Marine's office window, watching *Dawn Trader* rise on brilliant columns of energy before turning into an ever-shrinking dot quickly swallowed by a band of early morning clouds.

"If it is the Almighty's will, Colonel."

Before DeCarde could answer, Centurion Haller stuck her head through the door. "Sirs, Abbess, Government House just called to convene what the governor's secretary called a plenary conference for thirteen hundred hours. You're expected to be present. It's being held in the Colonial Assembly Hall."

"Did he say who else is invited to this plenary?" Morane asked. "The venue seems to hint at numerous attendees."

"No idea, sir. He didn't give me a chance to ask questions. A little full of himself if you want my opinion."

"His sort usually are, Eve. Please ask Major Kayne if he'd be so kind as to give us a lift. I'm sure he'll be part of this conference."

"Will do, sir." Haller vanished back into the battalion command post next door.

"We need to find our own ground transport, and soon," DeCarde said. "I should ask Major Salmin to dig through the depot's inventory and see if there are a few skimmers hidden behind the stacks of starship parts."

"Or you could buy some with those precious metals you liberated from the now no doubt late Governor General Klim."

DeCarde barked a laugh. "I completely forgot about that. Eve must be sitting on the crate, waiting for orders. I suppose we should think about securing our treasure chest, considering there's probably over ten million imperial marks' worth of ill-gotten gain."

"May I suggest you use your wealth sparingly?"

The Marine gave her a curious frown. "Why, Abbess?"

"Negotiating position. If the governor and her advisers, especially Speaker Hecht find out you're hiding this wealth, they'll be less inclined to discuss ways of regularizing your status as paid members of the Lyonesse defense forces. The reiver raid and your evidence from other worlds frightened them into accepting your protection as a necessary evil, but for many, we remain an unexpected and unwelcome burden. People don't like to hear their futures will not be what they expect."

"And Hecht will be looking for ways to separate us from the stash, just on of general principle."

"Precisely and please keep calling me sister. I am merely first among equals as current head of the Lyonesse Abbey, such as it is. Abbess is a role, not a title."

"Wilco, Sister." DeCarde turned to Morane. "Dress uniform this afternoon?"

"Can't hurt."

**

"Brace yourselves," Sister Gwenneth murmured as they climbed the Colonial Assembly Hall's steps, Major Kayne in tow. The hall, a gray, two-story stone building occupying a whole city block at Lannion's center served as both parliament, housing the Colonial Council in a sober amphitheater, and as a public meeting space.

The latter was in a high-ceilinged room with space for thousands. The sprawling lawn beyond massive transparent doors could accommodate thousands more.

"This will not be a pleasant exchange of views. I sense a great deal of hostility and fear as one would expect from people about to hear their universe is collapsing."

DeCarde almost rolled her eyes at the sister's remark, but then she felt it herself as they crossed the threshold and entered the grandiosely named Citizen's Agora. A large table had been formed by shoving two dozen smaller ones together. It was surrounded by a little over forty men and women, all of whom stared at the newcomers with expressions ranging from curious to cold while the buzz of twenty different conversations died away. More colonists sat in a semi-circle a few meters behind the table, bringing the total to almost a hundred.

Logran stood and waved them to four empty chairs across from where he and Hecht framed a lighter version of the gubernatorial throne they'd seen in Yakin's drawing room. Before they could sit, the governor's secretary called out, in a surprisingly loud and clear voice, "Her Excellency, The Honorable Elenia Yakin."

Everyone present climbed to their feet and assumed a respectful stance, except for the three officers, who came to rigid attention. Yakin swept into the hall and, with Logran holding her chair, sat at the midpoint between the table's far ends, facing Morane. As if on cue, everyone else imitated her.

"Good afternoon," she began. "At the request of Lyonesse's Estates General, I convened this plenary so Captain Morane of the Navy, Lieutenant Colonel DeCarde of the Marines and Sister Gwenneth of the Order of the Void may explain the reasons for their unannounced arrival, what they propose and why. For the edification of our visitors, the Estates General of Lyonesse is composed of the Colonial Council, whose leaders are at this table and whose members are sitting behind me; the mayors of Lyonesse's communities; the chancellor of the Lyonesse University; representatives of the Lyonesse Mercantile Association; senior administrators of the Lyonesse government; and representatives at large of trade unions, citizen's groups and professional associations. The Estates General are called into a plenary only on rare occasions when the government is faced with grave decisions concerning the colony's future. This is one of them."

Morane nodded once to acknowledge Yakin's explanation. "Thank you, Your Excellency."

"So far, only a few heard what you told us and saw your evidence, Captain, though everyone knows the gist of your purpose. And of course, everyone on Lyonesse knows of the debt we owe you and your people," she continued. "If I could impose on you to repeat your story and answer any questions. My secretary is prepared to display the recordings of those unfortunate colonies." Yakin pointed at a giant screen dominating the one wall not pierced by transparent doorways.

"Certainly, Madame." Morane stood and let his gaze roam over the assembled colonists, meeting their eyes without embarrassment or nervousness, no matter how hostile they might seem.

Then he spoke in slow, measured tones about a subject few seemed able to grasp and even less accept as fact — the violent end of a social and political order that had lasted longer than a dozen lifetimes.

And how they could salvage humanity's future along with their own.

Ashes of Empire continues with
Imperial Twilight

About the Author

Eric Thomson is the pen name of a retired Canadian soldier with thirty-one years of service, both in the Regular Army and the Army Reserve. He spent his Regular Army career in the Infantry and his Reserve service in the Armoured Corps. He worked as an information technology specialist for a number of years before retiring to become a full-time author.

Eric has been a voracious reader of science fiction, military fiction, and history all his life. Several years ago, he put fingers to keyboard and started writing his own military sci-fi, with a definite space opera slant, using many of his own experiences as a soldier for inspiration.

When he is not writing fiction, Eric indulges in his other passions: photography, hiking, and scuba diving, all of which he shares with his wife.

Join Eric Thomson at: http://www.thomsonfiction.ca/

Where you will find news about upcoming books and more information about the universe in which his heroes fight for humanity's survival.

Read his blog at:
https://ericthomsonblog.wordpress.com

If you enjoyed this book, please consider leaving a review on Amazon, at Goodreads, or with your favorite online retailer to help others discover it.

Also by Eric Thomson

Siobhan Dunmoore
No Honor in Death (Siobhan Dunmoore Book 1)
The Path of Duty (Siobhan Dunmoore Book 2)
Like Stars in Heaven (Siobhan Dunmoore Book 3)
Victory's Bright Dawn (Siobhan Dunmoore Book 4)
Without Mercy (Siobhan Dunmoore Book 5)

Decker's War
Death Comes but Once (Decker's War Book 1)
Cold Comfort (Decker's War Book 2)
Fatal Blade (Decker's War Book 3)
Howling Stars (Decker's War Book 4)
Black Sword (Decker's War Book 5)
No Remorse (Decker's War Book 6)
Hard Strike (Decker's War Book 7)

Quis Custodiet
The Warrior's Knife (Quis Custodiet No 1)

Ashes of Empire
Imperial Sunset (Ashes of Empire #1)

CPSIA information can be obtained
at www.ICGtesting.com
Printed in the USA
LVHW051310010723
751278LV00010B/856